W9-BDX-544

STORIES

# FRACTUS EUROPA

EDITED BY ERIC C. ANDERSON AND ADAM DUNN

with a Foreword by Peter Heather

dunn books

FRACTUS EUROPA

In Memoriam

Eric C. Anderson & Oriana Fallaci

*Avevi ragione*

"The value of a thing sometimes does not lie in that which one attains by it, but in what one pays for it—what it costs us. I shall give an example. Liberal institutions cease to be liberal as soon as they are attained: later on, there are no worse and no more thorough injurers of freedom than liberal institutions. Their effects are known well enough: they undermine the will to power; they level mountain and valley, and call that morality; they make men small, cowardly, and hedonistic—every time it is the herd animal that triumphs with them. Liberalism: in other words, herd-animalization."

—FRIEDRICH NIETZSCHE, *Twilight of the Idols*, 1888

## CONTENTS

# FOREWORD

BY PETER HEATHER

*PETER HEATHER is a Professor of Medieval History at King's College London. He read for a BA in Modern History at New College Oxford and completed his doctorate on relations between Goths and the Roman Empire at the same venue. After a (very) brief stint in HM Treasury, he has held teaching positions at University College London, Worcester College Oxford, and King's College London. He is a specialist in the dynamic, mutually transformative interactions of more and less complex societies in the first millennium AD, publishing extensively on the subject, including* The Fall of Rome *(2005) and* Empires and Barbarians: Migration, Development and State Formation in the First Millennium *(2009). His current project is a thousand-year history of the development of European Christianity.*

European democracy was not born in Greece. No democracy was. Two-thirds of the population of Athens consisted of slaves who had no rights and no political voice. It was actually born in the much more recent past, in the same historically specific conditions that gave rise to the nation-state.

Starting in the eighteenth and nineteenth centuries with Britain and France, European governments drew on their growing demographic and economic resources with greater intensity than ever before to fight each other at countless points across the globe, in an age of expanding literacy and communications. The—accidental—result was the idea of the nation-state, which claimed and exercised new rights over its citizens: literally to the point of death in the era when mass conscription first reared its ugly head. The obvious advantages of this new, much more powerful kind of political entity caused it to spread like wildfire, until, by the early twentieth century, nation-states and would-be nation-states were slugging it out right across the European landmass.

Which is where we get to democracy. As a payoff for the mass carnage inflicted on their citizenry in the nineteenth century, between 1914 and 1918, and again between 1939 and 1945, European elites slowly but surely gave way to demands for increased, then full, electoral suffrage, and for unprecedented levels of social care, starting with pensions before moving on to health care and income support. On one level, all this came with the evolving ideological territory of the nation. The new national narratives being taught to entire populations for the first time ever, as mass schooling came into being, justified unheard-of degrees of citizen sacrifice by portraying the inhabitants of one's own European nation as a special breed: heirs of an imagined community stretching back into the mists of time. If that were the case, and especially once they were being turned out regularly to fight and die, the imperative took hold that, in return, it was only right to build lands fit for heroes.

Two further developments made it possible to do so. First, the emergence of modern nation-states coincided with urbanization and industrialization, creating enormous quantities of surplus wealth, which was relatively easy to tax, since production took place in physical factories, firmly located within defined national boundaries. Before industrialization, the most that even prosperous states could manage was to wage the occasional war. Pre-modern agricultural economies produced so little surplus that maintaining an army consumed about 70 percent of all potential tax revenues. The previously unimaginable tax revenues generated in the modern era now means that military spending generally accounts for no more than 2 percent of European national budgets, with vast sums left over for other purposes.

Second, and this is obviously no accident, Europe's nation-states were born in an era that saw the establishment of European, then more broadly "Western" (including the major new entities created by European migration: Britain's "White" dominions, and, above all, America) domination of the planet. Europe's nation-states could mobilize resources more intensively, arm themselves with the fruits of industrialization, and on that basis dominate vast tracts of the planet.

Even through post-1945 decolonization, global economic dominance remained. Raw materials were traded cheaply to the West, whose manufacturing industries added huge economic value to the finished products, which were sold not only in the West, but back to the rest of the world. As a result, the West's overall share of world GDP continued to swell, until by the year 2000 a staggering 80 percent of global GDP was being consumed by one-sixth of the planet's population: not least to fund all the measures—pensions, health care, social benefits, etc.—on which the functional, social and political cohesion of Europe's nation-states actually rested. From a historical perspective, practical European democracy was based on the relatively equitable distribution of a vast flow of wealth from the rest of the planet.

All of which explains why it is currently in so much trouble. The most discussed challenge to cohesion is immigration from Europe's old imperial territories and beyond. This began as deliberate policy: to fill gaps in the post-war European labor market. That gap widened subsequently, because one direct effect of all the new health and pension spending since 1945 was to increase longevity and lower birth rates. As a result, European dependency ratios—the number of non-producers to workers—has skyrocketed, with migration filling the subsequent gap, sometimes in very specific ways. Most Western health care systems avoid the costs of training sufficient professionals by sucking in the already-trained from the developing world. Europe actually now depends on a flow of migration, but it has disrupted the cultural cohesion produced by the mass educational structures of the nation-state.

The current pushback against migration has still deeper roots, however, in a much more fundamental problem: deindustrialization. This gathered pace in the 1980s, in the Reagan-Thatcher era, when the liberalization of financial controls allowed Western corporations to outsource production to the developing world, where labor costs were much lower. This kept asset values and corporate revenues high, as well as, in the short term, reinvigorating governmental tax revenues to maintain and even increase levels of social spending in the 1990s. The European middle class remained gainfully employed managing and administering the new processes, but, as has now become clear, the working class was left behind and has become increasingly desperate, with social cohesion taking a huge hit. If a large portion of the European population is being offered an effective choice between working at McDonald's or living on benefits, there is a serious problem—especially as benefit levels have been declining and, for one fundamental reason, are likely to face continued downward pressure.

For if certain Western interests initiated the shift of manufacturing, the developing world is increasingly taking over the process. The rise of China, India, and so many others cannot be easily reversed; America can't just be made great again, because the fundamental building blocks of global wealth and power have shifted. Since the great crash of 2008, the West's control of world GDP has slipped by a quarter (from 80 percent to 60 percent) and that trend will continue as developing economies continue to expand.

In overall terms, the structural conditions that made European democracy possible—enough wealth to build functioning social cohesion among culturally unified populations—are being undermined. Many Europeans remain extremely wealthy, but the overall distribution of wealth is becoming increasingly uneven, as economic opportunities for the less educated continue to dwindle. Nor is government spending likely to fill the gap. Financing rising levels of government debt and a growing loss of fiscal control over wealth-generating multinationals who are no longer conveniently located within the confines of single nation-states are putting extra pressure on both health and social spending levels, posing still greater potential threats to cohesion. European democracy is certainly the product of an evolving set of ideas, but also an unprecedented inflow of wealth, which funded their practical realization. That flow has begun to dry up, with 2008 the moment when the significance of the underlying changes first became clear. The effects of the fundamental challenge have only begun to be felt, but it is clear that European democracy will not survive without clear-sighted responses to the existential threat that is beginning to unfold. In their different ways, all the stories in this volume deal with the individual experience of living in a time of huge upheaval, and with different attempts either to meet that threat or to pretend it doesn't exist. . . .

# BELGIUM:

## The Paper Trap

BY CONRAD ZIELAN

*CONRAD ZIELAN is a journalist and polyglot both well-traveled and known under a different name to NGO types, former soldiers, spies and police on the European continent and beyond. He has worked closely with all of the above to report on drug trafficking, the slave trade, political corruption, and, in the meantime, he has also anonymously aided journalists in the art of masking both meetings and communication. And for now, it is best to leave it at that.*

Who was this great mother of Africa? This "Ma Mere" who dared wave her finger at a man such as he? This exuberant, beastly whale of a woman railing about the whites—about the pale, cold murderers from the rainy lands a continent away?

Ah, great mother. How she would challenge him. How she would provoke them all.

"And you tell me that you would live among them?"

"You speak their language just as do I."

"Lingala is my language. The tongues of Kinshasa are my language. The rest . . . " She waved a great, inflated hand as if to ward off spirits. "The rest is the white corruption that has brought us here. Brought sinners such as you to eat at my table, to dine and connive with my little fox of a son."

The son, slim, quick and worrying in his own right, kicked back his head in glee.

▪ ▪ ▪ ▪

## (MAY 1, 2016)

The girl came to him with great deference, having swayed up the narrow stairs to the roof with the grace and innocence of a first-time prostitute. She bore the plate of fried plantains with both hands, offering them as a Chinese would his business card—with a smirk just behind a blank façade that meant: This is no introduction, friend, but a ticket. To anything, everything. Or, as the Chinese had said, "*A tout a tout le monde.*" But instead, the girl had simpered "also a beer?"—even as Marveille Feza had ignored her, as he had twitched his index finger off the trigger of the Truvelo rifle to remind her to keep silent, to set the plantains and mayonnaise and piri piri sauce upon the stool just off his elbow so that he could fucking *watch.*

And concentrate.

And wait.

White boy in Africa. A boy Fang had promised would be easy to find. Easy to kill through the blare of amplifiers from the Ndombolo bar, to drop cold and splattered among the hundreds of ghosts bobbing soulless to the rhumba of Marie Louise in the eerie green neon of the Truvelo sights.

"*Twey faceewul,*" Fang had said. "*C'est la rewanj. Twey, twey faceewul.*"

Fang babble, he called it. The Chinese bargaining, cutting down the price with a mix of bad French and endless Chinese blather. And Marveille Feza, as rangy as he was scarred and restless, had wondered about the words—was still wondering even now. What revenge? Revenge for the boy's meddling in Chinese money? For the sins of the president? For those of Leopold and the Belgian nation?

For the wars in the east? Severed limbs since the very beginning of time?

Not for the first time, Marveille Feza—mercenary, assassin, refugee and fugitive from a list of war crimes—had the urge to spit.

*Revenge*. A demonic word. And Fang repeating the word again and again. Negotiating in his fashion. Which meant never shutting up.

And still, he took it. From this Fang who owed him money. Papers and a passport to Europe.

Diamonds, even.

Marveille Feza shifted to a knee. The rooftop was cramped, maybe six meters square and cluttered with the flotsam of the family restaurant below. Old shoes. A deep-oil cooker in need of repair. A basketball and pile of bird cages corroded with the guano of the jungles. In silence, the girl slipped through the junk and laundry lines and hanging white linens so that the plate alighted upon the stool without so much as a scrape. Or maybe there was a scrape—the crack and sizzle of oil—but Marveille Feza could not hear this above a cacophony of music, the shouts and teases of the street. Saturday night in Kinshasa. And across the great river, Brazzaville, begging for sleep.

The girl, slender in her t-shirt and flowered print dress, bobbed a curtsy that he just caught out of the corner of his eye. Marveille Feza touched his brow to the night sight of the Truvelo—a bad habit of old—realized she was still there and whispered.

"As you want, child. Bring me a Simba. But just one beer. And then do not bother me again."

The girl bit her lip, curtsied a second time and played her hip as she turned to sway down the stairs—hoping, he knew, to be called back.

*La petite flirt.* Staring through the sights, mumbling his irritation at the sweat bleeding into his good eye, Marveille Feza did not see this as much as he sensed it. "*Une biere. C'est tout,*" he cursed. For what was one winsome *biche* in this madhouse of ten million? One more *putain* in a world where young girls were carried off on a man's shoulder. Where they were raped, cut and left for dead. Abandoned in retreat and found again when the raids went the other way.

Such had been in the war in the east.

Marveille Feza felt the tic in his bad eye. Prayed a four-word prayer that he would no longer remember, that the things he did remember were not him. Then he said to himself out loud: "Just shoot this white boy and be done with it."

A deep, precise breath. He panned the sniper rifle a degree left and then right, the film screen of dancers below shifting in tens of meters, the sweep exponential so that he had to concentrate not to over adjust.

Strange. In all of the raids and battles and kidnappings and killings, Marveille Feza had never shot a white man. Never killed a Belgian or even taken a shot.

Time to change that, *absolument.*

Pan left, pan right. Find the boy and be done with it. He assumed it would be like the last time—the time when he found the boy but could not shoot for the gendarmes, for the crowd and lack of cover. But otherwise the same. The Congolese bobbing, shifting, gyrating in time, but the boy, the thin, weak-ass European jerking out of rhythm, his white face and arms and hands casting a strange glow in the lens of the sight so that he could not be missed.

Marveille Feza swallowed hard, panned left and right, then took his eye off the sight with that tremble of a queasy stomach like the last time. The distaste of it, he thought. He had seen his fellow countrymen, women and children and mercs from all over Africa killed and maimed in so many various and bloody atrocities. Grenades. Land mines. Machetes. Limbs gone, bodies torn, brains blown out. But the thought of white blood—white meat and bile—again turned the milk in his gut.

Then he thought of Fang. The reek of the small, corrupt Chinaman and the diamonds he did not yet have in his stomach. Odd, he thought. All of these years of killing, and now the stomach.

"The beer, *monsieur.*"

The girl again. Silent and beckoning by his side. She had padded up the stairs with the spycraft of a cat, and yet he had heard her, sensed her again, her messy scent, and all but tasted the rut of a woman in the night.

Resigned, he let out a breath, flicked a hand at the girl and then pointed to the stool and the untouched food.

"You aim, but you do not shoot."

"I aim at no man this night."

"If he does not come—will you visit us again?"

Marveille Feza pulled back the weapon, gave the girl not a glance and began to break it down, stripping it as would an old soldier, part after part slipped deftly into the case with the body and stock braced against his stomach and knee. It was well after midnight now, and they were far away from the embassy quarters. He had found a bar in some other slum of the city, or he had stayed in to fuck and found no bar at all.

The girl stood before him, pigeon-toed, light-skinned and young knees almost touching, but again afraid to speak as the pounding beat of Ndombolo washed over them. What was she? Nineteen? Twenty? The same age of the NGO girls that ran with the boy?

At that age, he had run with no one. At that age, he had run after, run from, had booby-trapped and ambushed and shot.

The gun went in the case, the case into a gym bag that, as he stood, Feza casually swung upon his back. He took a long swig of beer then placed the glass three-quarters empty on the ground.

And said, "Fear not, my heart. I shall not visit you again."

▪ ▪ ▪ ▪

Laurent Desmet arrived in Kinshasa at the tender age of twenty-three, bright-eyed and bushy-tailed and absolutely, completely abashed by the Belgian ambassador and the intrigue of what he was about to do. For he had expected the trivial, the unbearably mundane. Greeting and grilling poor Congolese begging for visas to Europe. Degrading his highborn French with the Creole phrasing of Africa and occasionally hacking through the Flemish that had from childhood seemed forced if not unnatural.

Then again, he expected most conversations (and conflicts) to be quite simple, and to accompany the red stamp authority expected by an embassy employee of his youth and class.

*Paperwork incomplete. Visa denied.*

Yet this was not to be. For Ambassador De Clercq—shiny and rose-pink in his navy pin-striped suit—stammered through the mission with the conviction of both the unnerved and the appalled.

"You will dig, my young friend. You will unearth. You will confront and point fingers and in all circumstances great and small, you will only and infallibly report back to me."

"I will, Mr. Ambassador. You can count on me."

"Of course, I can," said the ambassador. The man turned his whole body—once again, Desmet was surprised by his superior's girth—to switch the second fan to a higher setting. It kicked into a faster gear, the blades syncopating to a watery thump. "Now, where will you begin?"

Desmet pursed his lips. Was this a test? A trick question?

"The passport ring was external."

"We have all read the papers, Desmet. But yes, the passport ring was indeed external. Money shifted to the president's family. The entire, unseemly debacle linked—tenuously, I might add, to the otherwise unblemished corporation, Shrinar."

"Yet, you truly suspect that our own embassy has been sullied?"

"Have you been listening, dear boy? Of course, I suspect. This is exactly what I suspect. Shrinar has a monopoly on security papers, on holographic passports. Shrinar now supplies the Congolese and the Belgian government both. And it is under suspicion of diverting revenue to the Congolese for this very right."

Desmet did not so much shrug as twitch his thumbs.

"Dear God, boy, do you not see? We are infiltrated to the core. Personally, I would begin with an audit of all visas supplied, not to mention an audit of all passports issued to dual citizens of Congolese nationality. I would not be surprised to find the family of the president and his minions to be heavily favored with both lengthy visas and new passports altogether."

"I see," said Desmet, although he was not completely sure he did.

"And do you see that I, as the very ambassador sent to represent Belgium in this deeply troubled country, cannot be seen to be drudging up evidence in order to tarnish the president's very family?"

"Of course not."

"But I can be surprised, dear boy. Pleasantly surprised by the resourcefulness and independence of my staff."

Desmet saw the wry nod, mimicked it back as best he knew how. Then he was ushered out the door, pointed to the office of the military attaché (but not without an admonition to "hurry, boy, hurry—for we need results") and was on the job.

Brave new world, thought Desmet.

My third day in Kinshasa.

Brave new world indeed.

And perhaps, looking back, Desmet had surprised himself. Six weeks into his mission, he had doggedly, if not perversely, failed to interview the Congolese secretary of the interior, utterly failed to even make an appointment with the vice minister of the interior, and had been unscrupulously and vociferously ridiculed by none other than the six-some-odd female and male secretaries of both. And such failures had hardly stood in isolation: they had been spliced quite profoundly and ineffectively among a host of miscellaneous officials, running from the ministry of state security to the ministry of defense to local officials such as three city councilors, one Kinshasa power company executive and even the vice head of the sanitation commission for the local mayor.

Yet here he was, waiting patiently (if not perversely) for the vice minister of the interior himself.

Desmet glanced at the clock, an ungainly white, schoolroom disc hanging off-center over a black bookcase topped with ebony carvings of antelope and crocodiles in Egyptian style. A secretary darker than either typed in short bursts, then paused to beam the friendliest smile on the continent, then went back to typing again.

And Desmet, sweating in a gray suit, wishing in God's good name for water, a fan, anything to deal with the spring heat, glanced back at the clock.

▪ ▪ ▪ ▪

"So, what did he do next? With whom did he speak?"

Fang handed Marveille Feza a shot of whiskey, leaning forward so that Feza could smell the unwashed-ness of the foreigner that was not unlike the dandies of the slums. In the second room, Feza had seen the other Chinese. He had also seen the two whites. Maybe Belgian, maybe South African, but he recognized them for what they were. Hired guns. Just like him.

Marveille Feza said, "He spoke to the girls. He danced with the girls. Then he left with the girls."

"And you saw this?"

"I saw nothing. I have told you twice now. This comes from my cousin, Reya. She works the SkyLounge on Du, makes good money. But you, Fang, you waste my time. You send me far to the slum of Matete where I watch. Where I wait. Yet the boy is not there."

Fang sipped his whiskey. Touched his ear lobe, gave it an odd tweak. Marveille Feza, loose, legs straight and his upper body slumped in the easy chair of the communist mission—the Chinese Friendship and Trade Mission—downed his whiskey in a gulp.

"Bad intelligence," muttered Fang. The Chinese touched his ear again, then his hair, which was thin, greased back so that to Feza's eye, he seemed Vietnamese. "Yet you say he left with the two girls. Why did he leave with the two girls?"

Marveille Feza could not resist.

"To fuck them until they cry."

Fang frowned. Yet again tweaked his ear. Marveille Feza had the impression that for all of this scheming and meddling, Fang was delicate indeed.

"Is there something wrong with your ear?"

Fang sat up straight, cocked his head. "My ear has no troubles. No troubles at all."

Feza chuckled. "There must be something wrong with your ear. You hear bad intelligence. You ask the same questions again and again. You do not listen to me when I say I must be paid."

A second frown. "What do you want?'

"I want money. Not these fucking diamonds. What the fuck will I do with diamonds? And I want the passports you promised."

With that, Marveille Feza raised his finger, pointed it a Fang and twitched his thumb as if firing a pistol.

"That is exactly what I want."

▪ ▪ ▪ ▪

"So what did he do next? With whom did he speak?"

Bar Cheetah in the Matonge district. Milongo the journalist spoke in earnest, leaning so close to Desmet that he was slightly repelled. Black, scrubby beard, a shard of shrimp or fish or onion in the tangle. On his shoulder hung Boisson, also a journalist, and a local fixer, Arnaud, who Desmet guessed could not have been more than sixteen.

Behind them both stood *Les Sapeurs*, the slum dandies Valdano and Carhel, both impeccable in outrageous suits, Valdano's a glowing maroon, complete with matching vest and a fiery orange tie, and Carhel's a more studied brown, over a gold, pin-striped shirt and the tie a dapper rose and yellow. The journalists were short, the dandies, wiry and tall. Arnaud was something in between. Slim, coffee-colored and as fierce as he appeared delicate.

Not unlike the beautiful NGO hippie girls Jeta and Claire.

"Trust the journos," whispered Jeta. "Trust most of all the child, Arnaud. Nobody has sources like the child Arnaud."

Desmet nodded in a fashion—how would he describe it? Yes. Dutifully. He nodded dutifully. For Jeta was exotic and some Creole mix of Congolese and anything else that made him gasp. As did Claire. As did the both of them when either chose to whisper wisdom into his ear.

Damn, he thought, as Jeta took him by the arm, only being polite to show I'm listening.

"But the men in suits?"

"Yes, they have sources," said Jeta. "Dangerous sources who will tell you the truth—but whom you should not trust."

Thus, Desmet listened. And absorbed. And the crowd of locals, hippies, NGO types and general bohemian hangabouts closing in concave and curious on the terrace of Jeta's ground-level apartment left Desmet sweating, nervous as if trapped in a pressing den of animals.

Or a very cramped and smoky bong.

"The vice minister laughed at me," said Desmet, sneaking a glance at Jeta. "He grinned and spoke in Lingala and Kikongo, but even when he spoke French, I could barely understand." Desmet glanced at Jeta. Half-Cuban, half-Congolese, she brushed back a mane of kinky hair and whispered conspiratorially to Claire, an Angolan volunteer who, for all practical purposes, could have passed for her sister. Claire's eyes narrowed slyly, and she put her hand over her mouth to cover a giggle. Desmet wondered just what that could mean.

"You cannot let this stand," said Milongo.

"Cannot let?"

"You see the state of our people? You see what they do—the family at the top?"

Desmet splayed his hands wide. "I've been asking questions."

"But you said he laughed at you," prodded Boisson. "And how could you even understand that if you could not understand his tongue?"

"Oh, he laughed at me; I understood that."

Valdano, king of the *saps*, slipped to the fore, a thumb and finger on his chin as if to study some strange, newly discovered bug. "The vice minister is corrupt," he said. "This is quite known. And yet you asked him about Shrinar? About passports and accounts?"

"I asked him about why the government of the Democratic Republic of the Congo should pay such high commission fees to the very offshore account our dear Boisson published in his paper," said Desmet. "I asked him how he expected a Congolese to pay two hundred and sixty-five Congo francs for a new passport—and a third of that sent to an offshore account? How could this possibly be justified?"

"Brave, but unintelligent questions," said Valdano, still studying him as if he were some new subspecies of bug. "The vice minister—all of the ministers—have faced such questions before."

"Then I asked him to aid me in retrieving the tax records of Stephen Demuto."

Gasps went up from the journalists. Even Valdano stepped back, eyebrows raised high. He glanced at the second dandy, Carhel, who with his mouth—with his entire face—made a tiny "o" of surprise.

The journalists gasped with incredulity.

"Stephen Demuto is the cousin of the president."

"Yes."

"Stephen Demuto is rumored to have owned offshore accounts in Luxembourg and the Channel Islands."

"Exactly. Both of which can be subpoenaed under know-your-client laws and anti-money laundering regulations. I only let him know there was the quiet, diplomatic option, or the more overt, potentially explosive approach through the proper legal authorities."

"And you have the backing of the embassy of Belgium?" asked Valdano.

A pause. Everyone who could trade glances with anyone did just that.

And Desmet said: "I'm not exactly sure."

A roar went up. A journalist whom he did not know shoved a beer into his fist, spilling it down the front of his pants. Valdano turned away, making a great show of being impressed.

But so much more interesting, Jeta alighted to his right and took his hand. And Claire alighted to his left and put a hand on his knee. African-Creole girls. Short, coffee-brown, delicate and nimble and altogether beyond his experience. Valdano eyed him and laughed. He placed a 1920s fedora on Desmet's head. Jeta glanced down, bit her lip in barely suppressed hilarity and then removed the hat and placed it squarely on Desmet's crotch.

Claire placed a reefer against his lips. Desmet was sure he'd glowed the entire disco red.

He tried to change the subject and nodded to Carhel and Valdano. "It's so hot—why do they dress like that?"

Jeta shrugged an answer as if to say, Okay, we can speak about whatever you like.

"In Kinshasa, we only have the now," said Jeta. "The dandies live the now. Ignore the suits, the sparkle of belts and buttons. They have the now and only the now. But yes, they are not the same. Like us, like everyone, they have nothing, but they have nothing in style."

"I can see that."

"But they are very interested in you," said Claire. Desmet glanced from Jeta to Claire and back. They seemed very close to him, and he could feel Jeta now had a hand gripping like a tiny claw upon his knee.

Desmet stuttered, "Why would they be interested in me?"

Jeta said, "All are interested in you. You provoke the ministers. For the Belgian government. But it is the Belgian government that lobbies for companies like Shrinar—companies that overcharge the Congolese for anything they can and then feed bribes back to the president's family."

Desmet nodded, attempting to focus his thoughts, his brain, his eyes and mouth to seem intelligent. Claire held a rough roll of ganja to his lips; as if swimming through an ocean of smoke and youths dancing and the big beat, he saw the *saps* Valdano and Carhel leaning close, the first smirking, then frowning as he spoke to the second dandy in some conspiracy. With the quick nod of a soldier, Carhel disappeared. Desmet felt Jeta's claw move higher upon his thigh. Or was that Claire?

He decided he really loved the Congo.

Which is when things got a bit weird.

Exactly how he arrived in their apartment, he would never remember. There were colors, blurred tones and bits of conversation repeated and slowed down. There was teasing, the devilish eyes and then Jeta upon him (or was that Claire?) and then the wrestling, the fleeting panic of not knowing where he was or whether or not he was wearing a condom and then the release of passing out warm and again swimming only to wake cool and absolutely calm with Jeta's head on his shoulder, her palm on her chest and Claire asleep, but clothed, against his other arm.

"The foreigner awakes," said Jeta.

Desmet took a deep breath. Jeta tapped him a kiss, and his stomach jumped. His eyes darted around the room. Just what he had expected from a pair of volunteers. Slight disarray. Maps on the walls. A flowered wreath as if Christmas had met Easter in Africa. A portable hanging rack for blue-jean shorts and white blouses that in the half-light of the coming morning were as lacy as lingerie.

Desmet turned his head to Claire. The tip of a finger touched his chin and brought him back.

"Let her sleep," said Jeta.

"Of course."

Jeta said, "We've had quite a night."

Desmet bit his lip. "I suppose we've had." He glanced at Claire again, turned back to Jeta and was tapped for another kiss.

"I have questions for you," she said.

Desmet nodded. So did he. As in: Did we really do this? The three of us? But why is Claire fully clothed? And did I use a condom? I really like you—both of you—but this is Africa and I hope I used a condom.

Then, noticing the baby-blue suit hung on the door, remembering the mindless, drunken wander with Jeta, Claire, Valdano and the dandy Carhel, Desmet thought:

Did I really buy that?

Jeta took his chin in her hand and bought him back to earth.

"Do you know you are being set up?"

Wait.

*What?*

Desmet swallowed hard. Not what he was expecting.

"You're kidding. Is that how it is?"

"What?"

"You are telling me you want money for this?"

Jeta rolled her eyes. "I'm going to ignore that, Laurent. No. I'm not going to ignore that. I'm going to file that for a later date. And on that topic, we will speak for once and for all. But not now. I'm talking about your ambassador."

"Ambassador De Clercq?"

"Do you have another?"

Desmet slumped lower in the pillow. As hard as he was trying, it always seemed that everyone—make that every single Congolese he met—was four or five steps ahead of him.

Jeta kissed him on the tip of his nose. "Don't be like that. Don't you understand we are worried for you?"

Desmet laced his fingers so that his hands were flat on his bare chest. "Look . . . I'm not an idiot. Shrinar is Belgian, and Shrinar is making millions. And we—I mean the Belgian embassy—are here to help Shrinar make money."

"Yes."

"Don't be like that. I'm going through the motions, I know. I'm not so naïve to think Shrinar is not lobbying the ambassador."

"And how would that work, Laurent?"

"What do you mean?"

"No. What do you mean? Delicate suggestions over tea? A letter-writing campaign?"

Desmet chuckled despite himself. "No. I suppose not."

"Shrinar set up offshore accounts for members of the president's family."

"We don't know that."

"You don't know that because you don't want to know that. Milongo knows that. Boisson knows that. Every journalist and political activist in the Congo knows that. But what De Clercq is worried about is complicity. Favors for Shrinar—which would mean favors for the president's extended family."

Desmet turned to meet huge brown eyes. This was unlike any pillow talk he had ever imagined.

"What kind of favors?"

"Money is one thing. But money is nothing without European villas, shopping, trips to Paris and London."

Desmet said nothing.

"I mean visas, Laurent. Half of the president's family is under one cloud or another. Yet they receive visas to anywhere their pure hearts' desire. Trust me, it's not only Belgium we are talking about."

Desmet stared at his thumbs. "They told you this?"

"Stop worrying about the 'they.' But you should speak to Valdano. Valdano has much to say."

"Valdano?"

"Valdano is in the know. Carhel is in the know. How do you think they afford the suits? They will speak with you if I ask them."

"Ask them about what?"

Jeta sighed. "Passports are small change. You should speak to Valdano about diamonds. Not about visas and your ambassador, but about your ambassador and the Chinese."

Desmet's eyes bugged wide.

"The Chinese?"

"Such a serious boy," said Jeta. She slid atop him, her body cool and longer than he could believe. "Maybe for this morning, we should focus on the less serious."

Desmet said, "We could do that."

■ ■ ■ ■

In the year 1898, the Pole Conrad wrote about the blood of the country. *Heart of Darkness.* The white man's journey into the depths of the black. The white man appalled, horrified by what the white experience. Not the black experience, but the white experience. The white man retreating. Retreating after writing a celebrated and muddy book full of implications and perhaps, for the white man, horror.

Marveille Feza had read that book in a deportation center in Calais. He had read it and marveled and scoffed, having been equally shocked and amazed by the fact that this book—this classic of English literature—had been tossed to him by a Belgian nurse three days before White Christmas and four days before his twenty-third birthday.

And later, in the slums of Kinshasa, in the kitchen, with the big woman dipping and stirring her soup, he had told the boy this. And he had merely grinned and whispered to his mother who had boomed:

"Ah, the prodigal had nothing on you, Marveille Feza. No, the prodigal had nothing on you."

And despite himself, Feza spoke of how he had struggled through the book in English, how he had used it as a guide and pamphlet.

How he had lost it when the Chechens came, when he had drawn a smuggled machete and killed them right in the camp in Calais and bloodied up the entire shack.

And yet it was nothing to what the Belgians had done to his country. For at least in his country, history was undiluted, unrevised.

In the year 1885, Belgian King Leopold II had, in the name of expanding trade, created the Congo Free State. And set the stage for the first, true African genocide. Fifteen million killed. White gendarmes, black capitas teaching the Africans how to enforce discipline. Screams and severed hands. And now, one hundred years later, the bush wars, the full genocides and trivial one-offs had never stopped.

And later, Feza pondering the darkness he kept even from the mother and her son. How he had grimaced, there on another rooftop, this time watching the boy kiss the first girl and the second. White Boy in Af-ri-ca. White Boy fucks Af-ri-ca.

From the beginning of time.

And Feza would wonder about this. How they came here and plundered and fucked. About the fucking. How his retched orgasms came in the deportation camp. The cold and rain. The slutty NGO girls wanting to do their part, to sympathize and empathize and finally fuck a refugee.

That was the second time. Three times, he had tried the "honest way." Three times into France and three times stuck at that nightmare shack-up in Calais. Each time caught, each time deemed a risk of one kind or another and sent back until the third time when the pixie of a white girl told him there were files on him in the Congo, files on him in Belgium, files on him in France.

He had not disbelieved her. The whites were meticulous, and why not? For what he had done, there were files on him with God. And anyway, she was doing him a favor, sending him back, she said. Otherwise, he was looking at endless time in the camp. Then deportation and prison.

So, they had done their thing, Feza prostituting himself and all for papyrus interruptus—this being the hang-up of a paper trap that meant deportation instead of records passed to Interpol and the French police.

That is what it was, in fact. How they got you.

The great paper trap. Funny how he had never thought of it this way.

And oh, how the great, buxom woman in the kitchen had laughed. How her whispering son had grinned, had muttered to the mother in some dialect before she had boomed.

"All of this misery for some pale white. And I tell you, you take your money and borrow a dandy suit. And you buy any Russian biche you want at the Hotel Grand."

And maybe Feza considered this. But Feza also considered the pixie, considered that all of this endless movement—the blacks, the Muslims, the whites—all of it so sexual, so Freudian. And even he, Marveille Feza, falling into it, preyed on by the girl. Frail. White as porcelain, but frail. A child preying on the weak and desperate.

No, that was the mother talking.

But yes. It was the first time Feza had ever considered it this way.

Which is when he muttered out loud, "Why the fuck you want a passport to Europe?"

Belgian even . . .

Which is when the mother and her son burst into laughter. Even as he remembered the bush. The diamond camps. The shooting and slaying and raping and . . .

Which is when his mind went back to what he would not say. Not in the kitchen. Not on the rooftops with a rifle in his hand.

Paulo and the mercenary Rafael raping the amputees. Young girls with no hands bleeding out.

And again, thought Marveille Feza, why the fuck would you stay?

But to hell with it. And all of this fucking, all of these memories—all of that four days ago. Over the past four days and nights, he had followed orders for Fang, had watched the white boy appear and disappear. Had returned to Fang and argued that he did not want diamonds and then had gone back to shadowing the boy, pistol in hand, before peeling off to follow the *sapeur* with the patch over his eye.

To catch him surprised with his whore in the alley.

With the girl that Feza had bought and paid for . . .

With Fang's money.

And all so that he could shoot the one-eyed dandy flat in the back of the head.

■ ■ ■ ■

"Roll your tongue," said Jeta. "Like this."

Desmet was transfixed. He said, "Do that again."

"Stop it. You want to speak Lingala, pay attention."

Jeta rolled her tongue.

"Do that again."

This was the conversation, Sunday afternoon, the Belgian young-and-upcoming diplomat and the beautiful half-Cuban volunteer sitting in plastic chairs on the porch of the Matete youth center, both sipping warm Primus beer from the bottle with notes and a handbook on dialects of the Congo atop Desmet's lap. Then Milongo arrived, then Boisson, the two competing journalists suddenly united, severe.

Jeta narrowed her eyes.

"What's wrong?"

"Valdano comes."

"What's wrong with Valdano?"

Later, in hindsight, Desmet was shocked by the simple fact that there was nothing wrong with Valdano. He did arrive, prim and proper in the wet heat, a Christian Dior suit set off by an equally flamboyant G-Star tie. And Desmet would remember this: Death does not affect Valdano. Valdano never sweats.

Valdano pointed at Desmet. "Carhel said to speak to you. He would have wished it."

Then there was the mutual shock, that of a discordant, non-functional family coming together over the loss of their own. *Did you see those starving kids? Did you see the mother with no hands and feet?* Yes, but this was *Carhel.* This was the infamous, one-eyed dandy, supplier of ganja and curious grins and, most of the time, wistful silence. Thus, over the afternoon, the course of the evening, the hippies filed in, cursing, waving fists and thin wrists and expressing profound and earth-moving outrage.

Some went to Valdano. Others gave him the most serious nods. Milongo, with no leads whatsoever, planned a full investigative piece into the murder. Not to be outdone, Boisson planned a feature on the dandies, on their cliché and niche and how no matter their fight for dignity, their historical demand for a government of the people, the realities of Kinshasa would not leave them untouched.

None but Desmet and Jeta heard what Valdano had to say.

"Diamonds," he began.

▪ ▪ ▪ ▪

"Diamonds," cursed Marveille Feza.

The hell was he going to do with diamonds?

Feza fingered the tiny stones in his pocket. Cursed Fang, the diamonds and Africa, and then Fang all over again. Deep in his pocket, he felt the tiny stones slide around his fingers like sand. Days of plotting, of waiting—only to commit yet another atrocity, one more forever unforgivable sin—and Fang had poured six tiny diamonds into the palm of his hand.

Feza dug into his pocket, scooped them into his fist. Pockets were not a safe place to keep tiny diamonds, but what was he? A diamond smuggler? He had no connections, no . . . foreign distributors.

The fuck was he going to do with diamonds?

"You get cash," Fang had said. "You get cash next time."

Feza passed through the Matonge district with the loose, natural gait of an athlete. This time it was Fang who had tipped him off, and not for the first time he wondered at the Chinese's sources. Avenue Du Kasai to Tombalbaye. The Ethiopian food stall on Tombalbaye and then the singing urchins on the corner of Des Travailleurs. He guessed he was maybe ten minutes from Kin Delicieux, so he still had plenty of time, when what he saw stopped him cold.

The second dandy, moving quickly and with a purpose, not to the lunch bar and the boy, but cutting down Ebeya in the direction of Hotel Memling.

It was odd enough, these chance happenings in such grand chaos that was Kinshasa, but Feza remembered the *sapeur* well. He had seen him many times in the hunt for Carhel the *Sap*. And he had never seen this second dandy so hurried, so *determined.*

He abandoned the hit and followed Valdano instead.

Followed him not to the Memling, but much further. Followed him straight to the Hotel Grand. Followed him right past the bored Russian whores and the animal carvings and the strange palm-tree arch into the lobby, knowing from experience that the boy and his mother were wrong; that, in his cheap suit and sandals, he would soon be ushered out. But still, he followed him just far enough to see Valdano conferring with the same pale white mercenaries he had seen with Fang.

My, he thought, isn't this getting complicated?

Feza retreated back out into the heat, thinking, Why not? It would be the easy way. Tail him and hunt him and shoot the cool dandy just as he had his friend.

Until the thought: I shoot for pay. Only for pay.

No name.

No shot.

Valdano lives.

▪ ▪ ▪ ▪

On the twenty-fifth of May, a young and impetuous Laurent Desmet strode into the High Office of the Belgian Ambassador, all but unannounced. His steam was up; he was full of vim and vigor and he was in the right.

He indeed had something to report.

But the ambassador spoke first. "Did you schedule a meeting?"

Desmet swallowed hard. He said, "Mr. Ambassador, as you well know, I have scheduled scores of meetings. Maybe close to one hundred meetings to little avail."

The ambassador perked an eyebrow. He was tempted to roll his eyes and begin reading the latest *le Monde*.

This was when Desmet said, "But I now have a key informant."

Ambassador Chris De Clercq gave pause. There was a hint of a sparkle in his eyes. Resigned humor? Desmet could not say.

De Clercq said, "Well, then. Congratulations. And just what does this new informant have to say?"

Desmet brightened. He had been warned to have his doubts, but once again the ambassador seemed not just interested, but in the finest tradition of elderly patriarchs, sincere, wise . . .

Patronizing.

Still, the young diplomat-in-training rushed it.

"It's not only passports," Desmet said.

"No?"

"If only that were the case; this goes far deeper."

"Go on."

"I was shown a photo, Mr. Ambassador."

The ambassador perked his eyebrows. Desmet recognized this as the first sign of irritation.

"A family of four, the father a doctor known in Kinshasa."

"Dear boy, could you please get to the point."

"They were murdered, sir. Murdered as part of a visa scam that has infiltrated this very embassy."

The ambassador went silent. Fingers resembling pink carrots rolled taps on his desk.

"We know from the press that the president's cousin, Stephen Demuto, has raked in proceeds off the printing of new Congolese passports. Shrinar obtained the contract to print all new Congolese passports on the condition that thirty percent of total fees would be paid in quarterly sums to the president's family. So now the Congo has the most expensive passports in Europe."

"The press," huffed the ambassador.

"But the president also has a second cousin, Alain Mwanza. He controls the visa trade. This family knew that it had almost no chance to emigrate to Europe simply because the doctor in question had little in terms of savings. Yet he also received threats for having treated rebel soldiers. So, he paid eight hundred francs with the guarantee that he would receive a visa in this very embassy. It is a considerable sum, sir, for a modest, emigrating family. For that is eight hundred times four. Yet, during the planned delivery of the visas, the family—the entire family—was murdered and left in the bush."

The ambassador nodded with a smirk. His message was clearly one of extreme disappointment—as if he were quite inclined to say, Dear God, why has this imbecile been foisted upon me?

So Desmet pressed ahead.

"This is not all, sir."

"No? Are you quite sure?"

"Quite sure, sir. Are you familiar with the firm Tamtax?"

"I believe that is a Chinese company, is it not? Rather scandalous, in fact. Blacklisted for the diamond trade."

"Exactly, sir. Blood diamonds from Tshikapa, sir," Desmet repeated. "Which brings us back to Shrinar, which has been forced to reduce passport fees—following the stories in the press, of course. But

Shrinar must pay its debts—so it by necessity came up with a solution to keep the money flowing to the president's first cousin, Demuto."

"Go on."

Desmet nodded. Rushing again. It was apparent, he realized, to the both of them that, at this point, he could not have stopped babbling even if he wanted to. "Tamtax, meanwhile, wants to be removed from the blacklist of companies trading in blood diamonds. Thus, Tamtax pays the equivalent of lost revenue to an offshore, Stahet, which belongs to Demuto. So, passport fees have dropped, but the contract remains in place with the Congolese, so Shrinar is happy."

Desmet nodded, serious as a schoolboy. "I hope I've made that clear, sir."

Rotund and oddly blushed red, the ambassador shook his head and said, "Indeed you have not. I see no reason for Tamtax to pay this . . . equivalent, as you call it."

Now full-blown impetuous, Desmet cut him off. "Ah, yes, sir. Forgot that part, sir. This is where our—erm, the embassy's role, comes in. In return for Tamtax's equivalent—for assuming debt, as it were—Shrinar is now lobbying quietly with the help of someone in our own embassy to get Tamtax removed from the blacklist."

Desmet all but beamed, then shrank before the oversized indignation of his superior. Ambassador De Clercq drew a deep breath. He turned and glanced out the window and then turned back to Desmet and drew another. Yet over the infinity of silence, the red fluster that had swelled the ambassador's neck began to wane, replaced by a condescending smile.

"Let me see if I have this straight. Shrinar paid, but no longer pays, offshore to the president's family. This payment has been assumed by Tamtax, who are Chinese. The Chinese have nothing to do with visas but wish to resume exporting diamonds. Thus, Shrinar is now obliged to lobby with mysterious support from our own embassy to remove said Chinese from said blacklist in order to export blood diamonds to Europe, through Belgium, I assume."

Desmet wondered if the ambassador had been listening. Neither the visa scam nor the dead family seemed to have made an impression on him. Instead, he said, "Yes, sir. That's the most important part, sir."

A pause and frown that lined the ambassador's face to the bone.

"I see you have been hard at work, Desmet."

Desmet's shoulders sank. The ambassador was infamous for stating this very thing before taking his staff down a notch.

"You do see, however, that this is a very serious accusation."

Desmet gulped. "I—I do see that, sir."

"An accusation that includes the complicity of our embassy, a major Belgian company that we still must assume is in good standing—"

"But the newspaper reports—"

"And which is all based upon a source that cannot be named."

Desmet's turn to frown. To the bone.

"Yes, sir. I do see that, sir."

"Very much like the sources in the press."

Desmet had to give him that. "Very much, sir."

"Then perhaps you do see," growled the ambassador. "For at this point in time, your statement is nothing short of unchecked and unsubstantiated slander. Which will become embassy-supported libel as soon as we orchestrate a report. But if you would rather join the not-so-esteemed ranks of the Kinshasa press core than pursue a career as a young diplomat, please let me know."

Desmet nodded. Then shook his head. Then he nodded and realized he did not know whether to sit or stand, whether to speak or creep away like a rather disgraced and hideous spider.

"That will be all."

Aha. Spider it was.

"Yes, sir. Of course, sir."

Desmet left the room. He made his way down the hall with his fists balled up. Perhaps if he had been a bit older—perhaps if he had arrived even a year earlier, if he had been blessed with a shred more experience—he would have remained a few steps from the ambassador's office, for, secretary or no secretary, the ambassador was so flustered, he didn't bother to shut the door.

Instead, he picked up a cell phone unregistered to the diplomatic services and dialed a European number.

"We need to speak," he said. "Our resident boy-genius has reckoned it out."

▪ ▪ ▪ ▪

There are meetings and words and signatures on paper, and then there is trust.

Marveille Feza had never believed in signatures on paper. Marveille Feza had long placed his belief in handshakes and payment when a job was complete. And he had believed in monopoly—for this was the stark necessity of the trade.

"You have not paid me as agreed."

"You have not finished the job."

"And you have told me that I am your only shooter."

Fang hesitated, then said, "I tell you this again. You, Monsieur. I deal with no other."

Feza raised a finger and pointed at the man's chest. "And these white foreigners? Are they not shooters just like me?"

Fang's face went blank as China. The fallback position, Feza knew, to anything from negotiations to lies to politics or even the truth.

Fang said nothing, twitched the corner of his mouth. The pair sat staring at each other in silence in the backroom of the communist mission as Marveille Feza studied the flat moon face with intent. He had long ago learned all there was to learn about trust. In that you could never trust. Life is a judgment call, he thought.

As is, whether by the hand of God or man, each and every death.

▪ ▪ ▪ ▪

The wheels of justice grind, thought Desmet. The wheels of injustice spin greedily into action.

Three days after the killing of Carhel and only one day following Desmet's confrontation with the high ambassador, the Hope for Young Women Foundation lost its license as an NGO. While this meant little to the general populace (apart from a two-paragraph story written by the gracious Boisson), it also meant that both Claire and Jeta were at that moment unemployed. Barely had they returned to their apartment when the *Police Nationale* arrived to inform Claire that her visa had been revoked.

Claire stuffed books, undergarments and jeans into a rainbow-striped suitcase. Jeta did her best to remain calm and make tea. The two police appeared no different than the average soldier. Claire and Jeta barely spoke, both fearing rape. Instead, the soldiers were formal, good-natured to the point that they allowed Claire and Jeta to hold each other, Jeta crying like a child while Claire patted her on the back to console her fear.

Then they drove Claire away, and she was gone.

For the rest of her life, Jeta would pray that the gendarmes had spoken the truth. That Claire had simply been taken to the processing center. That she had survived temporary arrest and had boarded a plane or bus to return home to Angola. That she never heard from Claire again meant nothing. This was Africa. People swirled into your life and then swirled away. For all she knew Claire was dead. For all she knew, Claire could have romanced one of the two police, could have run away to Madagascar or Morocco or the Maldives.

Milongo was not so lucky.

There was no wake, no drunken morbidity as there had been with Carhel. The hippies of Matonge had lived in Africa long enough that there could be no clinging together. Chaz had escaped the worst of Rwanda. Arthur had been shot in the leg in Kenya. No, when the soldiers came—when any soldiers came—it was every man for himself, every woman for herself. Every child you saw on the side of the road that you could not possibly help.

And no, maybe this was nothing. Certainly not Rwanda. Maybe this was just some private drama that was not even the slightest itch among the scars of Kinshasa.

All the same, there had been calls in the night. All the same, Desmet opened the morning papers and had the stomach-dropping urge to vomit.

Renowned Journalist Sidney Milongo Found Dead.

That was the headline, but the picture was worth a thousand words.

Desmet staggered from the kitchen to the bedroom of his apartment. With only a whisper, he woke Jeta (had she slept a wink?), and not unlike Claire (although he would never have known this), he threw his clothes, his undergarments, laptop and books into a rollered suitcase. The baby-blue dandy suit he left hung up on the wall.

Jeta was fully dressed. Silently, efficiently, she went to packing what food Desmet had in the pantry and refrigerator into her bag.

Desmet said, "I'm calling two taxis, Jeta."

"Two?"

"Tell me where to meet. I must speak with the ambassador—I must go to my embassy. But tell me where you'll be. Where to meet."

Jeta stared at Desmet in disbelief. Claire had not had a choice, but Desmet was proving himself the fool.

■ ■ ■ ■

Marveille Feza put his sights on the boy, saw him kiss the girl, and watched her slip into the taxi and ride off. He then watched the boy pay a second taxi a symbolic fare for no ride.

Then the boy made off on foot.

"A fool," Feza said to himself. With speed and efficiency, he stripped the sniper rifle and packed into a gym bag, never taking his eye off the boy's route. Before the boy hit the end of the street, Feza was bounding down the stairs to the ground floor. Then the heat, car horns and bustle of the thousand tribes of Africa hit him, and he was off, jogging at an easy pace, thinking, It's time to end it. To kill white men once and for all, and for once, justify his pay.

■ ■ ■ ■

Desmet half galloped, half ran in the general direction of the Belgian embassy. On foot, it would take him an hour. At a run, maybe twenty minutes. He did not trust taxis, not after Carhel and Milongo. It was best to treat all drivers as informers; although, now running, now knowing all that he should have never known, he was as conscious of skin color as he had ever been in his life. Ebony blacks, coffee blacks. Arab blacks and Belgian-French Creole. Yet there he was, slightly tanned at last, but in comparison, pink as a pig and running as scared as a piglet with reality standing the hairs upon his neck.

He stopped. Hailed a taxi on Boulevard Du. Rode past the golf course, directed the driver deep into the Lingwala District.

For taxi or no taxi, he was running for Arnaud.

Jeta had told him much of the teenage fixer. Arnaud was one of those teenage salesmen who provided cigarettes for the army, booze for the officers, women for politicians and information for all that lay in between.

If anyone could tell him the truth about the ambassador, it would be Arnaud. And for once in his life, Desmet had to know.

In truth, Desmet did not expect to make it to Arnaud's apartment. Perhaps he expected arrest, a gunshot—mercenaries with machetes—or perhaps he had no idea. Yet the building rushed upon him sooner than he would have believed, Desmet having abandoned the taxi; having cut through alleys and backyards to lose even the curiosity of the driver; having been snapped at not by dogs, but by chained hyenas belonging either to a visiting gang or circus or both.

Desmet slid to a halt. He drew the wadded paper out of his pocket, unsure as to whether this was really the place. They had visited once before—Jeta, Claire and Desmet, inseparable (although Desmet could still not remember the threesome or if it had truly happened) and slightly high. The boy-fixer lived with his grandmother, a jolly spinster who seemed to live to cook briny soups full of African squash, goat meat and badly scraped bones. The woman, massively bosomed, black as night, had loved Desmet on sight, the skinny Belgian now remembering how she had all but lifted him off his feet to crack his spine with hugs and unintelligible greetings in Lingala.

In that moment, thinking about the woman and the small apartment reeking of inedible soup, Desmet held to the illusion that he would be safe.

There were no dogs, but the front yard was a haven for free-range chickens. Desmet reached over a gate of sticks and flotsam wired together and unhitched a metal latch. Taking care not to set free the chickens, Desmet slipped into the yard, called out to Arnaud and "Mama Arnaud," and banged upon a half-open door. No response, but the door was not locked.

In Kinshasa.

Desmet glanced back over his shoulder. On the trash-strewn alley of Rue Itaga. Passersby with heavy loads on their shoulders, heads, and backs made their way with not so much as a glance. Desmet nudged the door with his toe.

Stepped inside . . .

To the reek of feces and death that he had not yet encountered in his diplomat-to-be career.

Down the stairs rained liters of blood. Masses of congealed lymph or brain or Desmet did not know what. The boy in him retched, a hand going to his mouth to hold it in and somehow not defile a scene that had been desecrated for life. And still, he could not help himself, and in his natural state of awkwardness, slipped to a knee. A hand went into the wet—instinct put his hand to his shirt, then to the wall, then back to his shirt so that he would not leave a print. But on standing, he saw that his knees, his khaki pants and white shirt were bloodied maroon black in the dark. Shaking, Desmet managed to stand without touching anything, without even bracing himself on the rail.

His steps went to the very edge of the dilapidated staircase and he plodded upward, unsteady and tip-toeing to the side of what was now a stepped-waterfall from the murder above. Desmet hyperventilated, tiny breaths puffing in and out of his mouth to avoid the smell, but the retch jerked up into his lower throat, forced him to swallow it back down and then jerked up again.

Still he refused to vomit, at one point gaining just enough control to spit a bile of fluid over the rail. Then he stood in the door, saw the state of Arnaud and Mama Arnaud, and whirled away with a gasp.

Which is when he would have, should have lost it. Only the instinct of disgust and vile repulsion were erased with a jolt of abject fear. For there was a lean African on the stairs staring up with an expression akin to a mix of concern, irritation and his own disgust that no, once again, he was not in the least surprised.

But most importantly, the African brandished a gun.

Marveille Feza spoke the question with a dry rasp so that it rang cold and factual. "They are dead, no?"

"Yes," said Desmet. "They are dead."

"The boy Arnaud and his mother both?"

Desmet nodded, his jaw beginning to tremble.

Feza said, "I must see this thing."

The African who was Marveille Feza easily navigated the stairs. Desmet saw that the African was not in the least troubled by the blood. He sidestepped Desmet with the grace of a dancer, paused and said to Desmet's back (for the Belgian had not the strength to again face the carnage behind him):

"Large-caliber weapon. Unnecessary and loud."

Desmet said, "Are you the police?"

Feza was suddenly before him, a wide smile and the raised eyebrow of bemusement. "No. Not the police. But they will come. I'm surprised no one is here already. But the dogs will come. They will smell the blood, and then the people will come, and then the police will come."

"We should call them."

Feza put a machine pistol to Desmet's forehead. "No, white Belgian. We should leave."

Desmet had never faced the specter of true violence, and this was not the violence of even the previous night. The tales of Valdano, the newspaper headlines and frantic phone calls since—this had been surreal. Yet the blood of Arnaud and his mother, the cold cylinder of the machine pistol to his head, this snapped him out of surreality and into the abject and stunned resignation of a servant.

"Where should we go?"

"You have blood on your clothes," said Desmet. "You cannot travel such."

Desmet removed his shirt, balled it up in a fist. "My apartment," he said.

"I know where you live."

Feza marched him down the stairs. Just as Feza predicted, the dogs had come, as had a shaky old man. Feza held the pistol to the old man's head.

"What do you see, Grandpa?"

"I see no man."

"Let us remember that."

The stick fence was open, the wire contraption of a door hanging as loose as a broken arm. They passed through this, blended into foot traffic and then the cars and carts and mopeds of Rue Itaga. They were moving easily now, Desmet strangely gliding atop the notion that if he broke away, he would be shot, that if he approached the embassy with an assassin in tow, they both would be shot. That if he brought the assassin to Jeta, they would also both be shot. So, the apartment it was, and to the apartment they ran.

Street after street. Alley after alley. Back at the unnamed corner on the edge of the district, back before the hyena-circus men who called out to the assassin with the greetings of friends.

"You know those guys?" blurted Desmet.

"Kinshasa is my home."

Again, the wide-toothed grin. Desmet had not expected an answer. He did not know whether the assassin was truly an assassin or secret police or even why, for that matter, they were running for his apartment when all he had left for clothing there was the baby-blue dandy suit.

So, he stopped in his tracks. Smack in the center of Avenue De La Region. There were sophisticated people here. Good taxis and business people and Feza did not waste a second. He pulled the machine pistol out in full view and put it to Desmet's head. Whether this was seen or reported or whether the citizens of Kinshasa reacted at all, Desmet would never know. He simply nodded and again began to run.

They made it to Desmet's apartment a hair before ten in the morning. Outside, the sun had the blinding glare of the second coming. Inside was a memory of cool respite. Of Jeta and Claire and a time as a kid when he had treated the embassy as a curious day job. Feza drove him into the apartment, the machine pistol back out in full view so that Desmet fumbled with the lock. Then he dropped the keys.

"You will shoot me in my own apartment."

"I will do no such thing."

Desmet glanced at Feza in disbelief. He kneeled to scoop up the keys and found his legs were gone. Feza hooked him under an arm and easily drew the boy to his feet.

Desmet said, "Then why the pistol?"

"Open the door."

"Why the pistol?"

"I have killed one man today. I can still make it two."

Desmet stood his ground. "But you did not kill Arnaud?"

A second voice boomed low and cheery behind them.

"No," said Valdano. "He did not kill *famille Arnaud*."

Feza perked an eye, saw the dandy brandished a pistol of his own.

Feza shrugged and said, "Open the door, Monsieur *Dezz-met*."

And Valdano also said, "Yes, Laurent. Open the door."

Thus, Laurent Desmet opened the door.

Slow and delicate, the three traipsed inside. Desmet strode to the far wall, but when he turned, he saw that the assassin had not dropped his gun but held it loosely, uncaring at his side. How they take it, thought Desmet. How the threat of death—how death itself—fazes them not in the least.

Not knowing what to do, Desmet said, "My clothes are with Jeta." He nodded to the blue zoot suit on the door. "I only have *that*."

The assassin surprised him then. He grinned wide as if he could be anyone and put a thumb to his lip. Valdano eyed the suit and nodded appreciatively, and in that surreal microsecond of a moment, Desmet actually worried that he could have offended the man.

"That will do," said the assassin.

"Yes," said Valdano. "That will do."

Desmet nodded and took the suit with the hanger. He made for the bathroom, and the assassin said, "Leave the door open, Monsieur."

Desmet shrugged, confused that he was taking orders by a stranger who was himself being covered by Valdano. Half-expecting—no, make that expecting—a gunfight behind his back, Desmet stripped to his undershorts, rinsed the blood from his hands and chest and elbows and knees and then donned the suit, silver vest and all without a shirt.

He stepped out of the bathroom in his blue suit and socks.

Feza said, "Put your shoes on, Monsieur."

But Valdano spoke to the assassin, "You knew the boy Arnaud."

Feza glanced at Valdano and held his stare.

"He was my friend."

"Mama Arnaud was your friend. A *holy woman*, but the boy—no, Arnaud was nobody's friend. Arnaud was a demon and his mother's shame."

Desmet, frozen in his blue dandy suit, watched in fascination, Valdano, speaking facts, cool with the pistol steady in a dandy suit of his own, his voice rolling fruity but monotonously, as if out of boredom.

But, for the first time, Feza raised the machine pistol. He trained it on Valdano and said:

"Arnaud Ilunga was my friend."

Valdano cocked his head. Offered a shrug of his own and stowed his pistol inside his coat.

"As you will," he said. "But tell me, Marveille Feza, whom have you shot today?"

Which is when Feza pursed his lips and shoved the machine pistol into the rear of his pants.

"A fucking liar of a Chinaman," he said. "That is whom I shot."

▪ ▪ ▪ ▪

Perhaps the son was in hell. Perhaps in purgatory for sins that were those of whispers and not of his own hand. Perhaps one day he, Marveille Feza (whose sins were always of his own hand) . . . perhaps one day, he would return for the two blood-cold whites who had killed the son and the mother both.

But not on this day.

No, on this day, this fool's day of April, he, Marveille Loic Feza, son of Regis Feza and Mireille, stood side by side with the dandies in the bluffs. Stood in solidarity along the river and wondered in silence when the boat would come.

White-child dandy in a baby blue suit. The elegant dissident-*sapeur* in a peppermint striped creation of his own. And Feza, chuckling now, pistol in his pants and sniper rifle in his gym bag, but anxious for the first time in his life.

For now, he had finally listened to the great mother of his life. Now—on payment of blood and sin—he had finally come to a decision.

So, he thought:

When comes the boat?

So, he worried:

Will the white-child keep up?

So, he was tempted to mumble aloud:

And if the fixers do not lie—if they dodge the patrols and the police and slip into Brazzaville, what then? The white Belgian to the refugee camps? Valdano to the merchants and traders?

Absurd.

And what about me? he thought. A killer with no more taste for killing? A soldier sick to death of the bush? And what of these two white shooters? Fang's guns for hire? Killers of Arnaud and his mother both?

His chuckle went grim. *Rewanj. Rewanj* for another day. Then his eyes went back to the baby blue suit and, shaking his head, he knew he would take the boy under his wing.

Life is a judgment call, he thought. Make your decision and worry yourself silly, but it is not always about death.

Which is when the dandy Valdano said, "Tell the truth now. All of us. We journey together. Maybe we die together. So, what do we have in our pockets?"

All eyes went to Desmet. White as a sheet, probably fearing he would be robbed, he stared at Valdano and took a deep breath.

"I have four hundred dollars," he said. "I have four hundred dollars and this old Nokia phone."

"Four hundred dollars is good," said Valdano. "But if you have used the phone, throw it in the river. We will soon find you another."

Desmet half-nodded, half-slumped. He held up the phone in resignation, whispered Jeta's number to himself and prayed that he would never forget it. Then he threw the phone far out into the churn.

Valdano turned to Feza. "And you, soldier who will now lead us, I shall not tolerate a lie. What do you have in *your* pockets?"

Feza broke into a smile. This Valdano was living up to his name. "You first, dandy brother on the run."

Valdano licked his lips and stared across the river to the wilds south of Brazzaville.

"I have a Varan pistol with one clip," he said. "I have two hundred and seventy-five Congo francs. I have a gold watch in my pocket and three sets of cufflinks that I plan to sell. But apart from this, I have nothing but my style."

Marveille Feza laughed. Out loud. He was tempted to reach behind the boy and slap this serious Valdano on the back. This *elegant.* This new *copain* whose friend he had killed. Good dear Mama Arnaud, he thought. In the end, we are all such trusting souls. But Dear God Above, what if one day he should tell the truth? The whole truth? Ugly and damning and . . . And yet, this was enlightenment. For it had occurred to him that he, Marveille Feza, child of war and sin, had not tasted true laughter in years; that now that he had finally abandoned this *error magnifique*—this misplaced dream of Europe; that perhaps finally after all of this murdering and killing, there could be a time to heal and forgive.

So when Valdano abruptly faced him, wanting an honest answer, for once in his life, Feza was not afraid to tell the truth.

"What do I have in my pockets, brother? That is all you want to know?"

Valdano spread his hands, imploring with a sigh. The Belgian Desmet, stateless, having now abandoned more than Feza and Valdano both, swallowed in the heat and put on a brave face the best he knew how.

"I have passports, my friends," Feza began. "Passports from a dead Chinaman. Passports that we shall *adjust.*"

Desmet glanced at Valdano. Valdano glanced at Desmet.

Which is when Marveille Feza said:

"And I have diamonds, brothers." He laughed. "Hundreds upon hundreds of them."

## GERMANY:

## Shifting Syrian Sands

BY CONSTANTINE BOUCHAGIAR

*CONSTANTINE BOUCHAGIAR is a journalist and TV producer living between Düsseldorf and Corfu Island. From 1994 on, he worked for TV Corfu as a journalist and cameraman, and six years later became a correspondent for MEGA and Alpha Channels and for Reuters. In the process, he set up Technorama, his own TV production studio, which he still heads today. Highlights of his career have been the production of short films, with his first production,* Sand Chronicles, *earning him a distinction for his role as Director of Photography at the seventh Festival of "Fantasy Cinema." In 2012, he participated in the production of* ILLUMINAM, *in 2013 of* Life Shadows, *and in 2015 of* Itinere.

Ali Rashid Hamas Abdul al-Boutros Muhammad Shadmanesh Pasha decided to shorten his name. Not only was it difficult to pronounce for Europeans and Americans, but for a refugee just arriving in Germany with the endless Syrian human caravans, it could be associated with everything negative—from petty crime to extreme terrorism, or from forcing women to wear veils to beating and raping them.

Furthermore, he did not want to be associated with a refugee problem that was contributing to significant tensions in Europe—resurgent nationalism, racism and right-wing politicians who threatened to shatter the European Union.

On a personal level, having "Muhammad" or Mohamed in your name immediately caused Westerners to conclude you were a Muslim religious fundamentalist. "Hamas" connected you to the terrorist organization fighting with Israel.

So, instead of "Ali," the twenty-eight-year-old considered two common German names, Aldo or Aldous. Aldo meant something like "the wise elder," while Aldous translated into "old and wealthy." Both names had positive connotations, so he could play with them according to circumstances. He could even shorten them further to Al. The English-speaking world, especially Americans, would love it. Al, short for Alan. You know, like Al Capone or something.

No, no, no! Get gangster names out of your mind, Ali Pasha. They will consider you a gangster anyhow, so don't be so stupid as to encourage them.

At one point, he considered adopting the first name Adolph. He thought that was very typically German or Austrian. However, friends who knew better advised him not to tempt fate—Adolf Hitler was never far from a German's memory.

He certainly kept Pasha as his surname. Altering it would have caused considerable complications with his documents, as well as suspicions. And it was not a bad name. In the Turkish and Arab worlds, *Pasha* was a very distinguished title accorded by the state.

It meant a nobleman, a regional leader, a governor, a rich guy, the equivalent of a lord or duke in English. So that wasn't bad; rich guys rarely suffered from discrimination. And he loved translating Pasha as "Lord." It was so noble-sounding, even vaguely Christian.

Ali Muhammad Hamas Pasha (the shorter version of his Arab name) had been fortunate enough as a young man to learn some English, to acquire basic computer and internet skills, and thereby indulge in English-language film binge-watching. He realized that people arrived in America from all parts of the world with hideous-sounding names, unpronounceable, and quickly changed them to blend into a "melting pot" dominated by a conservative white majority.

He saw how the Greeks shortened Papahajinikolopoulos down to Pappas, the Japanese reduced Hitokoshima to Hit or Hito, the Germans turned Heidelburger into something like Burg, and the Spanish took their lead from one of their most famous countrymen—Pablo Picasso. After all, Picasso's real name was far worse than Ali Pasha's. It was Pablo Diego José Francisco de Paula Juan Nepomuceno María de los Remedios Cipriano de la Santísima Trinidad Ruiz y Picasso.

Furthermore, Ali Pasha was not black. He was light brown. No minor advantage—for decades, there had been brown people in Germany, and the Deutsch were used to their Turkish "*gastarbeiter.*" The "guest workers" who did the "Three-D" jobs—the dirty, dangerous and demanding occupations.

Ali Pasha was among several hundred thousand Syrian refugees who, in the summer of 2016, made it across to Europe, hoping to settle in Germany. Anything to escape the horrors of a seemingly endless Syrian civil war. He had done so just like everybody else: long marches and endless bus rides. All headed to Greece, the easternmost member of the European Union. Allah praise the EU. Once they crossed into Greece or were dumped on any one of its hundreds of islands by well-paid human traffickers, the refugees were immediately accorded human rights. It meant that the worst part of the exodus was over, that they were more than halfway to Germany.

They were taken to specially built refugee camps in Greece, which, though by no means perfect, provided safety, food, shelter, warmth, basic sanitation and even some pocket money. All of it at European Union and American taxpayer expense. After a few weeks or months, European Union agencies and human rights activists were to help them get to Germany in an organized manner.

Ali Pasha knew Germany was the most powerful country in Europe, the richest, and that he had some hope of getting a job there. With the large diversification of nationalities, he saw it as something like a smaller version of the United States, within Europe. With a pronounceable name, good manners and a fair mastery of English and German, he felt he had a chance to make a life for himself. He did not want to be just one more ant among the insects marching endlessly with their burden of belongings.

The young Syrian was also concerned that he would be perceived as a potential troublemaker. Anything between a criminal and a terrorist. There was already fierce debate within Germany on the wisdom of admitting this sea of refugees. Chancellor Angela Merkel was engaged in a fight for her political career. Confronted on the right for admitting this unwashed mass, and on the left for failing to provide more "humane" services to the displaced. The "bleeding hearts" of liberal humanitarians caused him no concern. Bricks, bats and crowbars wielded by right-wing crusaders were a whole different matter.

The paranoia about refugee-imported crime in Germany reached new heights when Donald Trump turned migrant lawbreakers into a campaign theme. While Trump focused on the United States and its South American immigrants, he made sure to blacklist Germany on his way to the White House.

In short, Ali Pasha was in a quandary. How to quickly gain the confidence of the locals, be accepted in their factories and homes, and get a job so he could send some money back to his relatives in Damascus? That was what emigration was all about. To earn a living and sustain family remaining in the homeland.

Money and pride. No one wanted to send a letter home admitting to defeat. They wanted their friends and relatives to think that they had succeeded. They didn't want them to think they were scrubbing floors, cleaning toilets or just taking care of disabled elderly people.

## DOWN TO BUSINESS

Ali Pasha first tried to make himself useful upon reaching the Greek island of Lesbos. This island gave the international name to Lesbians, because in antiquity, when the Greek men went off to war, the lonely women turned to each other for love and comfort.

This was irrelevant to Ali. What was important was his fair knowledge of English—he became "the translator." The man who dealt with bureaucrats, law enforcement, military security and clueless humanitarian do-gooders.

He became so useful that he evolved into one of the most identifiable persons in his own refugee camp on Lesbos Island. Officials and guards would seek him out when mired in a language problem.

"Hi, Al," they would often call out to him. "Hi, Johnny," he would call back, a beaming smile on his face. He knew Johnny was one of the most common names in the Western world, and thus resorted to calling most English-speaking men Johnny. He caught on to calling almost all women "Mary," and then, as he became more confident and brazen, he used that phrase so often heard in American films: "Hi, baby." That made the women giggle.

He also picked up other little gestures of international significance, which helped his communication skills and general popularity. Thumbs up to message that everything was OK; a high five when passing by a younger official; or a touching of clenched fists once a deal was made.

"How are you, Al?" soldiers and police would call out to him. "I'm good, I'm good," he would beam back, thumbs up, with that big, ear-to-ear smile.

Most of the other Arab men stared at Al Pasha in bewilderment, wondering how on earth he had managed to make himself something of a star in such a short period. They spent a lot of time praying to Allah, but that did not seem to change their fate. However, they convinced themselves that this was the Will of the Almighty. He was still looking down on them. *Inshallah* (If God Wills It), or *Allāhu akbar* (God Is the Greatest), they would constantly mutter to themselves, just to make sure they did not forget their Arabic and to assure God they were not forgetting Him.

## TRANSLATIONS

The first job that Ali Pasha found to do on a regular basis was translation. He would attend small groups wanting to communicate with the relief forces, and then would be taken on by individual Syrian families. Particularly the wealthier expats who had managed to slip out of the country with secreted bundles of money. They would offer payment in cash, which at first surprised him, and he politely refused. But he then came to think this made sense. After all, he had expended considerable effort to learn languages and internet skills, and he *was* making a difference in assisting the future of these destitute people.

They would not remember him once they were settled, would they? And he wasn't begging, was he? He was working, right?

The relief agencies were not giving him money, but they came to appreciate his services so much that they give him useful gifts in the form of clothing, a good transistor radio, a portable TV and a smartphone. By listening to TV and radio programs in English and Arabic, he stored up a trove of knowledge as to what was going on, which was to prove extremely useful—in business.

Hardly any of the other refugees were so well informed. He was taking the global pulse, a measure of international comings and goings.

For his translations, he estimated that he was making about €300 or $300 per month, a respectable amount for an unemployed refugee. He now considered himself an official translator, a respectable profession.

## OFFICIAL LETTERS & BUREAUCRACY

This led him to a second job that was directly related: translation of documents. At first, Ali Pasha only dealt with verbal translations. With constant practice and the endless needs of the refugees, he could translate in what they called "real-time"—almost as quickly as the words were spoken. The other Arabs found this impressive.

Although his written English and German had not been as good as his spoken skills, he was inevitably called upon to complete their documents. Documents put them on the map. Turned them into real people instead of drifters.

Applications became his next job. Helping them fill out applications—for jobs, housing, long-term employment, medical assistance, schooling, adoption, anything. People clutched to their folders of papers and applications—they were just as important as food and clothes.

In the process, Ali Pasha learned the terminology and what exactly agencies were asking. Clear answers written in legible English or German earned prompt attention. When an official read them, he or she became more sympathetic to the applicant. Now here is a well-meaning and cultured person, they would think, nothing like the terrorists we were told of. In fact, many of them appear to be much better than our good-for-nothing hooligans who spend most of their time drinking and watching soccer!

So now Ali Pasha had two professions, two small businesses: translations and bureaucratic services. From these two jobs, he was making €600 to €700 per month, sometimes more. Far more than he could ever hope to earn in Syria.

## TRADING

The twenty-eight-year-old man noticed that many of the refugees lacked the small basics necessary for proper paperwork. Clients appeared without pens, paper, staplers, paperclips, plastic folders and so on. These were vital. Without these, their papers, their world would fall apart. Bureaucrats have no sense of humor or patience.

So he got another idea.

When going into nearby cities, a small number of refugees were allowed to accompany the police, soldiers or social workers. Ali Pasha became the indispensable translator.

He came to see the cities of Northern Greece—Drama, Kavala, Alexandroupolis and Salonica. This city was also known as the "Queen of the Balkans." Or the "Paris of the Balkans." He loved those broad and bright boulevards by the sea, shops with their tantalizing displays, supermarkets overflowing with products that made your mind boggle.

Most surprising of all, there was no fighting. No bombs, no bullets, no destroyed buildings, no bodies in the streets or smoke billowing in the distance. No jets screaming overhead or jeeps speeding up and down the streets with soldiers either shooting in the air or at people. Salonica was what Damascus used to be.

He went into one big stationery shop and purchased dozens of ballpoint pens, black, red and blue. Then erasers, packs of paper, staplers, paper clips, glue, sticky-tape, folders, ink, string and a roll of wrapping material. He even bought magnifying glasses for those who could not see small print.

When Ali went back to camp, his predictions were proved true: all these items sold like hotcakes. Everybody needed them. The refugees even bought more than they needed. Not only for themselves but for their children. Pens and paper to keep them occupied and quiet. If only he could have bought more!

Within two weeks, he realized he had to have a separate tent just for the products. A display bench outside his prefab was insufficient. The officials allowed him. After all, he was providing a useful service, as proved by the lines that formed almost all hours of the day. They had to impose an afternoon break in the "shopping hour" to give Ali a rest. He was exhausted, but he was a happy, happy man.

So now he had four professions: translator, handler of bureaucratic services, trader and shopkeeper. In the next month, he had doubled his income to about €1,500 per month. He had to buy a heavy, metal safe to keep it protected from envious intruders, and he cemented it to the ground in his shop-tent so it could not be carried away.

It was during these shopping sorties to the cities, always in cooperation with European and Greek police authorities, that he developed another, hidden trade: that of a police informer. Casually at first, then more intrusively, the Europol authorities tracking refugee crime asked him for information on various individuals. Ali had no problem surrendering such data . . . perhaps by the siren call of authorities promising to assist his fellow countrymen.

Gradually, Ali became fully aware of his role as a police informer. Since he was popular, played an important role in meeting refugee supply needs, came into contact with more individuals than anybody else, and spoke their language, he was an important source of reliable information. Furthermore, the refugees trusted him.

Ali, quite rightly, realized that his role as an informer was good for business. As the police found him useful as a channel of information, they were willing to turn a blind eye to a few peculiarities in his business practices.

## MAGIC MACHINES

By the time of his next trip to Salonica, he knew it was time to join the twenty-first century.

Back to the big stores—which he adored—and this time, he returned with two prize pieces of equipment. One was a small multi-purpose machine for scanning, faxing, photocopying and printing. The other was a computer with a large hard drive.

His customers loved the photocopier. They made more and more photocopies, far more than they needed. Now that this service was available, everybody in a family could make duplicate copies of their documents. The more folders with documents they had, the safer they felt.

The lines grew longer; sales of pens, staplers and folders to keep the photocopies together rocketed. Ali found himself safeguarding a seeming mountain of five- and ten-euro notes. The computer and printer were the largest sources of cash. Ali standardized applications and translations and literally churned out asylum requests. And then the internet came to the refugee camp. Almost overnight, he went from living off the printer to submitting emails across the EU collection of humanitarian organizations.

Ali Pasha had the next stroke of genius. Skype! He could arrange for refugees to appear in front of the computer screen and actually speak and *see* their relatives and friends back home. And it was live! For the overwhelming majority, it was an experience they could hardly have imagined. And all this only for one euro or one dollar for five minutes. They could only be given five minutes per shot on Skype because the lines were piling up, and people were impatient.

Many of them came to call Ali the "magician." As if he had developed magic powers.

Ali hardly had time to count the money. He just stuffed it into a lockbox secured to a cement block secured beneath his cot. He had to go to a bank to turn all those small denominations into bigger bank notes so they could fit into his "safe."

The young Syrian (could he call himself a "businessman" now?) convinced himself that it was not a question of greed. "Crises can create opportunities," went the popular saying. Well, in this case, the hell of Syria led to a near-paradise in the Western world. He couldn't wait to get to Germany and settle into a proper apartment.

He was now a professional translator, handler of bureaucratic services, a trader, shopkeeper, computer expert and provider of internet services. In effect, one business with *six* divisions. As for his role as a police informer, Ali found another professional phrase that soothed his conscience: public relations. He saw himself as maintaining communications between the refugees and authorities, for the security and wellbeing of all sides. Simply good public relations.

▪ ▪ ▪ ▪

Ali was on his eighth shopping spree in Salonica when he was approached in the street by two men. They were polite, introducing themselves as "Greek merchants" Niko and Yanni. They told him they noted the large quantities of goods he was buying and wanted to suggest some alternatives with better prices. Yet there was something wrong with their accents. They didn't sound like Greeks. More like Albanians. And if they were lying to him from the outset, how could he trust them?

When they said they were interested in doing business with him, in providing supplies at *half* the price he paid in shops and supermarkets, he decided to pay closer attention. They convinced him to join them for a quick coffee—"just fifteen minutes"—and wasted no time coming to the point.

Yes, they were Albanians, Niko admitted. He then repeated their promise for half-price goods but also requested Ali consider "very cheap" alcohol, cigarettes, and medicines. And if he wanted light drugs, primarily marijuana, they could also provide that.

Ali kept calm and friendly, but politely rejected most offers apart from the cheaper market goods. He also said he could take cigarettes, which were popular among the Syrians, but rejected alcohol as being contrary to Muslim habits. He also rejected drugs.

He told them he was heading for Germany and, once settled there, would be very interested in doing business with them. Niko and Yanni—their real Albanian names were Artan and Ilir—gave him samples of their products and refused payment.

"Just a small gift from us"—they feigned generosity—"and may God be with you"—even greater hypocrisy, coming from a pair of self-proclaimed atheists.

Acting as an informer, Ali promptly reported the incident to Europol police. They told him not to worry, and that henceforth they would handle the Albanian mafia members themselves. But, they said, should they get in contact with Ali again, he should let the business develop.

Ali was somewhat surprised but guessed that the police must have their reasons. And business was business, above all.

## FEMALE ASSISTANCE

Ali Pasha realized that he could not keep going at this pace. What was the point of making all this money if he collapsed from exhaustion? He hardly had time to eat, usually grabbing a sandwich and coffee or Coke while standing up. Eating with one hand and taking money with the other.

He just had to take on an assistant. But whom could he trust? He had no relatives in the camp, since his own family had been killed. And, as far as he knew, all businesses were family businesses.

He just had to get an assistant, preferably a female. This business needed a female presence, a female touch. Someone who, preferably, also did not have a family. Because if he brought her family in, he knew he would ultimately be doomed. They would rob him blind and then get him out of the way for the sake of their own family clan.

He had noticed a pretty Syrian girl who often came to his shop (or "trade center" as he sometimes called it). He estimated her to be somewhere between her late teens and early twenties. Reserved, but not too reserved; shy but not too shy. She usually wore a pretty light-blue headscarf that framed her bright face, and an almost perpetual smile. She made a pleasant difference compared to the hundreds of black-scarved women in their camp, who showed very little of their faces.

One morning he casually asked her name. Jasmina, she said. Jasmina-Adara. Jasmina was beautiful, simply because it was a traditional Arabic name that meant jasmine flower. Adara meant "the Virgins." Great. In chats with the Frontex combined European border forces there, and with his other customers, he easily found out her full name: Jasmina-Adara Al Muhtar Hassan Mashdala Aisha Badriyah Samsara. Aged twenty-one.

Problems again. This name was unmanageable in the Western world. Very non-commercial. Jasmina as a first name was fine, and pretty. The surname Samsara could be turned into Sammy, Shady, or Sadie, or even Saudi. No—Sandy; yes, Sandy! Jasmina Sandy. Beautiful. Perfect.

"Free for you," Ali told her the next morning, when Jasmina eventually got to the front of the line and asked for the cost of a pen, a writing pad and a bar of chocolate.

Jasmina blushed. She sensed an ulterior motive. "Why?" she asked in Arabic. "You have never done this before."

"Because only now did I discover that you have no family," Ali answered readily, since he had rehearsed a dialogue in his mind. "I learned that they were all killed in the war. That you have no one here at the camp, just like me. In a way, that makes us related, like brother and sister. Please accept these. I have many more."

Jasmina could not argue with that. She took the goods and walked away, still embarrassed. But Ali had succeeded in his objective. He had broken the ice. She could not ignore him next time. This bridge-building served as the beginning for more chats, and soon he formally proposed that she work for him. She explained that she had never worked before, only had a basic secondary school education, and hardly knew what to do.

"It's nothing," Ali countered cheerfully. "Just watch me, and in a day, you will know everything. After that, you can focus on the computer. Just one piece of advice: learn English and German; it will be absolutely vital for your future."

Jasmina said she would think about it. Ali said that he insisted and that she should see him like family, like brother and sister. He had found her soft spot, her Achilles' heel. It was that argument that always melted Jasmina's resistance. She felt she needed a family, especially an older brother, who would take care of her.

Ali offered her fifty euros per week, or €200 per month, a pittance, really, compared to what he was making. But she was delighted—started work the next day.

## AN ARAB MAN AND WOMAN

The plan worked. The presence of a young woman in the tent-shop made everything far more attractive and efficient. It improved Ali's mood, enabled him to get some rest, and boosted business. The lines got longer, one line for Ali and one for Jasmina. Ali's image was enhanced even further among the refugees and officialdom. The Arab refugees felt it was truly wonderful of him to take Jasmina in, offer her protection and money, plus guidance. Like a real elder brother.

The truth of the matter was that Ali was infatuated with Jasmina. Maybe he was even falling in love. He had never had a woman before, since dating was rare in the traditional Arab environment he was brought up in. Ali was a virgin at twenty-eight years old, but he fantasized and masturbated almost every night in the back of the tent behind the crates, whenever he felt he had some privacy. He wondered how all the other men managed with masturbation, considering that they had even less privacy than he did.

So was Jasmina a virgin, of course. In Syria, marriages were arranged, and property negotiations, a dowry, almost always came into it. "Dating" in the Western sense was almost unheard of in her community.

Jasmina-Adara carried her second name—the virgins—with pride. In Syria, there had been no chance of a young man approaching her and asking her out, even to a movie. It could only be for marriage, and the proposal would be made through the parents. Of course, she had seen things on the internet, things that had absolutely shocked her. Quite unbelievable that men and women could roll around on a bed and do such things to each other. Not only were the women not wearing headscarves and veils to cover their faces, but they were completely naked! They were doing terrible things with their hands, bodies, mouths and even with their—what was that? Was it their bottom or not? She was confused as to what went where. And when the films sometimes showed three or four men and women together, she got utterly confused as to what fitted where!

She would turn her face away in horror at such sights, but gradually got used to it. She would stare out of curiosity. What else on earth could men think of? But whatever her shock, Jasmina the Virgin came to realize that there was a different world out there.

So, when men began to flirt with her at the tent-shop, she was not that surprised. It was really the first time she was free from the constant surveillance of the family with whom she had been placed in a large prefabricated room, with a toilet and wash facilities alongside. She had strange, confused, mixed feelings when complimented by men—especially by those who were more cunning in their approach. But she was still shy, embarrassed and reluctant. She would turn them down, her most common tactic being to act as if she did not understand. But the tingling of womanhood had begun to stir within her.

## THE FIRST EXPERIENCE

Ali Pasha got in there first. Not surprising, considering that the young couple were working together and in close contact most of the day. Very much like a boss with his secretary, and the frequent adventures thereof. Whenever there was a break, they would chat and giggle together, gradually feeling more comfortable with each other. Nighttime would cast its magic spell. When they eventually zipped up the tent entrance at night (there was no door with a lock), they would become strongly aware of each other, and of their relative privacy—even though the voices of nearly one hundred people could be heard outside the tent. They were also very tired, anxious to get some sleep—wouldn't it be nice if they could cuddle up to each other?

Ali Pasha was shy and inexperienced as to how to make the first move, and Jasmina even more so. They would lie down to sleep on the makeshift beds they would roll out in the tent—as far from each other as possible.

The trouble—or the fortunate fact for them—was that they would touch quite a lot during the course of business. There was often a rush with clients, and they would brush against each other as they squeezed through to get products for them. Their hands would touch when they exchanged money or gave each other something. Ali would hold himself close to her as he helped her up a ladder to bring a box down from a shelf. Her young budding breasts would be right next to his face, and it is there that he would linger longest. Jasmina would also take her time coming down from the ladder. She would feel a warm tingle between her legs and was not quite sure how to handle it.

The situation developed one night while they were watching a film in the tent. It was a film with Brad Pitt and Angelina Jolie, and there was a lot of kissing. Then heavy petting and eventually sex. Ali and Jasmina sat there gaping wistfully while acting as if they were cool about it. They then exchanged glances and giggled. Jasmina fell asleep watching the film, and when she woke up, Ali was next to her. No reaction. She liked it.

The next night they watched another film. Jasmina made Ali a cup of tea, and she held it for him so it would not spill. Their hands touched for a long time. Ali kept it there. When they resumed watching the film, he put his hand on hers. She did not withdraw it. Then he clasped her fingers. No reaction. He picked up courage and put his arm around her. They stayed that way and watched the rest of the film, again falling asleep next to each other.

They worked happily through the next day, eagerly waiting for night to fall. Hugging at TV time became natural. Then Ali leaned his head on her shoulder, moved closer and gave her a timid kiss on the cheek. He got bolder and planted one on her lips. This was the first time that either of them had kissed someone on the lips.

The nights that followed grew increasingly passionate. They touched each other and felt their excitement. Jasmina could not even consider taking off her clothes. But she allowed Ali to take off his own—always giggling, pretending it was a joke. It was the very first time in her life she had seen a penis in real life, and she was fascinated. Ali eventually thought of how he could make her loosen up, maybe help her lose her inhibitions a teeny weeny bit. He told her he had a new fruit juice product, made of concentrated juices. A mix of cherry and pomegranate juice, he claimed. In reality, it was a liqueur, strong in alcohol content but sweet and easy to sip.

Jasmina the Virgin became intoxicated within minutes. Ali was naked and rubbing himself against her, his erection looking twice as large as usual when the effect of alcohol made Jasmina see everything double. He told her he would help her stand up and go to her own bed. Instead, he bent her over a table and, as she stood there with her arms splayed from one end of the table to the other, lifted up her dress and pulled down her panties. He had no previous experience, but his instinct took over, and, rubbing hungrily against her buttocks, he eventually found his way inside her.

"Ali," she only managed to gasp. "I thought we were brother and sister. Is this allowed?"

"God has wanted us to be like this," he gasped back. "Now I love you even more than a brother."

Ali's moans and groans became louder and faster as his pleasure increased, while Jasmina-Adara remained silent. He just had to keep as quiet as possible, so as not to be heard by the refugees outside the tent. A client might come at any time, seeking some emergency service. Eventually, he felt a sensation that began in his groins, rose to a climax and exploded simultaneously inside Jasmina and in his own mind and body. He was trying to suppress his screams of ecstasy, never imagining that it could feel so good, far better than his daily self-satisfaction.

When he had finished, Jasmina stumbled by herself to her own bed, not sure of how she felt. The next morning she said she was ashamed of herself. She felt extremely guilty, even dirty. And she decided to drop her second name, never again calling herself "Jasmina the Virgin." Just plain Jasmina.

She was silent and brooding when serving customers that morning. She felt that she could not look them in the eyes. Where had all her Muslim principles gone?

## GOOD NEWS STRIKES—GERMANY AHEAD

The self-critical hours did not last long. It was noon when a rumor, and then the real news, buzzed through the refugee camp. It then took on the energy of a tidal wave of joy. The green light had come through from Germany! The first two thousand of them were to be taken to Germany, including Ali and Jasmina, to be followed by two thousand more every week. They had five days before they would be taken by coach or train to Munich. They were elated.

"You see," Ali told her. "It was the will of God that instructed us to make love. Could it just be a coincidence that the gate to heaven has been opened to us, on the day that we made love as brother and sister?"

Jasmina liked that argument. It was convenient. More than that, it almost made her feel holy.

That night Ali and Jasmina did the holy act again. And this time without the encouragement of cherry liqueur. And they did it every night over the next five days, sometimes twice. They did not yet dare attempt all the experimentations and entanglements they had seen between couples on TV. But it still felt even better, even more cleansing, than prayers. They had discovered a new world and new sensations to look forward to.

▪▪▪▪

The future was promising, but also fraught with uncertainty. Ali knew that building up a business in Germany would be far more difficult. He was lucky that he had a "ready market" with the tens of thousands of Syrian refugees around him. But maintaining it, especially within a German environment with stricter supervision and a generally hostile population, would be more difficult. He would have to double his efforts. He knew that a good reputation was important, but making money was even more important. It was vital because money bought respectability, a good reputation—which in turn brought even more money.

He started reading about the refugee situation in Europe, particularly in Germany, and what the problems were. How this was an extremely divisive issue among European governments and peoples. How it caused severe tensions, especially during election periods. He noted that crime was on the rise in Germany and that, rightly or wrongly, the immigrants were being blamed for most of the increase.

Paradoxically, the refugee crisis in Syria had led to his personal enrichment and a spicy private life. Now, he wondered, how could he benefit from the crime in Germany among immigrants? How could he turn it to his advantage again? Especially considering all the negative information and statistics that had mushroomed in the German and international media?

The general environment and public mood had worsened with the advent of Donald Trump to the American presidency. His fiery pre-election speeches had focused considerably on Germany, which he targeted as an example of a "crime mess" to be avoided, one overwhelmingly caused by the immigrants. He used Germany as an example of what can go wrong with an open-door policy on refugees, describing Chancellor Angela Merkel's approach as a "disaster." He insisted that crime there rose to levels "that no one thought they would ever see."

That is why, Donald Trump concluded, America needed a wall on its borders with Mexico to keep the illegal immigrants out.

The situation was almost as bad in neighboring Austria, Hungary, France and Holland. The governments of Austria and Hungary, like Donald Trump, repeatedly spoke of building walls and of sending refugees back as a means of curbing crime and unemployment. In France, over the years, there had been the meteoric rise of ultra-rightist Marine Le Pen, employing anti-immigrant sentiments as one of her strongest bases. Centrist and moderate parties had to scramble in last-minute coalition formulas to prevent her from coming to power.

In Holland, ultra-rightist nationalist Geert Wilders was the fastest rising politician, and in the March 2017 elections came in second, only 2 percent behind the leading party. His campaign focused almost exclusively on Islam and the migrants, and the multiple dangers thereof.

In that month, a fierce row had broken out between the Dutch and Turkish governments. Wilders, quickly mimicked by other Dutch parties in order to stem his influence, said that if he became president, he would ban all Turkish government officials from the country if they attempted to stage political rallies. Wilders went on to declare he would ban the sale of the Koran and close several mosques and Islamic schools.

"We are losing control of our country as we struggle with Islamic fascism," he kept warning.

In order to counter Wilders's influence and as a response to Turkish provocations, in March 2017, Holland's governing moderate coalition of centrist parties banned the Turkish Foreign Minister from heading a political rally in Holland. They then put the Turkish Minister of Family Affairs in a car and drove her out of the country.

There was a furious backlash from Turkish President Recep Tayyip Erdogan, who slammed Holland as "Nazi fascists" and murderers of Muslims at Screbenica in the Bosnian war. He discredited the whole country as a "banana republic." The Dutch prime minister, reminding the world of the Nazi occupation of Holland and Rotterdam's destruction by German bombing, described the accusations as "disgusting . . . Hysterical . . . a re-writing of history."

It appeared that the intensity of the unprecedented political clash between the Dutch and Turkish governments would have an effect for many months—if not years—ahead. It also reverberated through neighboring Germany and further contaminated the whole refugee issue. Ali, like a majority of Syrian refugees, was worried.

## GERMAN CRIME STATISTICS

Ali concluded that Germany, the economic colossus of Europe, remained by far the largest focus of his interest. Sadly, he also realized that, according to media reports and research institutes, the political climate there was worsening—a reaction to the mounting flood of refugees.

One can only imagine his dismay in reading newspaper accounts claiming that Germany's Federal Criminal Police Office found the number of crimes committed by refugees in 2015 had gone up by 92,000 compared to 2014, a 79 percent increase. In 2016, they totaled about 285,000. This was the equivalent of 780 crimes a day—a further increase of nearly 40 percent over 2015.

The statistics were highly publicized, and Chancellor Angela Merkel was under heavy pressure. Barbed wire fences were going up on borders, and demonstrators were taking to the streets demanding that refugees be expelled. Hate crimes against refugees were increasing as well. There were 3,500 attacks on them in 2016.

In October 2016, thousands of protesters massed in the Eastern German city of Dresden to mark the second anniversary of the anti-migrant and Islamophobic movement Pegida. Carrying flags bearing slogans like "Refugees not welcome," the crowd chanted, "Merkel must go."

Chancellor Merkel repeatedly called on the media and the public not to exaggerate the statistics, insisting that crime by Germans was far more than that of the refugees. She pointed out that crime had gone up considerably following the unification of Germany and the arrival of three million refugees of German origin, while it had not gone up much following the arrival of one million non-German refugees. She insisted the refugees had "not led to a surge in violent crime."

Indeed, the statistics from Germany's Federal Criminal Police Office showed that refugees did not get involved in heavy crime or gang warfare. The nature of the majority of offenses appeared to be minor: 28,712 cases of riding on public transit without paying the fare, 52,167 incidents of forging paperwork in a bid to get money, 85,035 cases of theft, mostly shoplifting.

In the "medium-range" category were assaults, robberies, and what Germany classes as "predatory extortion" and "offenses against personal freedom," including threatening behavior. This doubled in 2015 with 36,010 cases, accounting for 18 percent of the crime total.

Sex crimes remained low, under 1 percent. Logged in 2015 were 1,688 cases of sexual offenses, including against children, and including 458 rapes or acts of "sexual coercion."

The Criminal Police Office report went on to state that there were 240 attempted murders by immigrants in 2015—doubled compared to 127 in 2014. In two-thirds of all cases, perpetrators and victims were of the same nationality. One German was murdered, while 27 immigrants were killed by other immigrants.

Syrians are officially listed as making up the bulk of Germany's asylum seekers—48 percent—with these being suspected of "only" 24 percent of the total number of refugee crimes. To the contrary, Serbians account for 2 percent of refugees but are suspected of 13 percent of the total number of crimes.

The report said: "Syrians, Afghans and Iraqis are the largest groups of immigrants, but are less frequently delinquent in relation to other groups of migrants.

"Proportionately more offenders were found among immigrants from the Balkans (Kosovo, Albania, Serbia), Eritrea and Nigeria."

As to terror suspects hiding among genuine refugees, the report stated that there were 266 instances of individuals *suspected* of being "fighters and members of terrorist organizations abroad."

Of these, 80 were ruled out, and 186 cases were still being probed. The report called the infiltration of militants into the country "a growing trend."

Ali concluded that under these circumstances, the climate was certainly not good for the Syrian refugees arriving from Greece and elsewhere. Even official reports that tended to underplay the fears were not trusted by the public. People would write in to the media and blogs and strongly argue that the refugee crime problem was, in fact, much larger. They said published figures concerned only incidents that were reported, recorded, or actually led to court decisions. They argued that the majority of incidents simply went unrecorded and did not enter the statistics mix.

▪ ▪ ▪ ▪

Ali's and Jasmina's enthusiasm was somewhat curbed by the statistics and vitriolic accusations. All the same, the trip to Germany was both interesting and exciting. Some of the refugees were taken by train, others on coaches. Military and police vehicles accompanied them as they were taken in ships from the Greek island of Lesbos to the port city of Salonica, of which Ali had many fond memories. From there, the trains and coaches went through Bulgaria, Serbia, Croatia, Slovenia, Austria, and then into southern Germany.

On the way, the mood was considerably improved compared to the Lesbos island camp. The refugees felt much freer, would chat like excited kids as they admired the scenery on the way: islands, endless coastlines, mountains, friendly people. . . . So, so different compared to the oppressive and life-threatening situation in Syria.

They talked and exchanged ideas without fear of being overheard, of being misunderstood, of being arrested and vanishing in some police dungeon or military camp. The younger ones, in particular, giggled and laughed in a way they had never done before.

Ali and Jasmina inevitably remained key players on the trip. They always had supplies of goodies to eat and also items useful in terms of daily needs. Nor did they waste any time in promoting their services. For example, since they were on the move most of the time, Ali and Jasmina taught, for those who didn't know, the virtues and uses of smartphones.

Jasmina was useful in another way, as well. The young girls gravitated toward her, as she had become a role model. She was happy, well-dressed, and talkative. She never wore a headscarf, and she put on a dab of makeup, which made her look even more beautiful.

Gradually, with Jasmina's encouragement, the girls picked up enough courage to ask her questions about sex. She enjoyed this role, encouraging them to try it, explaining that it was a gift from God, and they should not be ashamed. "To give and take love is Allah's wish," was a favorite cliché she used to overcome their hesitations. She taught them how to respond to young men—and older ones—when they looked at them with desire. How to dress in a more fashionable way, without resorting to extremes, and how to use basic makeup such as powder, lipstick and eye shadow. How to talk to men on an equal basis, to understand that women had equal rights.

Jasmina was no hothead, no cheap little thing that had suddenly discovered womanhood. For she also emphasized to the other girls the importance of education, of learning the key languages of English and German, of computer and smartphone skills. Of keeping clean and sweet-smelling.

Eventually, she showed them condoms, explained their function, and the overall importance of contraception. She explained about the contraception pill, and how much more convenient this was for all concerned. And she emphasized the dangers inherent in unprotected sex, especially among foreign communities in Germany.

Jasmina told them that sex before marriage was not a sin and that everybody did it in Western Europe and America. "That's one of the reasons they are great places to live," she would tease. And they would burst out laughing when filling up the condoms with water in the girls' bathrooms, to see just how big they could get before exploding.

Jasmina had become a leader in her own right.

▪▪▪▪

The caravans of Syrian refugees eventually exited Austria and stopped outside Munich in southern Germany, where reception centers and a refugee shelter had been prepared for them at the town of Neuperlach Süd. The locals had agreed to it, but soon afterward had secured court permission to build a thirteen-meter-high wall around it, so as to separate the foreigners from the locals. It was taller than the Berlin Wall.

Ali and Jasmina looked around, wondering how they could continue their business. They still had no idea how to organize it all so it would be accepted within the broader German economic system, not only in the refugee environment but in the "real world" outside.

The very first move Ali made was to name himself Aldous. He would state this to everybody in the most emphatic way and would fill in all forms accordingly. Who would notice the difference between Ali, Aldous—or just Al for short? He was right. No one did.

▪ ▪ ▪ ▪

In the days and weeks ahead, the couple realized they could not compete with the facilities within the refugee center that had been prepared by German authorities. And they could not compete with the supermarkets, mini-markets and stalls that sprung up everywhere around and within the refugee centers. They realized they had come face to face with the "German machine," far superior in terms of organization and standards than any they had known before.

The Greek islands had offered blue skies, sparkling seas, majestic coastlines and wonderful weather. Munich had nothing like this. Instead, the area seemed to be enveloped by an umbrella of gray skies, constant drizzle and penetrating cold. But it was superior in every other way, and the refugees realized this was "home" henceforth, barring any major political surprises.

Ali and Jasmina looked over the list of professional activities they had operated so far. Time for a change.

## THE GERMAN-SYRIAN FRIENDSHIP SOCIETY & NEWSLETTER

It was then that they had the idea of forming an NGO, a Non-Governmental Organization. This would purportedly be a non-profit and, as such, would legalize several activities and provide an initial cover for their business interests. They called it the "German-Syrian Friendship Society of Munich." This allowed for the distribution of market goods to the refugees and also facilitated services between the camp and local German people. The nature of many of these services was difficult for German police to detect and control. And having a registered NGO enabled them to disguise many of the profits as humanitarian fund-collecting.

However, Ali had also learned the importance of democratic procedures—at least on the surface. Local laws made NGO elections necessary every two years. So, in the very first ones, organized by Ali, Jasmina and their closest associates, and held inside his office premises, he was elected president of the Friendship Society with an overwhelming majority. Jasmina was elected treasurer, while a half-blinded young man from the Syrian war was elected secretary-general. All nine members of the NGO's board led various sections of Ali's businesses and were financially dependent on him.

The establishment of the NGO Friendship Society offered two other advantages. First, it allowed Germans to become members, thereby offering even broader inroads for Ali's businesses. Second, it allowed for the use of a large number of "volunteers." These men and women were happy to offer their services free of charge in return for food, clothes, something to keep them occupied during the day, social recognition, and—above all—the hope they would soon be integrated into German society.

Just recall, not everything is as it appears. Ali remembered he had read somewhere that the creation of Friendship Societies was one of the main methods used by the Soviets to infiltrate and undermine Western countries. The Chinese had tried a similar stunt with their "Confucius Institutes."

Ali also knew that influencing public opinion through the media, by spreading information and disinformation (*dezinformatsiya*), was a key method used by the Soviets to achieve these goals. To try to establish a mainstream newspaper would have been suicidal in terms of costs and also survival among the powerful German media, even at a local Munich level. Furthermore, Ali and Jasmina had a specific target audience—the Syrian refugees and other peripheral Arab nationalities in the Munich area. So, how best and cheaply to inform, organize, guide and influence them and German friends than through a low-cost weekly newsletter and website?

The weekly newsletter of the Friendship Society was produced in both the Arabic and German languages. Apart from news, it carried such attractive features as a TV guide, sources of news from Syria, and gatherings or events of interest to the refugees. It also provided valuable information on legislation and the means of processing their residency and naturalization documents.

The newsletter was an instant success. It was a respectable means of providing information. Furthermore, it was a great mechanism for strengthening Ali's role in the community and with German authorities. The locals loved to see their names and photos printed in the newsletter. It made them feel important—and grateful to Ali and his team.

The local German police were also able to "plant" stories in the newsletter—for example, information on how many refugees were arrested and punished for breaking the laws. That scared the foreigners. And there were features on the power of local technology and the potential for listening and watching the activities of refugees and their international communications. All attempts to "cow" the refugees. An invisible hand of fear.

The newsletter was distributed free of charge, in thousands of copies. It was handed out by the Friendship Society's volunteers at train and bus stations, supermarkets, kiosks and street stalls. Little did anyone realize that much of the advice shepherded readers toward Ali's businesses—for which they paid.

## EXPANDING THE BUSINESS

Ali concluded the time had come to activate his Albanian contacts operating in Northern Greece. He was not sure how this would work with the police, but he remembered well that he was actually encouraged to develop business with the Albanians—for reasons he just could not understand.

He notified Artan and Ilir that he had arrived safely in Munich and was ready for business. Ali invited proposals, products and services, as long as the Albanians themselves found ways of delivering to Munich.

Ali and Jasmina then proceeded to set up base in Munich. With the money they had amassed, they rented a nice apartment in Neuperlach Süd, just a few minutes' walk away from the refugee center's entrance.

Once settled, they ventured into Munich. It was a move that was going to change their lives even more dramatically. Starting at the Munich international train station, they came into contact with a far greater number of nationalities than they could possibly imagine. Plus, a significant number of people seeking a place to sleep, even outdoors, scraping for a living with methods that were barely within the borders of legality.

Mixing with the crowds, supermarket clientele and street vendors, the Syrian couple soon realized there was a whole new world of business outside the refugee camp. They also rapidly concluded competition was fierce.

Selling stationery and photocopy services were petty capitalism. The greatest profit was in marketing young women, cheap cigarettes, alcoholic drinks and medicines. Jasmina was asked by many men if she had "girlfriends to introduce to us." She did so and had soon set up several of her friends with wealthier Germans, irrespective of age. Some of them ended up as private mistresses, others as waitresses in clubs, and others took low-key jobs such as housemaids or babysitters.

Jasmina was given gifts for her services, and then money. Soon she was running a full-fledged escort service. The number of girls she "assisted" grew by the dozens, and eventually exceeded one hundred who had become full- or part-time sex workers.

This led to the discovery of another important need: finding babies for childless couples. Some would-be parents were desperate after finding medical assistance would not solve their problem. And adoption was a very difficult process in Germany. So, when some of her Syrian girlfriends got pregnant (they didn't listen to her advice on precautions, did they?), she assured them that they did not need to resort to abortions. She would find a good home for the babies.

That particular coup was probably the most profitable of all. The minimum selling price of a baby was €100,000. And once the goods were delivered, everybody was happy. Or at least the new parents; she never knew how the birth mother might react.

▪ ▪ ▪ ▪

Within a month of contacting Niko and Yanni in Salonica, a truck full of goods arrived in Munich. How they got through customs, Ali would never know. Bribes, he assumed. Over the next few months, the number of truckloads increased. Soon, he had to rent a warehouse.

He was now employing fifty associates, almost all of whom worked without legal paperwork. However, they were all proud card-carrying members of the German-Syrian Friendship Society of Munich, which gave them a certain respectability when stopped by police in the street for identity verification.

Crates on the incoming merchandise trucks would have foodstuffs, clothes and children's toys on the top surface layers, thereby concealing the cigarettes, alcohol and medicines that constituted 80 percent of the crate content. He paid for them at 20 percent of their retail market prices and sold them at 40 percent, making a 100 percent profit but still offering a deal to the general public—less than half the price of the official, taxed brands.

It was only once the tenth truckload was delivered that the Albanian crime group in Northern Greece suggested that he start buying drugs from them. He agreed to test this proposal, so he imported marijuana from Albania. When that went without incident, he then also imported very small quantities of cocaine and heroin. The venture proved equally successful.

These highly profitable new activities led to the development of parallel businesses, offering logistical support. For example, courier services and security. The couple by this time were employing a large number of people—Syrians, Germans and a sprinkling of other nationalities. They needed bodyguards and a fleet of cars, trucks and motorbikes. These were used not only to protect and service their own businesses but also to protect the homes and offices of wealthier Germans, and of the local merchants they cooperated with.

## THE POLICE MEETING

Back in German police HQs for the South Munich region, a high-level meeting was convened to see how far they should allow the Ali rackets to function and expand. So far, there was almost unanimous agreement that the advantages outweighed the disadvantages. They certainly knew of the drugs, including the small quantities of cocaine and heroin. But allowing him to develop ties with the Albanians had been a smart move. In this way, they had located much larger "fish," ringleaders heading the production and supply mechanisms within Albania. And their networks in Europe.

Within the Munich area, police also learned the identities of many Germans who were dabbling in drugs and other crimes. Allowing the trucks to get through had revealed an entire network of smuggling and corruption among customs officials that spread from Albania to Greece, Italy, and the former Yugoslav states.

So, let Ali and Jasmina continue, the police chiefs decided. After all, they were cooperative and a very valuable source of information within the Syrian refugee movement. The creation of the "German-Syrian Friendship Society" had proved an excellent mechanism for keeping the Syrians under surveillance, for spotting talent and developing an even larger army of informers feeding Europol and German authorities.

As for the prostitution, most of it under the guise of a dating and marriage service, they found that this was also relatively harmless because it did not cause any significant social disruption. Privately, they all knew that many of the police officers enjoyed the fruits of this activity. Ali and Jasmina could afford to be generous, particularly with law enforcement authorities who provided a "blind eye."

Police are corrupt everywhere in the world; it is only the degree that varies from country to country. Ali was happy to provide cash bonuses, but offering a young Syrian woman as a treat was always welcome. The girls were also quite willing. They felt that sleeping with a policeman was quite a privilege because it afforded them a sense of security and of association within the German state mechanism itself. Above all, they hoped, this kind of association between the sheets would one day help them achieve their ultimate target: German citizenship.

The meeting of the Munich senior police officers was concluded in harmony and with broad smiles. Yet again, there was an almost unanimous feeling that activities of the kind conducted by Ali and Jasmina should be closely watched, but allowed to continue. The advantages for Germany far outweighed the disadvantages.

## MAN OF CHARITY & POLITICS

Ali was evolving into a master entrepreneur. Within three years, he had almost two hundred full-time employees, very few of whom were formally registered as such. The overwhelming number were "black labor" or, at best, part-time labor. However, they were card-carrying members of the German-Syrian Friendship Society, with their role often being that of "volunteer."

Ali had become ruthlessly ambitious and continuously sought expansion. Yet, he was cautious. He would not get involved in deals if he suspected trouble at the end of the line. For example, he turned down the Albanians' offer to ship him a few guns for sale to businessmen.

Ali also wanted to be regarded as a respectable businessman. Not only *known* to be respectable but also to *look* respectable. He had long learned that in Germany, it was extremely important to have a good external appearance, irrespective of what was going on in your heart and mind. For example, he always shaved, washed, and cleaned his hair. Unshaven brown faces looked so unprofessional and dangerous.

Then came the suits and ties.

There was little surprise when he started being invited by mainstream German organizations to speak in public about the Syrian refugee movement, to discuss the advantages and disadvantages for German society.

It was then that he had another idea—charities. He would give part of the proceeds of his businesses to charities—not only to destitute young Syrians, or those who wanted to study, but also underprivileged Germans, specifically, physically handicapped children.

The image of the well-dressed, silky-tongued Syrian refugee who had risen from rags to riches, and was now donating to charities, mesmerized the broader German public. He was invited to appear on TV shows and was featured in publications. He was becoming a celebrity, not only among the Syrian refugees but also among the broader German population of Munich.

The financial impact these moves had on Ali's businesses was far greater than the cost of the donations. The indirect publicity boosted his products and services, with sales soaring and tens of thousands more euros pouring in. Donating to charities had proved yet another profitable business.

Ali was becoming so popular and respected that he attracted the attention of local politicians. He was invited to become a member of the Social Democratic Party and to head a newly established department on Refugees and Social Welfare. It was another stroke of genius. Ali was elected a member of the local government, with votes that came both from mainstream Germans and from ethnic Arabs who had become German citizens. Two years later, he was made a Deputy Mayor in Munich responsible for refugee affairs.

## . . . AND A HERO BACK HOME

Within seven years of starting work in Germany as a coordinator for refugees, Ali Pasha had become a real pasha. He was handling tens of thousands of euros or dollars every month, and the sky appeared to be the limit. He was a true chameleon, changing colors according to circumstances. As far as anybody knew, he was involved in translation services, private teaching, public relations, distribution of market products, courier services, security and physical protection services, imports, and IT and communications.

What people did not know was that he also ran operations for smuggled counterfeit cigarettes, alcoholic drinks, medicines, and drugs. Through his girlfriend, Jasmina, he headed a highly lucrative prostitution and baby-selling ring, always under the guise of a dating and marriage agency.

Through his newsletter, he had an influence on the flow of news to the refugees and from them back to the Arab world. And he was a collaborator with German police, a snitch, a spy on his own people.

Yet there was not a blemish on his record. From a penniless, innocent young man with dirty jeans, tattered shirts and sweaty, matted hair, he had evolved into a silk-tongued young entrepreneur and politician wearing expensive suits, radiating hope and friendship with his beaming smile and cleanly shaved face. He had become a real central European, with a shade of brown skin that he dismissed as being the result of his lengthy holidays under the Mediterranean sun. To anybody who asked, he would say that his mother was German and his father Syrian, but he himself knew very little of Syria, nor did he care. He told them what they wanted to hear because that increased his political acceptability—and his business.

■ ■ ■ ■

The news of his success reached Syria and was published in a weekly magazine that specialized in covering news and features on the fate of Syrians abroad who had fled the civil war.

The capsule presentation of his activities, which in effect he himself had written, ran as follows:

> While first based in a refugee camp in Greece, he commenced a correspondence course with a German and British university, specializing in Arab languages and the interaction of the European Union with the Arab world. He launched a successful translation service and helped thousands of refugees, almost always free of charge, to complete their documents, which secured them residency and working permits in Germany and other countries.
>
> In due course, he launched an employment agency that provided jobs to thousands of Syrians. Due to the wealth of writing material he had to handle, he developed writing skills and became an acclaimed journalist and then an author and publisher.
>
> On the business side, he opened an import-export agency and a chain of supermarkets where he specialized in importing Syrian and other Arab products popular with the immigrants and Germans. His specialty was the importation of fresh fruits and vegetables, supermarket goods, and office supplies.
>
> This successful international trade led him to expand to the importation of medicines, where he specialized in cheaper generic products and mass quantities, thereby bringing down the prices for the sake of the needy refugees and then for other lower-income strata of the German population.
>
> In the course of this meteoric rise, he never forgot his humble origins and the hardships that he himself

had gone through. He therefore initiated and developed social welfare organizations that specialized in helping young women and the adoption of babies or young children whose parents had been lost through war or other tragedies.

To make this possible and better organized, he founded the German-Syrian Friendship Society of Munich, of which he was elected its first president. Through this network, he donated extensively to charities.

In recognition of his significant contribution to many sectors of public life, Ali Hamas Muhammad Shadmanesh Pasha was invited to join the German Social Democratic Party. At his very first elections, he was elected a Deputy Mayor responsible for immigrant welfare and integration.

It is expected that at the next local government elections, he will stand as a candidate for mayor of Munich.

It was an interesting and objective report, at least Ali thought. Not a word about drugs, prostitution, baby-selling, counterfeit cigarettes, drinks and medicines, or on his spying on the Syrian refugees for the German police.

In a recent statement, Mr. Aldous Pasha said: "I have never been interested in political power or money. My life has been committed to helping the refugee populations of Europe because I will never forget that I was a refugee myself. I will continue to work closely with all sectors of refugee life."

Asked if he had eventually found a brand name for all his diverse activities, one that could be reflected in an all-embracing single company name, he said: "Yes, I will also keep that simple. Just 'My Lord Pasha International Enterprises.'"

# THE BALTICS:

## The Promised Land

BY PRESTON SMITH

*PRESTON SMITH is an American expatriate and polyglot who achieved notoriety in Central and Eastern Europe (CEE) as an investigative journalist willing to take on organized crime, the political elite and money laundering operations in the UK. The first foreign-born licensed detective in Poland, Smith's experience includes exposing offshore money laundering, forced prostitution, the killing of expats, kidnapping and political corruption. His reports appeared in media ranging from* Poland Monthly, BiznesPolska, *Polish and Czech dailies, Russia's Interfax News Agency and Australia's* The Bulletin *magazine, where he was nominated for a Walkley Award for his work with Eric Ellis in locating Abraham Goldberg, at the time Australia's most infamous white-collar criminal, wanted for embezzling more than one billion AUD.*

The hands—that's what you remember. No matter the deal, no matter the technique, you always remembered the hands. Furtive, darting. Cutting and dealing and dividing. This during the *kukulis*, of course, during that moment of the bribe when nobody but nobody looks the other in the eye. And later, he would think of this, how the others focused on the money while he watched their hands, the Latvians speaking bad Lithuanian and the Lithuanians translating for the Austrian and the Estonian and the Pole.

"These are your coupons," said the Austrian. "They have no names, need no signature. For all practical purposes, these coupons function as legal tender. But they are only redeemable in person, only payable on-site."

A murmur of agreement. Then the mutual grumble of irritation about needing to travel to an Austrian bank—this, followed by the *de rigueur* shit translation, the ripple of nods and grunts until it was clear all understood.

And the Pole had said, "*Lapówka. Lapówka.*"

Shrugs all around. The Pole had seemed the simplest yet the surest of the bunch. So later, the minister had made a point to ask about the meaning—the Polish word sounding so much more foreign than *kukulis* or the *kyšį* of the Lithuanians.

"*Lapówka,*" said the Lithuanians. "Bribe in Polish. What did you think it meant?"

"Yes, yes. But what of its origins? Just where does it come from?"

"*Lapa,*" came the answer. "Paw."

Ah yes. Of course.

Hand of an animal.

And suddenly it did not sound foreign in the least.

▪ ▪ ▪ ▪

He descended the ravine, fingers splayed and freezing, clawing through the new growth of pine and black alder and wondering just how he had strayed off the path.

What had she told him? Twenty meters from the road marker. A sharp left and two hundred meters east. And that's how he'd walked it, ankle-deep in snow, burrowing under the first purples of sunrise and now lost-as-fuck in the trees and brush so that maybe three hundred paces in, he'd glanced back and up and had stopped cold, his heart skipping, his feet submerged in the spring runoff of the slope.

*Holy—*

Sentinels on the ridgeline. Silhouettes of Kalashnikovs and military fur hats.

Kaspars's jaw clenched. His breath came short. It seemed an eternity before he raised his hands out to the side, first his fingers, then his wrists and elbows—movements telegraphed, executed in millimeters—as the border guards stared him down.

*Holy—*

Two soldiers and a civilian. Well-fucking armed. But no shouts, mind you, no commands—the soldiers resolute, the civilian smoking a cigarette.

And Kaspars all but praying. Thinking, move slow. Whispering, *little steps, eye contact,* as he backtracked down the slope.

And they were indeed little steps.

Make that tiny, toe-to-heel steps.

Until he'd slipped a second time—until he'd stumbled hard and sideways against terror and tree roots and ice.

*SHITE!*

Out zinged his feet, the flats of street shoes parallel as he struck the side of the ravine hard with his face. Then came the microseconds of bare terror as he flailed against the five-centimeter current and tried stupidly to call out, "From the Ministry. No cause for alarm."

Which was absolutely not true. For at least in Kaspars's mind, there was plenty of cause for alarm. There was *kuce*-bitch *maita*-dead-carcass as hell cause for alarm. As much cause for alarm as he had ever seen in his *laiza-dirsus*-kiss-my-ass you *mauka*-whore sixteen years as a Riga cop.

For it was at this moment, precisely—half drowning and slobbering in the runoff and dead leaves—that Kaspars looked up and saw the body.

And *that,* he knew to the depths of his grizzled soul, was truly cause for alarm.

It lay at one o'clock, just above him and half under a mound of sticks and earth. It was a wonder he spied it, a wonder he'd almost missed it coming down. A wonder for that *kuce*-bitch murderously bad job of it—the legs exposed, straight and stiff for a coffin. The unnatural blue of jeans and tennis shoes disgorged by snow.

Kaspars struggled to all fours, desperately aware. Wet to the bone in his gray business suit and coat and just staring at the body, then jerking his eyes up at the soldiers on the ridge, not believing it, really, this loss of dignity, this abject fear—this first day on this bastard of a new job.

Whispering:

*But where the hell's the guard box?*

*And if this is the border, where's the other damn border?*

Or make that:

*Those are Russians, not Estonians.*

*God bless . . .*

Then:

*Do not get your fool self shot.*

Kaspars rose against the bank of the ravine, careful to keep his hands high and wide, telling himself, ordering himself not to run. Shivers became tremors, shudders, the rattle of his teeth. Fuckin' *directions.* Fuckin' *international incident.* But *she's* the one who'd told him. Twenty meters in, two hundred meters east. And now he was East all right, scared to hell, freezing and wanting to piss.

And above him, the Russians, the pure, black silhouettes of them, just waiting for him to move.

So, fuck it; he moved, instinct going for a non-existent gun.

And thank *God.* . . .

Thank the *good Creator above. . . .*

The Russians did not react.

Or maybe one soldier did react. Maybe he cricked his neck to the side. But as for Kaspars . . . he would to the very end remember this moment: how in this God-awful forty-third year, his stomach had truly dropped; how out here on the border, lost confidence had gone to panic as he jammed his fist into his coat, as his fingers dug into empty pockets to come up instead with a shiny, new government business card—a fuck-this-useless-shit *atpisies* card that reminded him he was now no more than:

KASPARS JANSONS, DEPUTY HEAD OF THE
LATVIAN DEPARTMENT OF LAWS, REGULATIONS
AND QUALITY SECURITY

In other words, a drone subject to the direct authority of the prime minister, the minister of justice, the Ministry of Justice as an institution and, in all reality, to just about every department head, veteran bureaucrat, professional clerk, administrative assistant and possibly down to even the intern in his two-man office that he had not yet met.

Yes, a drone. A nobody standing in deer-shit muck with his name printed morosely in faded black ink.

But if he could just show it to them, he thought—if they could possibly see it from their distance—maybe they wouldn't kill him.

Or maybe . . .

Kaspars put the card in his teeth, fished out a cigarette of his own and found a lighter to ward off the smell of decay. He gave a hard stare to the Russians. Not my first body, you bastards, he thought, but nonetheless his hand shook. Still, he flicked twice, three times. And nothing. None of them reacting—not just leaving this to him. Just *overseeing*. Yes, that's what they did all right. Three Russians on the crest above. *Overseeing*. And just like a body to turn up now. Now being after his first-ever midnight call on the job.

Christ, he thought. *Just focus*. Just put them out of your head. How many times had he searched for bodies? How many times had he conducted sweeps for a dealer shot and frozen in winter or some mafioso's wife or even that of a little girl?

Ten times? Twenty? Yes, that's it. Calm down. This was the job. The old job.

Just never under the guns of Russians.

A deep breath. Kaspars lit the cigarette. Spied the ravine up and down for clues. And if only for a moment, he rode the adrenalin—if only for that quick tug of a cigarette, it was almost good to be back.

'Cause Russians or no Russians, it was like that with bodies.

Even back in Narco.

Even back in the States.

How they always turned up . . .

*Precisely* when you didn't need them.

▪ ▪ ▪ ▪

Twenty minutes later, at *precisely* 6:42, Kaspars entered the clearing, traipsing in from the wrong direction—out the Russian zone—to catch the captain off guard. Once again, there was no warning shot, no shouted "Halt" or "Who goes there?" Just Kaspars out of the woods and now the two of them facing each other in muted shock, both raising eyebrows, the captain wide-backed and mustached, offering maybe a shrug, but otherwise one poker face greeting another at a distance, twenty meters off. Kaspars, maybe mid-forties and gawky, the captain thick-set, maybe younger, maybe not.

Then finally, the captain calling out, "The fuck happened to you?"

Good question, thought Kaspars. A call in the dead of night. A three-hour drive to Viļaka for a lost walk in the woods. Then almost drowning in five centimeters of water. Or almost getting shot.

*The fuck happened to you?*

"You are Captain Nauris Berzins?"

"The one and only."

"I'm Jansons."

"So we gathered. Why are you all wet?"

Kaspars sighed. "Where are they?"

The captain ignored him back. "You shouldn't be out there. Cross the warning signs and the Russians will grab you for sure."

"And the Estonians?"

Berzins motioned left. "They are further off. Nervous as hell since the agent."

Fair enough. Kaspars drew himself up, a muddy official. He was three steps across the clearing before he saw the second guard. Apart from a Kalashnikov, he was much like the first, typical *Valsts Robežsardze*, sauntering heavy and bored, laden in the heavy green-gray and military boots of the army.

The second called out, "Not smart, civ. Everyone's on edge since the war."

Kaspars kept his eye on Berzins.

So, the second called out, "You saw what they did in Ukraine? Little green men and now they're here."

Kaspars said nothing. So the second border guard called out a third time, "They kidnapped the Estonian in the summer. The Russians came across and got him, said he was a spy."

Then:

"Why are you all wet?"

Kaspars ignored that too, freezing but playing it cool, cigarette down to the nub. Saying nothing about the body, but thinking, Okay, you border shite, just what do you see? By the suit, a minister or secret service agent. By the soiled pants and jacket . . . bitter work on a bitter morning. Or a fool. . . . Street shoes that skated clownish, slipping on remnant ice.

*Fuck me.*

A new suit. A new life.

Paid and played. . . .

And mum as a dead man.

So Kaspars said, "Where are they?"

A grunt. "Who wants to know?"

Kaspars trudged forward as dignified as wet socks would allow. "Me. The ministry. An embassy or two."

The captain held out a paw. Kaspars met him, his own arm outstretched, overly formal, and noticing that Berzins did not remove his glove.

The captain said, "This is Lieutenant Jans Olzos." Then a nod off toward nothing at all. "The detained are behind the barracks."

"You keep them outside?"

"Brought them outside. Just for your *Ministry* self."

▪ ▪ ▪ ▪

They were outside all right, and whether brought outside for Kaspars or simply left to freeze in the weather, the three Vietnamese were now well beyond misery. Clad in little more than pajama pants and US varsity football jackets, the three shifted from one foot to the other, oddly just out of time as if bound in an arrhythmic dance. On command, a pair of unnamed border guards forced them down to their knees, and here they stayed, understanding nothing as Berzins stepped from one to another and pointed out identifying marks.

"Suspect Number One," said Berzins. "Missing finger, two gold teeth." He paused. "What else?"

Olzos stepped in and took a clipboard from the third guard who jolted the suspect this way and that to match the marks so that the fourth guard could take pics as Olzos read them out loud. "Suspect One. Passport, Russian. Name, Phuong Hep Duy. Age, thirty-one. Missing ring finger. Snake tattoos on neck and back. Three gold teeth, not two."

As he spoke, the third guard bent the prisoner forward, pulled the wrists high to show nine fingers. Then came the lifted jacket and shirt, the roughly cocked-back neck, and finally, the guard used two gloved hands on the prisoner's head to pull back the Vietnamese's upper lip. Kaspars caught an ugly view of purple-brown gums and tooth rot, but yes, he could still make out the two gold teeth. Funny, he also could not see the third. The fourth guard nodded with the click of each photo snap.

"I believe you," said Kaspars. "There is no need for this."

"Of course, there is a need," grunted Berzins. "We finally have enough light for pics. Anyway, just look at them—how do you think we keep them straight?"

Kaspars ignored this, knowing the border was not for the politically correct—and also knowing the headache of dealing with Vietnamese. Ever since Donbass—ever since Ukraine had gone to chaos—they had come sneaking across, bouncing from transit country to transit country in their endless migration west. First, the drug runners, later the human traffickers with their desperate clients in tow.

"Prisoner Number Two," continued Olzos. "No passport, no name. Seems to answer to Nu or Ngoc. Missing little finger. No identifying tattoos. Burn scars on stomach and upper arm."

Kaspars said nothing. Berzins said nothing. Getting no reaction, Olzos stepped to the last man. "Prisoner Number Three. Latvian passport. Name, Nguyen Tan Dinh. Now get this: age, seventy-four."

"Seventy-four my ass," muttered Berzins.

The guards cuffed prisoner Number Three on his head. "I'd make him twenty, twenty-five tops," said the first.

"Never can tell, sir. Could be fifty for all we know."

"Well, he's sure as hell not seventy-four."

Kaspars was unimpressed, his mind tripping on stiff legs in the forest yet somehow still fumbling for the joke. Something about immortality and the Vietnamese in Latvia, but he could never remember the phrase. It was bad enough that they barely seemed to age, but for years the Vietnamese immigrants had held almost no funerals, no wakes. It was common knowledge in Narco that a dead Vietnamese meant a vanished body, the passport going to whomever new managed to slip in.

"No scars, no missing fingers," droned the guard. "Similar snake tattoos, neck, arm and back."

"This all of them?"

The third Vietnamese snapped curses in his language and jerked away. The guards cuffed him across the back of the head with Olzos stepping in as if to give them the back of his hand.

Berzins also stepped forward, ready to pile on. Then just catching it, his head snapped around to give Kaspars a sneer.

"What's that you said?"

Kaspars scratched his chin. "This all of them? There was not a fourth?"

And Captain Berzins said it to the others, just like that: "Look at him, the minister's boy. Still thinks he's a cop."

▪ ▪ ▪ ▪

Driving back, teeth chattering, in his wet clothes and wondering how close he'd come, Kaspars finally muttered to himself:

*Dear God. What am I going to tell Krista?*

Likely, not that much—considering the last time he was in her presence, he could barely speak. Raven-black hair, green eyes and the milk-chocolate skin of the Circassians, Krista was just not the typical boss. Hell, technically speaking, Krista could not possibly be his boss, as his true superiors climbed through a complicated web of bureaucracy that led straight to the vice minister himself. Yet Krista was the messenger, and when she had first met him, the message had been clear: your job description is whatever and whenever I call it that.

And in those first, ecstatic seconds, he had hoped she would call with all her might.

But now . . .

"The detective," she'd said when they had first met. "I must say I admire your work."

"My work?"

For what would she know about Operation Taiga? About the follow-up heroin bust and the mafia feelers back in—

"Your decisions under stress."

Ah.

*Those* decisions.

*Smart* decisions, or so she called them.

But getting less smart by the day. Kaspars leaned forward on the wheel, strained his eyes against a mid-morning fog. Forty minutes out of Riga and he was continuing to run through the incident in his head—how he'd almost come to blows with Captain Berzins and the rest of the *Valsts Robežsardze* over evidence he'd claimed but didn't want. British passports. Pistols. Estonian stock certificates. In a human trafficking case.

Why the hell would you smuggle Estonian stocks into Latvia?

Then the fight over the evidence. Berzins rightly claiming the evidence for the border guard, and Kaspars rightly threatening to call in the secret service. Then Olzos, shoving the old newspaper in his face, reading the name of the bank out loud and mocking Kaspars that he'd gotten a promotion out of it.

Kid stuff. Bullshit jurisdiction squabble that he could handle.

Then the last passport, which is when things got weird.

"Take it," they'd said.

"Take it? What do you mean, take it?"

"Just look at it. Is that a Vietnamese or what?"

Which is when his jaw had dropped at the likeness.

His likeness.

His *exact* likeness.

Which is when—back in the car now—Kaspars had eased on the brakes, careful not to slide.

*Kuces dcis.* Kaspars glanced forward and back, ignoring the rearview mirror and jerking back over his shoulder to tap the brakes on and off and warn the driver behind. All he needed now was to wreck a government vehicle.

The SUV ahead slowed to a crawl before Kaspars saw the markers and the police. Dead moose on the highway, and a three-car pileup that said he'd gotten his own.

Kaspars saw a wrecked Mercedes, then another SUV, and a completely destroyed Skoda off in the ditch. The police waved him past, but he saw the body, the carnage, how the driver had come through the windshield, and then the moose itself, huge, legs broken and splayed but otherwise seemingly asleep. Some great prehistoric thing that had wandered blindly into the modern world.

Nearsighted, prehistoric and blindsided.

And down everyone goes.

Kaspars could relate.

And he might as well have been the moose, stumbling exhausted and confused into Krista's office at exactly 11:23. Which was no less than fifty-three minutes late.

"A good morning to you," said Krista.

She was sitting at her desk, which was itself angled just enough to reveal a short black skirt, heels and gray business jacket over a low-cut blouse. A modern girl dressing in the fashion of yesteryear's commies. Kaspars turned to the hat rack, attempted to doff his overcoat, thought better of it (how to explain the muddied knees?), and turned back to a perked brow and blazing green eyes. The air rushed out of his gut. Kaspars wiped his unshaven chin and again considered the moose, but before he could speak or even begin to explain himself, Krista quite prettily lay her chin to rest on crisscrossed fingers.

"He was expecting you earlier," she said.

"I was delayed."

"The border is like that."

"I don't know why I was even out there."

Krista sniffed. For some decimal point of a second, she clearly did not like what she'd heard. Then the wide smile, teeth as blinding as her eyes.

Kaspars melted despite himself, grinning back and hating himself for it.

And Krista handed him a manila envelope and said, "I'm sure you'll find out soon enough."

"What's this?"

"Your tasks for the day, my friend."

"Tasks? I've been up since two."

"That's when I like to go out."

"I'm not kidding, Krista—"

Krista cut him off, cocked her head as the former cop winced and tried to explain. "On a first-name basis already," she said.

Oh bloody hell, thought Kaspars. Bloody Latvian commie-formality hell.

"I meant no offense, Miss."

"And now it's Miss, is it?"

Kaspars glanced at the manila envelope, feeling stupid and knowing that every answer, any answer at all, would be wrong. He frowned at the door behind Krista and gave a slight shake of the head.

"I've been up all night."

Krista also eyed the door and said, "And justice never sleeps." She reached across, cat-like, to tap the envelope with the tip of a nail. "These are not true audits. Just bureaucracy at work. Checklists, that kind of thing. You will find everything you need in the folder. Both destinations and both of last year's audits. Ojars will drive."

Blood red nails, a long dark wrist and a pair of silver bracelets as thin as snow. It took his breath to watch her settle back behind the desk.

Finally, he gathered himself, said as gruffly as he knew how, "Who the hell is Ojars?"

Krista smirked.

"Good," she said. "First-names after all."

▪ ▪ ▪ ▪

Maybe he was exhausted, but Kaspars hit the halls of the ministry as giddy as a schoolboy, stunned by the ant-like activity, the rush of aides and directors caught in an intensity so very unlike the Latvia he knew. Such a tiny country; how much could there be to actually get done? At headquarters, there had been the cops and the cons and the grumps (i.e., the detectives)—and yes, there had always been hallways jammed with family members or the accused, some in cuffs, some not. But all of them waiting, everyone always waiting. Waiting on paperwork, the prosecutor, the next appeal or trial or release. Everything oriented about some infraction or act of violence in the past.

Not like here. His second day on the job and he could already sense it. The police, *that* was the past. But politics—no, that was the future. New laws, new regulations. New politicians and new scandals that would have new headlines and bylines and that maybe one day, someday, just might bring the old cops and the detectives back into it. Been there, done that, he thought. The grizzled, nicotined fools, who in two or three years would just about, almost seriously, get down to digging into what happened on this very day, long lost and expired.

For on this day, soon to be in the past, here he was, his second morning on the job, a million miles from a murder and already harried and co-opted, shoving his way through. Recognized by some—by more than he would like—but still skidding forward, out of control just like everyone he ever knew. Or not like everyone he ever knew, but just *as* everyone he ever knew, the whole fucking lot of them well bloody off the path.

In these endless, Orwellian halls.

Ojars Kristens. Room 514. Or was it 415?

Then:

*Fuck me.*

*Who the hell is Ojars Kristens?*

But first, he had to deal with Lagunov.

The old man was waiting for him—not outside his office, but inside with his entourage, the Russian gaunt and gray and sitting before Kaspars's desk, his three goons standing behind and around and above with hands crossed bouncer-style over their belts, broad backs taking up the room.

Not expected. Kaspars shouldered past, wondering why his door was open, angry that some fool had let them in. No, not expected. And no less than embarrassing—the office as bare as a witch's cupboard. In the corner, his few, transferable files (still in boxes). On what was effectively an oversized elementary school teacher's desk, nothing but a pack of new business cards. And a Rolodex that simply would not turn.

Which is why he sat behind the desk and dutifully (and much like a politician) said, "Mr. Lagunov, what brings you to the ministry today?"

The old man cricked his neck. Kaspars stifled a gasp; he had worked as a detective for eleven years, but the face was a shock. The old man was recognizable, what was left of him, but the broken nose, stoved-in head—yes, the beating had been severe, but *just look at him*. It was beyond grotesque. More like sideshow circus; a wonder the man was still alive.

There was a cough, a heavy stutter, and the old man replied, "What is the protocol here? Do I speak Latvian or Russian?"

Kaspars fought the urge to stare. Instead glanced at the goons hanging like icebergs over his head and was equally taken aback.

"Speak how you like."

Lagunov made a hitching motion with a shoulder and spoke in Russian. "You were not so kind in the past."

"Probably not." Kaspars's eyes narrowed as he replied in Latvian; two could play this language game. He motioned to a goon at the CEO's side. "Don't I know you?"

Close to two meters tall, black-bearded and scarred, the thug was as wide as a sail. He did not speak, but rumbled as bodyguards rumble: "I shouldn't think so," he said and held out a business card. Which read:

IGOR DANILOV, HEAD OF SECURITY,
AMEX HOLDING

Liar, thought Kaspars. He knew him all right. Or did he? *Danilov*—wait a minute. Him but not him. These guys all look the same. Or maybe from Narco. From one of the discos on the outskirts of town.

The wreckage that was Lagunov cleared his throat. "I also give you—" but that was as far as he got. There was a gurgle, a rattle of phlegm, and the old man collapsed into a fit of hacking coughs. No one went to his aid. Instead, a somewhat elderly woman appeared from behind Danilov. Her hair was frizzed, dyed blonde to offset horned-rim glasses. Ignoring Lagunov just as did the goons, she stepped forward with a card of her own.

"Liga Krumins," she said over the din.

"Our new CFO," growled Danilov.

Kaspars offered a hand to the woman, noting both the Russian accent and the Latvian name. Lagunov was meanwhile hunched in two.

"Mr. Lagunov?"

Lagunov gave a small nod. He wiped his mouth a second time, but it was the towering Danilov who spoke.

"Mr. Lagunov remembers," he said.

"Remembers what?"

"Your sincerity."

"My sincerity?"

"And he wishes to add—"

Lagunov jerked. An age-spotted claw gripped a handkerchief to his mouth, the coughs jerking his body so that his forehead all but banged on the desk. Kaspars toyed with the cards, glancing from Danilov to Liga to the goons behind them both. Nobody moved to help; nobody seemed fazed in the least.

Danilov began again. "He wishes to add—*dammit.*"

The thug was putting it on now, flinching his shoulders, going for effect, but distracted by the old man. Finally, when the coughing simply would not stop, Danilov grew irritated, cupped a great mitt and clapped the geriatric, the president of Amex Holding, hard on the back. He did this two or three times. When that did not work, he growled in Russian so that the larger of his henchman left the room in search of a cup of water.

"The man recuperates slowly," he said.

"I see."

More coughing. Danilov clapped the old man harder, the *boom, boom, boom* muffled but seemingly violent enough to break ribs. Upon the third slap, Lagunov reached forward and supported himself on the desk. The first henchman returned with a paper cup. With great effort, Lagunov straightened out of his hunch. He drank greedily and wiped his mouth.

Kaspars glanced back at the cards. *Igor Danilov*. Him but not him. Ethnic Russian, but quite unlike an ethnic Russian, no patronym.

And Danilov, pounding on the man's back, said, "Mr. Lagunov wishes to add to his previous statement."

Kaspars looked at Danilov, Lagunov, the clock. Dear God. A murder this morning, two audits for the afternoon, and now this.

"This is the Ministry of Justice, not the police."

"The Ministry of Justice is above the police. It tells the police what to do."

"No. Not so simple as that."

"And Mr. Lagunov remembers. You, in particular. After the first assault."

"There was a second assault?"

Danilov was not a man of tact. "Just look at him."

These Russians. They could wear you out. As for Lagunov, it was by now pathetic, as the president of Amex had all but collapsed and was bracing himself on the edge of the desk—his stoved-in forehead ugly and concave and all but in the detective's face.

Shit. The man was about to fall out of his chair. A baseball bat will do that, Kaspars thought. On the other hand . . . incredible the old man could walk, function, speak.

Then again, he was not doing much speaking now.

"When did the assault—"

There was a rap of knuckles at the door, and Kaspars was cut short. With a creak, a slight, balding clerk in a brown tweed jacket slipped into the room—Ojars, no doubt. Just the type to be roundly ignored by all. Or all but security. Lagunov's men squared to face him, hands going into their coats.

Kaspars's went to his business card.

"Tell me when," he said, but all the while thinking, they have guns in the Ministry of Justice. They came in here with guns.

Danilov raised an eyebrow. "Seven months ago," he said. "We thought you had the case."

"You thought wrong." Kaspars reached to tap Lagunov on the shoulder, ignoring the caved-in crown, thinking, I'm not leaving here without a gun. Lagunov's head was now on his forearm. For all Kaspars knew, Lagunov could be comatose or dead. He gave the man a shake. Lagunov shuddered something between a gasp and a snore.

"Is he all right?"

"Does he look all right?"

Ask a stupid question. "You understand, this is not the police. I am no longer the police."

Silence.

A shrug. Danilov said, "Like the last time, only worse. Six assailants. Two drivers. Four with bats." A thug leaned to Danilov's ear, whispered something in Russian slang. "Correction. Three with bats. One with a telescopic club. One of those Arab, metal things."

"That's what did that to his head?"

"Hard to say."

Kaspars narrowed his eyes and glanced at Ojars. The clerk stood frozen in the corner; horrified or fascinated, Kaspars had no clue.

"I investigated the first assault," Kaspars said. "But I had no knowledge of this. It must have happened after my . . . departure."

Another whisper in Danilov's ear, but Danilov brushed it off.

"Your departure. Yes, we know about that. The bank. The Americans," he said. Then with a sneer, he added, "And you got a promotion. Hmmph. Had no idea."

▪ ▪ ▪ ▪

Ojars hit the A8, talking a mile a minute. Kaspars swigged from a flask, utterly failing to hold off both a migraine and fatigue—and astounded by the clerk's aggressive driving and questions to match.

"You knew his head of security, didn't you? A famous detective like you, I could see it."

A sip of vodka. "I thought I did. Now I'm not so sure."

"Then he lied to you. Said he'd never met you before."

"I told you, I'm not so sure. Lots of Igors in this world."

"Igors. Yes, yes, many Igors." Ojars's eyes were as wide as his lenses were thick. The way he arched his spindly frame over the wheel left Kaspars wondering whether the clerk could see anything at all. "Yes, definitely too many Igors for my taste. Do you know how many stateless we have now?"

Lord, thought Kaspars. An egghead racist. All he needed in a chauffeur.

"Do you mean stateless persons or Russian stateless in Latvia?"

"Russians in Lativa, what did you think? What do I care about Africans or raghead terrorists?"

Another swig of vodka. Great. Nothing to do but go along. "Approximately four hundred thousand."

Ojars was incredulous. "Phenomenal! I did not expect you to know that. But can you imagine? Four hundred thousand ethnic Russians without a Latvian or Russian passport in this tiny, impoverished country. Four hundred thousand without any nationality at all. Rather hard to believe, no?"

A third swig of vodka. His holster and pistol uncomfortable and unnecessary and poking against his kidney. Kaspars leaned forward, lowered a gimpy shoulder, and, in the morbid aches and pains of premature aging, removed both pistol and holster, shoving both into the glove compartment. Ojars either did not care or was not inclined to cut the babble if he did. Kaspars considered that, for most of his life, he had waited for people to surprise him, and they oh-so-rarely did. Yet here he was, the unsurprisingly racist, academic Ojars swerving out of the city, banging Kaspars's bad shoulder into the side door as he plunged the fifteen-year-old Mercedes into yet another endless forest.

Ojars babbled on. On the straightaway, Kaspars put his forehead to the passenger-side window, wondered if maybe God would save him and allow Ojars to strike a moose—then remembered Russian mafia collectors beating and cajoling witnesses in Riga; how these were invariably stateless Russians, a minority far more abused by fellow gang members than by "the system" or police.

"I believe it," said Kaspars.

Ojars had gone geek-ecstatic. "Wait—what do you mean? Do you mean what I said about highway corruption? Tenders?"

"Stateless Russians. I stopped listening after that."

"Ah! Aha! Do you agree? Do you, indeed? And such a cynical voice! You've seen much, my friend. Oh yes, you've lived the real life. No doubt about that."

Kaspars was tempted to drink the rest of the flask in one gulp. "What's that supposed to mean?"

"Oh, don't play coy, Detective. We're all friends here. And everyone talks about it. You and the bank. How many millions passed through it, and suddenly, out of nowhere, there you are. Some unknown cop, right smack-dab in the middle of the case."

Kaspars came slowly off the window to give Ojars the most menacing grimace of his life.

Entirely non-plussed, Ojars waved a spindly finger in the air. "Do you want to know corruption? I can tell you about corruption."

The menace drained out of Kaspars. In truth, he thought, *Oh no.*

Thus began an hour-long prattle of scams, schemes and the murky tide where business met state interests. The bait and switch turned into VAT flips. Fake trash disposal and returns on everything from meat to vodka. Accounting anomalies and fake payroll scams. Fake printing ink scams that should be kept in mind for the coming audit. As much as he hated to admit it, Kaspars was impressed.

He was also near catatonic. By the time they hit the first factory, his heart beat arrhythmically, a far more worrying anomaly that he attempted to cure with the flask and cigarettes. Otherwise, it was standard drill. Sign in at the factory gates. Obligatory vodka with the branch CEO and a tour of the grounds while Ojars went to work.

"Windshield wiper fluid," Ojars whispered. "Great opportunity for bootleg alcohol mafias, VAT flippers and label makers." He paused wistfully. "Danger, danger, danger."

With that, he scuttled off. Kaspars did the ministry official thing, sitting on a fake leather couch in the secretary's office until he lolled his head back and fell asleep.

The second "audit" was forty more kilometers north. Kaspars did not even try to hide his exhaustion, and after the second obligatory shot of vodka of the day, he found a second, near-identical couch and passed out shamelessly with a newspaper over his face.

Three, two, one . . . and he was falling. This was not sleep, but the steep drop into the void, complete with the swirling, falling sensation brought on by a good drunk.

Hands. Feet. Legs of bone and gristle protruding from a bank of snow and mud.

And then there was light, the dully white neon of the lamps above, followed by the hard slaps taken by the drunk and homeless any given night of the week.

"No snoring in the office, Detective."

Kaspars came up, shielding his face with his elbows. "I'm not a detective. I now—"

"You now work for the Ministry of Justice. We get it. And we are most impressed."

Kaspars rolled to a sitting position, the combination of alcohol and slaps seemed to have moved his brain forward in his head.

"Danilov?"

The Russian on the corner of the secretary's desk. "The one and only."

Kaspars rubbed his eyes. For the briefest moment of eternity, he could not remember just where he was.

"You follow us out here?"

Danilov's beady eyes gave little away, but for an equally brief moment, he appeared confused.

"Quality control," he said.

Kaspars steadied himself, struggling with the buzz. "That's why we're here. Where is Ojars?"

"Your colleague is inspecting. He is quite diligent."

"I should check on him." Kaspars tried to stand. A hand pressed on his shoulder, and he sank back down on the couch. He was at once aware that they were not alone in the room. Nerves of old turned over his stomach; he could not at this moment hide behind either badge or pistol.

"Is there a topic to discuss?"

"Only follow through."

Kaspars gazed up to his right and left. Goons might as well have been the redwoods of California.

"I work in the ministry," he began.

"That you do."

"That was what was offered."

Danilov gave the slightest of nods. "And that is why you are here?"

"You could say that. Did it look like I was here to investigate?"

A chuckle. "Papers to sign."

"Not me. My colleague handles that."

"Then, I believe that your colleague's tasks are complete."

"You let him know that already?"

Danilov's lip curled just short of a snarl. "You will be going now," he said.

It was about time to take the hint. Kaspars stood, tipped his flask to Danilov and the henchman and put on his coat. Yet just as he turned to go, the henchman offered his hand.

"You know, Detective—for I will always think of you as a detective—I thought you learned how it worked back at the bank."

"How it worked? How what works?"

"Business is complex. Life is not. A man faces a choice. Take up an offer or refuse."

"I can see that."

"Can you? Take up an offer or refuse. There is no third way."

Pretty simple when you thought of it like that.

■ ■ ■ ■

And now freezing and exhausted and out in the car, Kaspars dearly wished Danilov was wrong. Agree to ride back to Riga and listen to Ojars's babble or head for the bus stop in what was now freezing rain. No, considering they were ninety kilometers north of nowhere, Kaspars could not see a third way.

"Dirty boys, dirty boys," said Ojars.

Kaspars rolled his eyes. Fucking Ojars.

"Oh, yes. Dirty, dirty. So very dirty."

"You mean what?" Kaspars was hungover and white noise was not his priority. Then again, from where he was sitting, this was not an irrelevant question.

"The typical red flags. Efficiency and production up, but rejects and breakage and logistics anomalies galore. Yes, my friend, what goes in the trash does not always stay in the trash. Not in Latvia, at least."

Kaspars took that in. And he wondered about Danilov's presence so far away from Riga.

"So, what are you going to do about it?"

"Who me? Why, I'll put it in the report, of course. Summary of findings. Accounting anomalies. Disposal anomalies. Anomalies galore. Now that you are here, we can finally start producing real reports."

"You're crazy."

"No, no. I'm dedicated. Determined. Out to leave my impression on the world. I mean, look at these guys—are you going to let undocumented Russians further impact the productivity of state-owned companies?"

"Have they ever been productive?"

"Productive? Oh yes. Quite. But profitable? Not very. But it's all about details, is it not? Details galore. I'm sure you Sherlock Holmes–types understand that far better than me. For example, your Igor friend—did you notice he has a new tattoo?"

Kaspars shifted in his seat. "On the inside of his left wrist."

Ojars's eyes grew wide enough to fall out. "Ah! Impressive! I fall further under your influence, Detective. Inside of the left wrist. I noticed out in the production hall—when he rolled up his sleeves to hit me."

"I saw it in the office," said Kaspars. "Wait—was he really going to hit you?"

"I do believe he was."

"I can see that. What did you do?"

"I complimented his tattoo. The Virgin Mary and a dragon right up his forearm. New and old. Ugly faded blue. Truly quite authentic for that perfect, prison wanna-be look."

"And he didn't have this back in the ministry?"

"Hard to say," Ojars was trying to conceal obvious glee. "But no. You said so yourself."

"I said I didn't notice it before. In the ministry, he wore a suit and sleeves."

"The dragon's tail extends over his hand."

Good point, thought Kaspars.

And later, he realized it wouldn't be the last time he thought this.

Especially as it was the last thing Ojars ever said.

Kaspars's head struck the back of his seat as the Mercedes lurched forward, jarred from behind by what might as well have been a tank. Ojars bounced back and forward so that he struck his chin on the steering wheel, his forehead shattering the windshield as the tail of the Mercedes kicked out and a blinded Ojars did his best to wrestle for control.

All to no avail. The SUV behind them hit the Mercedes a second time, the oversized bull bars of the SUV caving in the rear doors and sending the Mercedes into an irreversible spin. Kaspars's head shattered the passenger window even as he punched the glove compartment for his gun. He saw the SUV flash past, then the second vehicle, a red hatchback, plowed into him, knocking the holster and pistol from his hands.

Then they went over the edge of the guardrail and rolled.

▪ ▪ ▪ ▪

"Kaspars," came the voice. "Kaspars, can you stand?"

He less heard her voice than remembered it through the knife-ammonia cut of smelling salts; through the vague sensation of blood running down his face, down his chest and into the crotch of his pants. Some strange prism of time. For he was already standing, already walking with arms supporting him and the gruff orders called out by someone behind him to "be careful with him," to "lay him flat in the car."

Yet still, he heard her voice. Well, after he was already standing, staggering and again passing out to awake not in the hospital but in a luxurious study. Fireplace against the wall. Hardwood shelves of seemingly thousands of books in Russian and Latvian and English.

"Kaspars, can you stand?"

Kaspars glanced up to see her hunching over him, felt her lean close to cradle his head and neck as she eased him to a sitting position to raise his arms above his head.

"Where am I?"

"Enough now. There. Raise your arm higher."

The bandages went under his arm, over his shoulder and back under his arm. Krista leaned close again—he could smell the fruit-smell of perfume and beyond that something native, perhaps the smell of earth. He moved and felt something grind in his ribs.

"Where am I?"

"At the home of a friend," said Krista. She ran her hand over the back of a British Chesterfield sofa. "Don't worry. A nice, elderly friend. One of those British chaps who thought he could make money in real estate here. He took care of me, though—when I first arrived. Sometimes you need someone to take care of you, I think."

Krista touched his face. Kaspars, confused and more indelicate than he meant to be, drew her hand away.

"Tell me what happened. And Ojars—where is Ojars?"

"Ojars is dead, Kaspars." The smile faded, and Krista rose from him, seemed to float a few inches off the floor to alight at the whiskey cabinet centered in the library on the far wall. Kaspars felt his torso and neck. Bandages everywhere, some of them still wet.

"We were struck from behind, run off the road."

"Yes."

"And you must know who did it. . . . And someone sent you to help, or I wouldn't be here."

"You are the detective, still."

Kaspars touched a palm to his eye. "This was a hit. On me. Not on Ojars. There was no point in hitting Ojars."

Krista returned (did her feet ever touch the floor?) dusky with her black locks trailing over her shoulders. "I don't know if you should drink this. You were cut up quite badly. You may have a concussion."

"Yet, I'm not in the hospital."

"You refused."

"I seriously doubt it."

"You refused."

Palm away from his eye, Kaspars was finally able to take in his surroundings. The apartment was plush, all right. Swords on the walls. A yellowed, antique globe by a matching desk in the corner and a coffee table just at his knees. It was if he had been plucked from the sordid world of unwanted detectives to be dropped in his underwear into the parlor of an English country home.

A coffee table magically appeared under his glass. For the first time since the bank, Kaspars set aside the whiskey and poured himself a new glass from a decanter of water. It was an effort not to physically attempt to wave away the fog.

"I found you very brave," said Krista.

Kaspars didn't feel brave. He didn't have the faintest idea what she was talking about. Instead, he thought, My gun? Where the hell is my gun? Instead, he half mumbled, half begged, "Krista—"

"Others have been so brave," she said. "May I tell you a story?"

"A story?"

"Do you know the kara'im?"

Kaspars strained to focus on Krista, nimble and standing in jeans and a white button-down on the far side of the table—and now he thought, perhaps more than a little crazy—and shrugged in a wounded cross of confusion and despair.

"Do not know the kara'im."

"They were a beautiful people," she said with a flash of a grin. "Like me." Then the bit lip, the child of her hopeful. "Dark skin, black hair, narrow hips. But the men were warriors. Some believed them to be of Tatar stock; others, most of us, knew that they were of a lost and wandering tribe of Israel. The true blood of Abraham dodging wars and pogroms, until finally, they found the lakes of Streva and Trakai."

"Lithuania."

"Lithuania. Poland. Russia. Lithuania again. Names of states that did not apply. For here, there were endless forests and lakes. Meadows of flowers and deer and clear water that you could take to drink with your hand. On so they survived, and in their small, fierce and beautiful way, they thrived."

Krista rocked from heel to toe, her hands crossed in front of her so that for the first time, Kaspars truly wondered about her age. Even younger than I thought. Even more caught up in it. Kaspars tried to swallow, but when he spoke, his voice was thick.

"Until?"

Krista's hands went to her sides, balled into fists. "Until the apocalypse of all they held dear. The true war when the Nazis hunted down my great-grandmother and my grandfather and my grandmother. Until the children hid in the forest from winter to winter, only coming out in the summers to watch the fighters dance across the sky."

"Your mother."

"My mother and her sister."

"What happened to you, Krista? Why did you come for me?"

"Yet, I am still Latvian," she said. "Part of me, at least." Silence and a bit lip. "Let me show you."

Hands went to her blouse. As she undid the buttons, he saw the startling color, the detail of a princess with a crown.

Then later, hours later, an endless flash of eternity later, she woke him, clinging to his side so that he had to cock his head just to look her in the eye.

She said, "You are bleeding again."

"Yes."

"You should be in the hospital."

"That's what I said."

"You can't go back."

"Is there a third way?"

More silence. Eyes so big and coal-black in the night that he knew there was no tumbling out.

"Printex-Lat," she said.

"What?"

"Your next audit. You know the name?"

"I know the name."

"Secure paper. They print money, stock certificates, bond papers. Not just for Latvia, but for the whole region. The company belongs to your friend Mr. Lagunov, but I suppose you knew that."

"Yes."

"They almost killed him in the spring."

A kiss. "Thank you."

But she wasn't finished. "Ojars knew what he was speaking about. Estonian mistakes. To be incinerated, but they never get incinerated in the end."

"Because Igor controls the books."

"That is what Ojars said."

"So, you understood Igor has control."

"Friends like these," muttered Kaspars.

"What?"

"A Russian CEO done in by his Russian security guards. Not the first time."

There is pain, and there is want, and as painful as want could be, Kaspars slid loose from Krista's grip.

"What are you doing?"

"I need to make a call. Your friend? He won't mind?"

"Depends on whom you call."

He would probably mind then. Tough luck for him. Kaspars dialed an overly long number, was rewarded with an operator and gave her the transfer number.

Krista was more concerned this time. "Who are you calling?"

Kaspars raised a hand just as he heard an irritated voice.

"Department of State. Caulson here."

"Chris?"

Static. Clicks as some greater someone was patched in.

"You've got the nut to call here."

"Chris, I would have called sooner."

"Bad idea."

"All I need is a minute—and I can trade for it."

"Trade what? Information? Kaspars, those days are gone. You made your choice, and should you need reminding . . ."

"I just need you to run a name, Chris. Igor Danilov. Patronym, I believe, is Sergey . . . Sergeyaveech."

"Call your friends in Narco."

"I don't have any, and it's not a Narco deal. And maybe it's not even Latvian. It's stocks, but counterfeit. Estonian certificates. Not my game, but I know we have Russians or the Ühiskassa."

"The Ühiskassa are Estonian only in name. The Ühiskassa are Russian mafia, my friend. Through and through."

Good. At least Chris was listening. "I've been dragged into this, Chris. Just like with everything else. Maybe that's not your fault, but you owe me."

"I don't owe you shit, Kaspars. We worked together, and you were working for the bank."

"I was never working for the bank."

"One day, maybe I'll believe you. But for now, good-bye, Kaspars."

"Chris—don't hang up. This isn't my beat." Kaspars paused, not sure if the line was not already dead. "I don't need you to come in on this. I just don't understand the game."

More silence. Kaspars was about to hang up when the agent finally spoke.

"You fake the certificates just like you fake land registries, acquisitions. Money flows in and out. Kid stuff unless the certificates are real."

"Got it."

"I doubt it. Little green men on the border, Estonia scared shitless and a buildup of tanks on both sides. But the Russians are smart enough—could be the government. Yeah, hell, why not take over Estonian companies from the inside? A threat or two, company owners tossed into the Baltic." Chris seemed to hesitate. "Is this oil? Infrastructure?"

"I don't know what it is, Chris."

A cough—or was it a laugh? "I'll pass it on. I appreciate it, which is why I'll warn you."

"Warn me what?"

"We have intel, Kaspars. Vietnamese. Human traffickers dead on the Lat-Russian border. Three to be exact. And you on the scene, my friend. You on the scene."

Kaspars braced himself, took hold of the desk. Listened to a line as empty and cold as space.

Until Chris said, "That's warning number one, Kaspar. Not that I think you did it. But now for warning number two."

"Tell me."

"You know that law on US citizens working for a foreign government?"

Kaspars gripped the phone harder. "I have dual citizenship. You knew that when I was in Narco."

"You are no longer in Narco, Kaspars. Or let me put it this way—you try to fly to New York or Boston, and they'll be waiting, brother." A pause. "And I will be too."

The line went dead. Kaspars's shoulders slumped, plan Z wiped out in a minute. What did they say about good deeds? Kaspars glanced at Krista, considered her tattoos, the reality of it all, which is when came the lilt of her cell.

Krista saw the number, poked out her tongue. A rough voice began before she could even speak.

"It's late," she said.

Monotone on the other end.

"It's late," she repeated.

Kaspars took her hand. "It's all right," he said. "All right. I understand it now. I understand it all."

▪ ▪ ▪ ▪

It was a strange night, her there by his side, her head on his shoulder as they drove the suicide road east. Once, he checked the glove compartment, his head so foggy he needed to make sure he still had the gun. Two times after that, he slowed to a stop on the side of the two-lane, terrified of lights behind him, pulling the gun and opening the door to step out into the night with the pistol at his hip as mere innocents passed.

The rest of the time, she spoke to him, held tight to his ribs and chest as if cloven to him to the end.

"There is a cabin near Verkne. We used to hike there—three days with my brother when I was a little girl. In the morning, the waters were golden. And my brother fished for pike as long as your arm.

"I know it is still there. It will be there just as it has always been, for a hundred years. The place where I long to return."

Such were her ramblings, the kisses on his cheek tiny and endearing. Yet Kaspars did not reply, did not say a word. Not once during the night and not until he saw the road marker that meant the tri-border was near.

"We're here."

"I don't want to go."

Kaspars again drew the pistol from the glove compartment. "That makes two of us."

This time, even in blue-black before sunrise, Kaspars knew the way. Twenty meters in, a sharp left where he's missed the path the first time and two hundred meters east. The path was wide here, the center tracked with bootprints so that he wondered how he had ever in that previous life become so irretrievably lost. Yet no longer, for this was how they walked to the clearing, an ex-cop and his half-Lithuanian girl, seeing the headlights ahead of them, shining out of the clearing straight at them, and then stepping out of the forest to find the customs guards loading a military truck in the snow.

Then Captain Berzins's voice, before they could see him. "You should put that pistol away. Good way to get shot."

"I rather think I won't."

The captain stepped out of the glare of headlights, an AK-47 at the ready. He was flanked by Olzos and a third border guard Kaspars had never met.

"We knew you'd come," he said. He grinned at Krista. "Pretty girl."

Kaspars ignored that. "You called; I came." He waved the pistol to the border guards loading boxes upon boxes from one military truck to another. "No Vietnamese this time?"

"Not this time."

"There was a fourth," said Kaspars. "I found him up on the hill the day we met. He ran, didn't he? Made it too close to the border so you left him there."

Olzos gave a quick glance at the captain, whose grin had faded to a sneer.

Kaspars said, "You should have given me credit for killing him as well."

"Wasn't our idea, putting it on you," said Berzins. "You can blame your friend for that."

"Danilov. Where is he?"

"Sergey or Igor."

Kaspars allowed him a nod. "Twins then," he said. "So Ojars was right. My guess is that it's Igor who runs the printing houses, Igor who ran me off the road yesterday morning. But I don't want to speak to Igor. I want to speak to Sergey."

"And Sergey wants to speak to you."

The Russian came out of the back of the truck, broad and sweating and clad only in boots, jeans and a muscle shirt despite the cold. With an easy hop, he alighted between trucks, the Virgin Mary tattoos a blue smudge, the epaulets upon his bare shoulders as sharp as knives.

Krista jerked Kaspars's hand, hissed "*Ühiskassa*," and all but pulled Kaspars off his feet. Kaspars held firm, yanked her back to his side. The Russian gave an appreciative grunt, held out an arm muscled-hominoid, making a show of it as a soldier helped him with his coat.

And Krista whispered, *"Shoot him. Shoot him. Don't you know what he is?"*

Kaspars dangled the pistol. He wasn't shooting anybody like this. Apart from maybe himself in the foot the way Krista wrestled so. Seeing she could not run, Krista cowered behind him, leaving Kaspars alone so that all he could do was to swallow his fear. For even in Narco, he had never seen true prison-epaulet tattoos.

Yet here he was, Sergey Danilov, Russian *vor v zakone*. Not just your ordinary thief-in-law, but lord of the gulag—in other words, a true Russian mafia king.

And no, he had not counted on that.

"A *vor* working with governments?" said Kaspars. "Isn't that against the code?"

"New times, my friend."

"Your brother almost killed me."

"Igor can be like that." The *vor* of the Ühiskassa gleamed a gold-toothed grin. "Indelicate. But tell me, bagman detective—or are you a minister already—why did you come?"

"You're not smuggling stock certificates into Latvia. You are printing them in Latvia, smuggling Estonian papers into Estonia. It's perfect. A government-approved, secure-paper printing plant with your brother beating the shit out of its ethnic Russian owner. Which means Ojars was right. You print the stock certificates, list them as flawed. Fake the incineration and ship across the border with the help of the Vietnamese."

The Russian gave a grunt, this time of disgust, and waved at the trucks, one Latvian, the other Estonian. "No longer. Human traffickers—just can't trust them for shit." He then pointed with his fist. "You can ask your girl about that."

Krista made herself smaller against Kaspars's back. Another story for another time.

Kaspars said, "You needed someone from the ministry to check off the books. That's the law, no way to get around it. You needed me."

"There is no third way."

"No, there is not."

"Why have you come, Kaspars Jansons?"

Kaspars worked his jaw, tried to find enough spit to continue to speak. Funny—now that they were finally getting down to it, he was no longer afraid, but relieved.

"You—your side—forced me into the bank deal."

The *vor* gave a shrug.

"How much did you make off that? Three hundred mil?'

Another shrug.

"I did my part, Sergey. I did my part, and we had a deal. But this—the stock certificates, killing the Vietnamese—this was not part of it."

"There is *no* third way."

"No, there is not."

Which was when Kaspars felt Krista release him, move away. He could just see her out of the corner of his eye, her face a mix of horror and shock. But too late now.

Kaspars said, "Do you have it?"

"As agreed."

The *vor* reached into the inside pocket of his coat. Despite himself, Kaspars tensed—it was all he could do to keep the pistol by his side. Yet the thief-in-law drew not a gun, but two different passports and handed them to Captain Berzins, who opened the first and read aloud.

"Thomas Alan Smith, citizen of the United Kingdom," he said.

Kaspars took the passport, saw his photo, how the document was perfect down to the aged and wrinkled cover. Then Berzins handed him a second passport.

"What's this?"

"Your Vietnamese double. As a keepsake."

"I see."

"Just so you know—we can find or put you any place, Kaspars Jansons. Any fucking time."

Kaspars tapped the passports with the barrel of his pistol. Yes, he thought, yes, they could. He eyed Berzins and the *vor.*

"Honor among thieves," he said.

"Honor among thieves."

Then he turned to Krista, the girl slight and trembling with horror. "I had to stay in or get out, Krista. No third way."

Her eyes were livid. "You—you *bastard.* You sucked me in, had me *hooked.*"

"Krista, listen to me. We're free. Wherever you want to go. Spain. The Bahamas. Wherever. I was locked in, but we're free."

*"You fucking bastard—"*

Or at least that is what she began to say—until the *vor* that was Sergey Danilov cut her off.

"Enough of that, Kris."

Krista balled up her fists, snarled at the mafia king with a pride so fierce that Kaspars was taken aback.

But Danilov barked, "Drop it, I said. Drop the damned charade."

And to Kaspars's utter shock, Krista took one bold step to the mafia king and held out her hand.

"Services rendered," she said. "Payment due."

Danilov shrugged indifference. "I hold with that."

Kaspars glanced from Krista to Danilov and back, incredulous, even as Danilov reached into a second pocket, came out with a stack of passports and flipped through each so that he could see the photos in the light.

"She played you, my friend. I mean, you are *conflicted.* You would have just gone to drink—and we couldn't wait forever. Now that you're finally out, we have a fine replacement on the way. A replacement with no qualms whatsoever."

Kaspars turned to Krista. "You ran me from the start."

"Of course she did," said the *vor*. "She spotted you, promoted you, led you on. From the bank to the ministry and still, you didn't see." Then he added. "Come on, friend. Since when does a ministry girl have tats like that."

And just like *that*, they stood beyond him, the *vor* and the former whore. For it was business now. Danilov handed the girl not one passport, but three. Then made notes, wrote numbers on paper. Kaspars saw he spoke to her kindly—and that she did not shrink in fear.

"We printed a Russian passport as well," the *vor* told her. "Just in case you change your mind."

Krista took the passports as if they were sacred, held them to her breast. Then she turned to Kaspars, and for once he saw her fully and forever, knew that a man should never in his life see into a woman so truly, so deeply. Not the prostitution, the fear. Not the clawing and the hope of the child within.

Which is when she came to him, as wary as a cat, and took his hand.

"To hell with Spain, to hell with the Bahamas," she said. "To hell with Russia even.

*"I know just where we will go."*

He didn't ask. No purpose served. So long as it was not here.

# ESTONIA:

## When Moscow Comes Calling

BY PETER GALUSZKA

*PETER GALUSZKA reported from Moscow for* BusinessWeek *magazine in the 1980s and 1990s. He also served as the magazine's international news editor in New York. A journalist for forty-five years, he has written for the* Washington Post, *the* New York Times, *Bloomberg News, and others. He published a book about the US coal industry in 2012.*

Kirk Palmer knew it was time to get up when he heard a steady "crunch, crunch" coming from the parking lot nine floors below. Dour women who might have stepped out of a Tolstoy novel were breaking up ice around cars with big shovels in the pre-dawn gloom.

Palmer's head pounded from the previous night's endeavors. He had been writing his piece about the latest crackdowns and threats. Yet, this time, his instincts were filled with foreboding. There had been plenty of provocations, threats, or troop and aircraft movements before. But nothing like this.

After he clicked the "send" button and got an acknowledgment from New York, his mind was still racing. He left the news bureau on Kutuzovsky Prospekt near Moscow city center and walked through the snow to his apartment. He pulled a bottle of vodka from the freezer, twisted off the cap and drank a large slug, then several more.

Palmer had been in Russia off and on for years. It had been a ride beyond belief. He knew the drill.

He started out back in the 1980s when Mikhail S. Gorbachev's ambitious but half-baked attempts to reform this country made for a profoundly exciting time. Who knew that Andrei Sakharov would be released from house detention in Nizhny Novgorod, then called Gorky? How about the smiling mug of Ronald Reagan flashing from a gigantic video screen on Novy Arbat, a main shopping street at the epicenter of the Evil Empire?

Up next, Boris Yeltsin had been doddering, yet, at times, decisive. Yeltsin never could catch up with the forces he had unleashed. The world's largest mafia state collapsed overnight, before transforming into a far more dangerous variant of the same.

During the ensuing *Dikaya Vremya* (Wild Time), privatized state wealth supposedly was transferred into stock shares held by ordinary citizens. The paper ended up in the hands of newly minted oligarchs. As their jealous rivals fought over the spoils, nouveau riche bosses made street shootouts as common as tram stops. Amidst the chaos, arrogant little shits from fancy Western universities urged painful and pointless "shock therapy" economic practices. That only alienated Russia's long-suffering citizenry and killed off many of the mediocre but free services they enjoyed while leaving nothing in their place.

As Yeltsin succumbed to age, alcohol, and painkillers, he somehow selected a strange little man named Vladimir Putin to be his successor. Of course, there was a veneer of an election. But it was clear to all that the former KGB officer with a modest career record would install an updated version of the *siloviki* (security) from the intelligence, military and law enforcement agencies that had somehow disappeared from the scene. All the while, wealth from extractive industries and weapons exports would flow into the offshore bank accounts of the oligarchs and their cronies. Putin's personal and carefully hidden riches were rumored to surpass $80 billion.

After twenty years of power, Putin had developed a modern version of Russian authoritarianism. At first, he brought stability, but he could not meet his promises. He failed to transform Russia from a Third World petrostate with rockets into a first-world industrial giant. His constituents were known for their ingenuity and durability—traits that save one from a Russian winter, but not the politicians. Putin and his cabal were too busy stripping assets to build on such admirable qualities.

There had been a time of breathtaking openness in culture and the media. But as kleptocracy emerged victorious, it ended. Critical journalists were shot, stabbed, had acid thrown in their faces or perished painfully in hospital wards as doctors tried to figure out what poisoned them. If any oligarchs challenged the concentration of power in Putin's Kremlin, they would be tried and imprisoned, sometimes a repeated cycle.

Reaching into the Russian psyche, Putin had fostered a modern concept of aggressive Russian exceptionalism and spiritualism. He drummed up popular support for bloody operations against the Chechens, Georgians, Ossetians, and Ukrainians. Russia faced a considerable threat from Islamic faithful, but, as in other countries, much of it was self-inflicted—brought on by absurd and/or discriminatory policies.

Partnering with the Russian Orthodox Church hierarchy, Putin evangelized that true Russians were pure, religious and best left free of foreign influences. This potent brew justified Moscow reaching out to take back land that had been lopped away when the Soviet Union disappeared on December 31, 1991. Putin's *Novorossiya*—former lands tracing back to the eastern flow of Orthodox Christianity—now included Moldova and a good bit of eastern Ukraine.

In his designs, Kiev, the Ukrainian capital, would be included as well, as it had been a critically important stepping stone for Orthodox religious domination. There were extensions to be thrown in for good measure, like the Balkan States, welcome for their balmy climates and laid-back lifestyles.

Putin knew precisely how to play to the uglier side: racism, paranoia and dog-like devotion to a leader with balls. Other than the intelligentsia, few protested when he banned sexual education (read Chekhov instead for guidance), gay "propaganda" (threatens the youth), Emo punk rockers, and yoga (they will invade us when we are relaxed). Pussy Riot—a female punk band—would be in and out of prison five times.

By combining strong-armed nationalism with extreme social conservativism, Putin made bizarre allies, including white supremacy groups in the United States. One was the Traditional Worker Party, a hard-right group that decried "anti-Christian degeneracy." Its leader called Russia "the great white power." America's "Identity Christians," who thought of themselves as the real "Jews," liked what they saw in Putin.

Suspicious foreigners, particularly Western diplomats and journalists, got a new taste of old-style behavior dating back to the Great Terror or the Cold War. GAI traffic cops would wave their *pazhalsta* sticks to pull over cars driven by select foreigners simply to harass them. Apartments were broken into by mystery men who left unflushed turds in toilets as mementos of their visits. On occasion, diplomats were punched out by gray-coated embassy police guards supposedly there to protect them. There were newer threats, too. Internet trolls and social media posts to spread false and embarrassing lies about targets. It was the era of digital *kompromat*.

The phone rang.

"You hear about it?" Yuri Smirnoff, a Russian reporter.

"Hear the fuck about what?" Palmer replied, head pounding.

"They're moving on the Baltics. Right now. Little green guys slipping past borders. Paratroops are massing. Motor rifle battalions. Just like Ukraine. Trump signaled it was OK. He doesn't give a shit what NATO says. He told his buddy—Putin—Washington's not standing in the way."

Russian strike forces had been massing for weeks in St. Petersburg and the provincial city of Pskov. Units of *Spetsnaz* special forces troops, *Desantniki* airborne soldiers, as well as heavy armor, including the latest M-14 Armata main battle tank that had only started coming off assembly lines in 2015. The buildup meant only one thing—the coming invasions of Estonia, Latvia and Lithuania.

That does change things, Palmer thought as he hung up. It just so happened he had planned on flying to the Estonian capital of Tallinn later that morning. Very doubtful he'd be allowed to travel now. But he really had to get there. He badly needed to meet some people.

He emailed the office in New York regarding his plans, pulled himself together and got a gypsy cab to take him to Sheremetyevo International Airport. Sure enough, airspace over Estonia had been closed. There were rumors of dogfights between NATO and Russian aircraft. A German F-16 had supposedly been shot down in international airspace over the Baltic Sea. Palmer's flight had been canceled. After some last-minute scrambling, he purchased a seat on a Finnair flight to Helsinki, where he would have more options.

▪ ▪ ▪ ▪

When Palmer landed at Helsinki-Vantaa International Airport, he found people calmly taking the news of impending combat just one hundred miles away on the other side of the Gulf of Finland with remarkable stoicism. In the back of everyone's mind was the understanding that things could go nuclear very quickly.

The Russians had plenty of missiles with warheads—even more after Putin had rescinded Russia's participation in intermediate-range ballistic missile treaties and thumbed his nose at other strategic arms pacts.

Putin had also introduced late model, nuclear-capable Iskander-M missiles and their truck launchers into Kaliningrad, a small Russian enclave between Poland and Lithuania on the Baltic Sea. He claimed it was just an exercise, but the missiles ended up staying there. Their range of four hundred and fifty miles threatened cities throughout northwestern Europe, including Berlin.

It was a time-worn strategy. Iterations of it had played out for decades. If NATO took out the Iskanders, they'd blow up isolated Kaliningrad and not Mother Russia, which would be more than ready to come back with a devastating retaliatory strike. Hitting European population centers would tend to delink the United States from getting involved despite its NATO obligations. Word-for-word, Leonid Brezhnev used the same ploy in the early 1980s. He placed SS-20 intermediate-range nuclear missiles in Eastern Europe to promote such a NATO delink. It lasted until Ronald Reagan deployed Pershing II and cruise missiles in Western Germany and the United Kingdom. In breakthrough diplomacy, he and Gorbachev subsequently negotiated most of them away.

The mood could not be more different now. After Great Britain's "Brexit" departure from the European Union, many wondered why London bothered with NATO. Continuing bloodshed by Islamic terrorists and the worst human migration in hundreds of years from shattered Middle Eastern countries fostered xenophobia not seen since Adolf Hitler and Mussolini. More European countries elected rightist nationalists as their leaders. The sense of communality that had crystallized with Maastricht was long gone. The ascendancy of an erratic, mindless blowhard like Marine Le Pen was a predictable next step.

Palmer took a cab to Makasiiniterminaali, Eteläsatama, on Helsinki's downtown waterfront. He then booked a ticket on the Linda Line Express. He was lucky—again. Ferry service to Tallinn was soon shutting down. But more ferries were needed to remove evacuees, so they still sailed a long-established route. It was brutally cold and windy as the ferry maneuvered around the harbor, but it managed to sweep up on its hydrofoils and roar southwest.

Palmer remained tired and hungover. He sipped four cups of espresso as he watched the satellite TV news in astonishment. No one spoke in the bar. Two hours later, the vessel slowed and approached Linnahalli Terminal in Estonia's ancient capital.

As he walked onto the wharf, he pulled out his cell phone and called Latta. She was his best contact in Estonia, a good friend and sometime lover.

"I'm here."

"It is finally happening," replied Latta. "I still can't believe it. I will be over soon."

By day, Latta worked at a website design company (tiny Estonia had some of the best information technicians in the world) and otherwise dabbled in progressive politics with an eye toward running for the Riigikogu, the Estonian parliament, at some point. With her thin, girlish build, light brown, partly reddish hair, and blue eyes, she would have no trouble with campaign advertising.

He had to get to his hotel and set up. His place was a strange choice, the Hotel Viru just south of picturesque Old Town with its red tile roofs and distinctive, almost Turkish-looking, minaret towers. Tallinn had always been a major trading spot, but the Viru was something else.

Post-Soviet Tallinn had plenty of splendid hotels. But they were booked solid with people anxiously preparing to leave as soon as they found passage. No one wanted to be around when the Russians came.

So, Palmer was stuck with the Viru. It was erected in 1972, during the middle of the Cold War. The KGB had realized Tallinn was a major meeting spot for people wanting to do business with the Soviet Union. Brezhnev was thinking about opening the door to foreign investment, albeit just a little. Plus, Tallinn was often included by tourism companies that led foreigners to gawk at the ostentatious art and architecture of what was then Leningrad just a few hours away by bus or train.

The Soviet government built a twenty-two-story tower to grab some of the business. But there was another reason. The hotel, operated by Intourist, the universally despised Soviet tourism agency, had one extra, secret floor—penthouse if you will—that was off-limits.

From there, the KGB operated an extensive surveillance system. Every hotel room, often every ashtray and lamp, was bugged. On the top floor, KGB officers worked shifts monitoring what went on in the bar, bathrooms and bedrooms.

The mystery floor was finally revealed after Communism fell. It became a museum whose artifacts included special red telephones to the KGB's headquarters operations in Lubyanka at the center of Moscow or at Yasenevo, the sprawling foreign intelligence center in a southwestern suburb.

Palmer had stayed there several times during the Hotel Viru years. Once, in the 1980s, he was there after he taped a breathtaking on-the-record interview he had with Estonian nationalists plotting the violent overthrow of the Communist Party and freedom from Moscow. It was high risk, life-or-death stuff. Meeting with them involved calls from random payphones and switching cars in a manner suggested by Alfred Hitchcock's classic film *Foreign Correspondent*.

They knew exactly what he was doing, of course. At one point, as he strolled the Old Town marking time before the meeting, he noticed a small Zhiguli car with four beefy men inside. They stared intently at him—heavy and obvious surveillance. They wanted him to know it.

Back at the Viru, he was so jacked up by fear and excitement that he transcribed his notes and made copies as quietly as he could in his room. Then he put away the better part of a bottle of whiskey out of sheer tension. Somehow, he was not searched when he flew back to Moscow the following day.

The next Viru visit was more pleasant, at least at first. He was squiring about with a curvy blonde who had taken a break from her job as an environmental journalist in Washington. After downing two bottles of decent Georgian wine at the bar, the giggling couple stumbled into their dark bedroom, where they enjoyed a delicious night. The mood changed when the sun came up. Groggy, Palmer looked beside the bed. On the floor were twenty-six used condoms—obviously not his. The KGB had left another calling card.

■ ■ ■ ■

Palmer unpacked, set up his laptop and got onto the hotel's Wi-Fi, which worked intermittently. He had multiple messages. A few were from worried relatives and friends. Most were from frantic editors in New York demanding immediate updates as they sweated out the latest round of job cuts.

The Baltic invasion seemed to have started, they wrote. The main target appeared to be Latvia so as to break apart its two neighbors. Officials at State and Defense did not know what to do with President Trump. What kind of deal had he made with Putin? Are we at DEFCON 3 or DEFCON 2? No one seemed to know where Trump was, but there was nothing out of sort at the White House or Trump Tower in midtown Manhattan. No helicopter dash to Andrews Air Force Base and Air Force One. No quick flights to Mount Storm or Weather or wherever.

After the Baltics joined NATO in 2004, Western troops, typically in small numbers, had rotated in and out of the Baltic states. German pilots maintained air combat patrols over the Baltic Sea and occasionally played tag with MiG-29s or Sukhoi Su-35s. American troops roamed around in Bradley armored vehicles or a few M1A1 Abrams tanks. Off the coast, Russian jets buzzed American warships.

There was a downside to NATO's generosity. Some natives of the Baltics were just as racist as their former Soviet masters and did not like African American soldiers, particularly at nightspots. Outside of a dance hall in Riga, two black American troops were assaulted by drunken local men. Their teeth were punched out, and both required emergency air evacuations to treat brain injuries.

It was all there for show. In the Bush years, relations with Putin were unsteady, but not awful. They came to be that way with Obama, particularly after the Russian "reset" failed miserably. Moscow retook Crimea and invaded eastern Ukraine. A new adventurism abetted by President Obama's tendency to "lead from behind" and avoid direct confrontations.

Trump, aided by Russian cyber manipulation of the 2016 election, was in rapture of his Putin bromance. That, and he was said to be secretly cooking up plans for a bunch of new Trump Towers and other real estate ventures from Vladivostok to Novosibirsk. They'd be bankrolled by Putin and his cronies. The scheme even included Yalta, the famous, subtropical garden spot in the freshly-Russian Crimea where, ironically, some say Franklin Delano Roosevelt and Winston Churchill sold out Eastern Europe to get Josef Stalin to agree to help put a final nail in the Empire of Japan.

The cold facts were that NATO couldn't make a difference. A RAND study showed that it would take Russian forces between thirty-six and sixty hours to roll through the Baltics, a flat area about the size of Florida.

Estonia would take the brunt of this blow.

Thirty-six hours.

Tops.

Estonia had a tiny army known for quaint but odd habits, like towing portable saunas into combat zones. Much of the border was simply marked by green and orange paint lines. A chain-link fence was planned, but it hadn't been built.

Despite the presence of company-sized units of American and European troops, they couldn't match what Putin had put together. Two years after seizing parts of eastern Ukraine and watching the West's impotence, he placed three fresh divisions—twenty-five thousand men under arms—on Russia's border with the Baltics and near Poland. NATO had just begun deploying an additional thirty thousand troops.

Not with Trump as president. He quickly nixed that plan as he plotted to take the United States out of NATO. Putin couldn't have asked for a clearer signal.

▪ ▪ ▪ ▪

The cell phone buzzed. Latta was in the lobby. He raced down. She was as beautiful as ever. Her surname was Koidula, the same as one of Estonia's most famous poets, whose work promoted a sense of Estonian identity struggling to survive amid various powerful neighbors. Smart as a whip, Latta emulated her namesake as a key player in one of the country's progressive parties and human rights groups. She was a fixer, a networker and one hell of a woman all mixed into one.

"So great to see you," Palmer whispered.

"Too bad for the circumstance," Latta replied, accepting his bear hug and kiss while gently touching his arm.

"What's the latest?"

"It's been tense for a long time. Pro-Russian demonstrations over a lot of make-believe ethnic abuse. A few days ago, there was a massive cyberattack. Took down numerous servers and routers. The net crashed and came back every now and then. No email, no Twitter, no phones. Television broadcasts came to a halt, like France in 2015. No one could do anything. Then the green men started showing up just over the line in Narva and later in Viro."

Latta's voice was suddenly drowned out by the shriek of a low-flying jet fighter, followed by the steady thump, thump of helicopters heading east.

"Can we get somewhere?" Palmer asked.

Latta led him to her car, an elderly VW Golf. They sat in it for a while, wondering what approach would be best. The two major immediate targets for the Russians would be Võru, a small town in the southeast of about thirteen thousand, and Narva, a border town, sixty thousand strong, about 135 miles due east. Eighty percent of its residents spoke Russian. Generally, the two populations had lived side by side. Ethnic Russians liked crossing the border because it meant three times the pay for the same work. In recent months, however, there had been mysterious beatings and murders of Russian speakers, whose bodies were always left in easy-to-spot places.

Narva was the obvious first choice. Palmer pushed it over Võru. Narva was a straight shot on European Route E-20. A favorite of trucks that belched filthy plumes of smoke, it also was ideal for Russian tanks and BMP and BTR armored personnel carriers.

Latta headed out of town, desperately trying to coax her radio to tap into the news. Ice and snow covered the roads, as city maintenance had shut down for the emergency.

As they approached Route E-20, they could see caravans of refugees fleeing the war zone. A rolling menagerie headed westward that included everything from goods-stuffed trucks to BMWs and even a few Zaporozhets, perhaps the worst automobile model the Soviet Union ever produced. It was nicknamed "The Soapbox" because it looked like one.

The eastbound lanes were nearly empty, save for Estonian, American or British armored personnel carriers and police cars with flashing blue lights. Every now and then, a helicopter in camouflage livery roared just over the vehicles.

"Your family OK?" Palmer asked.

"Mama and Papa are out in the countryside. They should be safe, but I don't know how they will get food if the Russians take Tallinn."

Her brother, Tatu, was another story. The strapping young man was a reservist with the Estonian armed forces and had just been called to duty.

Like all Estonians, Latta's family had been dealing with Russians in unpleasant ways for centuries. Her great-grandparents had been alive when Hitler signed a treaty with Stalin in 1939 to preserve peace between the two nations while dividing Eastern Europe into spheres of influence. The Baltics became Soviet, and the troops came down the very highway on which they were driving. The NKVD rounded up and sorted out potential troublemakers. Any resistance met with an immediate burst of gunfire—standard operating procedure. Her great-grandfather, described as a gentle, rough-hewn man, was put into a rail boxcar and taken to a gulag in Siberia. He worked chopping down trees . . . and never came back.

The pair traveled in silence. Palmer checked his cell phone, but there was no service. Filing his story was going to be a challenge—he needed to find a hard-cabled phone and good old-fashioned fax machine. He'd have to play that one by ear. They made good time to the town of Aaspere but slowed at Haljala. Then, chaos as Narva got closer.

A roadblock loomed ahead, manned by troops wearing either mottled green or snow-white battle dress. Most held American-made M4 assault carbines. Some had a new version of a handheld grenade launcher that looked like a shotgun with a revolving magazine. It resembled something that actor Steven Seagal, another Putin bromancer and honorary citizen of the Russian Federation, might use to blaze away at bad guys in a low-grade action movie.

A soldier with a military police armband waved them down. Latta rolled down the car window and chatted in her native tongue.

"No go," she told Palmer. "Too close. The Russians are in Narva. Paratroopers have landed there, and armored forces are coming across."

"Tell them I'm a reporter."

She did. More talk. Then a tall man in mottled brown and green battle dress and body armor walked up.

"So, you are an American? I'm Lieutenant Colonel Jack Collins, USMC. With a detachment from a MEU off the coast trying to help. It's a mess." The officer had a slight South Carolina drawl.

"Can we get anywhere close?"

"It's pretty hairy, bud. But if you turn back and take a right at the second side street, onto Rahu, you might be able to work yourself toward the town. You'll have to walk. It's a hike. Maybe a mile to the center. You got a camera?"

"Nothing serious," replied Palmer, pointing at the tiny Olympus digital plus his cell phone. "How much time before they break through to here?"

"Anybody's guess. Probably no more than an hour. Maybe less. They hit the riverbank and the bridge. Of course, there's no real border. Just a bridge holding up the parade. Look, your safety is on your own dime, but if you get the chance, I'd boogie back to Tallinn. Get to the embassy. They'll try to figure something out there."

"What are your orders?" Palmer asked.

"What fucking orders?" the colonel replied as he walked away.

▪ ▪ ▪ ▪

Latta and Palmer drove onto Rahu and circled back through big Soviet-style apartment blocks. Leaving the Golf, they slipped into Narva Lossipark, a city garden spot, through the snow. On occasion, an SUV would creep past, packed with people. In the distance, they could see about a dozen plumes of black smoke and hear the chatter of machine-gun fire.

Palmer had been in combat before—Afghanistan, Ukraine and Syria. He knew that the steadier, more mechanical thumping rhythm came from Kalashnikovs. Other weapons, American M4s and M16s, had a faster-paced crack. He couldn't judge lines of resistance by just the sounds.

They walked on, passing locals with backpacks who were toting suitcases or boxes as best they could.

"What happened?" Latta asked a plump, middle-aged woman.

"Slaughter," she said, replying in Russian, which Latta and Palmer understood.

Latta noticed an apartment that was familiar. She nodded toward it.

"I have friends here. Real patriots." She didn't say that they were part of a partisan team that had been training for years to harass invading Russians with guerilla assaults. They had caches of weapons, explosives, food, water and radios hidden all over the place.

Odds might have been a million to one, but Latta's friends were still at home in their strangely Soviet-style apartment block. Three men and two women were frantically stuffing laptops, tablets, and flash drives into backpacks.

Latta gave each a quick hug.

"Here are Ahti, Elmar, Joosep, Astrid and Saara," she told Palmer, who knew to memorize their names but not take notes and not seem too curious.

"Where can we go?" Palmer asked.

Elmar, a skinny man in his late twenties with dark hair and a bad complexion, replied in broken English, "Keep walking east. There's only one bridge downtown—the E-20 over the Varna River. That's where the fighting is. The Russians quickly took the bridge, but it is narrow and it takes time for them to get their armor across. We wonder why NATO doesn't just blow it. The Russians are also using amphibians to cross the river, and they have some mobile bridges."

"What are you going to do?" Palmer asked.

Saara, a blazing platinum blonde with piercing, ice-blue eyes, glanced at him. "We must get out. Stay ahead of their breakthrough and columns. Get to our friends. Try to make a stand."

That would be difficult, she added, because companies of Russian paratroopers had fluttered down into the countryside from their transports and were massing farther west to cut off Route E-20.

The group got back to their packing. Each gave Latta a hug as they slipped out of the apartment and disappeared into a side street. Before they left, Palmer managed to snap a photo of the group with his cell phone.

She and Palmer set out in the opposite direction. They ran from door to door, crunching through the snow, as they approached Narva Lossipark and the Restaurant Rondell.

A loud explosion ripped the air, followed by the sound of a jet aircraft pulling out of a dive. More booms. Palmer knew that one could get used to machine-gun fire. Bombs and artillery are hard to deal with. Shock and thunder—you never knew when and how large the munition.

"Make it stop," he silently muttered.

They finally came to what seemed to be the knoll that the Marine had been talking about. Hiding behind a brick wall, they could peer from time to time at the cityscape.

Dominating the scene was Hermanni Linnus, a famed stone fortress on the riverfront built by the Danes in 1256. The white walls of its distinctive tower were stained by soot.

Across the Narva River, on the Russian side, stood the Ivangorod Fortress, another historic structure. It, too, was smoldering.

The juxtaposition—symbols of Estonia and Russia—was startling. But it did make sense. Narva had been dealing with Russian muscle since the sixteenth century and the Livonian War. Soviet troops occupied it after Stalin's pact, and German forces captured the area in 1941. As a stop on the road to Leningrad, it held strategic importance. In 1944, the Soviet Air Force bombed the city, destroying its baroque Old Town district. By the end of the war, 98 percent of the third-largest city in Estonia had been destroyed.

Much was rebuilt with chunky, brutalist-style buildings made of shoddy concrete. About 80 percent of its citizens spoke Russian and read or watched Russian media. But there seemed to be no sentimental longing for the *Rossiya Matbuoti* the way there was in Crimea. Jobs paid more on the west side of the river.

From time to time, Palmer could make out figures running. The single bridge near the two municipal monuments was an obvious choke point. A line of tanks was backed up trying to cross. TOW wire-guided missiles fired by Estonian troops zipped into it. The turret popped off in the blast. The wreck was quickly pushed into the river by vehicles behind it.

Suddenly, another T-14 tank with its unusual turret and side-by-side cannons crashed through a fence. Palmer tried to steady his Olympus to snap some photographs. An eight-wheeled BTR rolled up next to it, machine gun blazing away.

Streams of red tracer fire crisscrossed the battle zone. From time to time, the bullets would ricochet against hard objects and fly off into a new direction. The tanks' cannons let loose with a roar as the vehicles bounced back from the recoil. Several figures were running. In a second, they were torn apart by the gunfire.

A section of the wall that shielded them exploded, showering brick, stone and red-hot shrapnel that burned through a sleeve of Palmer's down parka.

He and Latta were dazed and disoriented. They heard screams. They did not know from where. Then, gruff voices in Russian. A blast threw them both on the ground. Blood started trickling from Latta's right ear.

Figures appeared in bulky battle dress and helmets. They swung their AK-12 assault rifles at the pair as they cowered on the ground. A man dressed all in forest green with no identifying flashes and wearing a balaclava approached them. He was carrying a strange-looking weapon that Palmer later learned was an AS Val, an advanced submachine gun with a silencer designed for use by Russian special forces. The man studied Palmer as if he were an alien. Then he knelt beside him, and, very quickly, slipped a small computer flash drive into Palmer's pocket. He said nothing.

The small force vanished as quickly as it had appeared. Palmer struggled, helping Latta to her feet. They half crawled, half ran in the general direction of their car. Using walls and apartment blocks as cover, they saw the Golf. Luckily, it had not been hit. Palmer gently placed Latta in the passenger seat and used a rag to blot the blood that had stopped trickling from her ear. He started the engine and gingerly headed back to Route E-20 and turned west.

▪ ▪ ▪ ▪

Palmer retraced their route. The earlier NATO roadblock was no longer there—the Marine officer was gone. Latta had apparently suffered a mild concussion from the explosion. She was alert but silent. Palmer wanted to get her medical help, but he knew he also had to find a Wi-Fi connection so he could file a story in New York. Work was work, and he could provide a colorful, eyewitness account of the pounding Varna was taking. He had no idea what else was going on in the neighboring countries or if Tallinn had fallen.

Route E-20 westbound wasn't as clogged as it had been a few hours earlier, but it was still busy. Vehicles motored on. Trucks were overflowing with passengers dressed in puffy clothing against the cold. In the distance, smoke plumes licked the sky. From time to time, helicopters would hover overhead. At one point, Palmer heard a great roar and looked to the sky. A formation of white cargo jets, likely carrying airborne forces, moved with precision toward the west.

"How are you?" Palmer asked.

"Lots of ringing in my ears, but I'm OK," was Latta's only response. "Why did they let us go?"

"No frigging clue. They had to be *Spetsnaz*, the way they were dressed and armed. They were there and then 'poof,'" he replied.

"Are we heading back?"

"I don't know where else to go. Narva is torn to shit. I need to file. We need gas. Hopefully, they'll have some net access back in Tallinn."

"I am really worried about my brother. The last I heard, he was on maneuvers with US Army paratroopers from Italy. They were in Hellenurme running around in town buildings practicing urban warfare. Like it was Mosul or something."

"Hate to say it, but he's probably in the real thing right now. Hellenurme is right on the invasion route. God, I am sorry, Latta."

They groped along Route E-20 for four more hours before reaching the outskirts of the capital. Palmer tried to remember the route to Hotel Viru, but his vague memory required multiple wrong turns. With guidance from Latta, he finally pulled into the hotel's garage. He found the lobby crowded, but strangely quiet.

A crowd desperate for news. Nothing was clear on developments. Borders were shattered. Russian *Desantniki* had taken airports in Varna and Võru, but then ran into stiffer resistance. There were sure to be reprisals.

No one knew what NATO was doing, if anything. For some reason, the paratroopers hadn't attacked Tallinn's Lennart Meri airport. But there were reports of strange, oversized drones flitting about overhead.

Most seemed to be congregating at the airport, which billed itself as the "friendliest in Europe."

He and Latta tried to see a hotel doctor, but none was available. A paramedic examined Latta. Saying there wasn't much else he could do, he taped a fresh bandage to her head. The bleeding had stopped.

Palmer and Latta went to his room. Wi-Fi was intermittent, but Palmer managed to log on to his email, text messages, voicemails and Tweets. There were so many from the foreign desk in New York he simply couldn't read them.

Palmer had no interest in an intercontinental powwow at the moment. He could imagine dozens of questions for which he did not have answers. Stealing a line from Hunter S. Thompson, he banked on an age-old ploy and banged out a lively, highly descriptive account of the fighting at Narva (not mentioning Latta's insurgent commandos) and hit send.

The response was laudatory, along with anxious queries about where the fuck he was and what he was going to do.

Process information.

He spent time, while there was Wi-Fi service, reading up and trying to get a sense of what was happening. The Russians had taken Riga with an airborne attack while armored units rolled across Latvia's eastern border. Latvia was bearing the brunt of the assault. It made sense. Take the middle Baltic state and then use it as a jumping-off point to mop up Estonia and Lithuania. Reinforce Kaliningrad and sit on the Iskander missiles waiting for NATO to play the next hand.

But what hand was that? After Putin had revealed his aggressive intentions with initiatives in Crimea and eastern Ukraine, it was obvious the game had changed dramatically. Europe was in disarray after the Arab Spring had dislodged millions of Muslim African and Middle Eastern inhabitants.

At first, the EU tried to absorb these refugees, but a combination of weak economies and festering xenophobic hatred made a new type of fascist nationalism a political flavor of the moment. Knowledgeable experts predicted the chaos that now prevailed. Politicians ignored the advice, and paid the price in failed elections and, occasionally, assassinations.

Palmer scanned his laptop for any information about what the United States, Great Britain and Germany might do. Article Five of NATO's founding documents stated an armed attack on any one member was to be considered an attack on all signatories. The UK and Germany had gone to a war footing, called up reserves and appeared ready to deploy.

But what about Washington? President Trump, who had campaigned against NATO membership during his 2016 election campaign, didn't seem to be anywhere. According to the reports, some American military units had immediately gone to their highest state of readiness, but that was more of a reflex from seven decades of Cold War training than anything else.

Palmer found snacks he had bought on the ferry and offered them to Latta, who was sprawled on the bed. Nodding her thanks, she ate quietly and sipped the tea Palmer brewed. Soon, she had dozed off. Now was Palmer's chance.

▪ ▪ ▪ ▪

Moving as quietly as he could, Palmer packed his laptop and donned his parka with the ripped and burned sleeve. He took an elevator to the hotel lobby and hailed a taxi.

The first stop was at the National Archives, which, to his amazement, was still open for business. He nodded at the clerks and, with their help, was able to access an internal database. When no one was watching, he fingered the flash drive that the "man in green" had dropped in his pocket. A number of real estate deeds popped up. Fortunately, many were in English—his Estonian was non-existent, and his Russian, while workable, wasn't up to this kind of job.

When Palmer thought he had the real estate deeds of special interest selected, he attached a USB cable to an outlet linking to the Archives database. A few clicks of a button later, he was done.

Thanking the clerks, he took another cab to Eesti Pank, the Bank of Estonia. It, too, surprisingly, was open. He found the same level of cooperation as he did at the National Archives and access to an internal database for use by customers.

Once again, he set up his laptop and inserted the flash drive. Among its many functions, Eesti Pank established interest rates for unsecured loans. Besides this, it also had a major influence in determining an Estonian version of a prime rate base on negotiations for loans Eesti Pank established for other banks licensed to do business in Estonia. From this, the bank indirectly set mortgage rates for residential and commercial properties in the country.

He followed instructions from the flash drive and pulled up several screens of financial data he did not understand. Again, he plugged his USB cable into a link to the bank's database and hit "enter." As Palmer packed for a return to the Hotel Viru, he smiled at his own ignorance. "Did I just change the names on a whole lot of property deeds while also manipulating the country's mortgage rates? Nah." He let out a soft chuckle.

Back at the Viru, he found Latta asleep. That gave him time for one more chore. He opened up his laptop and connected it by wire to his cell phone. He transferred the picture of Ahti, Elmar, Joosep, Astrid and Saara and saved it, copying it to his flash drive. Miraculously, Wi-Fi was still on. After downloading an email from the flash drive, he sent the photograph on its way to that address.

Trying not to think of his breathtaking betrayal of Latta, he gently lay down beside her for a couple of hours of sleep.

▪ ▪ ▪ ▪

A nap that was short-lived. His cell phone started chirping away. An editor from the foreign desk in New York was on the line. The president of Estonia was due to speak within the hour. He had to be there.

Kersti Kaljulaid was the youngest and first female president of Estonia. She was to address the nation at Estonia Concert Hall, an elegant, cream-colored building with wood-paneled walls and rows of seats upholstered in dark blue cloth. Palmer and Latta made it past the huge crowd that had thronged at Estonia *puiestee*, a major street just southeast of Old Town.

Uniformed troops and police, along with obvious undercover men and women in tracksuits, formed a cordon around the hall. News media representatives with digital cameras of all sizes filled in the gaps. Palmer's credentials, representing one of the world's great newspapers, earned him and Latta ready access.

President Kaljulaid was fifteen minutes late—reasonable given the gravity of recent developments. Despite this delay, the crowd quickly quieted as she came to the podium.

"Citizens of Estonia, our beloved country . . ." she began in Estonian with immediate English subtitles flashing behind her. No minced words. "This is a supreme tragedy. The Russian Federation, under false pretenses and making false accusations of abuse of Russian-speaking residents, has undertaken a brutal invasion of our homeland. Hundreds, perhaps thousands, have been killed or wounded."

She continued, explaining that the invasion of Estonia was just part of an overall assault on the Baltic States. She had been in touch with Raimonds Vējonis, the president of Latvia. While Tallinn was intact, the Latvian capital of Riga had come under a full aerial attack, including a massive paradrop of Russian troops. Riga had fallen. President Vējonis was under arrest. There was no word yet on the situation in Lithuania.

President Kaljulaid then noted she was in contact with members of NATO's high command in Brussels. She was shocked to learn that

NATO was not immediately invoking Article Five and coming to the aid of Estonia and her sister states. However, a few units already posted in Estonia were fighting. These included Americans, although one of the reasons for the lack of action, she said, was that America's new president had not given a clear signal as to Washington's intentions. She did not know if President Trump was trying to use a backchannel to communicate with Putin. In short, she was not optimistic about the American president.

With that, she urged Estonians to remember what had happened throughout the centuries, particularly in 1939 with the Nazis and then in 1941 with the Soviets. Citizens of Estonia were warned they should be prepared to lay down their lives for the fatherland. That's what being free really meant. With that, she asked the audience to join her in singing the Estonian national anthem, "My Fatherland, My Happiness and Joy."

Palmer had to get back to the Viru to file his story. Latta, tears in her eyes, wanted to stay but said she'd call. Back in his hotel room, Palmer rattled off about one thousand words of the scene at the music hall. He was just sending his piece when the Wi-Fi went down. The room lights flickered on and off. His cell phone lost its connection. Then he heard a thunderous roar of jet engines followed by a series of very loud explosions.

■ ■ ■ ■

The *Desantniki* had come. Palmer hurried to Lennart Meri International Airport. His fearless cab driver ignored chaos on the streets. Palmer tipped him handsomely.

He was running toward a terminal and looked up. The sky was filled with white parachutes. There was a staccato "pop" and the whine of jet engines receding in the distance. Troops in winter battle dress swarmed about. Some quickly secured their parachutes while others cracked open cushioned tubes containing weapons and ammunition.

Also on the ground, shrouded in parachutes, were late-model BMP-4M tanks. Palmer had read about them. They were greatly improved versions of a traditional tracked vehicle the Soviets developed to support airborne soldiers. One IL-76 cargo jet could drop two of them.

The paratroopers briskly sprinted to the airport control tower, fuel depot and passenger terminal. Estonian police and troops put up sporadic resistance, but they were easily cut down by the Russians' assault rifles, rocket launchers and the BMP-4Ms. Huge picture windows in the terminals were shattered by shrapnel and bullets, but it was clear the fight was over before it began.

After the crackling of small-arms fire died down, Palmer, hiding behind a concrete fence, heard the steady "chop" of helicopters. Mi-24 "HINDs," the bug-like gunships famed for their slaughter of villagers in Afghanistan, came in first. After they flitted about, firing cannons and rockets, the next wave rolled in. These were heavy-lift Mi-26s bearing platoons of more troops.

Armored columns were likely not far behind. It was time for Palmer to move before he was arrested, interred or expelled. A phone call would have been the best way to reach Latta, but a cyberattack had shut down cell service. All Palmer could do was search out her aunt—somewhere outside of city limits. Latta had insisted he take the address in the event of an emergency. This was not just an emergency; it was a disaster.

■ ■ ■ ■

Palmer had no idea where the aunt lived, although Latta warned him it was about twenty miles southwest of Tallinn. A distance he covered, amazingly, with the assistance of a taxi driver who was charging triple while there was still money to be made.

The aunt, who knew some Russian, wrote down directions for Palmer. With Russian convoys fanning out from the airport, public transit had shut down. Palmer managed to thumb rides to the nearest village, Laitse. From there, it was a simple matter of reaching the Ruila LKA, a protected forest reserve perfect for hiding.

Palmer found some identifying areas that the aunt had described to him. He walked about in the snow, asking local residents if they knew Latta Koidula. He was so obviously an American that people actually helped him.

A long slog through the snow led him to a cottage that locals only identified as a "hunting camp." It was there he found the guerillas from Narva. All five—Ahti, Elmar, Joosep, Astrid and Saara—were still alive and weren't exactly delighted to see him, but knew he was close to Latta, so they confided in him. She was on her way.

Palmer said nothing and followed their lead. Right back out into the snow. After about forty-five minutes, they approached a small hill hidden among the pine, fir and birch trees. Palmer could barely make out an entrance, but he thought he could as they approached.

It was a cave whose rocky entrance had been well concealed by tree branches and earthen berms. Inside was livable but Spartan. The Defense League had designed it years before.

A cave equipped with battery-powered generators to provide warmth, as campfires would give them away. Communications, also carefully planned, included field radios with burst transmitters that gave radio direction finders only fractions of a second to home in. The slightest error in transmissions could be fatal. Russian drones were certain to be everywhere.

Saara served Palmer some tea as they huddled around a heater. Palmer described what had happened at Narva, at Tallinn and at the airport. In about an hour, Latta turned up, bundled in warm ski clothing. When she took off her fur hat, Palmer noticed a small bandage on her ear.

Latta said the Russians had Tallinn under their control. There were still firefights, and she had seen a number of bodies. It was difficult getting to the camp, but she managed to approach within ten kilometers and then cross-country ski. She had heard that next on the Russian list was the Ämari Lennubaas Air Base and also the small Navy base at Paldiski.

Nodding at the gathering around her, Latta explained that she and her colleagues were members of the Estonian Defense League, a paramilitary organization of volunteers who typically joined after serving their year or so as conscripts in the Estonian armed forces. Service was required of both men and women, so there was an egalitarian sense of common purpose, not to mention a widespread and basic understanding of weapons and strategy.

The immediate group was an elite within an elite. They had been picked to help form special Defense League teams that would first fight alongside regular armed units as support personnel. However, they were also prepared to go one step further and work with foreign special operations teams. Their mission was to gather intelligence, train resistance forces and strike the occupiers with ambushes and sabotage.

Ruila LKA was a good spot for their base. It was remote and uninhabited, save for indigenous wildlife—primarily moose and deer. It also wasn't far—within fifteen miles or so—of two of Estonia's most important military installations, Ämari and Paldiski.

The Ämari airbase had served Estonia off and on since World War I but had recently taken on new importance. In 2014, it had become thoroughly integrated into NATO's command structure. NATO and Estonian aircraft had begun flying surveillance patrols from the base. The Kremlin had been especially irritated when the United States moved in F-15C and A-10 airframes on a periodic basis. The former was one of the world's top interceptors, and the latter had 30mm GAU-8 cannons that spat out depleted uranium shells designed to penetrate Russian armored vehicles—including tanks.

Not far from Ämari was Paldiski, the naval base. The Russians had used it during the Cold War for coastal patrols and also to train crews on nuclear-powered submarines.

In the event of war, the Russians were certain to seize both bases as quickly as possible. Doing so would prevent NATO reinforcement.

Elmar glanced at his wristwatch and said it was time. He grabbed a collection of electronic gear and stepped outside into the snow. Returning within five minutes, he said there was a message. He downloaded the burst transmitter to a tablet and started decoding. Not that it was all that necessary. Estonian was a Finno-Ugric language, rootless in Roman or Slavic tongues. It was extremely difficult to translate. But with the Russians, one could never be sure—they had, after all, ruled the country for almost fifty years. Surely a few of Moscow's aging intelligence translators had been recruited for this campaign.

Once decrypted, the message offered optimistic news—the team was to prepare for an airdrop of special forces within twelve hours. They'd try to hit one of several clearings in the preserve that had been scouted long before the Russian invasion began.

The seven huddled in their lair as darkness settled over the forest. Outside, the snow continued to fall.

Palmer wondered what was happening in Tallinn and whether he should try to contact his editors. Reach the embassy? Looking around at the group, he knew he couldn't take the risk. At least not yet.

"Remember the last time we were here?" said Ahti, trying to bring some mirth to the awful evening.

"And Astrid vanished with Elmar?" Saara said.

"It wasn't for long," Elmar said.

"With you, it never takes long," smirked Astrid.

The plan was for the group to wait, rendezvous with the special forces, break off into several groups and hike toward Ämari. The point was to determine the runway's condition and what the Russians had deployed in addition to equipment flowing over Estonia's road grid.

The group waited, sipping tea and preparing their gear. But would the troops show up? Would Trump make that kind of commitment?

They took turns sleeping in down sleeping bags that had been arrayed around an electric heater. It was cold and moist in the cave, but not altogether unpleasant.

Latta was particularly subdued. She knew her brother was dead and had no idea about her parents. Palmer saw her despair and sat down next to her. He took her head in his lap and gently stroked her hair. He didn't see the point of saying anything.

At sunrise, the group prepared to move. They broke out weapons, Israeli Galils, Hecker & Koch pistols and a few AK-47s. In addition, there were a handful or two of old Soviet grenades and two Chinese-made RPG rocket launchers.

Loaded for battle, they broke into two groups. Saara led one and Elmar, the other. Traveling on Nordic-style cross-country skis made traversing the snowy forest easier, but also provided tracks for an adversary to follow. Palmer and Latta fell in behind Saara, and although he had nowhere nearly as much experience on skis as the others, he managed.

Palmer announced he had to make a call to nature, and he slipped behind a large fir tree. There, he got his cell phone, clicked it on and hit several buttons, making sure he was not noticed. He was back in thirty seconds.

The group started heading northwest toward a frozen bog that would make an acceptable drop zone. The two groups fanned out and took positions in the snow, their white outerwear providing respite from overhead observation.

They waited for more than an hour, shaking off the cold as snow squalls set in. Then, as if ghosts, men in white coveralls started to drop silently from the sky. They had rectangular parachutes that could be easily maneuvered. Chutes that were shed and buried immediately upon landing.

Commotion! Palmer heard several "FFFTT" sounds. Both Saara and Elmar were on the ground, their white smocks spreading with blood. The other paratroopers had the remaining five covered with silenced assault rifles. Death from above.

One man, obviously the leader, stepped forward. "My name is Major Yuri Zhdanov," in English nonetheless. Palmer knew he was the little green man in Varna. Now he was wearing white.

▪ ▪ ▪ ▪

A Russian Kamaz truck carried the surviving team members to Tallinn. In an incredible irony, they were driven to the Hotel Viru, which had been quickly converted into a high-end prison, its old KGB listening devices upgraded and switched back on.

Latta stared in disbelief at Palmer. He stared at the floor in silence. She was taken away.

He was led into a room with Zhdanov.

"You handled yourself well," he said. "We'll debrief you and then take you to your embassy. From there, you will be evacuated. You will have one hell of a story to print in your newspaper."

Palmer drank coffee and ate cherry blinis as he told the intelligence officers all the details of his adventure—from the flight to Helsinki to Tallinn to Varna and so on. He provided full details about Latta and the five Defense League members, plus photos he had snapped. He also said he had accomplished whatever mission it was, changing documents in the office building and bank.

He was dropped off at the US Embassy at Kentmanni 20 and made it past the Marine guards, attired in combat gear. The consular official appeared glad to see him. Seems he had received multiple calls from a certain newspaper in New York.

The embassy drove Palmer and some evacuees through downtown Tallinn to the airport in an armored Suburban. They were guarded by armed private contractors and a single Estonian army vehicle with a machine gun mounted atop the roof. Along the way, there was clear evidence of fighting. Some buildings were destroyed; others had their facades shorn off. Parking lots near some office towers were gigantic seas of broken glass after intense machine-gun fire and shelling had shattered windows on multiple floors. Everywhere were burned shells of vehicles and an occasional body. The detritus of war.

Lennart Meri was back in operation. Scarred with blackened walls and bullet holes. But charter flights were coming in and out. Palmer waited at a passport control point manned by Russian troops.

As he walked to his flight, he saw a sight that truly stunned him. A new era of real estate development was about to begin in Estonia, the Baltics and the rest of Europe.

Sitting on the tarmac was a Boeing 757 whose fuselage was painted with a white bottom, a dark red top and blue stripes down the middle. On the tail was a series of red stripes forming a "T."

The front of the fuselage was emblazoned with the word "TRUMP."

# HUNGARY:

## The Director

BY DAVID J. DOESSER

*DAVID J. DOESSER, a former intelligence officer of the Hungarian external secret service, graduated from the ELTE University faculty of law. He spent almost thirty years in the intelligence service and was assigned first to Western jurisdictions and later to Central Europe. When the "old regime" collapsed, he took part in transforming the service into a democratic institution and established successful cooperation with many major Western services. He left the service in 2000. He is married and has two children, and now lives in an undisclosed location in the EU.*

### WANT A JOB?

The jet-black BMW Z3 Cabriole stopped at a red light on Buda-side, close to the Szabadság Bridge. An old man, hunched and disheveled, walked over to the softly humming car and thrust out a red rose bouquet toward the bald driver wearing dark sunglasses. His passenger, a skinny girl with hydrogenated hair and artificial nails, was chewing gum with a bored expression. She paid no attention to the apparent bum.

"A small bouquet of roses for the beautiful young lady?" the man asked the driver and adjusted his used, discolored necktie on a stained light blue shirt of Fékon, a famous brand of the communist underwear industry. An adjustment prompted by a cursory glance into the deep décolletage of her opulent bosom.

"Thanks, not now," was the curt response from the billiard-ball-headed driver. A response that reflected weariness and deep immersion in one's own thoughts.

"Really, you could buy some flowers for me, at least once in your life," the blonde squeeze said with her querulous voice, tossing the gum out her window.

"Why do you need flowers, babe? They're just a vegetable, nothing more. I have bought you everything—jewelry, beautiful clothes and more stuff than demanded by a family of five. What else do you want?"

"I like these velvet roses; they must have a gorgeous smell," she said in her small voice, looking deeply into the man's eyes through the sunglasses. The bald man nodded at the old man, indicating he was ready to do business with him. The vendor went around the car hesitantly and shoved a red bouquet wrapped in cellophane toward the driver.

"You look like a brave man; I like that," the bald guy said while the electric window was doing its job. "You don't look like a Roma at all. I might have a business opportunity for you. Don't be afraid; there won't be a need to work hard. Clear business, no murky job. My manager has just left for good, and he left me in a bit of a pickle. I need a surrogate CEO, as they call them these days.

"As I said, it is a clear business, well documented, no tax issues. Look at me; I am a serious man. Only a few people have such a good car like this, but they are phony. I won't let you down; good money and a good car for a good director. What else would you want? Cell phone? No problem. . . . You will get two."

"Office?" the vendor asked timidly.

"No need. You can work from home. Your wife will be satisfied; so easy, you see."

"Home job?" the man asked back with wide eyes. "Look at me; where would my home be if not on the streets?"

"I am not curious about anybody's private life, am I right, sweetheart?" the driver said as he turned to the blonde and laughed.

"Curiosity killed the cat, ha-ha. Privacy is a holy thing to me. It doesn't matter where you come from. This is my 'Foreign Legionnaire' business policy."

Somewhere, I have already heard this term "business policy," the man thought and grabbed the bouquet firmly.

"And what would I have to do in your business?"

"Absolutely nothing, only managing my business. I am in urgent need of a manager," the bald man replied, emphasizing the word *manager*. "Nothing else, just managing."

"Aha, and what exactly does that mean?"

"See, you know the business ropes, don't you? You have a bright blue shirt, necktie, jacket and so on, a bit used, but my eyes don't cheat on me. I don't need to explain to you how to do business, or am I mistaken?"

"Still, what do I have to do?" asked the man a bit impatiently.

"Just sign some papers. It is clear work, as I said. My manager, the cretin, left me for good despite my first-class treatment. I had him eating out of the palm of my hand. But no, I've spoiled him, and he joined my competitor, a real shit. Yeah, I had lifted him from the dump; he was at rock bottom. Am I right, babe?" The driver turned to the bored blonde, who was staring at the red traffic light like a snake at a frog.

"Yeah," replied the blonde airhead, all the while combing her hair with those artificial nails.

## "FOND" MEMORIES

"Just sign, just sign," the two words echoed in his mind. "Just sign, just sign." . . . I know these words very well already, even in English: "Sign the papers!" Oh, my goodness, how many times have I heard this? They put tons of papers in front of me, and I just had to sign them while not knowing what I actually signed.

Everything started about ten years ago, immediately after the collapse of the communist system, aka political "change," in 1990. What euphoric times those were. Everybody was happy that the transition took place at the negotiating table; the old communist establishment succeeded in agreeing with the so-called underground "democratic opposition." Democratic, the opposite of communist, or as they called it, "socialist" system. I, myself, never liked this word "socialist" because I found it deceiving. There were "socialist" parties in the West as well, but they had nothing in common with the socialists in the East.

Well, we were happy that power was transferred to the opposition without a drop of bloodshed. That was—as we say in Budapest-style slang—"*not nothing*." Unlike the revolution in Romania on December 25, 1989, when the people's anger executed Dictator Ceaușescu (who called himself Conducător) and blood stained the streets. But we, luckily, had avoided the violence because our communist democracy was a "soft version." We were considered the "Happiest Barrack" in the communist camp.

However, the collapse could not happen without Gorbachev. This man, with the interesting birthmark on his forehead, had shaken the world with his one notion—well, rather two: *glasnost* and *perestroika*.

I remember very well what a large stone fell from our hearts when we understood that the Soviet Union would not intervene by force of arms in the Central European region, whatever would happen there. In other words, the superpower had washed its hands of its satellite countries. Everybody should manage their own affairs from now on was their motto. What a fantastic feeling it was. We realized freedom was knocking on our door. You ask me what "freedom" means to me? I could say all kinds of great words, but I will not.

Simply, freedom for us was equal to flying. Traveling whenever you wanted, wherever you wanted and staying there as long as you wanted.

Heavenly peace.

It wasn't so before? You might be surprised. We were unable to travel not only to the West but also to the East. We were allowed to travel to the friendly fellow communist countries once a year and a Western trip remained only a distant dream. In theory, you could have traveled to the West if you enjoyed the bureaucratic torturing process.

Think of it; you and your wife had the coveted blue passports in your hands, but not your children. They had to stay at home as hostages. Yes, it was a kind of guarantee to the State that you would return home safe and sound, as no parent would want to abandon their child, right? Smart system, wasn't it? Even if you were allowed to travel abroad, the amount of money that you could exchange from the only state-owned bank and take with you was a mere seventy dollars. So, the trip was not worth making, as you could not survive on this amount for a day, let alone for two weeks, in the West.

But do not worry. Go to Váci utca, the street in downtown Budapest, buy some additional "hard currency" on the black market run by some Arabic people from the "friendly" developing countries for double the exchange rate, and conceal the money in a safe place; let's say, in your wife's bra.

However, free movement was limited not only abroad but also inside the country due to prohibited areas. Namely, Hungary shares a border with Austria, and the West begins here along the River Lajta. The "Nirvana" for us began here, and Austria was named "*Lajtán túli terület*" (territory over the Lajta), a saying from the Austro-Hungarian Monarchy.

Well, the so-called *Vasfüggöny* (Iron Curtain) between the two economic and ideological systems that was installed here, the minefield that later became a wire fence, sounds very familiar to us, like the Berlin Wall for the Germans. Not only a physical barrier in its reality, but also a barricade lingering in our souls.

Absurd situation. I, as a local citizen, had to obtain special permission to be able to enter the area. I, as a Budapest resident, was prohibited from traveling freely to Sopron or other cities located in the border zone without special permission and even only then with a valid reason. Even though this restriction was canceled after the minefield was eliminated at the end of the '70s, it could not be erased from people's minds. Finally, the last communist government opened the Iron Curtain for East German tourists who were staying in Hungary and in September 1989 declared it free for us as well. The fate of communism in Hungary was sealed.

And the domino effect kicked in; the Velvet Revolution in Czechoslovakia, the collapse of the Berlin Wall and the disintegration of the Soviet Union. Once in my life I would still like to meet tovarish Gorbachev and shake hands with him. I would probably not have any language barrier because I had learned Russian for eight years. Others hated this language, hated it because it was compulsory in elementary and secondary schools and it was related to an invading power.

However, I liked it very much; I liked its softness and richness. I liked it despite the fact that I could not use it in practice because I had never been in touch with any Russian in real life. We learned the language from school books. I, however, had an LP, bought in the bookstore of the House of Soviet Culture in Budapest for a couple of forints in the '60s. Lenin was giving a speech on it. I listened to this LP on our old Soviet gramophone several times. I liked his fanaticism, dedication and enthusiasm, and he was as bald as Gorbachev.

Anyway, the "transition" was euphoric on all fronts. There was no revolution, as no one wanted to see blood shed on the streets of Budapest. Everything went peacefully. However, some fear was lingering in our minds. We had learned in school that the transition from capitalism to communism must be achieved through revolution. Yes, understood, but vice versa? Luckily the old regime and the new democratic opposition made a gentleman's agreement behind closed doors.

I remember seeing the first colorful Western-style edition of the brand-new weekly, *Reform,* at the kiosks. I have never been to Vienna before, but seeing the paper, I felt vicariously as if I was already there. I read in *Reform* that the new democratic minister of defense, a jovial old man, envisioned houses with red roofs like in France, and I fully agreed with him. Leaping from the gray into a colorful world.

Then came the telephone. Up until "the Change," we had to wait to get a line for eight to ten years . . . yes, years, until someone eventually obtained a telephone line. It was equal to a Lotto jackpot for us. However, the underground opposition had a "privileged" position; they could get a phone much sooner than the common people—not because the regime supported them, but because in this way it was easier for the secret police to eavesdrop on them.

Privatization of the communist estates had started. Western capital inflow was hyper-intense. There was no longer any need to wait for a landline. A few days of delay was enough, and then the mechanic knocked on your door. The Nirvana had arrived, no question about it.

And cell phones appeared within no time as well. They were of behemoth size, like a suitcase with a receiver, antenna and grip, but they were wireless. A businessman took one with him to negotiations, holding it in one hand and his suitcase in the other.

Fortunately, this did not last long because a cell phone that fits in your palm soon arrived. It was called a *bunkofon* because if you used it on the street, people who still did not have one were envious of you and made sarcastic comments that you were a "brute," and your phone was a "brute-phone," applying deductive reasoning to the issue.

Many Western chains opened shops in this country. There was no need to travel to Vienna anymore to buy bananas. They were available throughout the whole year, every day! The monkeys in the Zoo had a higher status in the old regime than we poor people because they could eat bananas every day, whereas we only had them once per year, around Christmastime, if at all. And then only in the capital and larger cities.

Prices were skyrocketing. There was no state intervention anymore. That would be incompatible with the free market notion. Gradually, staple foods cost twenty times more than before. Sometimes we got the shock of our life. I remember seeing an Austrian nightgown for 39,999 forints in a shop window. No doubt about it; it was very sexy. My salary was around 15,000 at the time. It was for my wife, Gloria. No problem, I thought, it is a market economy, after all, and it's not only America that is the land of unlimited opportunities; now our region was part of it as well. Oh, and one more thing—get familiar with prices ending in nine.

You can shove anything down people's throats when they are intoxicated with the notion of freedom. When the Iron Curtain collapsed, we besieged Vienna like our brave King Matthias in the Middle Ages, but we had no weapons, just Austrian shillings in our pockets. We wanted to buy Western refrigerators, color TVs, electronic gadgets called HiFi towers (those furniture-like, extra-large Philips, Sony and Samsung music centers that were the flavor of the month in the '70s and '80s). We were starving for this Western feeling, having Western gadgets, HiFi music centers, refrigerators and all the other clutter.

The fridge came from Yugoslavia? Who cares? I bought it in Vienna—more precisely, not even there. Austrian street vendors set up primitive, makeshift shops close to the border and were selling their goods of unknown origin, and we were standing in line to get the coveted gadgets. They sold like hotcakes.

The Czechs were traveling to Vienna after the Velvet Revolution to attend the opera, exhibitions and concerts. We, on the other hand, had occupied the Mariahilfer Strasse, Vienna's downtown shopping street. There was no need to have an interpreter present at the time; the common language was *Ungarisch* (Hungarian).

New, private car dealership companies were emerging like mushrooms after the rain, selling Western brands; however, the big business was not in these expensive cars but in that of used car imports. You could buy used cars such as Audi, Mercedes, Volkswagen, Opel and others in good shape for a pittance in Germany and The Netherlands.

We had to wait for a car coming from the friendly communist countries, i.e., Soviet (Shiguli), Czech (Škoda), Romanian (Dacia) or Polish (Polski Fiat), for five to six years in the old regime. When it arrived, you did not get what you wanted. You had no choice over color, for instance. My way or the highway. (By the way, the highway network was very poor prior to 1989). But smart people like the Hungarians took advantage of the miserable circumstances; they had considered it an investment, and a very good one at that.

It was a sort of communist stock-exchange; I must stress a "communist" one. After waiting five or six years, you got the car at the Csepel facility of the state-owned car importer—by providing a generous tip to the "facility manager" (side-expenses of the investment). Now you had a brand-new car with zero kilometers for 70,000 forints. You started the engine. All was running perfectly. You drove to the used car market ten kilometers away from the facility, and you sold it for 140,000 forints immediately. One hundred percent profit within five years.

It was a good investment, wasn't it? Even the sole state-owned bank, OTP, was unable to pay such a high interest rate. Everybody took advantage of the system. The state used your money for five to six years because half of the asking price had to be deposited in advance, at the time of purchase. I repeated this trick three times and bought a weekend house along the southern part of the River Danube close to Budapest.

Oh, and the multi-level marketing system, aka MLM, had appeared soon thereafter. We went to apartments in the evenings where a well-trained "presenter" demonstrated on a blackboard how we could earn big money and have a bright future if we joined the MLM system. The presenter did not want to bore us with the details but—"believe me"—following a winning formula . . . if you win five traders for the system, and each of them wins five again and so on, we could be millionaires within two to three weeks. Imagine the potential we could achieve within one year?

Swinging perspectives. There is no need to have difficult business plans, financial bullshit; it is enough to write your goals on a piece of paper and hang it on the wall (the best place is the bathroom) and read it every day in order to keep your MOTIVATION. It is very important, understand? You must be motivated wherever you are. Forget the old mentality.

America had only offered such an opportunity to the new settlers, nothing else. Whoever was able to grab it with both hands became a millionaire; those who snoozed lost out. This was the most effective path to "SELF-REALIZATION."

Of course, you must buy a package unit first to get the business going. It is only 39,999 forints (just like Gloria's would-be Palmers nightgown). You organize "MEETINGS" and sell package units like this. The more you sell, the more money you make. Finally, when you retire from this job, you will become multi-millionaires, if not billionaires.

"Please, do not forget that the whole set-up can be inherited, which means that the future of your children and grandchildren is secured. I was trained in the United States. Here is my house in Florida, my car and my golf gadgets." The presenter would let the projector skip ahead. "Now, I am here to help with your development, your future. Everybody in America pursues this business. This is the reason why the country is so rich. The whole country is a giant MLM. I could call it the United MLM Systems of America, ha, ha, ha."

Applause.

"Of course, there are always difficult customers. No problem, we just need to persuade them. Here is the latest marketing book from America, *Negotiating with Difficult People*, translated recently. Only costs 1,999 forints, very cheap." (Hmmm, it would have cost only 22.50 forints in the old days). "Let me read some parts of it. . . ."

Well, this was the moment I stood up, apologized to the presenter and left this legal pyramid-scheme venue that reminded me of some black magic bullshit.

I attended such a meeting one more time. Not because I wanted to join the scheme; it was more out of curiosity, and also because my friend wanted me to come along. Plus, we had time on our hands because our company was on the verge of privatization, and we both had no effective work.

Well, this was the epitome of bullshit. A young man from the States, third-generation Hungarian, was speaking the language with a heavy accent. We could hardly understand him, but he was always smiling. He added many English expressions to his presentation, which were translated into Hungarian by his beautiful assistant.

What did he sell? Vacation apartments. Where? Quite obvious, on the Caribbean Islands, maybe Turks and Caicos. It is not American territory? Who cares? We did not even know where these islands were. Well, the guy—like I said—was selling apartments. Only a legal part of the apartment had to be bought and you obtained the right of a two-week vacation. Amazing, isn't it? The money for it did not seem to be unattainable; even I could have afforded the price, but the big question was how to get there in the first place.

Who can afford plane tickets in this economy?

Then came the con artists from the West and mafia from the East and South. I remember reading stories about red mercury and snake poison in the newspapers. The Secret Service and the police were chasing these phantoms. We had rarely heard about "organized crime," "proliferation" and "drug smuggling." They were completely new words to the Hungarian dictionary, just like "Valentine's Day," "Halloween," "muffin" and "bagel."

My thoughts zigzag, but I have not yet mentioned anything about me. I worked for a color manufacturing company prior to the collapse and afterward. I was a branch-chief there, as it is called nowadays.

My wife, as mentioned before, is Gloria and she used to work for a pharmacy in the old days. She is a very clever and business-savvy woman. I would not say that she earned great money. Not at all. But she knew the way to make some extra dough; legally, I hasten to add.

Western drinks such as Cinzano, Martini, Campari, then the expensive cognacs (we call domestic brandies "*konyaks*") were unaffordable to the common people, but *we* could afford them. How come? Because Gloria and her fellow colleagues could "copy" the drinks.

They analyzed the contents, mixed the tincture together, bought some cheap red and white wine, stirred the mixture and there you had it. The Cinzano, Campari and Martini drinks were ready. French cognacs were easy to replicate, as well.

Moreover, they made fine sunbath-oils and body crème with genuine ingredients. It was a kind of private business venture already, but the whole "enterprise" had gone with the collapse of the Wall. There was no longer any need to play the alchemist because every genuine product appeared on the market immediately. Buying them was only a question of money; money that I had soon enough.

I am getting ahead of the story. These practices I just spoke of were the tricks of surviving communism not only in Hungary but also in the "socialist" region.

Several years before December 1989, at the height of Ceaușescu's regime, we traveled to Transylvania to visit a family friend of my father-in-law living in a small village close to Csíkszereda. The parents of the man fled from this village to Hungary in 1944 when the Soviet front was approaching Transylvania. They were able to cross the border and reach my father-in-law's house in a village in eastern Hungary and then anchored there because the Russian tanks were faster than the horses, and the front overtook them. After the battle noise died down, the family returned to Transylvania, but the friendly ties were maintained.

I have forgotten to mention that Hungary is in a privileged situation for Europe. No matter which direction you cross the border, you are still in the territory of Hungarian-speaking people because the land belonged to the Austro-Hungarian Empire before the Great War. However, the country lost two-thirds of its territory after the Trianon Peace Treaty of 1920.

Crossing the Romanian border, we stumbled into Hungarian signage everywhere and felt like we were back home. Reality returned with a jolt when we experienced the "offer" of the shops and lack of fuel at gas stations—to say nothing of long lines. Roads were in terrible shape, full of horse-drawn carriages and holes.

We left Kolozsvár (Cluj) when the heating unit of my Shiguli broke down, and the water escaped. I was pondering what to do when a Dacia stopped beside me, and a young man with a mustache jumped out, greeting us in Hungarian. He towed me to the next village to "Uncle Joe's Service," which was a small shed behind a barn, and all the tools there were made by Uncle Joe. So, Uncle Joe, who of course was a jack-of-all-trades, fixed the heating unit. I did not know how, but I returned home safely. The chief mechanic in my service at home summoned all his colleagues to demonstrate the perfect job Joe *"bácsi"* did, and I was happy because there was no need to replace the heating unit for a long time.

Well, my daughter, who completed her grammar school studies in the '90s, was admitted to the University of Economics, at the Foreign Trade faculty. We lived, the three of us, in an apartment at Stefánia Street, Fourteenth District of Budapest, happy and content until one day . . .

## WANTS AND DESIRES

"Sweetheart, please buy that bouquet of roses for me. Don't you see how poor that man is? Make this day happy for him." Whining from the blonde who was busily stuffing her mouth with another piece of gum.

"Keep quiet, honey, don't you see that I am having a business conversation with him? He seems to be a smart chum. Look at his clothes; he used to be elegant some time ago. . . . "

"But the traffic light will turn green soon, and I want this bouquet and . . . red is the color of love. You love me, don't you?"

"Yeah," the bald man murmured under his nose and turned his attention to the vendor again.

## NOT SO "FOND" MEMORIES

. . . Until one day, the new director of the paint factory summoned me to his office. As I mentioned before, the plant had been recently privatized. It was bought up by a US consortium. They had the company audited as a first step on the road to capitalism, which meant close examination of financial chaos.

Basically, they sacked the upper leadership and their deputies, but they left us. Some consultants from the US realized it was necessary to retain a few low-level management people who could navigate their way around the organization and were vaguely familiar with the company but not to the extent that they were able to meddle in upper management's business.

A meeting was convened with the board of directors on a sunny day in June. They started at nine o'clock. At 9:45, eleven big black cars appeared in front of the building on the street. It was so bizarre; I hadn't seen that many black cars parked there before. Around ten, the director general appeared in the main entrance, got in the first black car and drove away. This ceremony was repeated every ten minutes until the last black car departed. The execution was carried out by noon. No farewells, no goodbyes to colleagues, nothing. We who stayed there were shocked.

"Please take a seat," said the new boss, standing at the head of a just-polished conference room table. I looked around. Everything was replaced. The room smelled like a furniture shop.

"Are you sitting comfortably?" A question with a bit of accent in his voice. Although he spoke Hungarian well, he still couldn't pronounce the letter "ü" clearly. Without waiting for my response, he asked me another question.

"How would you like to become a managing director?" I must have looked at him in a strange way, because he repeated the question again.

"Would you like to become the MD of this sector?"

"MD, me? Here?" I mused. I have to acknowledge that I had a good understanding of the factory, but my knowledge also had its limitations. However, I'd been at the company for the past twenty years and thought, why not? I'm up for a challenge. Before I could answer, the new boss rose from a leather seat and went to his heavy oak desk. He picked up a piece of paper and stepped in front of me.

"Here's your new appointment. You are, as of today, this sector's managing director. I am your appointed consultant. We are going to register you with Companies Court Registry tomorrow. I have prepared all the relevant forms. Here's the amended Memorandum of Incorporation, your acceptance declaration, the lawyer's letter of authority, your signature sample and all the other important documents."

"How come you nominated me?" I asked tentatively.

"We have been observing you for a long time. You are an experienced colleague who knows a lot of people around here, and you also seem to have a good knowledge and understanding of the business you work in. As opposed to me who waltzed in from abroad."

"I get it, but does this mean that I will be your boss?" I asked with uncertainty in my voice.

"Let's cut the formal crap. In America, we are very informal. Just call me Rob. And yes, you'd become my boss. I will, of course, remain MD as well, but my HQ will be based in the US. I will only have a so-called delivery agent in Hungary who will be the company's attorney. Do you understand now?"

"Well . . . " I said, still a bit confused.

"OK, I will explain to you in more detail. It looks better if a Hungarian company has a Hungarian MD. My name is Hungarian, too, and I will remain an MD as well, but I will, on paper at least, be residing in the US. You will be managing the company. Don't worry, there won't be any problems. I will remain in Hungary and help you manage the company. I will provide you with advice, and you will make decisions. We will discuss everything. You understand? You'll get a brand-new Audi, a swank office and two cell phones. You will also get a decent managerial salary and everything else you want. Do you accept?" he asked in a questioning way.

"I'd like to discuss this with . . . ," I said, but Rob cut me off impatiently.

"With who? The wife? Look, women are not business savvy; this is gentlemen's business. You have been working here for the past twenty years and attained the position of branch chief. You are a valued member of this organization and have good people skills. There's no need to mull it over. The salary is more than respectable. You could even afford to buy a small yacht and enroll your daughter at a university abroad."

"But I do not have any experience in investments and financial affairs."

"Don't worry about those. Show me an MD who deals with such things. You'll see. Leave those to the experts. We will prepare everything. You will only need to sign some documents. We will be your guarantors. The American owner will be highly satisfied."

Rob spoke in a very persuasive and affable manner. Why wouldn't I take the job? My wife could stop working two shifts; one would be enough or, perhaps, even none would be necessary.

That night, when we were in bed, I moved over to Gloria and spoke to her in a quiet voice.

"Today, they have made me a managing director at the factory."

Gloria looked at me, unconvinced. After so many years of marriage, I have gotten to know her every facial expression. What followed was eerie silence. I could almost hear Gloria's brain racing. It felt like a few minutes had passed before she responded.

"And you accepted," she said matter-of-factly.

"Well, yes, I did, but I did ask them to allow me to discuss this with you."

"So you accepted the position, and you are only telling me the facts. You are not interested in my opinion." There was anger in her voice.

"Well, yes," I said in a hesitant manner.

"They will deceive you," she said without even looking at me. There was a long silence again between us before I finally responded.

"I have been studying, working all my life so that we can progress as a family. At last, an opportunity has come knocking on our door. You won't have to work long hours anymore. We will be able to afford new things, and our daughter will be able to study at prestigious universities."

Gloria cut me off.

"We do not need it, Egon. This all sounds too good to be true. I am against it, but I will leave it up to you. Sleep on it, at least. We will revisit the topic again in the morning." And with that, she turned away from me and switched off the light on her nightstand.

I didn't sleep a wink all night. I was twisting and turning in bed. I only fell into a deep slumber early in the morning. Gloria had gone to her first shift when I awoke. She did not wake me, and we missed our coffee ritual.

I wasn't running late, but Rob was already waiting for me at the door.

"How are you, Egon?" he asked with that fake Hollywood smile of his. He smiled at everyone. This bothered me as I could not decipher his thoughts from that smirk. He didn't wait for my response, not that he'd care anyway, before he continued.

"Egon, we have prepared all the documents we mentioned yesterday, including a press release."

"Press release?" I asked astounded.

"Of course. We will send the article to both the Hungarian and English newspapers. Everyone should be made aware of your new position. This will be good for our business reputation."

## MOVING UP . . . OR . . .

"Take whatever you need from this dingy little office into your new CEO residence."

I have to admit, I parted from my old little office with a heavy heart. I got so used to it in the past fifteen years and grew fonder of the space as time passed. Truth be told, I was dreading the new challenges ahead as a CEO, but I did have sufficient self-confidence to realize that I would be capable of taking on the new challenges successfully. And then there was Rob, who would be able to help. He was growing on me, always so chirpy and generous.

Rob and a tall, slim, thirty-to-thirty-five-year-old blonde woman were waiting for me in the office.

"Egon, this is Clara, your new personal assistant; Clara, this is Egon," was Rob's mechanical introduction.

"Clara will assist you in everything; she is a very experienced secretary. We poached her from a multinational company. She speaks fluent English; she has spent twenty years in international business. Oh, and she is single." The last comment came with a wry smile.

"Very well then, we are going to start the first working day. Clara has prepared everything. Today all you need to do is just sign some documents. You will not have to do anything else. Simple admin work. I'll leave you two on your own," Rob said and dashed away.

"I hope, Miss . . ."

"Please call me Clara; everybody knows me by this name."

". . . yes, Clara, so everything will pan out all right, I hope."

"You can rely on me, boss."

"Call me Egon, please. Everybody in this factory knows me by this name."

She smiled. "I would prefer to use the word *boss* if you don't mind."

"It is up to you. Now, where are the papers that I need to sign?"

To cut a long story short, Clara placed the papers in front of me one by one. She only opened the last page of every document and, while so doing, explained to me what the significance of each document was. "This is the amendment to the Memorandum of Incorporation; the owner has seen it already and agrees with it."

"Well, if it is good enough for the owner, then it is good enough for me, Clara."

"This is your Acceptance document, boss, accepting your current position."

"OK, I thought as much."

"This is . . ." And that is how the rest of the morning went until midday. I would never have thought that a CEO had to sign so much crap. After lunch, Rob popped in.

"OK, my friend, you've been working too hard today. I'll take over from here. You should go home until tomorrow morning. Your new car is in the parking lot. You can use it as you please. Here are your two cell phones as well. I'll call you if anything crops up. See you later."

I had a strange feeling. It was as if I got the sack. I couldn't really enjoy my new Audi and my new cell phones. I will get used to it, I reasoned and put the car keys in my pocket.

I got home at almost the same time as Gloria. She just finished her morning shift.

"You're at home already? So early? You used to work until late in the old days." Gloria offered this observation with a bit of disdain in her voice.

"New position, new timetable," I retaliated, "Take a look at my service car instead," and I pointed toward the brand-new black Audi.

"Nice, but it's a pity that it doesn't suit you," responded Gloria and made her way toward the apartment.

I was in the office every day by nine o'clock, signed prepared documents and then had lunch. I was free in the afternoon. I didn't go home until evening whenever Gloria had the morning shift. I went to the movies, library, or just took the car for a spin. This was my routine for about three months. I then called Rob and voiced my concerns. I told him how my old colleagues were talking behind my back about my early departures. He calmed me down saying that the owner had promised Western European wages and that he would honor this promise. They had even received an advance.

After that, everyone thought I was attending some important business meetings in the afternoons and evenings. They did not care about my departures. Everyone was focused on the new investment plan. We received this from Head Office in due course. He also stressed my pay increase, which I could not dispute of course. The pay was good, I had to admit, but I wanted something more. I wanted to work. I had known the business very well. Rob suggested that I attend an expat reception the following Friday. He called it a cocktail party, if I remember correctly. He even told me to bring Gloria. Sounds good, I thought.

Gloria didn't attend, of course. In fact, she tried to dissuade me from going as well. But I went nonetheless. I forgot to mention that the relationship between my wife and I became more and more untenable. I felt the relationship go cold. Meaningless small talk, boring weekends. Our daughter noticed the change as well. She, on the other hand, was happy about my new position, unlike her mother.

This cocktail party was, in fact, a TGIF gathering (or "*tídzsíájef*" as they pronounced it in Hungary). As I found out, Fridays were "Thank God It's Friday" celebrations in the US.

Everyone was clutching a glass in their hands, and people were huddled in clusters at this small restaurant in Buda. Rob was in his element. He introduced me to a lot of people with whom I exchanged business cards. We then moved on. Rob eventually disappeared, and I was left on my own. I felt a bit awkward. I was expecting something else. I was deep in my thoughts when a tall, brown-haired woman stepped next to me holding a glass of champagne. She was in her forties, or so I guessed. She said hello in a thick Hungarian accent. Told me her name was Renata and that she worked for Voice Trading Ltd. I introduced myself as well.

Renata wore a red dress that was split open at the thigh. She had long brown hair and reminded me of Gina Lollobrigida. She had an amazing scent. I reckon it was Opium, the perfume, which was very popular in Hungary at the time. We exchanged business cards.

"Are you not bored?" she asked in a tantalizing voice.

"This is the first time that I've attended such an event. I need to get used to the environment." Spoken in a timid voice from within my new Hugo Boss suit.

"You'll get used to it. This is a very easy-going bunch. We need to behave accordingly. If you'd follow my advice, I'd ditch the tie. No one has a tie on, as you can see."

I followed her advice and took my tie off. We only spoke to each other for the rest of the evening. Renata was very understanding and provided me with a lot of useful tips as to how I should handle my American counterparts. She had been a participant in international business for a long time.

We drank champagne with orange juice. Renata suggested we drink champagne this way. She always drank it like that while she was in Prague and also in Moscow, but there with vodka, of course. I have to admit, the drink went to my head a little bit. We were well over the two-hour TGIF limit, but the group just wouldn't break off.

"Are you coming?" she asked me about 9:00 p.m. "I am leaving. Where do you live?"

"In Zugló, near the Stadium," I responded.

"That's funny, because I live in Zugló (Fourteenth District) too. We could take one taxi," she suggested. I didn't oppose the idea.

She exited the taxi first.

"Am I going to see you again, Egon?" she asked me, looking into my eyes with a questioning expression.

"It doesn't depend on me, Renata," I said with a sudden warmth in my heart.

There was no need for Rob to invite me to the TGIF event the following week. I went on my own volition and, of course, met up with Renata. I had a wonderful time with her. I didn't care about work anymore. I no longer had guilt about the fact that all I did was sign documents on a daily basis. Memories of her smile, smell and sensual appearance occupied my spare time. I grew fond of her chiming voice and reserved behavior. We took, of course, the same taxi home. Over a month had elapsed when, one night, she asked me whether I wanted to come upstairs to her apartment. She teased me that I shouldn't be scared; she didn't want to show me her stamp collection. She just wanted to talk. She was hungry for a decent conversation.

She had a nice little condo on the first floor. We talked until dawn. I realized that I completely opened up to her like I never did to anyone before. I confided in her 100 percent. I had verbal diarrhea, which I blamed partly on the drinks. It was a life-confession. I became calm. I did not have angst regarding my personal and work life. I felt strong, almost invincible. Renata brewed me a coffee. I washed my face, shaved with her lady shaver and took a taxi back to the office. The city was still sleeping, and so was the night porter on the ground floor.

"I do apologize, sir, that I kept you waiting," he said with a confused expression on his face. "How come you are so early?"

"I have a very important business meeting in the morning and need to check something beforehand," I mumbled.

I was awakened by Clara in my office. I slept on the sofa in my clothes and must have looked quite disheveled.

My days became mechanical. I was only looking forward to Friday evenings. I couldn't care less about the documents I signed. I reasoned that that responsibility lay with Rob. He knew what was best for the owner. I wasn't interested at all in the investment, the business plan and all the other company bullshit. The anticipated change would happen eventually. I acquired, without realizing, managerial attitudes. Renata drew my attention to it. She was the one who composed my outfits and showed me some useful managerial poses in front of the mirror. I was a good pupil.

I moved out of the matrimonial home and moved in with Renata. Gloria did not oppose this step; I was actually surprised she did not even cause a scene. She only said that the person who burns all his bridges is an idiot. My daughter didn't take my moving out well. She was upset and angry, but paying double her pocket money soon did the trick. She will soon be surrounded by her university friends, I reasoned. I was on an express train that whizzed away into an unknown direction with me.

My situation eventually stabilized. Rob even asked for my opinion at times, and on one occasion, he even sent me to Prague to attend an Eastern European managerial meeting. I was elated about this. The city was beautiful, the women were beautiful, and the beer was cold. What more did a man want?!

I returned to Budapest on the morning flight and went straight to the office. I received the shock of my life when I got there. Clara's eyes were red from crying. She looked down at the floor in front of her, avoiding eye contact. She burst out crying again when she finally looked up at me.

"Clara, for God's sake. What's happened? Did someone die?" I asked in an impatient tone.

She thrust a piece of paper in my hand. The writing was almost illegible from her tear smudges.

"The courier brought it this morning," she responded in a resigned voice, still crying.

*"You stupid bitch, did you really think that my darling Rob was in love with you? I have been having an affair with him for a long time now, and we get on really well. Goodbye, sweety. You won't see us anymore. I'm sure you'll get on well with that stupid boss of yours. Renata."*

Blood drained from my face and legs. My heart was thumping harder.

"Is this a sick joke? Are you playing a prank on me?" I asked.

I took out my cell the same way a Texas cowboy would pull out his Colt. In an instant, I hit speed dial for Renata. "The number can not be reached at present" message awaited me. I didn't try it again. There was no point. I knew she wouldn't pick up, no matter how many times I tried calling her.

I jumped into my car and drove straight to Renata's apartment. I rang the bell. No answer. I rang the bell again with full force. Nothing. I started banging on the door. The neighbor looked out. She was an old lady.

"Are you looking for Renata?" she asked.

"Yes," I responded in a croaky voice.

"You need not look for her. She has moved out for good. I don't know where though. She wouldn't disclose that information to me. The apartment is on the market again as of today."

I raced back to the car and drove back to the office like a maniac. Clara was still crying.

"Clara, for the love of God! Pull yourself together. Let's try and work out what the hell is going on here."

"I don't know, boss. I don't know. Everything has fallen to pieces. Things were working out so well, and I trusted Rob so much, and I'm still in love with him."

"Speaking of Rob, where is he?" I asked with suspicion.

"Most probably on one of the Caribbean islands with all the embezzled money."

"What embezzled money?"

"The monies they transferred from the company bank into their personal account."

An atomic bomb exploded in my head. I couldn't really ascertain how many tons had gone off, but it must have been quite a few because I developed an instant headache, which in turn made me light on my feet.

I spoke with Renata from Prague this morning. She told me she was looking forward to seeing me again. She told me she wanted to come and pick me up from the airport but unfortunately had to attend a very important meeting with Rob. She said she would wait for me in the evening in our quiet little snuggle spot, which was her corner sofa. I was happy and was looking forward to our meeting. I pulled myself together. I was the CEO after all. I needed to instill confidence in front of my staff.

"Clara, please bring me all the documents that I have signed in the last two weeks," I demanded confidently.

She placed a bunch of documents in front of me. I sprang up from my seat and started perusing them frantically.

"You have to start from the end, boss," said Clara in a resigned tone. "The last documents are always the most important ones."

I turned the papers upside down. My whole desk was covered in them. Clara stepped in front of my desk and pulled out a sheet from the bunch, which she handed to me.

"Authorization" it read. "I hereby authorize Robert J. Muller, Deputy Director General, to transfer the amount of 839 million forints to the Bank of . . . " I felt as if my heart was going to stop. My signature was promenading underneath the date. I cast my mind back. I remembered having asked Rob what this document was, what its significance was. He told me that the investment was a long procedure. He told me it was not necessary to keep the bank loan in our company account because it would only burn on the flames of inflation. He said the owner wanted this to be re-invested so that a healthy profit could be made out of it. We would start setting up foreign currency transactions. We would travel the money and make use of the exchange-rate differences. There are myriad broker agencies that specialize in such transactions. At the end of the cycle, the money would return to us, and we would be making a healthy little profit that we would share among ourselves. Everyone would be happy, as it is a win-win situation.

Somehow this sounded too good to be true.

"Sounds good, but what if the money comes back with a loss at the end of the cycle due to the unpredictable fluctuation of the currency exchange rates?" I retorted.

"Not possible," Rob had replied. "As I said before, some broker agencies specialize in such transactions. Are you seriously thinking that they would waive their own shares?" Rob said with a quizzical expression. He then continued, "In the worst-case scenario, we would just write off the loss and that's it. However, as I mentioned, this would be impossible. The owner knows what he is doing. He is never wrong. Our company is listed on the Forbes 500. We didn't start this business yesterday. We know what we are doing, and in any event, the owner is good friends with the new Prime Minister. They attended school together. They had a recent meeting where the owner assured him that our company will help in stabilizing the economy."

What followed was the hardest period of my life. The Privatization Regulation Authority lodged an inquiry into the scam, involving the police and the Public Prosecutor's Office. I was, of course, removed from my position, and a government commissioner became my successor. I was subsequently arrested but released after three months. I then attended court proceedings that lasted forever and a day.

It transpired that the Forbes 500 company I worked for was a small, Delaware-registered off-shore company with a PO Box address in Wilmington. The owners of the company were fictional characters. Rob was a known thief who tried to swindle profits from the economic and political instability that was prevalent in Eastern Europe.

I regretted not having followed Gloria's advice, namely that I should have instructed a consultancy firm to carry out due diligence and background checks on the company in order to ensure everything was kosher. I remember telling her not to be silly about suggesting such a ridiculous move. After all, this was a company for which I had worked for many years. She then gave me a small lecture about the dodgy business deals that were taking place in the pharmaceutical industry, including the privatization of pharmacies that did not exist. But I just waived the idea away with a one-hand stroke.

I ended up receiving a two-year suspended prison sentence. I could not go home, and I could not go to my relatives. They did not want to know me. I ended up on the streets.

▪ ▪ ▪ ▪

The traffic light turned amber.

"Here's a thousand forints," was his offer for the bouquet. He took the flowers from my hand. . . . "Let me know if you change your mind." He handed me a business card that had his cell number on it and nothing else. "Call me, buddy. It's legit business; you won't regret it," he said and sped off into the distance.

I kept staring at the business card for a long time. Thanks, but no thanks, I muttered to myself. I only trust flowers these days. I was about to re-arrange my flowers when a car stopped next to me. I heard the whirring sound of the electric windows as they wound down. A young woman peeked out of the car and smiled at me. My heart felt warm, and a teardrop started to ripen in my eye. It was my daughter.

"Please come home, please," she said in a voice that was also somehow quite emphatic. "Mum has forgiven you." I instinctively grabbed the handle and opened the car door. I sat myself on the back seat, and the car sped off, disappearing in the mingling afternoon traffic.

## UKRAINE:

## Frontier sans Medicine

BY DARIA SAPENKO

*EDITOR'S NOTE: We lost contact with this author during production, and her whereabouts and status remain unknown at the time this book went to press. We wish her all the best.*

A howl, unlike the wind or a wounded animal, and certainly a noise no human would emit regardless of physical or emotional condition. A howl that evoked fear through the ages—the air-raid sirens of London and Berlin, tornado warnings for Oklahoma, tsunami alerts along Japan's eastern coastlines. A howl that had now come to Kiev.

For elderly pensioners, the noise revived memories of Nazi occupation and Soviet air-raid drills. The youth had only television documentaries and war films to startle imaginations, to trigger fight or flight.

Thus it was the treachery of being born too late that found medical student Ivan Dragonov standing on a curb unsure what to do or where to flee. Five decades of a Soviet nuclear umbrella left Kiev a city bereft of mass evacuation plans or fallout shelters. There was no bunker in which to bury one's head in the sand. Reality arrived unfiltered.

No rational Ukrainian expected a Russian attack. Shit, Kiev had been all too happy to cooperate in Western efforts to rid its territory of Moscow's nuclear arsenal. Who needed such weapons in one of the world's most productive bread bowls? Fields of wheat and other grains sheltered from European meddling by a looming Russian presence. Ukrainians were much like Canadians—why worry about what is not going to happen? The Americans will never strike north; the Russians would not drive south.

Until they did.

Reality came calling for Ukrainian youth in much the same way World War II, Korea and Vietnam entered the psyche of American males—conscription. Mandatory mobilization. Ivan's academic career—dreams of graduating from medical school at the University of Lugansk—came to an abrupt halt.

All men to arms.

Ivan was called up to enlist in the Ukrainian army. Given the circumstances, Ivan expected no less—he despised the Russians. But that made him a minority. Most residents of Lugansk were pro-Russian. Cognitive dissonance in the ranks from day one. A cadre that would willingly die in the name of Ukrainian nationalism, compelled to train with an equally large collection of men who were raised to respect "Mother Russia."

Cognitive dissonance that certainly spent limited time confined to barracks. Within forty-eight hours, he found himself and fellow students rushed to the battlefront. Well, perhaps not the physical battlefront. In truth, they were held some fifty miles behind the lines for training. A distancing that news reports revealed was grounds for further fear and confusion. Had the borders been violated by Russian troops or simply pro-Russian separatists?

Not that this really mattered; Ivan and his fellow conscripts shared little more than film fantasy when it came to armed combat, bloodshed and dying. Truthfully, most of the new enlistees had never held a weapon until it was issued upon departing their initial barracks.

Point, pull the trigger, and hope an intended target stopped moving. Not courage-inspiring guidance. Nonetheless, Ivan found himself a new member of the mechanized infantry. Or the Ukrainian version thereof.

Within a week of departing the barracks, he was on the real front line, assigned to an armored unit, and specifically tasked to trail behind tanks tasked with fending off Russian-led adversaries.

His training guidance?

"Tankers die without ground support; infantry die without tankers."

Whatever the hell that meant.

Within two weeks, he graduated from medical student to combat veteran. Trial by fire. Moments of terror, hours of cringing in fear, and death—all accompanied by a cacophony of artillery, roaring diesel engines and the screams of mortally injured men. Sleep was a luxury frequently interrupted by nightmares or demands he awake to stand guard duty.

They retreated or advanced from day to day, hour to hour. Nobody really knew what was happening. Rumors flew as to the outcome of any engagement, location of one's next adversary and even Kiev's will to go forward with this war.

Citizens chased from villages and farms streamed west in the day. Men who longed for Moscow's return slipped east in the night. Aircraft fell from the sky—including a civilian airliner—or so the propaganda doctors declared. The only "fact" he and his fellow conscripts could believe was the fall of Crimea—Russia had taken back that which was already very much Russian.

They also knew that claims were made to Lugansk and Donetsk, claims based on the presence of a large ethnic Russian population. Claims viciously exercised and then realized by Russian-supplied militia posing as "suppressed" locals.

A witness to history, Ivan saw destroyed villages and townships. His own city of Lugansk was heavily shelled. The airport and railway station were destroyed; resupply and reinforcements became scant and hard to come by. A logistician's nightmare, the average soldier's reality.

Ivan's daily reality.

Ivan wanted out. Like everybody else, he lived in a constant state of fright. He wanted to live. He watched friends and classmates fall on the battlefield—some to be taken away on litters, others to be buried in local cemeteries.

Medical school rapidly became a fading memory—a yellowing newspaper clip that made sense to the reader but was no longer applicable to an outside observer. In place of learning how to save lives, he learned how to take them. There was no other option. He learned to use handguns and rifles, and then machine guns. He discovered—and so did his superiors—that he was a good marksman. By his hand, men quit fighting; by his hand, men began dying.

As did his soul.

What would he do when the war was over? Go back to the university medical school? Not likely; war had laid to waste the university and hospital.

There was no "home" awaiting his return. Both parents were dead—placed in graves when he was just a boy, victims of an influenza epidemic that his country was ill-prepared to prevent or contain. . . . Much like this war.

That left the army.

He looked at the Makarov PM revolver on his hip and the FORT-301 sniper rifle secured over his shoulder. Best friends one could ask for in battle. Kill and killing—these were the new skills he had learned. He knew how to clean and assemble both blindfolded.

He was no longer an angel of mercy in training. He had become a merchant of death. Angels, he knew from church, learned much about suffering. Merchants, he learned from experience, become fat and wealthy.

Better to be a merchant.

Gradually, Ivan acquired detailed knowledge of every man-portable weapon in the Ukrainian military. The FORT-12, the PB, the Makarov PM, the PSM pistol, the Stechkin AP, and the Makarych.

The submachine guns were mainly German MP5s, the Ukrainian VEPR, the AKS-74U and the AK-74. Then there was the FORT-221, SAIGA-12, FORT-301 sniper rifles, Barrett M82 sniper rifle, and the FORT-401.

He had become the merchant of death—a walking encyclopedia of knowledge on weapons intended to do one thing: kill.

## ALL GOOD THINGS MUST COME TO AN END . . . EVEN WAR

We come to miss the familiar. Children miss departed parents—despite years of abuse. Dog owners miss the mutt once it runs off—despite a tendency to bite without warning. Drivers miss old cars—despite frequent breakdowns. Soldiers miss war—despite the death and destruction.

Ivan's war came to an end.

Ukraine had come a long way from the March 2014 Maidan square demonstrations in Kiev. Posthumously renamed the Revolution of Dignity, but whose? The damage was done, the dead were dead, and democracy appeared no less likely to go off the tracks.

Dignity indeed. What would all the demobilized young troops do now? Where would they find jobs? Schools were closed, shops shuttered, and there was little call for skilled sharpshooters. Yet, rent was to be paid, food placed upon the table, and clothes found suitable for placing employment applications.

Dignity lost at the personal and national level. Russia was no longer a benevolent giant, and the West offered a paltry panacea. Questions in cafes and the marketplace. Had America and NATO done enough to help?

Ivan recalled President Petro Poroshenko appearing before the European Parliament—bearing a blood-stained Ukrainian flag riddled with bullet holes. Brandishing this symbol of sacrifice, he thanked the European bastards for sending blankets, rations and other supplies, only to then mockingly complain, "But you cannot fight a war with blankets. We need military hardware."

Good fucking luck.

Oh, the CIA sent their agents to offer moral support, intelligence and backroom kibitzing. This had been exposed by Russia, but it was to be expected. Spies always report on other spies. Washington monitored Moscow, and Moscow watched Washington. An endless game with little utility—other than generating headlines when one side or the other sought to win the moral high ground.

Kiev was no place for spy-versus-spy. Located out of NATO—Moscow would never accept such an incursion into its backyard; the Ukraine could only go begging with hat in hand. A pauper among the prosperous—most of whom depended upon Russian natural gas to get through the winter. Good luck finding solace in the gilded hallways of Western Europe.

That said, no man or nation is an island. (Save, perhaps, North Korea.) Indirect methods were found; American money and NATO hardware began to flow in under various guises. And there was training. Soon the Ukrainian military was in a much better condition to face the enemy, but would always remain an underdog. Diplomatic pressure on Russia was imperative, and was, surprisingly, forthcoming. A trade embargo imposed by the US and European Union kicked Putin in the balls. Russia's economy now staggered like many of its drunken citizens.

But Crimea remained lost. An island of Russian expatriates re-joined with Moscow in an annexation no prettier than Hitler's acquisition of Austria or the Sudetenland.

Ivan, after more than a few beers at a local bar, would often decry, "America is not going to go to war over Crimea! They will not risk trading Boston for Berdiansk." A war cry that typically found him ousted for public drunkenness.

Tossed curbside, he would sulk off to a local internet café and generate online sulks with his fellow former conscripts. Once a soldier, always a soldier—at least in times of need and misery.

## LAWYERS, GUNS AND MONEY

Wishful thinking. What if? How could I? There must be a "right" and "wrong." All mental masturbation.

Left to his own devices, that is to say, locked out of the barracks and access to at least three steady mess-hall meals, Ivan had time to mope, contemplate, and contrive.

Contrive a means of paying his way. . . . Not only his, but that of his fellow conscripts. There was no "Blackwater" waiting to hire unemployed Ukrainian trigger pullers. Shit, there was no call for even lowly security guards. Employment opportunities in post-war Ukraine dried up faster than a whore's twat forty-eight hours after payday.

That left Ivan to contemplate his plight and that of fellow soldiers, as he sat on the edge of a bunk bed in a small, one-room Kiev apartment provided to him as a reward for his participation in the war. He was supposedly a "veteran," even a "war hero," and people looked at him as such. Although he was tempted to milk this sympathy, the udder went dry before he was satiated . . . before he was eating a decent meal more than once a day.

Here he was, twenty-six and unemployed. No prospect of continuing his studies, and few chances of getting a job. The financial crisis ran deep.

And then there was a knock on his door. Nikolai, a neighbor whose parents in Donetsk had gone missing in the war. Nikolai was nothing if not a conniving bastard. Said crime was rising sharply in Kiev and other cities. Theft was rampant. Argued they were missing out on a unique opportunity.

Indeed.

What Nikolai really wanted was a gun, no questions asked. No sweat in America; a real pain in the ass when one lived in the Ukraine.

Gun ownership was outlawed, and therefore most purchases only happened without documents.

Shit.

Paperwork was a benchmark of socialism and even the post-Soviet world. Heads of government came and went, the fucking bureaucrats never died . . . and they wanted official papers. Gun ownership was a long way off for an honest Ukrainian. The pragmatic were in far better shape.

Purchase today, paperwork tomorrow . . . if ever.

Seeing profit, a good meal and decent vodka in his immediate future, Ivan promised a gun to Nikolai . . . as soon as he returned to his army camp for the next training session.

"Training." An excuse to pilfer Western food aid, a few blankets and weapons. It was all about the weapons and ammunition. Senior NCOs turned a blind eye; officers simply stood by with open palms. Guns dispersed at "pennies on the dollar," to use an American phrase.

Medical school never promised to pay like this . . . a 3,000 percent return for thirty minutes of sweat. Ivan traded his soul and returned to Kiev with Nikolai's toy. No remorse. He didn't even bother to inspect it. Too many bad memories. Violence. Death. Absent social mores.

Welcome to the new Ukraine.

Nikolai said he wanted to pay, offering Ivan $300. Not yet the entrepreneur he was about to become, Ivan settled for $250. Gun in hand, Nikolai turned to him and demanded another, one for his cousin.

So began a life of theft and black-market deals.

Go to the camp for a drill, steal a couple of rifles, return home and sell. Ivan quickly lost his socialist education—capitalism paid well at $300 per weapon. Shells went for an equivalent of twenty-five cents apiece.

He actually came to find a friend in Nikolai.

▪ ▪ ▪ ▪

As the weeks and months went by, the demand for weapons blossomed. Ivan Dragonov became known indirectly, through friends of friends of friends of cousins. He was a conduit to arms—first in singular deliveries, then by the dozens.

He no longer took public transportation to the camp; he compelled Nikolai to drop him off in their latest acquisition—a 1998 Toyota Camry. Not a thing of beauty, but it ran well and drew little attention. Two attributes that served their purposes—swiftly moving a trunk-load of weapons without police intervention.

Demand began to outstrip supply. Handguns were the most sought after, but in one or two cases, buyers wanted submachine guns.

Then, crime statistics began to surface. Guns don't kill people; people kill people. Or so Ivan would tell himself—without realizing he was borrowing a line from an old US National Rifle Association grassroots campaign.

Regardless, it became clear that gun ownership emboldened would-be criminals.

Break into a pensioner's house and shoot the residents—no witnesses for the police to interrogate. Walk into a supermarket and have the cash registers emptied into a shopping bag—so what if an overzealous clerk died? . . . There were more applicants than jobs.

By far, however, the crème de la crème of shoot-and-run took place within Ukrainian banks. Kiev was reliving John Dillinger and his ilk seventy years after the mobsters were dispatched by American law enforcement.

Not surprisingly, the private security business mushroomed. Would-be tough guys in dingy leather jackets loitered outside shops and any institution that handled cash. Men with a lot of muscle on their bones, but little brain between their ears.

In a world of "rent-a-cops," the badged officers rapidly found other means of making a living. Military conscripts were not the only ones with access to guns. Weapons pulled from crime scenes rarely showed up in evidence rooms. The guns were sold before an arresting officer made it back to his or her station.

Even with business turning at a pace he never expected, Ivan's name and background remained unknown to 95 percent of his customers. To those close to him, to the conduits, he became known simply as "Ivan the Terrible." Within two years, Ivan had moved into a villa on the outskirts of Kiev. An imposing structure with a tall stone wall thoughtfully crowned with barbed wire and broken glass. What the physical dimensions could not deter, electronics supplemented. Surveillance cameras and floodlights. And, of course, bodyguards.

This made for an interesting double life. The Ivan who sipped champagne and entertained expensive whores behind guarded walls. And the Ivan Dragonov of old, the gentle and popular former medical student who supposedly lived in a very simple apartment near the city center.

He and Nikolai were drinking buddies . . . two men supposedly looking for work or taking on menial day jobs. Carpentry one day, bricklaying a second and unloading trucks on the third.

In fact, not even Nikolai knew the full scope of Ivan's enterprise. He was just another conduit for Ivan's gun sales. He had no idea Ivan was now a nationwide entrepreneur . . . a man who had little tolerance for sloppy security or fiscal incompetence.

The villa became Ivan's operational headquarters. All communications were screened for potential wiretaps. Email always went via Tor (The Onion Router) and was encrypted. Cell phones were forbidden. Business contacts were always done in bars or hotel lobbies. Deliveries no longer figured in his schedule—let some poor "mule" go down should an honest policeman suddenly appear from nowhere. (Not a serious concern, but why take the risk when there was a sea of young men willing to prove their worth?)

Medicine was now a figment of his ancient imagination. Why spend forty years tending to the sick when the same money could be made in three weeks being chauffeured through the streets of Kiev?

## LIES, DAMN LIES, AND STATISTICS . . .

Optimism springs eternal, or at least at midnight on December 31. The next day may seem less rosy.

So it was the Ukraine entered 2017. Despite predictions to the contrary, there appeared little hope of a complete end to hostilities between pro-Russian forces and the Ukraine. Outsiders began to refer to Kiev's woes as a second Balkans, the media went searching for headlines elsewhere, and the average Ukrainian appeared resigned to surviving as a witness to violence.

Perhaps "resigned" is too passive a term. Were it not for a shortage of cash and psychologists, the Ukrainian population would be better characterized as a petri dish for Freud's legendary couch. Angst, generalized angst. Fear of death, not finding employment, and even starvation.

Criminologists are quick to note that the poor are most likely to prey on their own. A phenomenon that made Ivan an even wealthier man. His contacts now included members of the business, criminal, political and social elite.

Pervasive fear is a great equalizer. Even the wealthy and well-connected wanted weapons—if not for themselves, then for a bodyguard. The days of intimidation via a man's size were gone—now all the goons carried guns, and even the scrawniest pistol waver was deemed preferable to former bar bouncers. Not surprisingly, the social wall that once separated reputable authorities from known criminals rapidly evaporated. Each depended upon the other for profit and protection. A real prisoner's dilemma of tit-for-tat. Ivan offered protection. But he also needed protection.

The solution was to offer to law enforcement information on would-be competitors in exchange for a "blind eye," or occasional backup when rivals decided armed force was preferable to bribes.

Ivan, the medical student, now became Ivan, the politician. His survival depended upon knowing who to call and when to call them. Less politely, he was accused of knowing who to blow and how much dick was going to require stroking.

No mean feat in a nation with multiple law enforcement and security agencies.

▪ ▪ ▪ ▪

Never underestimate the power of learning, nor the consequences of comprehending the lesson. Ivan had an insatiable appetite for languages and computer skills. Already fluent in Russian and Ukrainian, he set about learning English—the native language of Google and many other search engines. Add to these talents a zest for statistics, and we have a sophisticated gunrunner.

Unfortunately for the paltry set of morals remaining within his twisted value system, this quest for knowledge revealed Ukraine was rapidly descending into violence that transcended the battlefield. In 2010, Ukraine had a murder rate of 4.3 per 100,000 in the population. A little mental math—know the population size and do the division—suggested something in the vicinity of 2,000 violent deaths in one year. That grew to 5,900 in 2014 and in 2016 rocketed to 8,200.

Now he was caught between his inner angels and demons. Abet escalating violence or discontinue living in style. One can guess which side of the debate succeeded. Ivan—the moralist beset by capitalist ambitions. Money always wins—particularly when you are young, single and have an endless list of wants or desires.

A wiser man might have quit reading or turned to fiction. Ivan kept digging. Much to his dismay, Ukraine was not only becoming the murder capital of eastern Europe—but it also appeared poised to make the Greek system look pristine.

His Google-abetted imagination soon stumbled upon the fact that in 2014, the Transparency International Corruption Perception Index ranked Ukraine 145th out of the 175 countries investigated—on par with Uganda. In 2015 it improved very slightly: 130th out of 175 countries.

Coin of the realm—but US dollars were preferable—was the only sure means of securing public services. Payoffs for everything from utilities to marriage licenses were considered "customary and expected." The highest corruption levels were found in vehicle inspection and permits (57.5%), the police (54.2%), health care (54%), the courts (49%) and higher education (43.6%). In total, 10% to 15% of the state budget ended up in the pockets of officials.

Made gunrunning seems altogether an innocent crime. He actually spent time contemplating how he might tap into the vehicle inspection racket but was quietly informed that organized crime had a monopoly on that cash cow.

None of this should have come as a surprise.

As Google noted, even the US State Department found post-conflict Ukraine bereft of a societal conscience. According to the United States Agency for International Development (USAID), "The main causes of corruption were (and continue to be) a weak justice system and an over-controlling, non-transparent government combined with business-political ties and a weak civil society." A fetid recipe for disaster.

Pah, a pox on politicians and their statistics, was Ivan's silent rant. Time to start avoiding the guilt mongers and pay more attention to profits. A bit of mental gymnastics that stumbled over his discomfort in knowing that apart from the financial crisis and sharp drop in living standards, his sale of weapons was clearly attributable to the 100 percent increase in crime in a short three years.

Things were now so bad that the American embassy issued a travel advisory for US citizens contemplating a trip to the Ukraine. "Expect theft, break-ins and carjacking—at gunpoint."

Subtle, like hitting a brick wall at sixty miles per hour. Ukraine—the home of beautiful women, sweeping plains of grain and simple farmers—was no longer a haven for tourists or its own citizens.

And, there in the thick of it all, sat Ivan Dragonov. A one-time medical student who now specialized in serving up instruments of death.

"Fuck," he mumbled. "Damned if I stay and condemned if I leave."

Drug dealers seemingly had more options. At least their customers could be counted on to overdose or finally flee to rehabilitation. The arms market was less forgiving. Customers tended to stay and become increasingly dangerous. More than once, he returned home with soiled underwear—a consequence of staring down the barrel of a weapon sold not less than a week earlier.

Purchase one gun and then come back to steal another.

Returning to medical school was out—his lifestyle depended upon a steady income. The custom suits, Mercedes and villa were now a standard of living not to be exchanged for blue jeans and a student's humble single room in a ratty apartment building. That, and his bribes to keep law enforcement at bay, meant leaving the weapons business was unthinkable. He would be in jail long before the first semester of medical school ever came to fruition.

Nor was he alone in this dilemma. The days of 300 percent profit and ready access to military stockpiles were coming to a close. He was not the only wise guy who latched onto this underground business, a business that enjoyed protection from politicians, the police and thugs.

When he began, his competitors could be named and numbered. Now there were hundreds, perhaps thousands. All with the same goal. Profit.

Killing was not their business; that was left to the petty thieves and hitmen for hire. Divorce plummeted—spousal deaths skyrocketed. Easier to kill her than keep her.

But that made Ivan and his ilk the middlemen of murder. Perhaps in a pre-conflict Ukraine, this would have been unthinkable. Today it was normal. He had become a merchant of death. A lord of war.

## THE FIRST RULE OF CAPITALISM—ALWAYS SEEK TO EXPAND DEMAND

Brides or bullets?

A common question circulating through Kiev's diplomatic community. The internet ensured the damn Ukrainians could be counted upon to continue peddling their daughters to the highest Western bidder. But now the same was true of weapons. What the

Russians left behind, or the Ukrainian military would not secure, went for sale on a global scale.

Sleep in the wake of "fight or flight" is always elusive. Combat veterans often lament an inability to rest a weary soul—awakened repeatedly by the screams of the wounded and dying or simply "jazzed" by the prospect of more action. Cowards frequently suffer the same insomnia—but theirs is caused by guilt.

"I should, I could have," crossed Ivan's mind in an endless game of tic-tac-toe. At his every turn, there was a loss. Tic—should have stayed in school—alas, there was no cash for such an option. Tac—should have stayed out of gunrunning—but the profits paid his rent and put food on the table. Toe—never should have been in that basement—hindsight is 20/20.

Sleeping pills were out of the question. In this line of business, a drunk or druggie was certain to meet with an abrupt departure from the living. Nor could he turn to professional assistance. Psychologists were expensive witch doctors in his estimation. Physicians healed—psychologists simply held your hand and then demanded payment for twenty-five minutes of sympathetic nodding.

That left the church—Ivan was never going inside another church. Damn priests were a collective lot of gay men, pedophiles or rapists. He knew. . . . Lord, he knew. One of their lot took his virginity at age eleven.

He locked the door to his villa, instructed the guard to forbid all visitors and then slunk into a darkened living room to contemplate a new future.

Images of the dead child poured through his mind like a repeat cycle of a cheap black-and-white film. A loop that had only one soundtrack—that piercing scream. Even Nikolai could not pry him loose of this nightmare—and it was not for want of trying. His good friend tried everything: booze, women, and even the promise of a vacation in France.

The last option left him speechless.

"How the fuck are we going to afford France?"

Nikolai, oblivious to the gun price collapse, could offer no rejoinder. He simply offered, "It's only France. Short plane trip away . . . can't be that expensive." Poor Nikolai—like many in Ukraine's poor villages, he had rarely left his neighborhood, never mind the country.

Ivan dismissed him and slunk back into the cheap faux-leather couch. Out of here. . . . A tantalizing thought. A thought with little opportunity for realization—something like considering a return to medical school.

▪▪▪▪

Sunday morning—the bells tolling a call to services were an unwelcome wakeup call. Priests summoning their flock to slaughter, or a fleecing, all depending on the holy man's ambition for that week, day or hour.

He had to admit, the blonde lying there naked next to him was a welcome distraction—a birthday present for himself. A would-be mail-order bride who was skimping by as a "high-priced" whore on Kiev's angry streets.

The blonde was left to snore—she, at least, had satisfied one of his internal appetites. Sex was one thing, an animal passion easily resolved by a one-night stand; cognitive contentment was a whole different matter.

That thought in mind, Ivan took the last step he or his bodyguard considered an option—he headed for church.

Too late for services, he entered the Russian Orthodox Church of Saint Nikolai alone, took a rear seat, then gradually moved forward up the stained wooden pews until he sat in the front row.

Echoes of footsteps, a lingering scent of incense, flickering candles, depictions of Christ and a glitter of gold and silver used to highlight instruments of the sacrament. It should have brought peace—if not to human conflict, then at least to a solitary being. Yet, there was none to be found.

His subconscious kept awaiting the arrival of a poorly bathed priest wrapped in holy robes while reeking of vodka. Poor choice of an option for cognitive condolence.

A furtive glance to his left, right and behind. The church remained all but empty. A motley collection of solitary elderly widows mumbled prayers from their long-staked positions; all else was silent.

Then he heard that click—the one all gunrunners know so well, a trigger being cocked. Even the house of God was no sanctuary—a business deal was taking place just to the right of the vestibule.

House of God, my ass. Ivan left with his thoughts. Out of the corner of his eye, he caught the priest handing money over to a younger man—the morning's collection passed along for a Berretta 9mm.

Peace go with you, and so shall this weapon.

## ONLY IDIOTS PLAY BY THE RULES

There is never a good time to depart lucrative crime. Perhaps it would be more appropriate to argue that one frequently does not choose when to resign from a profitable illegal industry—it is more often selected for you. A lesson made all too clear, a short week later, when the Bossov twins, teenage sons of Kiev's largest gunrunning family, met a bitter end.

Partying on daddy's dirty money, the two nineteen-year-olds were bar-hopping by limo when the driver announced a fuel stop. When no one came out to service the vehicle, an impatient driver honked and shouted curses out his open window.

A few seconds later, service arrived—with submachine guns spitting fire in a never-ending hail of bullets.

No newspaper coverage—just pictures on Facebook and a bloody recording pasted onto YouTube. Made for a good watch. Car gets riddled, then the fuel tank explodes. Corpses are charred beyond recognition long before police or fire units arrive.

No mistaking the message here—or who was the sender. Civil wars are not civil—particularly when one side came claiming a blessing from Moscow.

Revenge was not rapid, but it assuredly came. Along the conflict zone that had once been the Russian-Ukrainian border. In one night, three known separatist villages burned. Children, men and women, gunned down as they ran out of flaming homes into the freezing night. By morning the only undamaged structures were churches. Seemed the priests played both sides of this coin.

■ ■ ■ ■

Rumor passed that "Ivan the Terrible" had returned from his self-imposed isolation. That he was conniving to retake the gun market. That he was now directing the efforts of former loyalists, who saw little other option than salvation by the barrel of a gun. Ivan, the former medical student, became Ivan, the taker of life.

Alone in the villa—no whore today—there was little doubt something was different. The rumpled Ivan, collapsed in a puddle of remorse over the death of an innocent, was, once again, back. A man with a mission—make money, collect political favor, and depart this shithole with a wad of cash in hand. To say nothing of the profits being quietly banked in Cyprus.

Blessed are the meek, as they shall inherit the earth. Unless the greedy and strong arrive there first. Ivan had no intention of awaiting the former; he was now squarely a member of the latter.

## NEVER THINK WITH THE WRONG HEAD

For a man of education and experience, Ivan suffered one fatal weakness—his cock frequently drove him to imprudent decisions. Once content to sleep with homely fellow medical students, he now bedded the finest that Ukrainians had to offer. Young or old—brunette or blonde.

He should have known better. A pretty, well-dressed, leggy blonde hanging out in one of the city's most expensive nightclubs. Oh, the warning signs were present. Bodyguards loitering in the shadows, a seemingly endless expense account at the bar and clothing that came off a designer's rack in Paris. He should have known better.

But he took her home anyway. Promised a long future together. And set about making peace with her father—a fellow gifted gunrunner.

Bliss, at least for a few weeks of expensive dinners and much rolling about in the sheets. Alas, it did not take her long to discover the other side of Ivan—as did her father.

It started when she noticed that he was not available some weekends. And when he was, he did not have enough sexual appetite. Then, she found long blonde or black hairs and could smell various perfumes in his bedroom. None of them matched her own honey blonde or her passion for Nina Ricci perfumes.

Then she discovered sperm on his sheets. She would not accept his lame excuse that it was just overflow when he was having wet dreams about her.

She pouted, refused to answer his calls and awaited an apology.

Ivan simply moved on. "Just another fish in the sea."

▪ ▪ ▪ ▪

It was yet another Sunday morning, bells pealing, when Ivan awoke with a blonde on one side and a much-tanned redhead on the other. Fucking women would never learn redheads don't tan, but Ivan liked her perky tits. So be it.

As was his new fashion—money bespoke privilege—the catering van was allowed to pass through the villa's gates, behind the high walls, and into his inner sanctum. Per the usual procedure, the caterers toted boxes into the villa.

A few more catering staff this day than his bodyguards thought usual.

Boxes were opened, making for a luxury meal laid out on a large trolley. Any unopened boxes, presumably a follow-up snack, were placed on a lower shelf of the trolley. This buffet was then rolled into

Ivan's bedroom and accompanying dining suite, everyone pretending as though the two half-naked women in his bed were normal protocol.

All very relaxed—no drips of sweat, no furtive glances, no sighs or racing breath.

All very cool.

The catering lady started with choices of cold and warm dishes, including makings of a very English breakfast. Various coffees were suggested, ranging from French filtered to Italian cappuccino and Greco-Turkish thick syrup.

Standing to one side was the catering team chief, a long, embroidered napkin over his left arm. He used it to cover a steaming, covered silver tray. Which, upon lifting, revealed an aluminum-foil-wrapped Makarov PM handgun.

Ivan the terrible, rendered speechless—shot twice, once in the heart and once in the forehead. Then the mayhem began. In a swirl of practiced motion, the unopened boxes were swept from beneath the trolley. Ivan's "dates" died next—rapidly followed by guards foolish enough to run toward the sounds of gunfire.

Ten minutes later, the catering van backed out of the compound. Ivan's gates were tightly closed and given a yank to ensure proper functioning. All a show for an unsuspecting sidewalk observer. And then it was gone—no police call, no witnesses, just another gunrunner come to an all-too-appropriate end.

Facebook shut down his pages after a month of no activity. The jilted blonde went in search of another sugar daddy. Typical week in the Ukraine.

# CYPRUS:

## Beaches and Banks

BY GRAHAM THOMAS

*GRAHAM THOMAS has lived and worked in the UK, Hong Kong, Dubai, Bahrain, and, currently, Cyprus, specializing in corporate finance and financial investigations. He also writes media articles on corporate financial corruption, including money laundering.*

Another sunny day on the Island of Love.

"How many mornings over the past three years have I thought that?" Jane Graham was mumbling to herself while driving her two children to the International School in Limassol. They'd lived there for just over three years. Tom Graham, her husband, had been headhunted by the Hellenic Bank to take up the post of deputy managing director, based in its new headquarters on the south coast of Cyprus.

Initially, Jane considered the move a blessing—escape from the drab skies of London to this idyllic island in the east Mediterranean Sea. Endless sun, safe for children, no crime, a large salary for Tom and a villa provided for the family. What more was needed? Ah, yes, friends to be made. No problem.

As she dropped off Gareth and Katrina, she saw one of her best friends, Mickey, another parent shedding a child for the day. In this case, her son, Danny. Jane had met Mickey Anastasi a couple of years ago while on the "school run." Danny was in the same class as Gareth, both being seven years old. Katrina was eleven and was the boys' mentor whenever they were together. And they were together a lot. The two mums had immediately been drawn to each other, even though Mickey and family were Americans from St. Louis, Missouri.

Since then, the two families had grown very close. Mickey's husband, Bob, was a large, strapping senior manager with the KPMG audit firm in Limassol. He and Tom had become close "buddies," as Bob would say. They were drinking partners and frequently enjoyed evenings at a local snooker hall. The families invariably went out together on weekends, whether to the beaches or a favorite taverna in the Troodos mountains.

"Hi." Mickey's standard greeting. "What're you up to today, anything interesting? Tennis? Mahjong? Gym?"

"No, I've nothing going on today," came Jane's standard reply. "So I might spend a few hours at the hotel pool, perhaps have lunch there. Top up my tan. What about you?"

"I'm off to have my hair chopped. It's getting hot; I need to get some of this off to help cool down."

As they spoke, the sun was arcing to its zenith, when the temperature on this cloud-free June day would be in the high nineties.

"Why don't you drop by the pool after the hairdresser's?"

"And sit next to you, competing for the eyes of those sexy Cypriot waiters?" retorted Mickey. They both laughed out loud. This was an ongoing joke between them, for Mickey was a short, plump woman who couldn't care less who thought or said it. In contrast, Jane was a tall, sinuous thirty-five-year-old with long, blonde hair. Mickey agreed to stop by the pool later, and both went their separate ways, Jane in her four-wheel-drive Pajero, Mickey in her Mercedes.

▪ ▪ ▪ ▪

Tom sat working at his desk. He was a handsome, dark-haired, thirty-seven-year-old man, a little taller than Jane, with an athletic body. He was an inveterate jogger, which kept him fit. He enjoyed his work at the bank, the third-largest in Cyprus, even though his boss, Costas Georgiou, was a lazy Cypriot who delegated anything remotely complex to the expat Brit.

Costas, of course, had not become managing director through hard work and banking proficiency. No, it was due to the Cypriot phenomenon of *mesa* or, in other words, having close contacts inside the power apparatus of the government or local banking sector. Costas's father-in-law was the finance minister in Cyprus, and his uncle was one of the Hellenic Bank's major shareholders. "Two *mesas* are better than one," was a favorite mantra of Tom's after a few beers.

Tom reflected on his initial reaction to being approached about the job. Cyprus, the mythical birthplace of Aphrodite, the goddess of love. Images of blue skies, sandy beaches, orange and lemon groves, and vineyards had immediately come to mind. But then he had read about the recent history of Cyprus, prior to the family's move to the island.

Following nationalist violence in the 1950s, Cyprus was granted independence in 1960. In 1974, Greek Cypriot nationalists staged a coup d'état with support from elements of the Greek military junta in an attempt at *enosis*, the incorporation of Cyprus into Greece. This action precipitated the Turkish invasion of Cyprus, which led to the capture of northern Cyprus and the displacement of thousands of both Greek and Turkish Cypriots. The north of the island was still in the hands of the Turkish Cypriots and the Turkish military.

Since 1974, despite continuous failed negotiations to unite the two sides and the "north" unilaterally declaring its independence as the Turkish Republic of Northern Cyprus (TRNC), peace remained the status quo and the island was perceived as a haven of stability and tranquility.

But was it?

In the 1970s, the Cyprus government began a program of low tax rates for offshore companies in order to attract inward investment. Over the ensuing fifteen years, foreign investors established over fifty thousand such investment vehicles. These new businesses created thousands of new jobs and brought in millions in annual tax revenues.

But Cyprus became an *entrepôt* for dubious business from the Middle East. Cigarette smuggling, illegal arms deals, and illicit oil trading.

In the early 1990s, billions of dollars of ill-gotten gains made by Serbian President Slobodan Milošević were spirited out of the former Yugoslavia to Cypriot bank accounts held by offshore companies.

Only to be followed by Russian kleptocrats and mafia, drawn by low tax rates, visa-free travel, a shared religious Orthodox heritage, and, most importantly, the ease of moving large tranches of money into the Cypriot banking system without drawing legal attention.

Russian businessmen bought huge villas, primarily in the Limassol area, and by the turn of the millennium, Cyprus was home to some two thousand Russian-owned offshore companies. It was estimated that $1 billion per month was flowing out of Russia into Cyprus.

And, of course, much of this cash was unclean.

In the late 1990s, the Russian mafia controlled over 75 percent of all business back in the motherland, according to *Izvestia*. Transferring the funds to Cyprus kept it safe from Russian tax collectors, dishonest bureaucrats, creditors, other Mafia members and dodgy Russian banks.

This increasing use of Cyprus as a Russian money-laundering haven led to international pressure on the Cypriot government to tighten up and start enforcing anti–money laundering or "AML" practices.

And, Tom mused, this is where I came in with the help of *mesa*.

The Central Bank required all Cypriot banks to adhere to international AML standards via diligence regulations. Thus, the banks needed competent bankers with prior AML experience. Costas Gregoriou did not fit into that category. He made his way to the summit of the Hellenic Bank through whom he knew, not what he knew. Explaining the headhunt for Tom—he'd specialized in the AML area with Barclays in London.

During his first few months at the bank, Tom was amazed at the general lack of skills exhibited by many of the senior managers at the bank, and specifically in the laundering area. He was also astounded at the incompetence of the Central Bank. Tom had met on several occasions with the inexperienced governor and her similarly incompetent minions. He had come away from meetings with a mixture of stupefaction and distaste. And with the need for a stiff drink.

Still, he had concentrated on the main thrust of his work: AML procedures. He had built up and executed a framework for AML operations and checks.

▪ ▪ ▪ ▪

Bob Anastasi was spending that day at the Bank of Cyprus headquarters in Nicosia. Bob was coming to the end of a two-week stint at the Bank of Cyprus, where he was helping the bank's IT department implement a new risk-management system.

Bob had been loaned from KPMG's St. Louis office to KPMG Cyprus almost four years ago. He specialized in audits within the financial services sector. And, being the son of a Greek academic professor who had moved to the US in the 1970s, he spoke fluent Greek.

Originally, he had been appointed for two years, but as he and Mickey had enjoyed the lifestyle so much, he asked to stay for another two years. This extension was coming to an end in three months. Bob had been offered another extension, but after much discussion, he and Mickey had decided to return to the States, to the KPMG Boston office, where Bob would hopefully be promoted to partner from his current senior manager status.

As he was packing up for the day, he ruminated about the decision to return. They had fallen in love with Cyprus and would miss it dreadfully. The large salary and concomitant expatriate benefits, combined with the laid-back Cypriot working environment, made for an idyllic lifestyle.

He thought of the hectic, frenzied fifty- to sixty-hour workweek environment to which he would be returning. Still, at the age of forty, this was the time to rejoin the KPMG US practice and go for a partnership.

He looked at his watch and decided to call it a day. An hour's drive down the highway to Limassol, a couple of beers at his favorite beach bar, and then home for dinner.

▪ ▪ ▪ ▪

While Bob was spending the afternoon in the BOC offices and Tom was laboring away at the Hellenic Bank, their wives were sunning themselves poolside at the luxurious Elias Beach Hotel. They had family club memberships at the hotel pool. As they lay on sun loungers, sipping brandy sours, the two women discussed what they should do this coming weekend.

"How about a trip up to the Troodos on Sunday for some cooler air and a good liquid lunch?" Mickey's favorite option. "We haven't been up there for a few weeks."

"Good idea," Jane replied. The two families typically lunched at the Village Pub in Kakopetria, a beautiful Cypriot town not far from the mountain peak.

"Why don't y'all come round to our place for a liquid breakfast around nine?" Mickey continued. She was renowned for her strong "breakfast cocktails," a habit brought over from the States. In fact, on a few occasions, the children were denied their trip up the mountains due to the breakfast cocktail hour stretching out into lunch cocktails and nobody being capable of driving.

"Love to, but I'll have to ask Tom. He's been grumbling about having to work Saturday afternoon on some project at the bank. He reckons he won't be finished till late, so he might not want to get up too early."

"Yuck, that's unusual, isn't it? Him working on a Saturday," retorted Mickey.

"He's been working some long hours lately, with quite a few Saturdays thrown in."

"I thought he'd finished that money laundering thing and was now a bit less pressurized."

"Huh, you know how lazy that Costas creature is. Tom's more or less running the bloody bank."

"Hey, he's not got another woman, has he?" said Mickey, spluttering over her drink as she chortled away.

"If he has a mistress, she's called the Hellenic Bank, and it's only her bottom line figure I need to worry about."

They both roared with laughter.

▪ ▪ ▪ ▪

Tom arrived home at five o'clock that Thursday evening, gave Jane a hug and kiss, poured himself a beer, and went out into the yard to play some table tennis with Gareth. Katrina was out somewhere with neighborhood friends.

Katrina came home for dinner at seven o'clock. It was a happy-go-lucky meal, with the children jabbering away about their day. Tom relaxed over a bottle of Cypriot plonk, which he shared with Jane.

After the children had gone to bed, Jane mentioned Mickey's invitation to come round for morning cocktails on Sunday before going to the mountains. Tom demurred, reminding her of his Saturday work.

"You poor old dear. Is it something special, this project you're now working on?"

"Not really, but the American FCPA people are coming down hard on US banks dealing with dodgy foreign enterprises, so the Cyprus

Central Bank is pressurizing all the island's banks to concur with new, stricter regulations."

"What's the FCPA? I really haven't a clue about all these things."

"The Foreign Corrupt Practices Act."

"But I thought you'd done all the hard work to get the money laundering stuff up and running at the bank."

"Yes, but there's a lot more to be done in other areas of the bank. And I have to do it. You know what Costas is like."

■ ■ ■ ■

Bob arrived at the villa that evening after a couple of very cold local KEO beers at the Kiton Taverna. Danny, as always, rushed into Bob's arms. Danny was a daddy's boy, adoring his father, and was the spitting image of him.

"Hi, young feller; how was school today?"

"Well, me and Gareth had a good game of tag at the morning break. Then we both scored a goal in the soccer game at playtime. We beat the other team five-three. Gareth played very well. Then me, Gareth and Katrina were picked up by Aunty Jane and taken to the pool for a while before we came home."

Later that evening, with Danny fast asleep in bed, Bob and Mickey sat outside on their patio, having a nightcap.

"You know," Mickey said, "Danny absolutely adores Gareth and Katrina; it's as if they were siblings."

"Yes. I don't know how he's going to cope without them when we leave."

"I was actually talking to Jane about that this afternoon at the pool. She thinks her kids will miss Danny too. Katrina was all over her a few days ago about us leaving and wanted to know why we couldn't stay."

"Well," said Bob, "we've talked through that for the past few months nonstop, and when you gotta go, you gotta go."

"I know, honey," Mickey said softly, "it's the right move at the right time for your career."

The following morning, Friday, Bob was in a rush. He had to pick up some papers from his office at KPMG before driving up to Nicosia for his last day of the project at the Bank of Cyprus.

▪ ▪ ▪ ▪

At the Hellenic Bank that morning, Tom was busying himself with some mundane matters when his boss, Costas, phoned and asked him to come by his office. What now? he thought. Does he want me to wipe his ass? Just grin and bear it.

He knocked on Costas's office door and entered the palatial, commodious space that was wholly appropriate for Costas as managing director. Or so Costas thought.

"*Kalimera*, Tom, sit down; how are you?"

"*Kalimera*, Costas, I'm fine. How about you? All well with the family?"

The small talk went on for a few minutes. Costas then turned the conversation onto work. He asked Tom if all the anti–money laundering procedures were operating well after the various wrinkles had been ironed out. Tom responded in the affirmative, without going into much detail. He knew Costas had no idea how the nuts and bolts of the system worked.

"Good, good." Costas looked cross. "Because we were having dinner with Agneta Dimitriou and her husband last night, and she mentioned there were some new regulations on AML about to come in from that, um, fatty lot."

Tom tried to conceal his smile as he heard the "fatty" word. Costas always mixed up the various entities in the financial regulatory world. "Fatty" referred to the Financial Action Task Force, or FATF for short, an intergovernmental body responsible for the development and promotion of national and international policies to combat money laundering and terrorist financing.

Agneta Dimitriou was the Cyprus Central Bank governor, appointed to this lofty post at a young age due to her brother's wife being the daughter of the Cyprus President—who appointed the governor.

Tom was bemused at this news, as he had heard nothing through his various international contacts of any new FATF rules or regulations.

Anyway, Tom thought as he returned to his office, Costas has probably got it wrong. Although didn't Mike mention something a few weeks ago?

Mike Ferris, an ex-colleague and drinking partner, was still with Barclays in London. He and Tom kept in touch by phone. But, Tom remembered, his mind had been elsewhere during that last conversation with Mike, and he wasn't taking in what his former colleague was saying. Yes, the conversation was on the Friday after that awful Thursday night.

▪ ▪ ▪ ▪

Bob bade farewell to the team at the Bank of Cyprus that Friday afternoon. The project had gone well and had finished on time. Another success on his KPMG career record. "US partnership, here I come," he told himself as he drove back to Limassol.

He stopped at the Kiton for a couple of beers. It was around 6:00 p.m., and on the horizon, the sun was sinking into the Mediterranean. Bob was admiring the view when there was a tap on his shoulder. He looked round to see Zoran Babic standing next to him.

## ZORAN

"Hi Zoran." Bob extended his hand to shake Zoran's. "Haven't seen you for a while; how are things?"

"Fine," said Zoran in his slight Baltic accent. "And you? How are Mickey and Danny?"

"Everyone's great. How is Georgina?"

"Same as ever; gorgeous, beautiful and still slaving away at Kaligirou's."

"And the court case?" inquired Bob.

"Just about there, hopefully."

"Sit down and have a beer; bring me up to date."

"I'll just nip to the toilet first, Bob. I'll order a couple of KEOs on the way."

As Zoran strode off, Bob reflected on his friend's experiences over the past fifteen years. Bob had first met Zoran about three years ago. Bob was undertaking an audit of a large Cypriot insurance company. Zoran was a Serbian who had come to Cyprus ten years ago. He was an accountant in the company's Finance Department. Not a qualified accountant, but a hard worker with a rapid brain. Bob took to him immediately, and a friendship formed.

Zoran had met Georgina, a young Cypriot girl, five years previously. They had fallen in love and, despite her family's shock and horror at Georgina not marrying a fellow Cypriot, tied the knot. Zoran was in his forties and Georgina in her early twenties.

After two years of renting an apartment in Limassol, they managed to save enough to put down a deposit on a small apartment in Fasoula, a delightful village about ten miles north of Limassol. They just about succeeded in keeping up with their mortgage payments, with Georgina's income from her secretarial job at a Kaligirou law firm.

They rarely ate or drank out, being happy enough to stay in and quench their thirst from the huge *pitharias* of wine bought from the nearby winery. Zoran occasionally stopped for a quick drink at the Kiton after work, as he knew Bob was often there. Bob had introduced him to Tom. Through time, the Babics had become firm friends with the Grahams and Anastasis. While the Babics tended not to socialize very much due to their money situation, they had been invited to both the Graham and the Anastasi abodes on a number of occasions for food and drinks. And they, of course, had reciprocated a couple of times.

Bob sipped his beer and thought of the financial struggles Zoran had experienced compared to his own worry-free lifestyle. However, Zoran was hopefully soon to be relieved of his fiscal worries.

Zoran's grandfather had built a very successful timber business in Yugoslavia after the Second World War. This had been handed down to Zoran's father, who, through shrewd but ethical business activities and sound investments, had become wealthy in the old Yugoslavia.

In 1991, when Zoran was in his late teens and working at the family business as a trainee accountant, the Yugoslav War started. Over the ensuing years, many of his father's investments failed and the family business deteriorated. In 1995, his father suffered a severe stroke and, after a short illness, died. This left Zoran on his own, as his mother had died of cancer a year before the start of the war, and he had no siblings.

Although the business was floundering, there was still a fortune in the bank. A year after his father's death, Zoran decided he had had enough of the war, as Yugoslavia had been literally torn apart. He resolved to close the company, leave the stricken region and head for England.

However, when seeking to transfer funds to Western banks, he found the various company and family savings accounts to be bereft of money. Investigation showed that many of the Yugoslav banks had been "robbed" of their cash holdings to fund Slobodan Milošević's money-laundering acts. A vast amount of this cash had been taken physically in suitcases, contrary to a UN embargo, to Cyprus and laundered within the island's banking system.

Much of this dirty money was then used to purchase weapons, thereby arming a Serbian army busily engaged in genocide.

Zoran calculated that around $8 million was missing. Despite many meetings with senior government and banking officials, it appeared there was nothing to be done. It was then Zoran decided to track down his money in Cyprus. He would somehow try to recoup the lost millions.

Thus, he moved to Cyprus and got a junior job at his present employer, moving slowly up the ranks. Of more importance than his day job was his "night" job. He spent long hours talking to local bank officials and journalists, attempting to follow the money paper trail.

Through sheer endurance and stubbornness, he managed to paint a convincing picture of where and how the "Milošević millions" entered and exited Cyprus.

Everything pointed to Marfin Bank. As he managed to put the last pieces of the jigsaw in place, Zoran wondered what he could then do with the puzzle. He could sue Marfin Bank for the return of his $8 million. But what about the legal fees? He had access to very little money. There were no savings, and he was living on his salary from month to month.

Then good fortune struck. He met Georgina at a church bazaar in Limassol. She was serving tea and coffee. A stunning vision; by the end of the afternoon, Zoran was afloat on coffee. But it worked. She was attracted to him, and they were soon seeing a great deal of each other.

He told her the story of his money-laundering investigation and frustration about how to proceed. She was working at Kaligirou's and said she would mention it to one of the partners.

A week later, at a partnership meeting, after Zoran had been invited to make a presentation, it was decided that the firm would act for him on a contingency basis. No win, no fee. The partners were amazed at his story, and even if the firm lost this case, it would certainly receive rewarding publicity.

This had happened just over three years ago, and, as usual with the Cypriot courts, the case had moved slowly.

Now, after Zoran sat down and took a sip of his drink, he brought Bob up to date on the case. It seemed the judge, just two days ago, had unofficially told Zoran's lawyers that he was coming down on his side. The judge accepted that Marfin Bank had been responsible for taking in large amounts of illegal spoils from Milošević, including Zoran's money.

There was just one piece of evidence missing: a statement from a banker in Serbia regarding the main account from which Zoran's funds had been expropriated. This would win the case. The problem was the banker, who refused to travel to Cyprus.

The only solution was for Zoran to travel to Serbia and for both men to swear a statement in front of a local judge. They had to be physically in the same room making the statement for a Cypriot judge to accept the evidence.

"That's brilliant news, Zoran. So when are you off to Serbia then?"

"In a couple of weeks."

Bob smiled. "I'm absolutely delighted for both you and Georgina. You deserve it after all this time." Bob reached across and gave Zoran a big hug. He was genuinely pleased for his friend.

Bob grinned. "I suppose this could mean the tapping of tiny feet in your apartment in due course."

"Yes, Georgina will be off the pill as soon as the judge has spoken."

"And it won't be an apartment your first baby will go home to. It will be a villa as big as some of those Russian ones up in the posh part of town!"

The laughter of the two friends exploded through the Kiton.

▪ ▪ ▪ ▪

Bob arrived home just after seven. "Sorry I'm a bit late," he said to Mickey, who had lit up the barbeque, "but I bumped into Zoran. Good news; he . . ."

"Whoa," Mickey interrupted, "I spoke to Georgina on the phone today. She told me about it. Just a trip to Serbia, and he's won."

Bob gave Mickey a kiss. "Yeah, I'm so glad for them; they deserve it."

After dinner, Bob read Danny a bedtime story while Mickey was stowing dirty plates into the dishwasher. Bob walked back out to the yard and replenished his and Mickey's wine glasses.

When she joined him, she said, "I was thinking last night after you'd gone to bed . . ."

"Come on then, Einstein; tell me your innermost thoughts."

Mickey collected herself, took a deep breath, and said, "You know how we've talked so much about missing the Grahams?"

"Yes."

"Well . . . um . . . do you think they'd ever consider moving to the States? I know they love it in Cyprus . . . so do we . . . but we're going back."

"But it's all about my career; that's why we're going," Bob said.

"Yeah, but what about Tom? Where's he going, career-wise, at the Hellenic? There's no way that creep Costas will ever be dethroned, so Tom will just remain where he is. And he's only in his mid-thirties. Surely it's time to look elsewhere."

"Difficult for him to uproot the family and go and live and work in the States. And even if he wanted to, there's the little matter of a green card."

"But Bob, I was thinking that perhaps you could help get him a position at KPMG. He's got a great banking background, with a lot of money-laundering experience . . . or should I say anti–money laundering experience?" Mickey grinned as she corrected herself.

"And with what you've told me about all the new AML regulations and the pressure put on the US banks, surely Tom could get a job on the audit or consulting side. You said the KPMG's Boston office was going to be the US hub of the firm's banking practice."

Bob was quiet for a few minutes. He sipped his wine and contemplated Mickey's idea. The Boston office was looking to recruit qualified staff over the next six months. "Mmm, you might have something there, darling.

"OK, I'll run it by Tom in the morning; see if he's interested. And perhaps you could mention it to Jane. Let's go for it from two directions."

▪ ▪ ▪ ▪

The following morning, at the start of another hot, sunny weekend, Bob and Tom agreed to take the children to the beach while the wives did a bit of shopping.

Tom picked up Bob and Danny and drove them all to a beach adjacent to the Kiton Taverna. As soon as they were there, the children slipped their outer clothes off and raced into the sea. Bob and Tom paid for a couple of sun loungers and relaxed in the sunshine.

The beach was already busy even though it was only nine o'clock. A mix of tourists, locals and expatriates.

Bob went off to buy the *Cyprus Mail*, the only English-language national daily on the island. When he returned, Tom told him he was going for a swim. Bob watched him as he walked down to the shoreline. Lucky bugger to be built like that, Bob thought after glancing down at his well-earned beer gut.

Bob noticed the heads of a couple of female beachgoers turn as Tom passed. Two long-legged feminine beauties approaching their mid-thirties. They had their children with them, but no husbands . . . and no bikini tops. Topless sunbathing was widespread on Cypriot beaches. One of these beauties nodded her head at Tom's retreating back, saying something in Russian to her friend, who laughed. Bob didn't understand what she said, but could guess. Bloody Russians, he thought—nice knockers though!

The *Mail's* front-page article was about a company in Russia, "Hermitage Capital," owned by an American, Bill Browder. Bob had heard something about this before. He read that top Russian police officials had embezzled $230 million from the company two years ago through an illegal raid on Hermitage Capital's Moscow office. Bill Browder had recently flown out of Russia in fear of his life, and the company's lawyer had been arrested and imprisoned. Torture was alleged.

Then he read the paragraph that prompted the article to be front-page news in a Cypriot newspaper. Browder claimed his lawyer's investigation revealed that over $50 million of the embezzled money had been moved out of Russia into newly registered Cyprus offshore companies via Marfin Bank. "Hmm," Bob muttered, "à la Zoran."

Tom returned from the sea and was toweling himself off. Bob grimaced and showed him the article.

"Some more revelations of bloody laundering into Cyprus. And it sounds like some poor Russian lawyer is in for it. If there was nowhere to launder the money, things like this wouldn't happen. Lives wouldn't be ruined. Thank God the authorities have told the banks to tighten up. And thank God experts like you are around."

Tom offered a disinterested response to the affirmative and promptly buried his head in a novel. Bob finished reading the paper and took off for a swim and a few games with the children.

Around eleven o'clock, Katrina asked her dad to help the children make a big sandcastle down by the water's edge. Tom excelled in beach castle architecture, and so was inevitably the parent sought out when help was needed.

"Not now, Katrina," was the short and sharp retort from Tom, "I'm finishing my book."

Bob, back on his sun lounger, looked quizzically at Tom. An unusual response from the normally mild-mannered Brit.

"I'll come down, Katrina," Bob offered. "I know I'm not an expert like your dad, but I'm always willing to give a new challenge a try."

Tom felt bad about it, but he had other things on his mind. He reached into the cooler box that Bob had filled with soft drinks and beers earlier that morning. He opened a can of KEO and took a large mouthful. He wondered whether this was his third or fourth beer of the morning.

Around noon, they showered and dried themselves and retired to the Kiton to have some lunch. Tom was going to the bank at one o'clock, and Mickey would pick up Bob and the children.

The children occupied a table opposite their dads', with Katrina playing the mum. "They really are enjoying themselves; it's going to be sad when they're on different sides of the world."

"They'll make other friends," Tom replied curtly, "it's not the end of the world."

This was the time when Bob was going to bring up the possibility of Tom and family going to the States. But Tom's obvious bad mood ruled out exploratory suggestions of this magnitude.

Mickey arrived to pick up the children and Bob. Tom walked to his car, agreeing to meet at Bob's villa for a trip up the mountains around half-past eleven the following morning.

Tom drove along the seafront road toward Hellenic Tower. The building overlooked the ocean, with wonderful views. He slowed at the Tower's parking lot. But he didn't turn in, instead continuing onto the highway and accelerating in the direction of Nicosia.

▪ ▪ ▪ ▪

While husbands and offspring had been at the beach, Jane and Mickey enjoyed recreational shopping in a couple of new malls that had sprung up in the last twenty-four months. As was now the case throughout Limassol, shop notices on windows, doors, and inside were in English, Greek and Russian.

Halfway through the morning, the two girls had a breather, sitting down for a coffee. Over a pair of lattes, Mickey brought up the subject of moving to the States. She laid it on thick. Talked of Tom's prospects at the Hellenic Bank—zilch. She mentioned the rumors about the flimsy state of the Cyprus banking sector. Would all the major banks survive? Doubtful. She praised the potential at KPMG—a first-rate future and big bucks. She talked about the beauty of Boston and its "English" background.

At first, it came as somewhat of a bombshell to Jane. Moving from Cyprus in the near future was certainly not on her wish list. And moving to the USA? She had spent a holiday with a boyfriend in California when she was in her early twenties. Tom had been on a few business trips to New York and Washington. That was it.

But the more Mickey chatted, and particularly when she stressed the positives of the two families sticking together and battling through a transition to the Boston area, the more Jane liked the idea. It was a possibility, but of course, in the end, the decision was Tom's. He had to think of his career first. However, a little nudge in the US direction was not beyond Jane's capacity—and feminine charms.

▪ ▪ ▪ ▪

As Tom drove up the highway, he mused about developments during the past few months. Not his work at the bank. Not his family life. But his experiences in Nicosia. And not in the south of the capital, but over the Green Line in the north.

Since the fall of the Berlin Wall, Nicosia remained the only divided capital city in the world, with the Greek Cypriots in the south and the Turkish Cypriots in the north. The dividing line was manned by Cypriot Greek military units and Turkish army troops—the invasion force, the Cypriot Greeks called them. A United Nations peacekeeping team refereed in the middle.

But why the Green Line? When Tom was researching Cyprus just before the move, he found that it was named after the color of a pen used by the United Nations officer who drew a borderline between the two communities.

There was one crossing that could be used to travel from south to north. It was at the Ledra Palace Hotel. Before the Turkish invasion in 1974, the hotel had been one of the largest and most glamorous on the island. The fighting in 1974 ended a few meters north of the hotel. It was now covered in barbed wire and bullet holes—serving as a barracks for some of the UN troops.

The two families had frequently crossed over to the north for a weekend day out. They would either drive on to the beaches of Kyrenia or visit one of the ancient castles and have a long lunch in a remote village.

Tom's thoughts as he drove past the brown, barren fields on either side of the highway centered on that first time he had passed through the rickety wooden portal of the Saray Hotel in the north of the capital. He had arranged a meeting with an HSBC Bank official to discuss AML software, which HSBC was installing worldwide. HSBC was the only large international bank with a presence in the internationally unrecognized TRNC, and Tom had taken advantage to get a first-hand look at how the software worked.

The HSBC man had proposed a meeting at the Saray Hotel in the old city of north Nicosia. An aging building in need of paint inside and out. But it had character and represented a perceptive visage of the "old" Cyprus. The meeting went well, finishing at around five o'clock. Mr. HSBC, a Turkish Cypriot—Tom couldn't even recall his name now—suggested a drink before the two men departed.

He led the way to a bar located on the top floor of the hotel—a bar that led into a casino. Tom was not really a gambling man, the odd bet on the horses and a lottery ticket being the extent of his wagers. As he drank his beer, he thought how amazing it was that casinos were commonplace throughout the north, yet remained illegal in the south. And Turkey, although a secular state, had a population that was 95 percent Muslim.

A few minutes after the two men sat down with their drinks, Mr. HSBC's cell phone rang. He had a short conversation, which, being in Turkish, Tom didn't understand. The call ended, and Tom's fellow banker apologized, as he had to leave right away. His wife was having car trouble.

Tom finished his beer and decided to have just one more before making his way home. As he received his drink, he looked over toward one of the three roulette wheels. One of the players was a very attractive young woman with a red, clinging, low-cut dress. Probably a high-priced Russian escort, he thought.

On a whim, he picked up his glass and walked over to the wheel. He stood, watching the action for a few moments—while furtively admiring the lady's deep cleavage.

To take his concentration away from cleavages, Tom decided to place a bet. He bought some chips and, to his credit, walked to another wheel where there would be no "cleavage distraction." Two hours went by without notice. He had won with his first bet and kept on winning.

It was only when a new payout was pushed in his direction that he glanced at his watch. Half-past seven. Christ. Jane would be worrying.

He dropped his chips into a plastic bucket conveniently placed for winning punters, took a phone from his jacket pocket and dialed Jane's number.

"Sorry I'm late, love, the meeting took longer than expected, but I'm leaving now, so should be home around nine-ish."

"No problem, darling," replied Jane, "I'll heat up some lasagna when you get in."

Tom quickly counted his chips. His eyes opened in astonishment when he found they amounted to over $1,000. Not bad, considering his initial investment of fifty bucks.

That was Tom's initial induction to the gaming tables of the Saray Hotel. His chips were cashed by a smiling cashier, and, as he was leaving the room, a tuxedo-clad Turkish Cypriot approached him, offering congratulations on his lucky evening. Tom was soon to find out this gentleman was the hotel's manager.

For the next two weeks, Tom kept contemplating his good luck at the wheel and the enjoyment of placing bets. It's all right, now and again, he thought.

However, "now and again" turned into a regular trip to the Saray. Sometimes, he was on legitimate banking business; then, the casino visit became an add-on. Other times, it was a Saturday visit, with work his excuse to Jane.

And "now and again" had an increasingly negative effect on Tom's bank balance. After that first profitable evening, his luck went rapidly downhill. Monthly credit card statements were littered with "Saray" entries. Only the fact that Tom took care of the bills kept Jane in the dark about his gambling habits.

Now, as Tom neared Nicosia, he remembered that fateful Thursday night a few weeks ago. He had been determined to extricate himself from this gambling obsession. It would end in tears, both from a financial and a family perspective. He had decided on one last bash at the wheel to try to make up some of his large losses. After that, he would have to stop, as his and Jane's savings were already down the tubes and his bank balance had turned from black to red.

That Thursday, he had an afternoon meeting at the Central Bank in Nicosia. It ended at half-past four, after which Tom proceeded to the Saray. He entered the ancient hotel elevator, which creaked its way to the top floor. He was going to purchase $500 in chips. . . . There was just no more to fritter away.

The cashier greeted him with her usual effusiveness. "Good luck, Mr. Graham; have a good evening." As he strolled over to his favorite roulette wheel—though "favorite" was hardly the most apt of adjectives now—Ozcan Kanburoglu, the hotel manager, greeted him. "Good evening, Mr. Tom; I am sure Lady Luck will be with you tonight."

"I hope so, Ozcan," responded Tom. They were now on first-name terms.

Tom placed a fifty-dollar chip on red and watched the wheel spin. He was willing the tiny ball to end up on a red number. A good start and he would relax. The wheel slowed and the ball lodged itself on 23 red. Tom's face lightened with a smile. "It's going to be a good night," he whispered to himself as the croupier pushed his winnings toward him.

After a further hour, Tom found himself about $1,100 up. He thought about calling it a day but decided to ride his luck with some betting on single numbers. Half an hour later, he had lost all his winnings and the original investment.

He stepped away from the table, dispirited that he had lost, but happy, in a way, that he had no more cash to lose. As he walked toward the elevator, Ozcan Kanburoglu approached him and gave him a beer. It was on the house, he explained, as Tom was such a good customer. Ozcan inquired why he was leaving so early. Tom said he had no more cash on him and lied that he didn't have his debit or credit cards with him.

"No problem," exhorted Ozcan, "we can open up a credit account for you. You're well respected in our esteemed establishment and, of course, a very reputable banker in the south."

Tom's immediate thoughts were to say no. He was finished with gambling. Time to get back to the real world. As he sipped his complimentary drink, he listened to Ozcan's continuous discourse about Tom's doubtless change of luck on the horizon. After much hesitation, Tom gave in, was provided a line of credit and went back to the wheel.

Looking back, Tom considered that night to be the start of his real troubles. If only he had walked away. But his gambling had continued with disastrous consequences. Now he was more than $300,000 in debt to the casino.

He was dreading his visit to the casino on this Saturday afternoon. He hadn't been for a few weeks and knew that his gambling addiction was over. It had happened suddenly. He did not miss it.

However, he had received a call at the bank from Ozcan. Could he pop up to the hotel in the next couple of days to discuss money?

It was a friendly greeting when he entered the manager's office. Ten minutes of chitchat before Tom's debt was brought up. Tom said he was now finished with gambling, but he could not pay back the money immediately. He offered to pay in monthly installments. That was not possible, was Ozcan's sharp response.

Tom indicated there was no other way for him to honor the debt. Then Ozcan mentioned "debt collectors" and "court proceedings." Tom's heart rate accelerated. He thought of his job, of his wife, all in a flash. "However," said Ozcan, smiling, "there is one way we could consider writing off your debt." His thick Turkish accent resonated around the room. "We would like to transfer some funds into various accounts we hold with your bank over the next week or so."

"Yes?" Tom's cautious response, wondering who the "we" were.

"These are large amounts, but we don't want reports going to your Central Bank about the source of these funds. No investigations."

"How much are you talking about?"

"Oh, six transfers of around five million dollars each."

"Impossible. They would not pass our laundering procedures. We would be forced to investigate. And at those levels, we'd have to notify the Central Bank."

Ozcan laughed. "But I believe you are the Hellenic's money-laundering compliance officer, aren't you, besides being deputy MD?"

"Yes."

"And the MLCO is responsible for reporting to the Central Bank.

So even if your minions at the bank spotted these transfers, it is you who ultimately signs them off."

"Well, actually, the MD is the final signatory."

Ozcan laughed louder. "Hah, that dickhead Costas Georgiou would sign anything you put in front of him. He understands bugger all."

Tom was bewildered at the man's insight on the bank. How and why had he come across this knowledge? Then he remembered Ozcan's mention of Tom being a reputable banker some time back. Plus, he had called him at the bank on his direct line. He wondered what the manager of a tin-pot Turkish Cypriot hotel was doing gathering information about the bank and him.

"I couldn't ignore these transfers; it would cost me my job if I were found out," Tom sputtered.

"But what would Jane say if your debts came to public knowledge? And think what their school friends would say to Katrina and Gareth. Poor kids."

Tom was stunned. This man knew about his family as well as his work.

Ozcan stood up, went to a liquor cabinet in the corner of his small, untidy office. He returned and placed a bottle of whiskey and two tumblers on his desk. He poured a large tipple into each tumbler.

"I think we both need a fortifier, don't you?" he said calmly. "While I give you some background."

He told Tom the hotel was owned by Russians, and the casino was used for money-laundering purposes. The previous manager had threatened to go to the authorities when Russians took ownership and he discovered money-laundering activities. That manager died in a drowning "accident," leaving a wife and three young children.

Upon his promotion, Ozcan wisely conformed to the owners' wishes. He had a wife and four children. However, the authorities were now beginning to clamp down on casinos. The TRNC wanted international recognition—allowing the operation of casinos that indulged in money-laundering and terrorism-funding activities would do nothing to assist in that aim.

So, the Russians decided to look south of the Green Line. But how? Not Marfin Bank, too risky. Then Tom and his gambling fixation and losses came on the scene. The right fool in the right place at the right time. He had been used. He had been set up. He was to overlook certain transactions, and his debt to the casino would be written off. There may even be a bit of spare cash to alleviate the red figures in his bank account.

▪ ▪ ▪ ▪

Tom drove home that evening, traumatized. Blackmail. But there was no choice. He had to go through with it.

Jane could tell Tom was in a bad mood within minutes of walking through the front door. Unusual for him, but she reckoned the strain at work was getting to him again. She reminded him about the day in the mountains the next day and went to bed early.

On Sunday morning, Tom woke with a throbbing head and a heavy heart. Was it all a dream? No, it was a living nightmare. He knew he couldn't put on a show of *joie de vivre* today and told Jane he felt unwell. He would stay at home to rest while she and the children went up the Troodos with Bob and family.

Despite Tom's absence, the two families had a thoroughly enjoyable time. Jane told Bob and Mickey that she had not mentioned Boston to Tom last night or this morning due to his disposition. She would see what he was like when they arrived home tonight. As she was talking, a huge cry of laughter swept through the open restaurant windows. They looked out and saw a bundle of arms and legs on the ground. The three children had been playing tag.

Mickey simply observed out loud, "Look at those three soulmates. You better convince that husband of yours that Boston is the pinnacle of the universe. Promise him more sex on the other side of the pond."

Later that evening, Jane broached the subject of Boston and KPMG with her husband. Tom's reaction was not what she expected. She had thought he would start to discuss the pros and cons of such a move. But he showed diffidence about the whole subject, just saying that he would get around to thinking about it during the coming week.

▪ ▪ ▪ ▪

When he arrived at his office the following morning, Tom was once again weighing his options. Resign and move from Cyprus? What would Jane say about their savings having disappeared and the large overdraft and credit card balances? Anyway, if he left without paying off the casino debt, wouldn't the Russian mafia's widespread connections find him wherever the family went?

Go through with the laundering transgressions? If he were found out, besides getting sacked, there would almost certainly be criminal proceedings, jail and divorce. End of story. If he were not found out, freedom of sorts.

He was confident he could deceive the dozy Central Bank people, who were too lazy to examine closely the intricate reports received from commercial banks. In addition, when they came to audit, they could easily be fobbed off by convoluted explanations and accidentally misplaced computer printouts.

▪ ▪ ▪ ▪

Bob walked into the KPMG's office, wondering what he would be doing during his last six weeks in Cyprus. After getting a cup of coffee and dealing with a few administrative matters, he strolled down the corridor to the office of his boss, Marios. After exchanging a few pleasantries, Marios congratulated Bob on a job well done at BOC. He told him that, starting tomorrow, he wanted Bob to join a team auditing a funds management company in Limassol for a couple of weeks.

▪ ▪ ▪ ▪

That week, Tom was on tenterhooks. Nothing happened until Friday, when a red flag appeared on the daily report he received concerning large transactions at the bank. One of his staff had written a questioning word next to it. "Investigate?" So, it had started. Tom had worked out how he could disguise these transactions to avoid having to report them to the Central Bank and to dispel any of his minions' concerns.

Over the next ten days, more came through the system. By then, the $30 million total mentioned by Ozcan was in various accounts. An enormous amount that had escaped AML due diligence, thanks to Tom's chicanery.

On the day the last transaction went through, Tom received a call from Ozcan. "I think you've done your bit, my friend," he said. "My Russian masters have heard nothing about the initial transfers, so I assume they have eluded AML investigation."

"Yes, and they won't be discovered by the Central Bank through our reports. Neither will their auditors find out what I've done."

"Excellent!"

"So, is my debt written off?"

"It will be as soon as we know all the transfers have been accepted with no problems. And you will be pleased to know there will be no more use of the Hellenic Bank. My masters like to spread their risk."

"OK," was Tom's resigned response.

"Goodbye, my friend; I hope to see you in the casino soon," was Ozcan's sarcastic signoff.

Tom slammed the phone down, sat back in his chair and closed his eyes. He had half expected the blackmail to continue, with further money transfers to be similarly dealt with. But no, thank God. All he had to do was fool the Central Bank guys, and he would be home free.

For the first time in ages, Tom relaxed and started to act like his old self. Jane noticed the difference in him. He even discussed Boston and asked Bob to make some initial inquiries with KPMG. The weekend came, and the two families enjoyed a riotous "chili cook-off" party in

Bob's yard on Saturday afternoon. Other friends were invited, including Zoran and Georgina. The former would be off to Serbia the following Monday for his crucial meeting that would close out the court case.

▪ ▪ ▪ ▪

Zoran looked out of the window as his plane descended into Belgrade's Nikola Tesla Airport. He didn't miss his homeland. He had no family there.

After checking into a hotel, Zoran hung up his suit and shirt, ready for the following morning's meeting. He went for a walk to locate a restaurant worthy of dinner. After eating, he made his way slowly back to the hotel for an early night. It was a pleasantly warm evening and now dark.

The hotel was in the city center but located on a quiet street between the main railway station and the River Danube. During the walk, Zoran's mind was totally fixed on tomorrow's meeting and his flight back to Cyprus in the evening. Georgina was to meet him at Larnaca Airport.

He was so absorbed in these thoughts that he failed to hear the quiet footsteps of someone who had followed him from the restaurant. He also failed to hear the male voice, which at that moment talked into a cell phone. He did, though, hear a car's engine splutter into life somewhere ahead of him around the corner. He heard the car coming down the hill toward him. He heard a higher engine sound and some screeching tires as the car accelerated. The car's lights came into Zoran's view, and it seemed to be swerving across the road toward him. *What the hell!* he thought. It was his last thought.

The following Sunday evening, Bob and Tom were at the local snooker hall. It had been a traumatic week after the news of Zoran's death had reached them.

"So the Serbian authorities haven't found the hit-and-run driver then?" was Tom's rhetorical question. He already knew the answer.

"No, and they never will, as you know," Bob answered bitterly as, for the third time in a row, he missed an easy spot. "Let's pack it in, pal, and just sit over in the bar."

"Couldn't agree more. This Zoran thing is upsetting everybody."

They moved to a table in the adjoining bar.

"A hit-and-run accident, say the police. Huh, it was certainly 'hit and run,' but it was no 'accident.'" Bob was railing. "That bastard Vgenopoulos is behind this, as we all know."

"Yep, no doubts whatsoever," said Tom, "he's managed to save Marfin from going under."

They then remained quiet for a while, each man thinking of Zoran and poor Georgina.

"That bastard Vgenopoulos" was Andreas Vgenopoulos, a Greek national. He owned Marfin Investment Group, which two years previously had acquired a large holding in the local Laiki Bank. It had bought the shares from HSBC Bank, which wanted to distance itself from Laiki due to rumors of continuous large-scale money laundering at the bank. The bank's name had been changed to Marfin Bank.

Vgenopoulos was considered a crook and a brute in local banking circles. He ran the Marfin Group as an oligarch. If the court case had finished in Zoran's favor, it would have resulted in a multitude of similar lawsuits. Marfin Bank did not have sufficient reserves to meet the potential claims and would go under. The bank being the jewel in Vgenopoulos's crown, he would do anything to keep it afloat . . . including hiring a hitman in Serbia.

Zoran's body was flown back to Cyprus the following week. The funeral was a distressing affair, with an anguished Georgina still in a state of utter shock. Afterward, Tom, Jane, Bob and Mickey went to the Kiton for drinks. The conversation was subdued. The wives were still tearful, and Jane actually sobbed when Bob said vehemently, "Poor Zoran, not the first, but probably the last victim of that bastard Milošević's money laundering."

Tom tried not to choke on his whiskey.

▪ ▪ ▪ ▪

On the following Tuesday, Bob received a call from his boss, Marios, who said he had a two-week job for him, starting next Monday. The Central Bank had requested assistance from KPMG in auditing the anti–money laundering procedures at one of the commercial banks. Marios didn't know which one yet, as this was to be a "snap audit investigation." He would be told on Friday so that the bank would not know the audit was to take place until the auditors arrived at the front door. Bob would be accompanied by a CB auditor.

Late Friday, Bob popped into Marios's office. He was told the audit would be at the Hellenic, and Marios stressed the importance of keeping it confidential until Bob met with the CB auditor first thing Monday morning.

As he left Marios's office, Bob smiled to himself. Hah, he thought, now I'll be able to find out how Tom and his merry men are cooking the books!

On Monday morning, as arranged, Bob met up with the CB auditor outside Hellenic Tower. They walked into the bank and asked to see Costas Gregoriou. Once inside his office, the CB auditor showed the MD the authorization letter signed by the CB governor. Costas phoned Tom and asked him to come to his office.

Tom looked at Bob in astonishment as he entered Costas's office. The latter explained it was another snap audit investigation by the Central Bank. Tom tried to hide his anxiety. He could fool the CB guy. But Bob was a different matter.

Tom caught Bob on his own a little later. He asked why Bob had not told him at the snooker hall on Sunday night that he was coming to the bank. "Confidentiality, mate," Bob responded, "and anyway, it would have given you time to cook the books." He grinned at Tom. "I know it's a bind for you, but we'll only be here for ten days or so."

Tom worked in dread over the next few days. Random sampling of transactions by the auditors meant his misdemeanors might not be found. If the CB guy found something untoward, Tom was confident he could pull the wool over his eyes. The same was not true of Bob.

It was late on Friday afternoon when Bob knocked on Tom's office door. He entered the room and sat down at Tom's desk with a collection of documents in his hand.

"There are a couple of money transfers of around five million apiece I've found. They seem to have gone through the AML diligence procedures without being picked up as suspicious," Bob said. "I've talked to Rita about them. She can't understand how they got through. She checked some printouts, which showed the red flags. But I can't find any documentation or anything in the system that shows any ensuing checks taking place. Any idea, mate?"

Tom felt himself reddening as Bob talked. Shit, he thought, how do I get out of this?

"Um, let me look into it next week. It's almost five o'clock, and I've got to finish off something important before I leave."

"Well," Bob retorted, "I should think this is pretty important, don't you? We're talking big money here." He paused and considered, "Oh well; it's late, I suppose. OK, let's go through it first thing Monday morning."

Bob turned to leave the office. "How about a beer at the Kiton?"

"Yes, I could do with a drink. I'll meet you at the Kiton at half-past five."

"Sure," said Bob as he walked out of Tom's office.

■ ■ ■ ■

Tom left the office immediately and was on his third beer at the Kiton when Bob arrived. He had pondered about what to do in the time he had had on his own. Could he get out of it? No, Bob had discovered a serious problem, and Tom would not be able to bamboozle his friend. There was only one thing to do.

Bob ordered a beer at the bar and went outside on the terrace to join Tom. Bob was looking pretty grim.

"Tom," he said, "I've just been looking at other transactions around that time, and I've found some more dubious ones. What the hell's going on?"

Tom looked down at the table as he spoke to Bob. "I've messed up big time," he croaked, "let me tell you what's been happening."

Tom took a deep breath and proceeded to reveal the story of the last few months. From his gambling addiction to the Russian blackmail and, finally, his banking indiscretions. Bob listened incredulously. This was his best friend admitting to personal recklessness leading up to dishonesty.

When Tom was finished, the two friends were silent for a number of minutes. Bob still couldn't take it in. Tom then asked Bob for the biggest favor his friend could ever do for him. He asked Bob to ignore the misdemeanors. He argued that nobody would find out. The inept Central Bank auditor was checking transactions from another period. And Rita in the office could be outfoxed.

"It's only money moving from one account to another," said Tom, "nobody will get hurt. And I'll still have a career, whether in the bank or with you at KPMG."

Bob shook his head and told Tom that he couldn't go along with it. He had his own career to think of. Tom pleaded, but to no avail. Bob was adamant. The two friends left each other at seven o'clock, both looking miserable.

▪ ▪ ▪ ▪

When Bob arrived at his villa, Mickey had already put Danny to bed. They shared a drink and sat down to dinner. Mickey could feel that something was not quite right. Her husband was subdued, which was unusual with the weekend coming up.

"Want to tell me about it, honey?" she asked, as they were clearing up the dishes. "I know there's something on your mind." He took hold of her tightly, gave her a kiss and sat her down. He then related Tom's story to her.

Mickey was as shocked as Bob had been. She thought of Jane and what this would do to her. She asked Bob what he was going to do. He replied that on Monday, he'd have to divulge what he had found to the authorities.

Mickey's mind reeled. Would it be possible to ignore it? she asked Bob. He repeated the words he had said to Tom—no way. It was a miserable evening at the Anastasi's.

▪ ▪ ▪ ▪

Tom had returned home, determined to tell Jane the truth. It would be hard work, but he couldn't keep it under wraps from her. After dinner, he told his wife he had something awful to confess to her. Jane immediately thought it was another woman. All those extra hours at the bank when perhaps he hadn't been working but . . .

When Tom related his story, Jane wished it had been a secret lover. She was appalled. She just could not accept that her man had been so stupid, so dishonest. She cried; he cried. They held each other, but Tom could sense Jane's reproof. Neither of them went to bed that night, both falling asleep on separate sofas.

As previously promised, Tom took Katrina and Gareth to a local camel park on Saturday morning. Jane was red-eyed with all the crying and in a state of utter despair. It meant the end of their cozy lifestyle and leaving Cyprus in disgrace. To say nothing of the possibility that Tom would be arrested. She was sitting in the yard drinking coffee when her cell phone rang. It was Mickey.

"I'm so sorry," said Mickey in a sympathetic tone. "You must be so distraught. Would you like me to come by? Bob's taken Danny to the barber's."

"I'd rather drive over to your place. I need to get out of the house. Tom's out with the kids."

Jane arrived at Mickey's, and the two gave each other a hug. They talked about the appalling situation. Mickey explained that Bob could not let the matter stay hidden; it was just not possible. Jane accepted this. Bob arrived home with Danny. He gave Jane a kiss and took her out into the yard, away from Danny's prying ears. They talked for a while, with Jane actually pleading with Bob not to report Tom. But Bob was having none of it. Money laundering was evil and caused so much misery in the world. He mentioned Zoran.

Jane returned home at midday, knowing Bob was right. She was still in a daze. The family arrived home around two o'clock. The children had enjoyed the camels, and it seemed their dad had been in good form.

The adults maintained silence on the subject of the bank. They would talk again this evening when they were alone, though Tom thought that everything had been said. He was going to have to face the fact that he had screwed up his, Jane's and the children's lives. Nothing could alleviate the situation. He spent a lot of time playing with the children that afternoon.

At six o'clock, Tom told Jane he was going for a drink. He needed some time alone. He kissed the children good night and gave Jane a brief peck on the cheek.

"I'll be back around eight."

"OK, but catch a taxi home if you have too many beers."

Tom drove away, but a mile further on, instead of turning onto his usual route toward the Kiton, he took a left onto the road leading to the Troodos mountains. It took him forty minutes to reach the top, where he parked the car and strolled into the Troodos Inn. He ordered a beer and sat there in the cooler air, contemplating the miseries of the last few months. He thought of his "best friend," Bob. Why couldn't the American have come to his rescue? It would have been simple for him to have collaborated. But no, not the high-and-mighty KPMG guy. Bob was going to ruin his life. You bastard, Anastasi, he thought.

Meanwhile, at six o'clock in the Anastasi household, Bob and Mickey continued to debate Tom and Jane's terrible predicament, while Danny watched television in the next room. They talked of the good times they'd had in Cyprus with the other family. They had fallen silent for a few minutes when Bob suddenly stood up.

"I'll do it for Tom," he said to Mickey. "I can't see them destroyed like this when I have the means to save them. And no one else will get hurt. Tom's gambling days are over. We can all put this behind us and go to Boston."

"I'm so glad," cried Mickey, clasping her husband with affection. "Give him a call and put him out of his misery. Thank you, honey. I love you."

"No, I'm going to drive over and tell him face to face, give him and Jane a big squeeze, and share a drink for the future. I won't be long. You put Danny to bed, and I'll be back for dinner."

Fifteen minutes later, Bob arrived at Tom's place. Jane greeted him and told him that Tom had gone for a drink. Bob told her the reason for his visit, and the two of them hugged, with Jane bursting into tears.

"He's probably at the Kiton. I'll call him," said Bob. However, Tom's phone was switched off. Bob said he'd stop by the Kiton on his way home. But Tom wasn't at the tavern. Bob called Jane to tell her and said he would keep trying Tom's phone.

▪ ▪ ▪ ▪

By half-past seven at the Troodos Inn, Tom had drunk four beers and a large whiskey. But he was as sober as a judge, with total clarity of thought. He paid his bill and got into his car to make his way back down the road to Limassol. Before heading out, he switched on his cell phone to make a call to Jane but changed his mind and left the phone on the passenger seat next to him.

About halfway between the top of the mountains and Limassol is the very pretty village of Platres. And just after the village is a very sharp left-hand bend. To the right of the bend, there is a vertical drop of about five hundred feet onto rocks below. It has metal protection barriers to prevent accidents. However, Tom had noticed on his drive up that, due to a wreck a few weeks previously, temporary wooden barriers had replaced the metal ones.

The road was quiet, and dusk was falling. About two hundred yards from the bend, Tom pressed sharply on the accelerator. The car sped up.

At that moment, Bob tried to get hold of Tom again. The latter's phone rang as the car raced along at seventy miles per hour. He glanced at the phone and saw who was calling. Tom screamed, "Fuck you, Bob," as his foot pressed the accelerator hard to the floor.

▪ ▪ ▪ ▪

Jane was worried. It was eleven o'clock; Tom still wasn't home. She heard a car pull up and thought, thank God. She rushed out to the front patio and froze when she saw a police car. Two police officers, one male and one female, got out of the car and walked toward her.

"Mrs. Graham?" asked the female officer, "Mrs. Jane Graham?"

"Yes."

"I'm afraid, madam, I have some bad news."

# IRELAND:

## Ode to a River

BY FERGAL PARKINSON AND PRESTON SMITH

*FERGAL PARKINSON is a communications consultant and former news journalist with more than twenty years of experience. As a North American correspondent for the BBC, he was part of the award-winning team that reported from New York following the 9/11 attacks. He has also covered many major domestic and international stories in recent years, including the death of Diana, the war in the Balkans, as well as the buildup to the Iraq and Afghanistan conflict. In 2007, he established his own consultancy and has since helped clients protect their corporate reputation and communicate clearly in a wide range of situations around the world.*

He sighted the barn, not by the gray wood slats or the high, wind-torn roof, but by the shape of the black cutout where the stars should have been upon the horizon. He had ascended the grade from the stream—the full twenty paces—had dropped into a thief's crouch and finally, making the sign of the cross, had wondered at his own idiocy; at the vast unlikelihood of finding the stash; at the sheer childishness of his system in the dark.

Twenty full paces from the bend in the stream.

Forty paces from the barn he could not see.

And no third marker to triangulate, to bring the cross to bear.

*Fuck me.*

Davin De Barra felt inside his coat, found a flask. One swig and in a smooth, unthinking movement, he both stashed the flask and crossed himself yet again. He was out in the open now, cursing himself for the broken night vision, for the politics and side games, and even then, remembering the time he'd been shot.

The time, just like this, when he had crossed the heath at night, knowing the British would have the Green Jackets or the SAS, or some fucker anyway, maybe a mile away—some bastard with night vision that worked—and how he had felt the eyes upon him, had shivered under the prickles up his back and, even before he had heard the shot, had known not only that he was in for it, but exactly and precisely where.

The prickle, the tingle, the itch that he had felt coming just below the hip. Then the shock of it, knowing he was bleeding like a pig, his leg broken, and how he had crawled and cried and whimpered until his brothers had managed to hold them off, to drag him away and escape in the turf ditch between the peat, De Barra not in the back seat where there was no room, but crashing and bleeding and gripping his leg in that cold coffin of the trunk, taking a second round in the foot, a potshot through the side panel from some other far-away wanker with gear they could not match.

And De Barra bleeding to death, drenched and suffocating from gasoline leaking out of a punctured tank—wondering, holy fuck, why they'd not caught fire, and praying to the Virgin for mercy, for a Green Jacket to take him with a final shot, but please, dear Mother of God, do not let me burn.

Ah, yes. *The good old days be damned.*

De Barra's hand went back to his flask. Three swigs in under twenty seconds, but it could have been hours or a month of moonless nights in that eternity of fear. He could almost feel the prickle, the tingle of an infrared on his back. Could almost taste the smelling-salts burn of gasoline.

Funny, that. How it always came back to fuel.

But courage now, he thought. Courage and a last swig of whiskey. Courage and whiskey, the blind trust that if he had to die in Northern Ireland, he would not die in this nowhere heath on the edge of Kinawley. Even as he blundered through the comical big steps of a child, hoping against hope that maybe, just maybe, "x" marked the spot.

De Barra limped up the hill, tried to remember the details of stones and the footpath of the last time he'd come. Then the fear passed as it always did, dulling into drudgery and exhaustion in the chill of a near-April night, until after much fumbling and muttering and nerve-jangling, came the scrape of spade on stone and then finally wood, which meant he'd found it.

Arms cache #NB27. Five pistols, three grenades, a useless Tommy gun from the '30s with a rotten stock, but still the prize—a clean-as-a-newborn M2 .50 Cal Browning, complete with stand and six hundred rounds of ammunition.

And De Barra thought, dear God in heaven, still fuckin' here.

Not stolen. Not borrowed. Not uncovered or rigged by MI5 or 6.

Who woulda bloody thought?

It was something akin to elation—for the first twenty minutes, De Barra laboring with the spade, and then digging with the smaller shovel and his hands (the elation long gone now) before the sobering realization of what he was in for and before he blurted out loud, "Dear Mother, an' I come on me own?" For it would be an hour more digging to get the cache fully open. Another half-hour to seal it back up, re-bury it and try to camo the upturned soil.

Then the endless slog, De Barra still wide-backed and strong, but knowing he was late, knowing he'd missed the pick-up by an hour or more. Knowing this and limping with a sodding Browning machine gun on this back, with the mount and stand and belts of ammunition draped over his shoulders *à la* Pancho Villa—and with his true heart racing, with every fiber in his body burning, as no matter how he prayed and cursed and counted the invisible beads of his sins, he knew that this time he was sure. Fate was upon him. Upon the very righteous traitor of his soul. Mercenary that he was, he had sworn upon this future of freedom and blood and now he was literally carrying the fight of it off on his weary back.

*Omertà*. Irish fuckin' *omertà*.

And De Barra remembering the song:

*Oh, damn ye all to hell, me brothers. Damn ye all to hell.*

▪ ▪ ▪ ▪

He was exceedingly tall for an Irishman, close to six foot seven with his head bent forward in the cab of a truck so that his years as a driver had deformed him: eternally hunched, his natural posture stork-like, both hands upon the wheel so that he could easily appear short-limbed and hollow-chested and afraid. Which, thanks to De Barra, was on this night—and most every night—exactly and forever the case.

Mickey Blake ran his palm down over his face and spindly fray of a red beard. Two trips 'round Kinawley and Swanlinbar and Clonliffe and no sign of De Barra but all the signs of a tail, and for Blake all of the stress and racing pulse of a near heart attack.

Four miles now, he thought. Four miles and it could damn near be anybody. The cops, the Brits. The bloody Continuity or the ex-Óglaigh or the Russians, not that he'd ever trust that lot.

What'd Seamus call them? Slops. Short for Slavic Wops, he'd said. Blake eyed the rearview mirror and considered what De Barra had got them into. Considered this and the hour, until a half-mile out of Clonliffe, just like that, there was no tail, no sign of lights in the rearview mirror of the lumbering Iveco truck, but instead the wave-down on the highway that signaled the peelers—the Northern Ireland cops.

To hell with De Barra and his river, thought Blake. To hell with the lot of them. All he'd wanted was a bit of cash—something to keep him good and drunk, but it was when they'd asked him to step out of the truck, when the police had searched the truck back to front and back again, that it had finally come to him.

"Petrol to burn?" quizzed the cop.

A loaded question, thought Blake. "Was burning oil. Tuned it up but need to get her right for the hauls."

"And you're just riding 'round and 'round. 'Round and 'round at two past midnight for the joy of it?"

A shrug. Believable stupidity, Blake looming over a cop in a glow-yellow jacket laid on the bottle-green—that on this night could have been black. Yes, he'd been riding 'round and 'round. Yes, that meant the tail had been the peelers or the Brits or both.

But better them than CIRA or the slops or the ONH.

"Don't believe you for a minute," said the cop.

Another shrug, Blake an ignorant stork. The officer, fat-necked and frowning with his billed hat down low, said, "On your way then. But I'd advise you that you're done for the night. One more trip around, and I'll have you down to the station."

Blake climbed into the cabin with his head down, his neck aching and his hands into that short-armed fold of a kangaroo. Harassment, he thought. Nothing more than harassment. But as the truck revved and lurched jerkily into gear, he thought, De Barra's still out there; now what am I gannae do? Thought this word for word, and shoulders half up by his ears, murmured out loud:

"Bugger De Barra and his damned river.

"Bugger it bloody all."

▪ ▪ ▪ ▪

Detective Sean McAuliffe was no more than twenty-six years old, having served exactly six years on the job, minus no more than twenty-two days and two-thirds of a shift, or six hours and twenty minutes, which meant, in the fiction of official hours, give or take two hours and forty minutes left. This was important, as six years was an anniversary he kept in his head, his brain as wiry and lean as his boxer's frame—each night's entirely official and misleading punch clock the essential math to the reverse countdown to retirement, still a good twenty-four years off.

But McAuliffe was like this, pedantic, impatient, a mathematical genius who couldae, shouldae spent a hair more time in school gunning for a stipend in London, but who instead had followed his blood into the confounded world of the Northern Irish Protestant cop. A world that he hated and loved and dreaded for the maze of intrigue that was as mixed as family could ever be. Orangemen and Ulsters. Smugglers and soldiers and serving cons.

And dear good God above, be merciful and save him . . .

But he loved every minute of it.

For work as a PSNI detective came with the mathematics of the damned. Break case after case after case, but toe the bloody line. Toss the dealers and pimps and foreigners into the can 'till death do them (and to the devil) part, but watch the alliances and the soldiers and the honor of family.

As in your sisters and your cousins.

Your mother and your soul.

Which meant McAuliffe rarely slept for the worry and intrigue, but mostly for the latter and sheer complexity of the game. How to gather information on smugglers and dealers while protecting both sides of the family? How to play a game secretly yet openly enough to remain well understood? For to become misunderstood was as good as passing along secrets—for which the price was clear.

A round straight to the patella. Or through the patella with the hollow-tip taking out the entire back of the knee.

That and to be disowned from all that a good Irishman held dear.

Which brought you back to mother, father, little sisters and their kids (although their husbands could happily go to rot).

If McAuliffe was lucky, of course. And if he were quick enough to gain the ear of Uncle Angus or his captain or any of the hard, unforgiving on both sides of his blood.

And if (God truly help him this time) he was able to explain to any of them this third bloody visit from none other than MI6.

Masquerading as MI5, of course.

"You do understand our concern—Mr. De Barra is wanted for his role in the poisoning of the Shimna River," Bistran had begun—or had tried to begin, the spindly shadow of him all but a mirror image of Agent Tobias James. McAuliffe shrugged—not saying and not willing to say aloud that he considered De Barra's role in the Shimna to be utter bollocks. And anyway, the pair of them seemed anything but concerned in this officially secret, but absolutely not secret in the least (after all, this was the Police Service of Northern Ireland), appearance in the officially (but doubtfully) debugged and secure office on Grosvenor.

"Davin De Barra is no concern of mine," McAuliffe came back, official and cold and all but praying that somebody, anybody (but hopefully the damned Continuity IRA chieftains themselves) were listening in. "He is a concern of CIRA and Óglaigh na hÉireann or both. Or so goes the gossip. God help him if the rumors are true."

"Which rumors do you mean?"

"Coy, the both of you, but don't play coy with me. De Barra, they say, abandoned them both—abandoned one and all to work with foreign petrol smugglers. One man against the world and all that."

James said, "You seem well informed."

"Well informed and not an informer, which is the way of the Irish, is it not?"

The two agents stared him down, but to hell with them. Not for the first time, McAuliffe wondered if pre-requisite to Her Majesty's Secret Service was the selling of one's soul. So, he said, "If I can only repeat that I have not opened a case on Mr. De Barra, that I have no interest in De Barra and that at this time and to the best of my knowledge neither does the narcotics section of the PSNI."

Nods in tandem. Bistran's pursed lips seemed to infect those of James. "Your clarity and absolute honesty are greatly appreciated," said James, "But once again, *we* were also *informed.* Of your wide and quite meticulous approach to smugglers of all types."

"Were you now?" McAuliffe shifted in his seat. Just who was doing the squawking this time? Which was otherwise known as passing the buck. After all, this was visit number three. McAuliffe had likewise remained informed that the Brits were coming, and he had quite logically managed to duck visits number one and two. Not this time, however, and by the looks of it, neither his captain, nor VAT scam expert Detective Ian McAllister was about to join in, come to his rescue or at least hang around to vouch for McAuliffe's absolute need to remain mum.

"We were indeed," said Bistran, neither put off nor impressed by McAuliffe's tone. "For your deeds precede you, Detective. Item one: you were successful against the Tanners. Item two, you were equally impressive in the Polish Jakubowski case. Considering that both resulted in seizures of illegal fuel, and that you have been an ardent investigator of the Shimna."

"The bastards who poisoned the Shimna River should rot in hell, much less behind bars—but they were neither the Tanners nor our immigrant Poles."

"Sure of that, are we?"

McAuliffe cut in, his mother's temper coming on. "Do you southerners know the phrase *sure as shite*? The Tanners were pikeys. Small-timers with no business in Northern Ireland. The Poles are troublemakers—and their shite locked up engines far and wide. And we only caught one of them."

"Yet, you made the case."

"Against one of them," said McAuliffe. "And he was not former IRA. Neither were the Tanners. And certainly not CIRA or Óglaigh na hÉireann—certainly not ONH. But you're missing the point."

Mutual frowns.

"This point being," continued McAuliffe, "that the Polish fuel was on the market. In the engines and seizing them up solid. The bastards who poisoned the Shimna were stuck. All dressed up and nowhere to go. As in fuel stuck in lorries—lorries vulnerable, I'd guess, so they panicked."

"The smuggling is a billion-pound-a-year business."

"That it is. And it will double with Brexit. Just you wait and see—Brexit means the border between the North and the South will go as hard as a coffin nail. Just you wait and see."

"And you believe the Shimna was poisoned by the Irish?"

"Belief has nothing to do with it. Neither does a witness that wants to live."

The Brits did not even trade a glance—McAuliffe wondered at that. Two soulless agents that might as well have been both sides of a mirror. Against such drones as these, it was hard even for McAuliffe to keep his temper up. Thus came the last unpleasant pleasantries, the reminders to stay in contact, followed by an Irish quip from McAuliffe that he had his patch *bloody well covered, thank you*—which did, in fact, lead to a final staredown as the two agents sipped the last of their tea. Then there was the proffered card from James. Not a typical business card, but a blank card with a number. McAuliffe made a show of putting it right into his wallet. And for a brief and indefinable moment in time, McAuliffe hoped that was that.

Or so it was until the pair of suits had sauntered out the door.

McAuliffe eyed the clock, synchronized his watch. At five-thirty, he made three phone calls on one of maybe four-hundred burner phones in Northern Ireland, cutting off each at the second ring. By seven-thirty-five, he had sent phone texts with no locations named upon the second of maybe four-hundred burner phones in Northern Ireland, which gave him exactly twenty-five minutes to pack files, lock shelves, consider and reconsider his standard-issue Glock 17 pistol, sign out with the night captain, and banter, bother and beg a low-ranker into driving him not five minutes away with himself slunk low in the back.

From there it was an amble down Grosvenor Road past the parking garage and the old Jury and on across the intersection to the Glass bar, where he gave a nod of recognition to the barman Kelly for a pint in return for not one key but two to the bathroom—a bathroom that just happened to be a flight of steps down, past the first and second bathroom for the customers and near-invisible at the length of a darkened hall. Such were the additional facilities, that the alternate pisser would be fitted with a second door that led to a staircase, which led to a private room healthily stocked with cigars, beer on tap and a full second bar, empty, as luck would have it—apart from a grizzled and bearded wreck of a man sipping on a pint in the corner.

Or so McAuliffe hoped.

McAuliffe pocketed the first key on the clatter down the stairs; the key was a false flag that worked on nothing he could remember. Once below and with the latch shut to the door behind him, he removed the side panel to the second door. This door *did* demand a key, and McAuliffe struggled with the task of unlocking the latch behind him then quickly stepping inside the secret door while hurrying to replace the panel. This was taxing and awkward, and the sheer irony of a cop growing nervous for using an IRA drinking hole made him sweat. Yet the panel slid in place, and the lock clicked back shut, and at exactly eighteen-thirty-five military time he was in. And marching up a second set of stairs so narrow they were almost scraping his shoulders.

The graybeard spoke up before McAuliffe was full up the stairs. "Glad to have you, Sean."

"Glad you were in the neighborhood, Paddy."

"Manky damned stairs, manky secret door," came the voice.

McAuliffe saw the man, Paddy "Ice Pick" McCabe, silhouetted before plate glass in the gloom. The plate glass was something English, Saint George slaying a dragon or something of the kind, but McCabe, despite a plastic foot below the knee, was still a large and heavy man, and McAuliffe could make out nothing but a tussle of long, uncombed hair, the shape of a beard and great, rounded shoulders. It must have been a tough slog up the stairs indeed.

McCabe motioned at the two-tap bar. "Make yourself at home, Sean. Go on—pour us a pint."

McAuliffe eyed the former soldier, and the man put his doubts to rest by guzzling the remaining half-a-pint in his fist. With a nod of appreciation, the younger man stepped behind the bar, dipped two new mugs in the rinse well, and set to filling the first with both precision and care.

"I reckoned you could skip the loo and the stairs," McAuliffe said.

"What? A second secret door? Special-like—for the old geezers like meself?"

"I'd believe it."

"You find it, and a Baby Power on me."

"Cheap bastard."

"Cheeky gobshite."

McAuliffe made his way to the table, slid McCabe the beer. The two grinned at each other, McCabe maybe twice McAuliffe's age and teasing him whenever he got the chance. McAuliffe had always liked it, had looked up to his first uncle since he was indeed a child. It was difficult to change face, to revert to cold mathematics. McCabe saw him struggling with it and cut in.

"In a hurry, are we?"

"I've two serious types asking about Davin."

"Davin De Barra had nothing to do with it."

"And I didn't say what it was."

"None of whatever they're askin'. Davin is his own man now; Devil bless him."

McAuliffe sat back in his seat. He had not expected such a reaction. In truth, he had not expected much of a reaction at all. His uncle was respected, a hero, a patriot of the past and perhaps at times a fountain of information, but generally, he only spoke on topic and once the topic was thoroughly defined. Nothing to do, thought McAuliffe, but to try harder.

"They reckon De Barra for Shimna poisoning."

"Bollocks."

"Not my reckoning."

"And you've tagged him for Lough Ross as well."

McAuliffe squinted disgust. The Lough Ross Reservoir poisoning was as infamous as it was reviled, but framing De Barra or anyone else was not his beat.

"I don't have him for the Shimna, and I don't have him for Lough Ross," McAuliffe said, meeting his uncle in the eye. "But I won't protect him or anyone else for either. Those are our waters, Uncle . . . "

"And I say De Barra is a waste of your time," barked the older man.

"This isn't politics—"

McCabe wanted none of it. "Don't you lecture me about politics, Sean. This is Belfast, and Belfast is always politics. You could have come on the list yourself, you know. But I stepped in—and so did your uncle Angus."

"I do not want to hear it, Uncle. Angus is Sinn Fein. Angus is politics, but if De Barra is a person of interest—"

"DE BARRA WAS A GOOD MAN."

McCabe's fist had come down hard, rattling the braces of the table. McAuliffe stared into his beer, uncomfortable at having drawn the man's ire. Below there was a scraping and clinking, and for the first time, McAuliffe was aware he could hear the music and life of the public bar. He wondered just how safe the safe chamber could actually be. McCabe saw the young man sitting before him, shoulders rolled in, and softened.

"De Barra chose his own way. He's in with the smugglers you so hate. None can protect him, and none should—but he has nothing to do with this, understand?"

"I got it."

"You understand me now?"

"I said I got it." McAuliffe glanced up. His vision had by now adjusted, and for the first time, he saw the hurt, the watery eyes and . . . odd that, . . . the desperation.

But all he said was, "I think I'll leave you now, Uncle. We'll share a pint some other time."

And he'd meant what he said. Even as he descended the secret stairs, even as he had again wrestled and dropped (and partially cracked) the secret panel in the bathroom. Even as he had stationed himself outside on the street, curious to know from just where the limping Uncle McCabe would appear.

He would never find out. McAuliffe glanced up the street then down and, as if a ghost, McCabe was already on the street, moving at pace and drawing McAuliffe as a tail for no reason but sheer effin' curiosity.

Which would leave him a witness to his good uncle's murder.

The motorbike sped past him, burdened by two lean riders in black leather. The second of the two gripped the tail bar with both hands in a fashion hardly smart nor stable. Yet as the bike slowed, he released the tail bar with his right hand and drew a pistol.

McAuliffe began to run. McCabe, hearing the bike and McAuliffe's shouting, also began to run. McAuliffe saw the rider line up his aim on McCabe's back. McAuliffe drew his own pistol and fired just as the rider did the same.

For all he could remember—for all he would ever remember—the rider fired only one shot.

McCabe was pitched forward at precisely the moment that the handlebars of the motorcycle went sideways, spilling both riders to the ground. McAuliffe fired again, realized he had hit the driver, not the shooter, understood the gun battle was on with the singing of a bullet by his ear.

Better sense—call it fear—kicked in. McAuliffe fired and ran, fired and ducked, and took cover between parked cars. There came a watery boom as first the windshield and then the rear window was hit. Then came the rev of the cycle and the shooter was off.

McAuliffe bounded into the open. He ran first to the downed driver, saw he was still alive. Training his pistol on him, he backpedaled to McCabe.

When he saw it . . .

Not in the back, but in the back of the head. McAuliffe jerked away, the child of him not wanting to see, not wanting to remember the atrocity of his dead uncle's brain. Instead, he plodded forward, legs weak, stomach turning and gun still trained on the driver. The man's legs were splayed out. One arm broken, contorted unnaturally behind his back. McAuliffe collapsed into the discipline of his kind, kicked the man's legs wider, put a gun to the faceguard of the helmet as he hollered, veritably screamed for the suspect to show his hidden hand.

The driver screamed back, his voice muffled and his face still hidden by his mask. McAuliffe kicked the man's arm out from under him, spurring a real scream. The man bucked in pain. Seeing the driver had no weapon, McAuliffe ripped open the visor to see bloodshot eyes, a brow heavy as thorny black caterpillars.

The rest was pure drama—McAuliffe shouting for answers, then pointing at bystanders to get back with the sirens coming on. The suspect made his own show of gasping, cursing and then swearing in McAuliffe's face.

"De Barra is a bastard," gasped the driver.

Then came the cry for his mother and a final cough.

And then there was just McAuliffe, shocked aloof, eyeing his dead uncle and the driver he'd shot in the back. And hearing nothing but some voice beyond him screaming. And feeling nothing—as if enveloped in white noise, as if his vision had gone flat 2D.

Until he knew that voice from beyond was his voice.

Until he shut it down, swallowed it cold. . . .

Until he was whispering:

"Shite. This is the real deal after all."

■ ■ ■ ■

The fish kill was worse than De Barra could imagine. So many times as a young man, he had waded this river, hooked sea trout with his father and brother, guzzled beer. Romanced this red-haired girl or that. Once he had even asked a lady's hand in marriage, so many centuries ago, and yet it seemed he could remember none of this, the carnage of dead fish and the stink pervading inside and out for miles.

He could still see it—wondered why it ate at him so and then knew he would be surprised if it had not. The sheer numbers of dead trout and salmon were an astonishment. So many times he'd had but a nibble, but by the thousands of dead, the silver and white corpses stiff as wood under a gray spring sky, you would have thought the Shimna to have boasted more fish than water. As if you could have crossed the river upon their very backs.

He remembered the crowds milling around on the banks, watching the peelers and the strange cosmonauts in their biohazard suits, even while the more pragmatic locals picked up a stiff trout or two to test the smell.

A shake of the head and a dead fish tossed in horror back to the river's bank. Killed by a fuel dump, every living being in the water so thoroughly contaminated that the whole Shimna could have gone up in flame.

And now, wife, off who knew where, his father dead and brother just as well—these were his memories, the death of a river eclipsing all that he had ever loved, the entire slew of remembrance torn from the vibrant to the gray and abstract.

De Barra pulled out a burner phone, whatever cause he'd ever held to now gone, but the soldier in him returning to the here-and-now, knowing nostalgia (or the want of it) could wait. Micky Blake had simply not turned up, leaving De Barra to leave the Browning and ammunition in a temporary hide and hitch to Clonliffe, where he had forked over eleven quid for one night's boozing.

De Barra dialed, not trusting the phone, the old Nokia handed to him by the slops. His finger hovered fat and bent over the dial. Bad burners always seemed to make their way into circulation. Penn's phone had gotten him arrested. Penn's arrest had led to McNeeley being tagged a traitor, for which he was shot.

But that was two years ago. Before the Lough Ross or the Shimna . . .

De Barra realized he'd misdialed halfway through. He hung up and began to dial again. Yes, the poisoning was eating at him. Funny, that's all it really took.

▪ ▪ ▪ ▪

"You've got no witnesses who will talk, McAuliffe—apart from those that put you somewhere in the back of O'Connell's pub for close to an hour."

It was as if he had come back from the dead, as if he had swum up from some deep ocean of cold dead black. He knew there had been the hour on the street. The sirens and medics and armored car and then the sheer army of police—and that had only been the beginning of the long night of care and suspicion and questions about relatives and phone numbers, until then it was suddenly over. Until he was suddenly traipsing back to work in a daze to face the one shock that could truly snap him out of it.

The Police Ombudsman Unit. Nasty buggers whose job it was not to be liked.

McAuliffe wiped his face, doing his best to stifle rage. The two heavy-set bulldogs were more British than Irish, pokers and prodders, their mannerisms and tactics learned in some stodgy, far away kingdom. McAuliffe knew they reported to the constable and to Crime Operations both, but a recommendation for suspension . . . Officers had been suspended for years, with the record holder coming in at five years on half-pay. They had also been prosecuted, but McAuliffe tried not to think about that.

Instead, he attempted to psycho-analyze, to divide and conquer. The taller of the pair, Anderson, was prone to standing too many steps back, almost in the corner of the room. The bad cop of the two, Ratcliffe, was the leaner, looming over McAuliffe as had McAuliffe so many times when grilling a suspect. McAuliffe had heard the stories, the bitterness in the complaints, but in his young, albeit semi-illustrious career, he had never had the pleasure of a good grilling by ombudsman such as these.

So indeed, he began to calculate, to add and subtract. Would they have tapped the burner? Would they have tapped McCabe's burner? Would McCabe have been under surveillance? Would the safe bar have been bugged? Would any or all of the above be true?

McAuliffe calculated the answer to each and every question—and all in tandem—to be 50 percent.

And said, "I was in the loo."

"For an hour, lad? Was it Indian, Turkish kebab? You tell me."

McAuliffe said, "Wanking takes time."

Ratcliffe reared back as if to give him a slap. Anderson stepped forward as if to stop Ratcliffe before things got out of hand. McAuliffe, smaller than either, beamed with pride, thinking that all he needed was a hothead to poke, push or shove him, and he could get the inquiry dropped and probably still take a swing at them both.

Which is when Anderson surprised him.

"We're not here to help you, Detective," he said. "And if you think this is good cop, bad cop, you've pegged us wrong from the start. What we have in our file is you, you and more you. Interesting relatives, including not only your uncle, McCabe—whom you probably shot—but also there's that Sinn Fein prick, your other esteemed uncle, Angus Browne, whose history goes straight back to the Real IRA. Then there is your third cousin and father—"

"My father passed away."

"Yes, he did."

"Keep him out of this."

"Hit a nerve, did we? Well, let's just tap another nerve, Detective. How would you make the case from where we sit? McCabe is a known sympathizer with a past full of every acronym you can find. REAL, CIRA, ONH, you name it. And you're a detective with a stellar record of breaking any and every case not connected to fucking sympathizers."

"So that's how you make it?"

Ratcliffe spoke up. "You can't account for your time or why you were in a high-risk district alone. There's nary a witness—not that we thought there would be—and no sign of a shooter or a gun."

"Piss off. The ballistics will show—"

"The ballistics show you shot an unarmed man, for all we know an innocent bystander, in the back—and the bullet fragmented to pieces in your good uncle's head. So, they don't show shite."

"A bystander with a motorcycle helmet?"

"Nobody saw a motorcycle."

"Bollocks."

"You may think that."

"Is this an internal inquiry or an arrest?"

Andersen stepped forward, replaced the ugly lean of his partner.

"Keep up the lip, and it will soon be both."

▪ ▪ ▪ ▪

On the street, McAuliffe's mind raced. He was truly thinking now, invigorated, threatened, alive. He could picture the case, the secret meetings, the intrigue. The late nights patching witnesses together, pulling in the anti-fraud team or maybe Bert at Scotland Yard over the next nerve-wracking months. Maybe Internal Controls was meant to frighten, but finally, Detective Sean McAuliffe was cut loose on the world. As in every man for himself. As in fuck the lot, I'm going to figure this out, cut no corners, be my own man.

That is not how it went. Not how it went at all.

He saw it first in the reflection of a storefront window. The unmarked sedan tailed him and slowed to a stop. McAuliffe's reaction was to pull for his gun, but in that teeth-grinding, stomach drop of a fraction of a second, he remembered he no longer had a gun—that Internal Controls had taken his gun while he was under inquiry.

So, he just stood there, blank-faced, his hands up as stupidly as a Kung Fu fighter, as the tinted window rolled down.

Which is when he saw Bistran and James from MI5. Or was it MI6?

Whatever the case, it was certainly James, who spoke coolly from the passenger window.

"Good evening, Detective."

"Same to you, gents."

"Care for a ride?"

"Not particularly."

"Get in the bloody car."

McAuliffe did just that, thinking as he opened the door that this was a decision he would certainly regret.

The sedan pulled away, Bistran guiding the Audi easily away from the station and then meandering to Victoria Square. They rode in silence for some two or three minutes before James said as an afterthought, "Your mobile?"

McAuliffe did nothing.

"It's only for the drive. You'll get it back."

McAuliffe drew it out of his jacket pocket, switched it off and handed it over.

Bistran jibed, "Good. We can all be ourselves now."

McAuliffe said, "What's this about?"

James scratched his brow, looked over at Bistran with a slight grin. From there, they were just two heads in the front seat. Against the coming night and the street lamps, there was the heavy outline of Bistran's jaw, the broken, Roman nose, but James was no more than close-cropped hair from the back, a white collar hiding a wide neck, and deep-set, coal-black eyes McAuliffe could occasionally make out in the rearview mirror.

"What this is about," said James, "is your utter pig-headedness—and possible redemption."

"He who casts the first stone."

"You takin' the piss? You are in trouble, son, and we know it. The entire world knows it."

"How do you mean?"

"How do you think? Local news. Two citizens killed by a Razzer, the first man shot a confirmed veteran of the IRA."

At first, McAuliffe said nothing, afraid to ask whether his identity had been revealed. Then he made the calculated guess.

"But you can help me—is that it?"

"We can help each other."

"Here it comes."

James nudged Bistran, said, "This one takes chances, eh?"

Bistran said nothing. He turned right, winding toward the marvelously clean and touristy streets near City Hall. James picked up where he had left off. "This information is deniable, my friend, remember that."

"What information?"

"Cheeky bastard," said Bistran.

"Chancer," said James.

McAuliffe said, "No, really. I want to know."

James gave a sigh as if he was considering giving up. "Useful information. Such as the fact that you, the assassins, your uncle—the whole crying shame—was caught on surveillance film. Which means you could very well be in the clear. You could just be an innocent man."

"I am an innocent man."

"Not without the film, my friend. Not without the film. But what's it worth to you? And I don't mean you, but your family. Your extended family. How much is it worth to be declared innocent, even a hero, in the eyes of McCabe's faction and your family?"

McAuliffe swallowed hard. There was no calculating that.

"What do you want?"

"We want Davin De Barra," said Bistran, voice cold as gravel. "We want him shut down, arrested, dead if that is what you have to do."

"De Barra? What's MI5 got to do with Davin De Barra?"

James said, "What's a card player got to do with poker? As in, the fuck do you bloody well care?"

"Is this the Shimna River? If you think I'll pin him for the Shimna—"

"If you think we care how you pin him, you're wrong, Detective."

"Not in the business of caring," said Bistran.

"Or empathy," added James.

"I want the bastards that poisoned the Shimna," glared McAuliffe. "It all points to ONH and CIRA, and as I'm sure you know, De Barra is not on their welcome list."

"Not on anybody's welcome list," said James. "Look, we'll come clean if you come clean," he said, suddenly with a warmth that McAuliffe did not believe. "De Barra has been under the eye for months. And sooner or later, he'll go too far. We've got Serbs and Poles and Russians buying muscle to smuggle in dopey fuel, and the further it goes, the more likely we'll see violence like nothing you've ever seen."

"Go scare your mother."

"You think we're kidding, do you? The vote for Brexit is in. That means the border between North and South goes hard, my friend. Which means the one-billion trade goes to three or four a year—and that's just fuel. It's enough to fight and die for, but you throw in joker cigarettes, and you might as well move to Bagdad."

"What's this got to do with De Barra?"

"He's recruiting protection for foreign smugglers. He's seen as a traitor to his kind. He's going to start his own little version of the Troubles that will spin out of control."

McAuliffe paused. Gave it a second of thought. Then just for the hell of it said, "Go scare your mother."

"Have it your way."

The Audi stopped in its tracks. Up popped the locks, and McAuliffe stepped out of the car without a word.

He moved at the quick pace of a man about to burst into a jog. He had reversed direction (why make it easy on them?) and when he spied back over his shoulder, saw that the black four-door was on its way, gliding and uncaring, into the night of the city. McAuliffe could not help but wonder if it were a setup. If they had him on film, nothing was stopping a second team (but was this MI5 or MI6?) from dogging him like a flushed quail.

Fine, thought McAuliffe. Dog on this.

McAuliffe gave way to a run. Street soles slapped on wet pavement as he hit Donegal and Castle. From there, he kept running. Nabbed a cab to the edge of the Falls District, where the driver checked his watch and begged off.

McAuliffe paid the fare; the adrenalin within him barely held back as he trotted with the tower of the Divis Apartments behind him, headed straight up Falls Road itself in the rain, then made a break on Cavendish Street, passing mural after mural, the old sofas on the corner of Violet Street before a quick left on Oakman. From here, he walked no more than a couple of blocks.

McAuliffe could pub crawl with the rest of them, and he went into Donal's bar, begged a beer for show and seated himself in the cavernous dark of the booth nearest the kitchen. When no one entered for the next half hour, McAuliffe gave a nod to the bartender and disappeared into the kitchen. He was out the back and into the alley and down two more bars in less than a minute. The right rhyme of a rap and he was into a second kitchen, greeting the two cooks and a drunken mate from school before exiting into a glorious evening rain on Iris Street. This street he followed to Forfar Street where he entered a third bar and then a fourth (each owned by a cousin or distant family member). In the third bar, he left a message with the bartender warning of his final destination.

He was, in fact, feeling rather sneaky. Rather confident. Rather untouchable. That is, until he ditched the beer and the bar, stepped back into the alley, was blindsided, hooded and tossed into the trunk of something fast and uncomfortable, which meant that most bloody likely his plan had gone perfectly or perhaps horribly awry.

And once again, he put the odds at fifty-fifty.

It was a bitch of a ride. He had never wondered about kidnapping victims—had maybe been too self-occupied and calculating to give it any thought. But for the first time in his short life, he felt the terror of constriction, the phobias of the truly trapped, of not being able to breathe through a mask, of sliding and bumping his head into the side of the trunk and then into the spare tire, with his hands taped so tight behind his back that they were soon swollen and numb.

The fear ramped up to ten when the vehicle stopped. Blew exponential when he heard no familiar banter, when the hood was not instantly drawn away. Instead, he was jerked out of the trunk by thugs who damned-near dislocated his arms before having him frog-marched with his head down à la the terrorists nabbed on TV.

Then all at once, he was slammed into a chair, cracked once in the ear with an open hand for no reason that he could possibly discern before the hood was loosened and yanked away to reveal none other than Uncle Angus himself.

"Good to see you, Sean," said the burly politician. "Have yourself a drink?"

McAuliffe bugged his eyes to the light, shook his head to ward off the bell-ring of the slap that was still with him. "You had to fuckin' hit me?"

Angus Browne reached forward, gave his nephew a much lighter slap on the cheek. "None of that now, Sean," he said. "We'll have no blasphemy here." Browne motioned to a body in the shadows behind him. "Get the boy a proper drink."

McAuliffe blinked. Wherever he was, this was not a friendly place. The light over his head reminded him of the interrogations in old-school American films. More worrying, the other men in the room wore the full hoods of the bad times, the masks of propaganda films and killings, and these, he knew, they were not keen to remove.

A drink appeared on the table between them. Not whiskey, but vodka or rum. Browne pulled out a butterfly knife and handed it in silence to a masked soldier. McAuliffe put his chest to the table so that the soldier could cut the tape.

"Did you have to tape me hands? They're red raw."

"Standard procedure, nephew. You never know what a man in panic will do."

"I left the message on me own—you knew what I was out to do."

"So, we hope," said Browne.

Ah, thought McAuliffe, a tremble running through him. God help him if they had their doubts, but drinks or not, Browne was not wasting any time.

"I'm in trouble, Uncle," said McAuliffe.

"Don't we all know it."

"Do you all know who shot Paddy?"

"We heard it was you."

"Bollocks to that."

Browne's eyes went sly. For his heavy build and wide jaw, he could have been a second McCabe—minus the beard and uncombed locks. Instead, gray curls were greased to the tight sides of a mafia lord, and the twinkle in his eye a far cry from the exhaustion he had last seen in Uncle McCabe. Yet the silence continued, and for the second time in under a minute, McAuliffe suffered a second twinge of fear.

Which almost dissipated completely when Browne finally spoke.

"My cousin was a good man," said Browne. "And the bastard who killed him will be punished."

"At least I got one of them."

"That's the story goin' 'round," muttered Browne. "But it's not why we brought you here, Sean."

"Not why—" McAuliffe huffed. Whatever fear still gnawed inside him, his temper gnawed with a sharper bite. "It was me who called you, Uncle. I'm under inquiry—inquiry for trying to protect our blood."

Browne waved this off. "And I commend you, Sean. Paddy deserved no less. But it's the green streak that has us worried."

McAuliffe's brow jumped. "I don't know what you mean."

"You've been asking questions for weeks. Tracking fuel deliveries all up and down the border."

"Of course I have."

"And where do you think that will lead?"

"Dear God, Angus. Did you see it? Did you actually go and see it? They killed the bloody river—whose bloody idea was that?"

Browne's face went from pleasant to cold.

"This isn't the fuckin' cause, Angus. This was our bloody river. And don't think you remember—for I remember. You and me, Dad and—"

Angus raised a hand. It was enough to quiet McAuliffe—and he hated himself for it. But when Browne spoke, his voice was beyond authority—it was in the quiet tone his kind used before a murder. "Enough with the foul language, I said. And whosever's it was, it's no business of yours."

McAuliffe bridled, but said nothing.

Browne said, "There now, son, get ahold of yourself. It's all for the greater good, you see? Until this damned notion of leaving, we had reached a bit of a separate peace, had we not? Sure, the troublemakers bomb and bully, but the past years have been nothing to the dark years."

Browne paused, waited for McAuliffe to bite. When McAuliffe simply sat with his lip out, Browne shrugged and continued. "You are a young man, Sean. You don't believe it, but you are too young to remember the days of an-eye-for-an-eye. You cannot erase the hate, but it's true; the violence, the atrocities, we slowed them down to a trickle. Yet, now what do we have, these bloody foreigners, interfering in local business of all kinds—and true-born Irishmen of the cause, splinter after splinter, leaving their brothers for their thirty shekels of silver."

"Are you talking about me, Uncle?"

A threatening chuckle. "Far from it, Sean. Far from it. But I am speaking of the chaos—of the influx of business interests without honor. And of persons of interest, as you like to call them. Persons who contribute to this chaos—a chaos that does indeed damage us all."

"You're speaking like a politician."

"I am a politician," countered his uncle.

"With guns at your back."

"And before me every day of the week," Browne said. "But you are a detective investigating the chaos, the consequences. Not the traitors upon whom you should hang the crime."

"Lough Ross, the Shimna, the poisoning of our waters? These are mere consequences, are they?"

"You could say that, and it is just beginning, only now set to explode. But the good men you have been investigating are merely caught in a situation not of their choosing."

McAuliffe eyed his uncle and then the masked soldiers behind him. They were getting down to it now, finally, after so much pomp and circumstance. Browne motioned to the rum.

"You can drink that if you like."

McAuliffe ignored that, said, "Name them."

Browne did something of the kind. He passed McAuliffe a list. Nine names, only one of whom he recognized.

"And I'm to arrest them?"

"It's the humane solution, is it not? None of us need the atrocities, the kneecaps and killings of yesteryear."

It was McAuliffe's turn to chuckle. The splinter groups killed and bombed, which left the politicals with their hands tied. Which left the humane solution of creative arrests. "You know I can't help you. I'm under investigation as we speak."

"Times change, situations change. But family, Sean, family is what you count on forever."

▪ ▪ ▪ ▪

The saying is Irish—not many people know that. Most believe it comes from the American farmer, which it does. But before this, it came from the mountains of Appalachia, from the high-mountain people who arrived to US shores with their lilts and fiddle tunes and sayings for every occurrence of the day.

*Forgetting a debt . . .*

McAuliffe raised his hand. The lass at the bar winked and vanished behind the tap. McAuliffe had not taken a drink since the death of McCabe. But he was damned sure he was going to start now. The barmaid swayed around the corner, brought him a shot glass and a bottle of Scotch.

"You wanted Scotch, not Irish?" she teased.

McAuliffe considered the night. Not thinking, his hand went to find his wallet, but his fingers touched the folded paper, the nine names, first. He shook his head, drew out his wallet, and in shock remembered the card with the number for MI6. Fuck me, good thing they hadn't discovered that. McAuliffe drew out a tenner.

"Sister, more of the bleeding Irish is the last thing I need."

"Have it your way, but don't have us carry you out of here—we've long ago had enough of that."

Sass, thought McAuliffe as he poured himself a shot. And drank. Now, what was he thinking?

*Forgetting a debt . . .*

He drew out the card. Nine names—shockingly, eight of whom were altogether unfamiliar to him. But should he be surprised? A billion pounds per year not counting tobacco. Sometimes it seemed that the very earth was being smuggled under his feet.

McAuliffe laid down the card, poured himself another shot. And drank.

Davin De Barra. The only name he knew. A name Paddy McCabe had been trying to protect. A name that had gotten Paddy killed. But for what?

McAuliffe poured another. And drank.

He did know De Barra. Knew him from his rap sheet and McCabe and tales of old. Not your typical muscle. A shooter prone to running wild. As a young man too emotional to get when the going was good, which had meant prolonged shootouts and being twice surrounded and once apprehended by the British. Apprehended and convicted, but as luck would have it, not a Green Jacket he had shot had succumbed to his injuries, which had meant that exactly seven years in, De Barra had been released.

And for the most part, he had not been in trouble since.

McAuliffe poured shot number four. And drank.

His thoughts began to run loose, to ooze and bleed anger, and in the way of alcohol, to bleed into those that were not quite his own.

For he was sincere about the job. Sincere about family, about Browne and McCabe and all of those bad hearts in between. But what did family have to do with poisoners and the river? And if the Brownes among them could not keep their business out of the waters, what was a young detective to possibly do?

McAuliffe remembered McCabe. Remembered him as a younger man in the kitchen singing to guitars. He'd been the good uncle he truly knew. The friend when his father—also a drinker—had gone and died on the road. And now what was family? McCabe's head blown open in the back. Browne passing him a list of names.

And how'd the saying go?

*Forgetting a debt . . .*

It's just the beginning, mind you. We'll be out, and we'll go to hell, sure as shite. First, the lakes and the rivers, then the true dumping will begin. I don't mean gasoline, but chemicals. Toxic waste. Sure as shite we'll be like southern Italy or Sicily an' worse.

McAuliffe awoke from his dreaming. This was not his voice, but a strange voice speaking to another, loudly, up at the bar. But McAuliffe remembered then. He remembered McCabe's pat on the shoulder. Remembered his father's exhausted smile. And maybe, just maybe, he remembered exactly whom he'd been brought up to be.

*Forgetting a debt does not mean it's paid.*

Yes, that's how the saying went.

Funny how he'd just remembered it.

McAuliffe made his way to the bar. There he bummed a phone off of his fellow greens, claiming no battery, blaming drunkenness and a worried wife.

Then he called the number on the card and left an address because, for the first time in his life, just maybe he was—or wasn't—willing to make a deal.

▪ ▪ ▪ ▪

On the night of April third, two-thousand-and-sixteen, Davin De Barra had seen enough. Whatever his original plan with the Browning, it was long ago shot, with Blake having failed, then tried and failed a second time, before finally rescuing him from that dank hotel in Clonliffe only for the both of them to find that the Browning was there, but the extra belts of ammunition were long gone. This had spooked Blake to no end, who was sure that it had been located and left as bait by the Razz.

De Barra was not so sure, was thinking local kids who were afraid to try to move such a monster of a gun without a ride—but he was scared when they'd found it and scared when they'd slid it into to the truck, the missing ammo belts having managed to panic them into full, and abysmal, flight. Not back to the slops, but instead straight to a rented brick apartment building below the Divis—in other words, the last safe house they had left.

And for his part . . . De Barra was also shocked. The slops would come calling, and all they had left was an empty truck (possibly compromised), their pistols (with nary a clip apiece) and an untrusty ArmaLite with no more than a fourth of a magazine and the Browning, complete with maybe thirty rounds max. So, De Barra drank and stripped the weapon looking for bugs or beepers while Blake, all but twitching with nerves, fried eggs and bacon and, in the effort, burnt the fuck out of the pan.

Hard to believe, De Barra thought, snapping the barrel support back into the receiver. He could never get used to the weight, the feel of the .50 caliber Browning in his hands.

How'd the saying go?

The operation was a success, but the patient died?

Because, yeah, right, the safe house. It was probably compromised, as well.

De Barra finished the beer, listened to Blake curse and scrape at the crud in the pan. And he watched the cell phone, waited and wondered about life abroad. Poland. Serbia. Russia, even. Wondered if, when it was all said and done, he might be rescued by the slops.

▪▪▪▪

They picked him up outside the Titanic Memorial Garden in the city center. It struck McAuliffe that these two MI5 (or was it really MI6?) agents were always available, always riding around. It also struck McAuliffe that he had not slept a wink in three days. And what a three days it had been. Killings. An ombudsmen inquiry. And threats from all bloody sides.

Bistran, once again at the wheel, said, "You called, we came."

"That you did."

Bistran pulled away. James muttered to him something unintelligible, and the agents headed into the west of the city.

"You've thought it over?"

"I have," said McAuliffe. "Long and hard."

The agents said nothing. James again tapped Bistran on the shoulder. McAuliffe was struck, and not for the first time, that the pair could have been brothers, how they communicated in grunts and taps with no emotions whatsoever.

"Where are you taking me?"

"Just where you need to go."

McAuliffe ignored that, calculating and content with his suspicions. "Then, back to your question. I have thought it over—but I need to know more. The truth now. Why do you want De Barra? Is it just MI6 monitoring Russians this time, or is there more?"

"We're not much for answering questions, Detective. You know that."

"Oh, do I. And I also know that every Tom, Dick and Paddy is after Davin De Barra, just like the likes of you. And yet it still goes back to fuel. Or maybe tobacco. What do I know? I'm just a young detective with Republican roots, eh? But I can tell you what I think. I think De Barra is the deal. The sacrificial lamb. I think you want peace with Brexit, and the De Barras don't fit into the plan."

James said, "You're paid to think, are you?"

"Call it a personal hobby. And what I also think is that someone's made a deal. Shut down the De Barras nice and peaceful-like to prevent a rehash of the Troubles. Or support the ONH or CIRA, or whomever you like, to run out the Slavic smugglers before Brexit takes hold."

Bistran chuckled. "Sounds like a conspiracy, Detective."

"That it does, Mr. Bond." McAuliffe hesitated, noticed how Bistran keenly navigated the streets, how he followed May to Victoria Street and Chichester, ambling the Audi in circles until he was going the long way around, heading back to Queen Street and Castle to finally wind all the way back to the Falls with the Divis Towers just ahead. "And me, being a son of a Republican, I can almost hold with that. Let the Irish troubles remain Irish. Or let's say I did hold with that until some bastard murdered my Uncle Paddy McCabe—with you two out there somewhere, getting the entire show on tape."

Bistran was past the Divis now. "And your point?"

"My point is, I want to know. And I want a guarantee. I take De Barra—although God help me find him—and you provide the tape, get the investigation dropped. But you give me charges, evidence for De Barra, and not only De Barra. If he's guilty of something, anything, I'll arrest him. He made his choices, and he can pay for them. But I want the bastards that shot my uncle Paddy. You don't help me there and—"

The vehicle stopped. McAuliffe was surprised. They had barely entered the Falls; McAuliffe had believed it would be further in.

"You don't need God, and we've already made our offer," said James, pointing ahead. "You see that red-brick set of flats? You just head up there and ring number nine. Second floor, number nine. Our good Davin De Barra is in there now, fretting away, I should think."

McAuliffe pressed forward so that his face was suddenly between the two agents where they sat in the front seat. "He's in there now? You know this?"

"Call it confirmed," said James.

McAuliffe stared up the street, then jerked to look back the way they had come. Drizzle and red brick. A few parked cars. But no surveillance van, no vehicle that would mean a crying thing.

"My uncle—" he began, but James cut him off.

"He doesn't figure into this, Detective. But arrest De Barra, and you're in the clear. That's the only deal you are ever going to get."

McAuliffe sat back in the seat, met James's eyes in the rearview mirror, but it was Bistran who spoke last. "It's a good deal, Detective. We'll keep tabs on De Barra. You call in the troops any time you want. You'll go down as a hero on all sides. Arrest a gunman in league with foreign smugglers. Make your fellow paddies happy by tossing a traitor in the clink. Move on with your life, and let your uncle rest in peace."

And McAuliffe considered this. Saw his whole life flash before his eyes—his listing as an informant. The knowledge of his actions eating at him, of the calls that would undoubtedly come in the future every time anyone needed a cop for hire.

Which is why he said, "Over there, you say? Apartment number nine?"

"That's right."

"Then let's not wait a minute," cursed McAuliffe. "Let's just go see what our good Mr. De Barra has to say right now."

There was muffled shouting—a *"no, you fool,"* and "our bloody cover"—as McAuliffe flipped the lock and stepped out of the car. Bistran tried to grab him, reaching back over the seat, but McAuliffe threw off his arm and marched in a straight diagonal across an intersection, then straight up to the tenement door. He did not look back to see Bistran and James glare at him, the pair of them on mobiles before the sedan backed away.

McAuliffe tried the door. No luck, but through a narrow glass window, he waved down an elderly woman who was maybe a year short of ninety. The woman pressed her eye against the glass and McAuliffe showed her his badge, and he was in.

Now for the hard part.

Or make that the easy part, for at this point, he was sure he had no choice.

McAuliffe marched up the stairs, found door number nine, and, taking a full step back, kicked it in.

He'd caught De Barra and a second man seated at a table before whiskey and scrambled eggs. Both in jeans and t-shirts, millionaire smugglers they were not. The pair reached for guns, and since McAuliffe had no pistol of his own, he reached for the sky. And for maybe a full second, the three were locked frozen, just staring at each other in disbelief.

Then came the rush. The larger of the two tackling him to the floor before he could get out more than *"Belfast Police. We need to—"*

He was not sure how it had meant to go—just not like this. The two soldiers were atop him, furious now, striking him in the sides, the cheek, the back of the head, even with a pistol jammed deep in his ear. McAuliffe did his best to keep his palms out, up, away, but when they rolled him over and poked him in the face, he made the dirty mistake of fighting back.

He caught a fist to the eye for this, then a second punch to the side of the neck. Then he was truly down, curled into a ball and crying mercy, and just like that, they were off him, the second soldier crashing shut the door.

McAuliffe flinched, thinking there was a shot. He saw De Barra backing away with the pistol trained on his head.

De Barra shouted, "The hell you are?"

"Listen to me—"

"The hell you fuckin' are?"

"Belfast Police. Just talk—we just need to fuckin' talk."

The barrel of a second pistol poked into his eye, the new voice gruffing, "We can't do 'im 'ere."

De Barra roared, "Shut it, you fool."

"We'll 'ave to take 'im with us."

"I said, shut it. You on the ground—talk, you say? The fuck is there to talk about?"

"Just let me—"

"YOU WANT TO TALK, BLOODY TALK THEN."

McAuliffe clenched his jaw, even now finding it near impossible to control his anger. "Me front pocket—take the list out of me front pocket."

There was a moment's hesitation before both men were back atop him, the second man on his legs while De Barra gave him a last punch before searching his pockets with fingers the size of carrots. McAuliffe felt the weight shift. Saw De Barra back and on his haunches. He had the list unfolded.

"Fuck me."

"What?" said the other man.

"They're on to us. On to all of us."

"Give it here."

"FUCK."

McAuliffe used his legs to push his back against the nearest wall. His hands were still up, although he wiped at blood and snot with his sleeve.

De Barra pointed the pistol at his head. McAuliffe saw the shake from six feet away.

"Why have you come?"

"In a bottle, mates," he said. "All of us in a bottle."

More of the rough stuff. De Barra and the second man dragged him to the kitchen, the second man jabbing him a light pistol whip along the way. Then he was at the table, the list of names in his face. The second man had already found McAuliffe's wallet and keys. These he dumped on the table, spreading the credit cards and the badge, which he held up by the tips of his fingers.

"He's telling the truth."

This seemed to throw the men into a deeper panic. That the list held their names was one thing. That a bonafide police detective had just stormed unarmed into their safe house with this very list was another.

McAuliffe held his eye as the pair stormed about the room. They seemed to take turns pointing their pistols at him, yelling at him, then grabbing their beards to think.

"Talk fast, peeler. You'd better talk fast."

McAuliffe did talk fast—or faster than he would have liked. He told them they were wanted. That they were pinned for Lough Ross and the Shimna both. That he knew they hadn't done it—this part was as fast as he could speak with both pistols jammed into his neck—but that he'd also been framed, and the only way out was to bring them in on his own terms.

"And how do you expect to do that?"

"As God is my witness—I don't bloody know."

More threats, the second man begging the first to just top him now.

"Don't do it, mate," said McAuliffe. "They know it's the two of you, and they saw me coming in."

This got blank stares from them both. And brought them back to the table.

"We didn't do the lake. We didn't do the river," said De Barra, not calm, but no longer shouting. Just desperate and talking fast. "The river's why we bloody left."

McAuliffe nodded, not necessarily believing it, but knowing it was best to give them the benefit just the same.

"You're working with who then? Russians? Poles?"

"One Russian. The others were Poles and Serbs," said the second man. "But we haven't done nothing. Just stood around, stood muscle for cash."

McAuliffe's hand was back to his eye. A pistol whipping was nothing like he'd seen in the movies. Apart from the blood, there was something loose and moving under the skin. Bone chip. He'd have to remind himself never to do that to anyone—unless they truly deserved it.

"I thought we'd call the telly," he said. "I know a journalist, but now look at me. Look what you bastards did to me. They'll think I'm a hostage."

"You'll be worse than that if you don't come up with something fast."

Not De Barra, the other one. McAuliffe gave him a hard stare despite the blood. He'd about had enough of this other one.

"Do you have a vehicle?"

The other one cut in. "Don't tell him nothing. Top him and run, I say."

"Shut your bloody gob. Nobody's toppin' anybody." De Barra's face sunk lower between his shoulders, a sincere attempt to meet the detective eye to eye.

"We do," he said.

"Close by?"

"We can get to it."

McAuliffe steadied himself on the table. He'd taken more of a flogging than he'd thought. It struck him that he was not sure that he could walk. "Tell your friend you can trust me. I'm in it deeper than you both. Just being here puts me in the sights of anybody you'd ever know."

It was the truth, McAuliffe thought. The hard, cold truth, and for the fleetest of moments, he thought, So, this is what it feels like. Be your own man. Fly and go free. Which is when De Barra did a funny thing. The soldier pursed his lips, still looking the detective in the eye, and reached over to pat the detective on his shoulder. And for all the angels in heaven, it felt just like his Uncle McCabe.

The rest was a blur. The two soldiers gathered weapons, ammunition and burner phones. Not trusting him, they marched him down a second set of stairs, out into a yard where De Barra stopped to wipe the blood from his face with the old lady's linens. Then came the frog march, half-stumble, half-skip down the alley to an old Iveco truck.

White cab, green box. "Inconspicuous, that," mumbled McAuliffe.

"You go with what you've got," said De Barra as he pulled down the gate and helped the younger man into the back. The second man, maybe it was Blake, maybe not, got into the cab, and they were moving, jerking backward into the alley before McAuliffe could get set.

"We started with the Russians first," said De Barra. "It was them shifted us onto the Poles and Serbs."

"Got it."

"We've got names—not real names, mind you, but we can pick them out."

"Such as?"

"Andrey Lazarov. Russian, just like the man said."

"I don't know him."

"We can pick him out."

The truck rumbled down the alley, as loud as an airplane, and McAuliffe wondered if MI6 would simply cut them off in the street.

"It got messy at the Shimna," added De Barra, feeling scared but good, as if there were a slither of hope with a copper by his side. "But we don't know anything about Lough Ross. Blake there—you might as well know his name—he got us in with his sister's husband. So we had the inside track, which means the ONH had nowhere to go, so they dumped it."

"Who in the ONH?"

De Barra hesitated.

"It'll be all or nothing," shouted McAuliffe. "You want crown witness? We'll have to finger players on all sides—me included—or we don't stand a chance."

De Barra nodded. And he began to name names.

And McAuliffe thought, All or nothing, all right. Crown witness be damned. The three of us will never be able to return to Ireland ever again.

But Blake, driving and in the front seat, was whispering into his mobile.

Neither of the two caught it, the noise of the engine and the mutual conniving getting the best of them. And long after Blake made the call, the two still suspected nothing, both of them staring out the back at the narrow streets, McAuliffe wondering aloud about patrols, but De Barra waving it off to say they had some way through.

Thus, at every twist and turn, under every mural and street lamp when McAuliffe was sure they would be stopped, they kept on. But just they slid down the clean asphalt of Grosvenor, moonlight shining off the drizzle, and onto the highway—at the very point that De Barra was shouting at Blake about how he was driving the wrong way—the truck pulled to the side of the road.

Which is when they knew.

"We've got to stick together," shouted De Barra.

"Fuck you, copper," shouted Blake through the cab.

"I said—"

"Fuck you too, Davin. Let the slops deal with him, that's what I say."

McAuliffe felt his heart skip. De Barra was at the Browning, the muzzle pointing behind them into traffic. McAuliffe saw Blake's ugly face, the sneer shouting obscenities through the cab window.

"'Ave you lost your bloody mind?" tried De Barra. They's 'ave cameras. The shades will be in here in a minute."

"He's a peeler, you arse!"

"We've got nowhere else to fuckin' go," shouted De Barra.

Blake's pistol thrust through the rear cab window to point at De Barra's face.

"Shut it, Davin. Now you shut it this time. We wait for the bloody slops."

Dear Lord, thought McAuliffe. Cops or ONH or slops, someone would hit them soon where they were parked out on this suburban highway—and it took no calculation at all to tell the detective that this was not going to end well. One eye blind, McAuliffe dropped to his knees, feigned fear, made to search the dark for a pistol, the ArmaLite—anything he could remember from the kitchen. He was on the floor of the bed of the truck, doing just this and pretending to cower when De Barra was lit up by headlights.

Which is when McAuliffe came up with the ArmaLite. Cops or slops, he was not going to go down without a fight. The two black Mercedes skidded to a stop, men in black crouching out by passenger doors. McAuliffe's first thought was MI5. Bistran and James. He even thought to call out to them—thought to raise the ArmaLite high to stop them before it was too late.

He would never find out just who they were. The shot came from behind him, cutting through his back and out his ribcage with a kick that cast him forward onto the truck gate. McAuliffe felt the horse-kick impact, gasped at the tearing, crackle of his ribs where he hung on metal and thought this is nothing like McCabe. McCabe went in a flash.

Then came the flash—the second shot from Blake—and then there was nothing at all.

De Barra whirled, couldn't believe it, spun back to McAuliffe, and then hit the deck as the slops opened up on them all. Maybe it was confusion, maybe it was the slops cutting their losses. All De Barra knew was that he was on his back, head between McAuliffe's feet, listening to cannon and clank and aiming back at Blake before he realized there was no point. Blake was dead with his arm hanging loose in the cab window.

"YOU LOUSY IRISH FUCK."

De Barra rolled and crawled to get behind the Browning. He had just heard the sirens when he came up firing from the back of the cab, surprising the slops as he raked engine and windshield and went for figures in black scampering for the backs of their cars.

Somewhere out there would be Andrey—oh, how he wanted to kill Andrey before this was done.

The Browning spat in the thung thung thung of an engine. But it cut out as soon as it began, thirty rounds blown in seconds, and De Barra scrambled back, shoved Blake from where he'd come, then pushed and pulled his body through so that he came down atop him in the cab.

The slops were shooting again, straight into the back of the truck. Maybe they'd seen him; maybe they were just aiming at the silver light of the cab window. De Barra tumbled ass over tits, stuck a hand into Blake's blown out face. Found his own head in the floorboards before pulling the side-door lever and dropping out to the side of the road. Somewhere along the way, he'd grabbed the ArmaLite. Somewhere along the way, Blake's pistol had fallen beside him.

Somewhere along the way, he had fuckin' lost.

De Barra saw movement on the shoulder and gave some poor sod a burst. He crawled forward, snagging the pistol, shooting with the ArmaLite, crawling on elbows and knees, and shooting again. The second Mercedes backed out from behind the first, pulled out onto the highway and fired back at him as it sped away. The first Mercedes was not moving, and at least two of the slops were taking potshots, cursing God above for all he knew and with one calling out in pain to the other.

De Barra listened to the second cry out, waited for another shot, and then pushed himself forward to the truck's rear tire. He lay flat, could just make out a knee behind the Mercedes. Andrey Lazarov—

oh, how I would love that to be you, he thought. But beyond Andrey, beyond the drama of all of them, dead and alive, there came the wail of sirens. Belfast police finally clued in, coming on hard from the south with the lights just beginning to show.

Fuck the peelers, thought De Barra, aiming at the shadow of a knee. Fuck the slops and smugglers—and fuck the fuckin' Brexit and all of those loyal Republicans, and fuck the good ol' IRA.

Then he lay the ArmaLite flat to the side, thought of his wife and a crystal river, and gave old Andrey a burst.

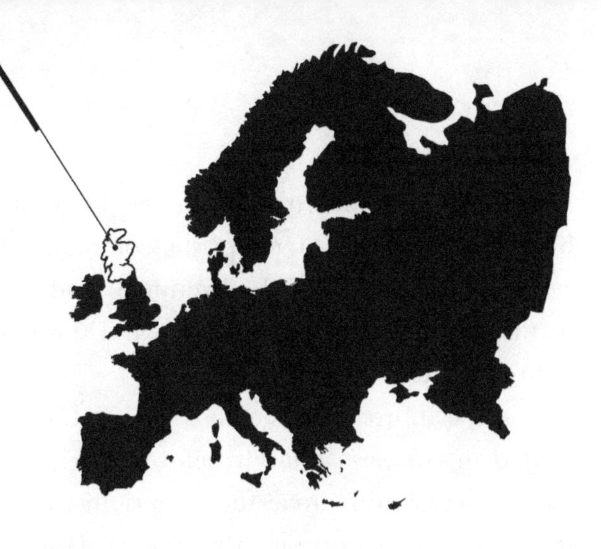

## SCOTLAND:

### Prose and Politics

BY NICK EADEN

*At the age of twenty-one, NICK EADEN was recruited into a covert special forces unit to track and trace high-value terror suspects internationally. Since leaving the service, Nick has utilized his former training to discover illicit money flows being siphoned through offshore structures to nominee subsidiaries, often for the benefit of malign state actors. Nick's recent experiences have focused on conducting investigations in the Middle East, Africa, Russia, and South America.*

As the fog lifted over the old concrete piers of Aberdeen Harbor, non-descript silhouettes moved like ghosts across the loading points that had long ago lost their purpose. Fraser Stewart walked slowly, head sunken to his chest to keep the cold wind from his eyes. An athletic man, six foot two in stature, Fraser was a man of nature. His rosy cheeks showed years of wind exposure.

Since the turmoil over oil prices, his well-being had suffered and his gut had refused to accept the commands from above to remain a secret traveler. His hair had thinned, and eyes had sunken from the torture of permanent uncertainty and the too-often dashed hopes of light at the end of the tunnel.

Fraser approached the door of the office, where he ritually briefly waited to compose himself before entering. As the rush of cold air chilled the greeting area, the receptionist raised her head to welcome the boss. "Good morning, Mr. Stewart. How was your Christmas?"

Fraser unwrapped his scarf and cheerily replied, "Ah, fantastic. The girls came to us, and we ate our body weight in turkey and tatties"—patting his disobedient gut. The receptionist heard the words but didn't believe them. Life hadn't been good for Mr. Stewart for some time, and she knew, as the rest of the office did, that he hadn't taken a paycheck since September.

Fraser walked through the desks, nodding and smiling at those already in. He spoke without breaking stride, fixated on locking himself into his glass office, which overlooked the rest of the staff desks. Closing the door behind him, he settled into his chair and poked at the computer before him. This was Fraser's most pivotal moment of the day. Clicking through the logins, he tracked his way directly to the trading screen. The display bubbled with color. Red and orange bars flashing with digits, sparks of points on the graph drawing across the screen like an electrocardiogram.

"It could be worse," he mumbled under his breath, knowing that this excuse had for some time now lacked comfort. As he settled into the back of his chair, another computer whirred into action. This one, however, brought confidence and purpose directly to its user.

▪ ▪ ▪ ▪

Andrey Pavlov moved the energy drink can to one side so as to slide his digits upon the ergonomic mouse pad custom-made to reduce the pain of his repetitive stress disorder. As a result of his dedication to this screen, Andrey's hands experienced a permanent cold and painful numbness. When off the plastic buttons, Andrey massaged his right wrist, a signal often confused for nervousness. He had rationalized this as an occupational hazard—akin to his father's black lung—which should be expected after thirty years of pounding on computer keyboards.

Andrey moved through his logins, never once with his true identity, to access a gateway to the rest of the world. The numbers appeared in rolling lists that danced across the screen, seemingly erratic, but with a deliberate cadence only he and a few others around the world could appreciate. There was a confidence in his keystrokes, resembling a conductor, with a speed and efficiency that demanded silence from the audience.

Andrey was contacted after the Prime Minister's Twitter account had been humorously hacked, sending out Tweets declaring his resignation and desire to become a professional photographer. While the rest of the world laughed, the Kremlin responded predictably with an aggressive commitment to offensive cyber development and increased digital surveillance against those who dared to challenge their authority.

Andrey ignored the cheap chat scrolling over the right side of his screen and scanned for the user identity he needed. There he was. "Ulysees." Andrey admired the wordplay on a former US president's name. The deliberate misspelling was an arrogant taunt. Andrey respected the hacker, although he had never met him.

Ulysees—You in?
DalieLama—bac. btw, boss loved your last hijack. LMAO
Ulysees—Walk in the park. What's next? zzzzzzzz running rings round these gamers.
DalieLama—They want you to get in $$ account. Credit with $1mil from some chump's offshore.
Ulysees—Credit?

DalieLama—IK! But that's what they said. They need to keep some guy alive.
Ulysees—W/E. send the tx deets.
DalieLama—Sweet

Andrey proceeded to enter the account details for both the donor and benefactor, then hit send. Ulysees confirmed receipt and went offline. Sitting in the low light of this windowless room, comforted by the perpetual murmur of the huge servers that protected his world, surrounding him like digital terracotta warriors, Andrey waited patiently for the confirmation from a virtual friend.

▪ ▪ ▪ ▪

Craig MacDonald sat hunched over a computer he did not understand. MacDonald had been checking his online banking every fifteen minutes for six hours now. The money coming in was needed for the campaign and was more necessary now than ever. He had been promised it weeks ago, but as usual, it was sent at the last moment.

Clicking the refresh icon, he finally exhaled in relief, leaning back in the chair, which rested noisily at the upper limit of its manufactured stress-tested capacity. MacDonald was back in the game.

MacDonald's constituency was Aberdeen North, the former Scottish nexus of the oil industry and a diminishing beacon of success in Scotland's economy. MacDonald was largely considered a mediocre politician, whose unsensational career had been assisted by the region's anti-Westminster sentiment. Since the downturn in oil prices, businesses had shed staff to stay afloat. North Sea oil tax contributed only £59 million to the treasury last year, compared to the £9.6 billion raised a few years ago. People were losing jobs and money at a phenomenal pace, and all of government was being blamed.

▪ ▪ ▪ ▪

Serhii Logvinov moved through another harbor, the bustling and fortune-clad port of Monaco. The white pavement provided pathways for the rich, and often anonymous, wealth of the world. Serhii liked the comfort of this discretion in an impersonal haven.

Serhii entered the office of Monaco's new resident, PetroScek. Walking into the complex on the edge of the marina, Serhii followed signs to the first floor. On arrival at the reception desk, a sleek and efficient brunette asked him to follow her through to the meeting room. After requesting his green tea, he sat alone for only a minute before the door swung open and a chic-looking executive entered with an all-too-obvious artificial smile.

"Good afternoon, sir; it's a pleasure to finally meet. I was surprised to hear you were in town. Is there something you wanted to discuss specifically?" Query from an executive servant who knew there was hell to pay.

Serhii snapped, "It take too long. I must know we are on track."

The executive inhaled to begin his defense before Serhii continued. It was a waste of time—Serhii was clearly out of patience.

"I will bring some guests soon. These guests are very important and need top-style attention." Without pausing, he continued, "When they come, no English speakers in office. And also, no CCTV and 'ears' in the room. Understand?"

Acknowledgment was a nod and scribble in a notebook.

"You will make arrangement for meal at Eden Garden, usual table. After, you take our guest to see Isabelle. Only girls from Crimea."

Nod. Scribble.

"Where are the geo reports?"

The charmless executive lifted his head and began to recite a script he had prepared the night before.

"We will be ready in two days. The final exploration hotspots are being pulled together, and the end product will create a lot of excitement. The methane results are compelling, to say the least."

"Don't be confident. Not too good, otherwise they not bite."

The executive's face signaled a sense of rejection.

"Of course, sir."

Serhii dismissed him with a flick of the wrist and reached for the phone in the pocket of his chinos.

▪ ▪ ▪ ▪

MacDonald's phone rang on the bedside cabinet. The private number didn't discourage him from answering.

"Mr. MacDonald! We talk a long time ago." the familiar voice echoed. MacDonald sat upright, pushing the stray blonde's leg away from him.

"Good morning, Serhii. It's been a while," MacDonald responded, now knowing why the number was private.

"This is true. We have opportunity for you. Or maybe no. I want to give you chance before I give to big company. I always like you, you know."

"That's very kind. To be honest, I didn't think you really had much time for me, just wanted a few harmless snippets here and there."

Serhii laughed explosively.

"Ha! You very funny, Mr. MacDonald. HA! I know small research company, they say they find big in North Sea. Gas, they say. Enough to make Iran and Qatar seem like fart in a *banya*." He deliberately paused to allow for the justified impact. "I think of you. Big opportunity for you to say Aberdeen, the energy of Europe, again. You interested or maybe no?"

Attempting to hide his excitement, MacDonald stumbled out his response. "Well, this is a turn up for the books. Yes, I would be very interested."

"We need plan, which means a few people to talk to. Do you have company for contract? But, ship no pipe."

▪ ▪ ▪ ▪

MacDonald remembered a pitiful man who wrote to him recently from Aberdeen. A man whose company had seen heavy layoffs. Fraser Stewart, a pathetic soul looking for handouts, he recalled.

"Oh yes, I have a canny firm in my constituency. Run by a very capable chap called Fraser Stewart. They have a lot of spare capacity at the moment."

"Good, we have meeting, talk through the detail. You call your friend Mr. Fraser next week. Come to see me in Monaco, maybe two week."

"That's great; I mean, really great. Tell me where you want to meet, and I'll bring Stewart. Perhaps best to do this off the record for the time being, you know, with expenses?" MacDonald optimistically suggested.

"Maybe good. This is fine." Serhii responded.

▪ ▪ ▪ ▪

New Task:
*Fraser Stewart*—Aberdeen Oil and Gas Logistics—
Pipe, no ship.
Keywords:
Gas+Scotland+NorthSea+PetroScek+Buy+Exploration+
subsea+drilling.
5 Days
End*

Andrey noted the location. The masters obviously had another interest other than whiskey and grouse. He'd been given the outline that morning but was "waiting for a call to happen." Andrey's screen flashed to life, and he pulled together the search terms for his crawlers. Each binary insect would retrieve a common digital thread, providing him with the yarn from which he weaved his stories. Andrey's mission was to send targeted but discrete messaging through to this "Fraser Stewart." Andrey was a force multiplier. What used to take multiple meetings with multiple spooks could be constructed from his desktop in hours. By sending ads, popups and media content from multiple, seemingly different sources, Andrey could plant and nurture his narrative. The only variable was time. He knew that the more desperation of the recipient to believe it to be true, the more dramatically reduced was the incubation period.

▪▪▪▪

Fraser paused, entered, greeted, nodded and smiled his way to his desk. Sitting in his chair, he poked at the computer, reaching for the multicolored markets' data. On accepting the status quo, he began to cycle through the news alerts sent through to his email. He dismissed many before a headline caught his eye. "Start-up conducts multiple visits to abandoned drill sites in North Sea." The article laid out a statement from an obscure helicopter services company claiming that business had been better since the exploration company had started using their services again. Fraser was always interested in this, because he never truly ruled out further finds in the North Sea, something he had spoken about and even written an article on for an online industry magazine a few years earlier.

▪▪▪▪

Days later, another headline then caught his attention:"European sponsor provides Scottish students grant for new subsea drilling templates."

Fraser had been in the industry too long not to spot that there seemed to be an undeclared interest in the North Sea bubbling, and his online alerts had been telling him there was something afoot for some days now. A ringing phone broke his train of thought—reception with some politician on the line.

"Mr. Fraser, Craig MacDonald here. It's been a long time. How are you?"

"Fine. This is unannounced. How can I help you?" Fraser inquired suspiciously.

"As you know, I work tirelessly for the constituency, and your letter really made me think. I have spent the last year trying to understand exactly how we, the local government, can support the market here in Aberdeen, like you suggested. As a result of this, I have discovered an opportunity I think you might be interested in. I have obtained a meeting with a new European exploration company very much interested in speaking with us. I can't go into details on the phone, but they have asked that we meet them in Monaco on Friday. Naturally, I told them if they were serious, they should cover our costs. They had no choice but to agree. I can be very convincing when I set my mind to it. Either way, I would very much like you to join me on the trip."

"Wait—so, just to confirm, North Sea exploration . . . new European Company . . . opportunities in Scotland?" Fraser asked, rising to the conversation.

"Yes, that's right, but it's all very hush-hush; we don't want the big boys getting in on it. Will you come with me to Monaco to meet them?"

"Well, if you think it's worth it, and I can offer value." By now, Fraser was well engrossed, and MacDonald could hear the speculation of possibility change the tone in his voice.

"Excellent, I knew you were the chap. Let's keep it hush-hush for the time being. Wouldn't want to let the cat out of the bag just yet."

■ ■ ■ ■

No more than forty-eight hours after his call with MacDonald, Fraser pulled up to a hotel in the French Riviera. As the taxi door opened in front of the pristine Fairmont, Fraser felt the heat gently wash over his face. While hardly scorching, he felt the reassuring comfort of the sunshine bring him to life. After checking in to his room, he showered, getting ready for his meeting that afternoon, per MacDonald's guidance.

He was curious to finally discover the details on this "opportunity," as MacDonald had been particularly vague and almost clandestine about the visit, continuously talking about the "big boys" and their unjust monopoly. Fraser decided to walk to the meeting. Even if it was to come to nothing, at least he could appear for a brief time an image of carelessness, although it was far from the truth. He entered the complex and was directed to an upstairs meeting room, past desks of analysts staring at geo-data and maps, where MacDonald sat slouched and sweating through his suit jacket.

They greeted each other in an overly familiar sense and sat in near silence waiting for their guests to enter. After five minutes, Serhii and the executive servant entered the room.

"Welcome, gentlemen. Thank you for making effort to see us. Mr. Stewart?" Serhii lurched for a handshake with Fraser, ignoring MacDonald.

"It's a pleasure to meet you, Mr. . . . ?" Fraser asked.

"Call me Serhii. Mr. MacDonald tells me you are good friend."

"He does? Well, maybe; I suppose we'll see today," Fraser replied, his eyes moving between Serhii and MacDonald.

"Fraser and I have been looking at the issue of underemployment in Aberdeen for over a year together. We think the opportunity we are here to discuss may be what we are looking for—a way to bring jobs back to the city," MacDonald interrupted, forcing his presence in the meeting to be acknowledged.

"Straight to business for Craig then!" Serhii exclaimed, deliberately using MacDonald's first name to flatter him. "So be it." His eyes gleamed with avaricious excitement.

"PetroScek—where we sit now, have made big discovery." Serhii said as he passed a document to Fraser.

As Fraser slowly worked through the report, Serhii continued.

"This not known to rest of world. But important to keep secret. We want to develop this, using trusted company who moves quickly. Now we are here. You see. Big opportunity," Serhii reiterated, pointing at the document in Fraser's hand. "Good for Scotland and Aberdeen. Change community for lots of jobs and happiness."

"The country more like!" MacDonald declared, showing the room his unbridled excitement.

"Well, maybe, Craig. This is new information for you, Mr. Fraser; you don't know this, but it is true."

"I'm sure it is. After all, I understand that you have put considerable effort into visiting the abandoned rigs and provided grants for new subsea drilling plate designs."

"Mr. Fraser, you have research, very good. We have not been very secret." Serhii replied, shooting his assistant an accusatory glance. "So, if you know, other men know. This means we move quickly."

Fraser leaned back, thankful that the assumption had been correct.

Turning to MacDonald, Serhii stated with some authority, "We like for the Scottish people. But Scotland give so much to London. London always take so much. It makes bad business sense."

"Business sense! It's criminal; bloody English bastards been stealing from us for years. The sooner we are independent, the better." MacDonald's response was spoken with more than a slight tinge of anger.

"YES!" exclaimed Serhii, grateful that MacDonald had got to the point faster than he had hoped. "The investor will not pay for London. They charge too much. Waste the money on immigrants and the lazy. If Scotland is independent, the investor pay, and we all very happy. Scotland, only Scotland. Then for us, we make great rewards for Scotland."

Still enraged from his last outburst, MacDonald leaned forward and slyly observed, "Well, once they know we have struck gas, no one will vote to stay in. And another thing, those European poofs will be begging us to join their poncey little club." Sweat was now streaming down his face onto the plateau atop his gut.

"Like I said, Craig, it is secret," Serhii repeated with authority. "If Exchequer think they lose billions of pound in tax, the independence vote will take too many years delay. If leave, the divorce very expensive because of gas. Must be secret until Scotland leave. If secret, Scotland very strong with . . . poof . . . Europe." To nodding agreements, Serhii asked MacDonald, "Now, you must make election leave. The people do not know anything of this, whatever it take, but you still make Scotland leave?"

"Ah, you see it's not that . . . "

Fraser almost unconsciously interrupted MacDonald, "I can." As the heads in the room turned to him, he wondered why he felt he needed to assure the audience.

Fraser continued, "My cousin is the Energy Minister, and he fucking hates the English." The curse was the first used in the meeting and created a clear impact on the audience that reflected the unknown cousin's hatred.

"He can get into the manifesto. He's told me before that it's all just numbers; they don't need to stack up. The Labour Party is the worst in British politics, and no one trusts a Tory; so, it's neither here nor there. He said the public are selfish spongers and don't believe politicians anyway. All the voters focus on is what's in their pocket, because when you've got nothing, that's all that fucking matters."

Serhii's face remained largely unemotional, except for a slight creak of sympathy. Exactly the face he wanted to portray. Inside, however, he was furious. Why Andrey hadn't discovered that Fraser's brother was Magnus Bridger MSP was unbelievable and almost unforgivable. With direct access to the cabinet through Fraser, they didn't need this bloated MP MacDonald. Serhii dismissed his frustration, safe in the knowledge the honey trap with Isabelle's girl that night would provide the *kompromat* needed to deal with him at a later stage.

"Okay, well, this is plan. Mr. Stewart, you will speak to cousin, tell him lots of gas for Scotland. But only Scotland. You know this is true from your research; you know as much as me. He must make voter leave, even if he lie to them for short bit. It is important for Scotland. Scotland more important than London. Investor want to make lots of money, for everyone. Craig, Mr. Stewart, Mr. Energy Minister. Lots of trip to Brussels, lot of more money for Scotland, for everybody from Europe. This all that matter."

After acknowledgment from Fraser, Serhii then sought reassurance that his firm could handle the logistics as it would be a supersized project.

MacDonald's glee was evident, despite being on the outskirts of most of the conversation and contributing little. He suggested they might have dinner and celebrate with a dram of whiskey. Serhii agreed and declared a dinner reservation would be set for that evening. Waving his guests away, he lifted his phone to his ear.

New Task:
*Magnus Bridger MSP*—Energy Minister Scotland
Keywords:
Gas+Scotland+NorthSea+Exploration+subsea+drilling
(Negative English Context)
End*

Fraser didn't stay on after dinner; he needed to clear his head and was fed up with MacDonald's gloating. A bloated pride that increased in direct proportion to the amount of wine the politician consumed.

MacDonald aside, Fraser knew this was the chance he was looking for and that he could deliver on a promise to get Magnus across the line. On the flight back, he rehearsed the conversation in his head over and over again until he knew all the arguments. Fraser decided not to mention MacDonald's part; as far as he was concerned, the man's participation would cast shadows over the legitimacy of the opportunity, and he knew how territorial MPs could be.

Fraser contacted Magnus and requested to meet the following week. Although at first curious about the call, he agreed to a sit-down in his office. Fraser laid out the situation after being assured of his cousin's confidence. Magnus was strangely warm to the idea, and it took a lot less explanation than Fraser expected.

▪▪▪▪

Magnus had made no secret of the inequality Westminster had shown Scotland. He scorned his seniors for bending over to every English whim. Like Fraser, he had also noticed activity through his email alerts about a European start-up interested in gas exploration over the last week. The idea of an independent Scotland with energy reserves sufficient to gain a favorable new deal with Europe burned passionately in his heart.

A final "screw you" for London after a successful independence campaign was simply too much to pass up.

Magnus had always known that leaving the British Union without a pot of cash would be impossible. He needed to make the voters believe they had the money. He knew there was no way they would ever know what was really in the pot until after the gas deal had come in. By then, he fantasized that he'd be too busy thanking people for re-electing him for anyone to care about a little white lie. The key, they agreed, was to ensure this was not something anyone else could take credit for—discretion was paramount.

Magnus began a campaign of discreet lobbying throughout the Party. His influence gained significantly as he declared to individual members that in his position as Energy Minister, he was reallocating revenues from gas and wanted their departments to have it. He pleaded that each member didn't divulge their new supporter for fear of accusations of favoritism. Each minister swore absolute loyalty to their new companion.

▪▪▪▪

On the understanding their budgets were to be increased, departments started to roll out revised pledges that saw their constituents receive more direct social welfare, provided increased government security against loans to small and medium-sized enterprises, and promised assurances of migration controls on the new hard border with England.

Health-care contributions stood to increase significantly, and large government subsidies for infrastructure developments were to become possible. Over time, the independence manifesto took a form that was almost too good to be true. The contesting parties predictably challenged the financial construct of the pact. And, as Fraser had stated in Monaco, the arguments were dismissed among a slew of claims and counterclaims often lost in the run-up to general elections.

The First Minister was briefly suspicious of the new financial optimism, almost to the point that she was going to order the Party to justify their positions. However, soon enough, the First Minister received new polls, which showed a huge swing toward the independence vote. It began to look like her name would go down in history as the premier that liberated Scotland from the oppression of Westminster. Her long-awaited calling to the history books had come.

▪ ▪ ▪ ▪

Andrey and Ulysees had launched a cyber campaign. Systematically, they released hacked details on the most credible opposition members in the Westminster cabinet. The Conservative Energy Minister, who had begun to make noise about the impossibility of the current energy reserves supporting the country's ambitions, had his bank statements leaked to *Newsdrop*. Bank statements that revealed sizeable rental incomes from his Westminster apartments. The cries for a criminal investigation were heard, headlined in news reports, and he was duly suspended.

The social media and press sites in Scotland experienced an unwitting optimization, filling the top search results with negative media on those opposing the independence campaign. As Andrey's social media engagement took control, Ulysees hijacked European accounts to support the independence campaign, with fictional well-wishers from the continent sending support for their European compatriots.

By examining online user sentiment, Andrey introduced likeminded users to each other through seemingly innocuous contacts. A "like" on a post would fire a flare into the network that Ulysees had created around the subjects, bringing support to the sentiment and centralizing core fanatics.

A speed dating of political rhetoric combined for the maximum commotion. The effect, he knew from experience, then propagated into the real world. Soon after, regional and then national news stations began to report the "facts" presented by bloggers of x and self-appointed representatives of y, who quoted with confidence the statistics of the oppressed, statistically confirmed by their many online contributors.

Andrey examined comments from investors on international markets, then sliced and diced the message to portray an unwavering commitment to an independent Scotland. Andrey and Ulysees bypassed the press and piped the rhetoric straight into the electorates' minds. Any competing press opinion was rejected by most, who were hearing ten Leave arguments to one Remain.

The battleground was scorched as voters rolled out in droves to the ballot boxes. Turnout was marginally smaller than the 85 percent in the previous vote, but the split was far more obvious from the outset. A majority rallied behind the independence slogans and waved Saltire and EU flags. Westminster lost control of the electorate. Media messaging fell on deaf ears. Any contest to the budgets of the independent manifesto was discounted from the start. The previously unimaginable became a reality.

■ ■ ■ ■

MacDonald was front and center on this "Momentous Independence Day," preaching to the constituents of the Hope and Glory public house in Aberdeen. One month from now, when his secret was out, he alone would be established as the savior of Aberdeen and likely given the key to the city.

Magnus and Fraser met the following day after Magnus had completed his celebratory duties with the First Minister.

"We did it. Now we can start building again. Have you heard anything from your friends in Monaco?" was Magnus's first question.

"Nothing yet, but I expect they will be in contact soon. Time is of the essence to keep the big boys out," responded Fraser.

"It'll need to be soon. The First Minister wants to begin discussions with the EU in two weeks," Magnus added impatiently.

■ ■ ■ ■

Serhii watched the ticker tapes scroll across the news screen. The last-minute push had consumed all their energy. Andrey and his accomplice had worked for twenty-four hours straight prior to the vote. He could just imagine a pile of empty energy drink cans under Andrey's desk.

Now that the die had been cast, they had one last flurry of punches to throw. Serhii was not pleased about being drawn into this personally, but the Kremlin left him no option but to tighten the cilice in repentance for his previous failings. He also knew this was to be his final act.

■ ■ ■ ■

Heidi Sheller woke to the news of the referendum outcome. A rotund MP in a pub declaring Independence Day before a group of Saltire-waving disciples. Heidi hadn't followed the independence vote closely, as she had been reporting on the bank statements she had received from an anonymous source a few weeks before. Still bathing in that success and successive hangovers, she crawled to the kitchen, placed a pod into the coffee machine and struggled to find the toaster—all on autopilot.

While the bitter stench of coffee roused her, she thumbed the power button that woke her laptop from the same point it fell asleep alongside her last night. She opened the email and buzzed through a list of alerts relating to her current stories. Heidi stopped when she noticed another email from "DalieLama," the source that had been so generous with the bank statements.

RE: Because you are worth it ☺

She opened the email, despite her better judgement. A raft of photos began to cascade down her screen. Image after image of pictures from some sun-drenched haven for the rich and famous. A group of men meeting at an unnamed restaurant appeared jovial and confident. A veil of recognition waved over her for one of the faces. A rotund man sweating in an obviously alien environment. She whipped her eyes to the TV set. The same man was standing on a table in a nearby pub. Craig MacDonald of Aberdeen.

The television went on mute as she scrolled through the remaining photos. It was him. It was the politician. Then she noticed another man appearing to pay the bill. "Jesus," she shouted at her screen. "Serhii Logvinov. What the fuck are you doing there? In fact, what the fuck are any of you doing there?"

Heidi knew of Serhii. He was a prominent Russian oligarch, closely aligned with Putin's St. Petersburg clan. Serhii had made his money racketeering in the aftermath of the Soviet Union's collapse. He was a lesser-known dealmaker, but a hugely powerful man who was rolled out in times when Russia wanted to exercise its foreign policy discretely. Heidi knew he'd been off the grid after the Maidan revolution in Ukraine put an end to attempts to keep Kiev at arm's length from Europe. Not surprisingly, he'd arranged for the now-famous "little green men" as his fallback option.

Her cascade of digital photos changed background settings in a dramatic fashion. The scene moved to what appeared to be a private room, with MacDonald. She struggled to make him out until a photo of him arching his back in pleasure and facing straight into the camera in a brief moment of ecstasy. The last photo seemed to show him apologizing to the female in the room before passing her a wad of notes from his jacket thrown across the chair in the corner.

Finally, she discovered an audio clip attached to the email. The audio sprung instantly to life with absolute clarity. So much clarity that the papers shuffling and toe-tapping were crisp and distracting.

"Bloody English bastards been stealing from us for years. The sooner we are independent, the better."

"Straight to business for Craig then! You good friend."

"We think the opportunity we are here to discuss may be what we are looking for."

"My cousin is the Energy Minister, and he fucking hates (inaudible). He's told me that it's all just numbers; they don't need to stack up. The (inaudible) are the worst in British politics and no one trusts (inaudible); so, it's neither here nor there. He said the public are selfish spongers, and that's all that fucking matters."

"So, this means we move quickly. The investor will not pay for Scotland. Waste money on immigrants and the lazy. Then for us, we make great rewards. Craig, it is a secret. Lots of gas. This is plan. Speak to cousin, lots of gas. Investor wants to make lots of money. Craig, Mr. Stewart, Mr. Energy Minister. Lots of trips, lot of money. This all that matter."

The audio stopped. Heidi pulled up a local broadcast on her laptop and replayed the politician's pub sermon. She played the audio and the news in unison, repeatedly. MacDonald's voice with Serhii and the remaining Scot was Mr. Stewart.

She loaded the internet search engine looking for familial connections of Scotland's Energy Minister—Search: "Magnus Bridger" MSP. The results spawned dozens of political reports on the minister's achievements and recent comments on the independence campaign with photos of him voting. She shifted the searches from his professional façade to his intimate personal environment. She searched "Magnus Bridger + sport." A few lines down on the second Google page a link appeared. The image in the article showed Magnus standing next to a tall athletic man. The caption below read "Cousins Magnus Bridger and Fraser Stewart dominate the game with six tries between them."

Heidi's searches on Fraser Stewart soon turned up the company profile of a local businessman in Aberdeen who had previously spoken to reporters on the opportunities that may still remain with untapped resources in the offshore industry. She continued to build her profile on him, including the dire state of his company financials. A desperate man.

Time was now of the essence; this story had to be filed. As quickly as possible for maximum impact.

DalieLama—AND SHE BITES!
Ulysees—I see. She's searching Bridger as we speak. She's hot; I would have delivered in person!

MacDonald woke from an alcoholic coma two days after the vote. As he peeled the thick blanket off, he swung his legs to the floor from his sofa and kicked aside an empty whiskey bottle he conquered single-handedly the night before. After shaking off the fuzz, he rocked himself to his feet and wandered lazily to the kitchen for coffee. He soon returned to the sofa to look for his phone. He'd been receiving congratulations in quick succession from people he thought barely liked him. He thumbed the keypad and dismissed the "battery low" banner. Suddenly the phone sprang to life, vibrating in his hand.

"Hello, Mr. MacDonald speaking."

"Mr. MacDonald, it's Heidi Sheller at *Newsdrop*. I wonder if you had time to discuss the independence vote."

"Oh, hullo. Well, you should go through the press office, but I understand if you want to speak to the organ grinder, not the monkey. How can I help you?"

"Indeed, sir, I'm looking to speak to the man behind the result."

MacDonald's posture straightened, to present himself as more statesmanlike despite the lack of audience in his apartment.

"Are you able to provide any details on your relationship with Serhii Logvinov and Mr. Fraser Stewart?" Heidi asked, attempting to hide any joy in the inflection.

MacDonald froze, paralyzed by the question.

Heidi continued so as not to lose momentum—anticipating the hang up.

"We have information to suggest that you are a business partner of Mr. Logvinov and that he was influential in support of the 'Leave' campaign. In fact, our information suggests you are so close that he lavished you with expensive meals and pretty women in order to influence the independence vote."

Silence.

"We will be running the story and hoped for comment from you. Sir? Are you there?"

The line went dead. Similar calls went into Bridger, Stewart and finally Serhii, with no comment from any party. It didn't matter to Heidi; she had the photos and was rolling hot as far as her editor was concerned. Legal signed off, and the printing press fired up.

"'Sponger' Scotland Sold to the Russians," a common headline in print and digital media.

The fall was, as often is, as swift as the rise.

MacDonald had barely moved in the last twenty-four hours, except to form a steady relationship with the "number disconnected" voice that was apparently looking after Serhii's phone for the foreseeable future. Bridger had been called into the First Minister's office as word spread among the Party. His pleadings that the audio was taken out of context fell short of a confession that he had agreed to do his cousin's bidding and inflate the manifesto budgets.

Fraser hadn't left the office since the call a day before. He double-locked the office doors, as the cacophony of telephone rings echoed around him. He knew as soon as he had received the call from a reporter that there was no discovery. There was no deal. There was no future, for him at least.

He'd shaken a bottle of pills to loosen the load. He had placed the prize whiskey, an award from his junior rugby club, next to his knee while he raised the pill bottle to his mouth. After the powder in this mouth had formed a chalky paste, he held his nose and poured the whiskey in as well.

The political whirlwind had begun before the bottle crashed to Fraser's side. The press focus shone intensely on the manifesto numbers. The Party failed woefully at defending themselves in the aftermath of apparent Russian interference.

Brussels called crisis meetings after the plot had been exposed. They had willingly believed the manifesto pledges and ruled out Westminster's protests as sour grapes. Scotland's biggest trading party was out of the EU, or soon would be, and the EU family, who had preached togetherness and unity, were now responsible for Scotland's well-being. Despite the unpalatable thought of enrolling another burden into the Union, the decision had been made, and Brussels could not change its mind.

In the weeks that followed, the Party tried to put on a brave face, but the truth remained that they entered the negotiations with manifesto pledges based on a fictional fiscal position. Brussels, naturally, imposed heavy terms on the contributions Scotland had to make to the EU for membership status.

Brussels wanted money up front for this group of "spongers." The increased contributions from Scotland placed an even greater burden on the economy, resulting in health-care cuts and the rollback of education pledges.

■ ■ ■ ■

Serhii relaxed on the balcony of his villa. He'd taken to staying in while the heat died down and canceled his travel plans after the story broke. He knew he was a distant pawn in the Kremlin's foreign policy. He would be sacrificed on the chess table when Moscow decided an alternative "fixer" would be more appropriate. For the moment, he basked in the knowledge that remaining here placed him safely under the protection of Article 6 of the Human Rights Convention.

A convention that had served his predecessors well when the Kremlin came knocking, which they always did.

# ENGLAND:

## Medical Care sans Money

BY PETER HEATHER

*PETER HEATHER is a Professor of Medieval History at King's College London. He read for a BA in Modern History at New College Oxford and completed his doctorate on relations between Goths and the Roman Empire at the same venue. After a (very) brief stint in HM Treasury, he has held teaching positions at University College London, Worcester College Oxford, and King's College London.*

"GOOD MORNING. . . ." Jonathan jumped abruptly into consciousness. He really needed to get a radio with a mute button. And set the alarm for an hour later.

Nothing like waking up to the grim tidings of a pert blonde reading yesterday's news.

Well, he liked to think she was pert and blond. For all Jonathan knew, the broadcaster was a dowdy housewife approaching her late forties. Still, a man can dream.

"It's 6:00 a.m. on Tuesday, December twenty-second. This is the *Today* program on Radio 4, and these are the headlines from the BBC. Scientists confirm that 2021 is set to be the warmest year on record. . . ."

More "good" news would inevitably follow. Hitting the off button on the radio and simultaneously dragging himself out of bed, he quietly mused that global warming was doing nothing for his fucking freezing bedroom. A room made even more chilly by his wife's insistence on leaving the window open all night.

Global warming my ass; Britain was in the middle of a brutal cold snap, and a great deal of it was now crawling up through his feet toward . . . Damn, now he needed to pee.

Helen was downstairs in the kitchen, working her way through a second coffee.

Naturally an early riser, she also started work before him and tended to avoid Jonathan, who was not a "morning person."

She, on the other hand, could be guaranteed to be wide awake, ready to chew over any issues that needed sorting out before plunging onto another day of work. He would listen, mumble over his coffee and reach for the paper. At least it did not yell at him or demand answers.

But at least the kitchen was warm. Blame Brexit; while oil prices had remained low, the pound continued a gradual decline to obscurity. The pence no longer was worth a pence—was actually about a quarter of its previous value—so they had to economize on heating.

Another reason the bloody bedroom is so cold, came into his head apropos of nothing.

"Have you thought any more about those school reports?"

Of course I bloody haven't, he thought. Having got in at ten-thirty last night, grabbed something to eat and gone to bed, he hadn't really contemplated anything more than sleeping off his minor buzz. A few pints with the boys, you know. Helped take the edge off the cold walk from a not-so-nearby Tube station.

What he actually said was, "They're a bit discouraging, aren't they?"

"Discouraging? They're a complete disaster. I've been awake most of the night thinking about them."

Trust the missus to fret.

The twins—boys: Jake and Andy—were seventeen with university on the horizon, but school was going gently yet titantically wrong. With all the slow inevitability of a garden tortoise, their grades had been heading toward an academic cliff edge for the last three years, and now it was getting serious. . . .

"One B between them in their mock exams, and the rest D. They're not going to get into any course worth having, and there you are. Life chances stuffed, aged eighteen." She was on a roll, one he had heard at least once a week for the last six months.

Helen could be jittery on caffeine, made worse by a lack of sleep, but he knew she was right. They were charming, hugely intelligent boys. They didn't do drugs or steal cars, they loved their mother, and everyone said what good company they were. They knew lots about lots of things and had a great sense of humor.

Starting work later, he usually did the school run, and they often had him in stitches, even at eight-thirty in the morning. But they were bored out of their minds at the local state school, where good teachers were few and far between (though not non-existent, hence that solitary B). Two young men stuck in a system that incentivized staff to get weaker students through and didn't have the resources to worry about anyone else.

Enough self-motivated ones—usually girls, channeling all that teenage anxiety—did it for themselves to give the school a smattering of the good results it needed to avoid administrative review from London. The inspectors stayed at bay, while lots of bright but feckless others—usually boys basking (although they didn't know it) in the glow of a temporary immortality generated by huge amounts of testosterone—drifted on to mediocrity.

He knew where this conversation was going next.

"We've got to get them out of there, Jonathan. You know as well as I do that these days you're competing with the brightest and best from across the whole damn planet. To have any kind of decent career, they need to go to a better school."

He hated the thought of private education. A state-school boy, he'd defined himself by that in his younger days, hugely enjoying outperforming all the smug, entitled products of the private sector, at university and beyond.

He looked up.

"I don't want to hear it, Jonathan. You went to an elite grammar, much more like bloody Eton than most state schools, and you've been unutterably smug ever since. You didn't see that look on Jake's face when he gave me the report. Real despair—in a seventeen-year-old, for God's sake. He knows. He knows he's not built to be an entrepreneur or a rock star. They both need to be professionals. But right now, they're going to have to pay a fortune for a grisly course somewhere awful, and then what's life going to offer them?"

They'd had versions of this conversation more times than he cared to recall. He'd fended it off in the past. Equality of opportunity was burned deep into his psyche. He despised private schools as much as he loathed private health care. His heart bled when he thought about the human experience behind the mortality rates of the developing world, and it was offensive to him that richer people in the West should have so much of an advantage where it mattered so much. Bigger cars and houses, fine, but longer, healthier lives? That was disgusting. Which is why he'd dedicated his working life to the National Health Service (NHS).

Besides, his own school results were pretty mediocre until he was about fifteen and found enough iron in his soul to take control. His sons were really bright boys; they'd make the same transition, and do just as well . . . perhaps.

Except they hadn't, and they weren't, and it was beginning to look terminal. It had also been dawning on him that his own triumphant narrative of personal achievement was miscast. Going to a good school with excellent teachers, the stimulation of intellectual excitement had been there for him on a plate, when he finally woke up long enough to notice, but if it hadn't been, he couldn't have done it by himself.

"I agree," he said.

Helen looked up in surprise, having heard that other line a dozen times.

"In principle," he added quickly. "But how the hell are we going to afford it? There's no point in sending them somewhere second rate, and a decent private school is thirty-five grand a year. We're barely making it as it is, so we can't remortgage. . . ."

Brexit hadn't made Britain cheaper but had made many a Brit broke. Crowded together on an island about the size of northern Michigan, with a population one-fifth the size of the whole US. Prices had only one place to go—up. Everything cost more—as the pound had gone down—except for their salaries. They both worked in the NHS, both in highly demanding positions, but there'd effectively been a pay freeze since the referendum, and taxes had gone up too. The government was not about to pay more for civil servants—Parliament saved the expenditures for American weapon systems and more police. Seemed broke citizens were more apt to be criminals.

They batted it back and forth—the "how will we afford this" debate—while the knot in Jonathan's stomach slowly tightened, and he watched the despair grow in Helen, tears rolling down her face. . . .

All for naught. She left for work. He slumped over a second cup of coffee.

■ ■ ■ ■

"Mail and water on your desk, Dr. Lawrence."

"Thanks, James. Situation meeting at eleven?"

"Then you can have an early lunch. Possibly. . . . But it's party time at 1:00 p.m., and the ambassador won't be kept waiting. Followed at four by the strategic planning group. Anything else you need?"

"No. If you brief me at ten forty-five, that'll give me an hour to get through the paperwork."

Jonathan sat down and poured himself some water, silently blessing the fact he had such a dedicated physician's assistant (PA). As usual, James had pared it down to the absolutely necessary, but there were still a dozen items to get through.

Primarily it was all a question of initialing or signing, but good administrator that he was, Jonathan made sure the bottom line was clear in his head.

That's why he was here, stuck at this desk most of the time. His original specialization had been oncology: "Bloody good I am—or was—too." Might as well stroke his own ego. . . . No one else was going to meet that need.

A good doctor, but a better administrator. He had a gift for the big picture, which, combined with problem-solving skills and a cheerily resilient sense of humor, made people willing to do things for him.

Even before Brexit, financial issues were pressing. An aging population, new treatments, ever-escalating drug prices—people just didn't get it. They wanted the NHS but didn't understand that an ideal service was impossible. The absolute best was always going to cost more than anyone was remotely willing to pay.

So he pared away, cutting away at fixed costs and redundant bits of the structure. All in an effort to free up existing resources, and make the best of any new monies politicians were willing to commit.

Which had brought Jonathan's finest hour. The Oxford Trust's post-Brexit Sustainability and Transformation Plan had been a triumph. Old premises shut down and sold off, but only to build new ones. And no compulsory layoffs; comprehensive retraining offered wherever necessary or desired. Greater efficiency in the use of staff time, and in reclaiming costs from patients ineligible for free treatment.

Of course, there had been a fuss—the NHS was a sacred cow, where change was perceived as an unnecessary evil. Nonetheless, his efforts helped ensure the Trust eliminated its deficit, continued to hit targets set by a rapid succession of Health Ministers, and received its due reward in terms of improved resources.

As did Jonathan himself. Whereas the salaries of all medical staff—consultants and downwards—hadn't really moved since the Great Crash of 2008, and in fact had been slowly declining with the pound, his package was generous.

Wouldn't stretch to private education, he thought, but it does at least mean we can live in a nice house with some hope of owning it. Or, maybe, our grandkids. These new lifetime mortgages get you on the property ladder, but defer real ownership more or less indefinitely.

Still better than Japan, where one-hundred-year mortgages were now a common practice.

The pile on his desk nagged for attention. Enough musing.

It was the letter with a foreign stamp marked *Private and Personal*—that caught his eye and was the first physical act of the workday. He pitched the damn thing into a trash can. He knew what was in it, having opened the first one last June, and similar envelopes had been arriving monthly.

Now for the mundane. The only thing he really stopped to think about was his copy of the Trust's report on non-national employees, which had been sent into the Home Office a short five days ago.

The report came with implications that were potentially toxic. Amber "Bloody" Rudd had started it. Rudd, an old Remainder trying to curry favor at the first post-Brexit Tory party conference, demanded firms should own up to how many foreigners they employed. It got shouted down at the time, but when the Ukippers returned triumphantly to the Tory fold, the new Home Secretary made it compulsory for all publicly supported bodies to file such reports.

Jonathan could smell blood in the water. This report was going to draw scathing rebuke for the Trust. NHS had not been training enough doctors or nurses for years. Instead, they stole skilled personnel from overseas. Nurses from the Philippines, doctors from Italy or Spain, and skilled staffers from India.

Some of this workforce, particularly doctors and nurses—Scottish ones as well after independence—had gone home when salaries became less attractive. But the DUK—the Disunited Kingdom as it was called—still paid more than the developing world. As for functionaries . . . ward assistants, cleaners, and porters—where the pay was too meager to attract enough locals—immigrants were his only hope.

Some. Not just "some." Forty percent of the Trust's employees were not full citizens.

▪ ▪ ▪ ▪

"Let's start with Accident and Emergency—A&E."

"Angela?"

"OK-ish, Jonathan. Waiting time currently averaging five and a quarter hours, so we're inside target."

It had caused a huge fervor two years earlier, but the Department of Health had finally accepted that the old four-hour target was undermining good practice in a world of tightening belts. Hospitals were just doing anything to get people out of Accident and Emergency within the limit, no matter how non-urgent the case. Or consequences for other hospital functions . . . like suddenly canceling cancer operations because someone with a broken leg, waiting for an x-ray, had to be shoved in the nearest available bed after three hours and fifty minutes.

Five and a half hours was now the target, and that had proved more manageable. For once, the politicians ignored public outcry in favor of logic. Too bad they had not been so brave when the question of departing the EU first emerged.

"Any pressures building?"

"Flu."

He'd known the answer before Angela spoke. "The cold snap is starting to generate more cases, and the worst ones are clogging things up. Last week, the average wait was under five hours, but it's going to approach the magic five and a half."

"OK. We'll have to watch this one carefully." Missed targets meant financial penalties and further trouble making ends meet.

"Bob, how about the bed situation overall?"

"Again, not too bad, really. We're more or less full, but about fifty percent of our patients are ready for discharge."

The Trust controlled about 1,300 beds.

"I've got my people all over social services and researching patient home circumstances to see who we can get rid of, and I'm hopeful it will be about a quarter. Which should free up enough beds for ninety percent of tomorrow's scheduled admissions, again just about within target."

In 2016, about 40 percent of hospital beds were occupied unnecessarily, and the figure had been slowly creeping up, despite the best efforts of hospital administrators to find ways—not far short of blackmailing relatives—to get patients out of the building. If it hadn't been for all the advances in keyhole surgery that allowed you to send people straight home, they would never be hitting the 90 percent target for scheduled admissions.

The reporting then turned to the hospital's individual departments, where the situation was reasonable. Only about 5 percent of today's scheduled operations had been canceled, and they'd been able to shuffle staff to make sure that these were mostly tonsils. Most of the cases with life-threatening conditions had been admitted on time.

"Thank you, gentlemen and ladies," Jonathan concluded with a parting grin. "Looks like medicine's back on the menu. . . ."

▪ ▪ ▪ ▪

"Welcome, everyone! It gives me the greatest pleasure to welcome you all here today for the opening of NHS Oxford's newest treatment center."

Jonathan really was happy about it. Despite all the financial problems, they'd managed to get their hands on one of the new-generation linear accelerators from the States, even if it had taken a bit of help. Pride before the fall . . . and all that other crap aside. Often made him think politicians should be required to take the Hippocratic Oath.

"And let me now invite Ambassador Farage, who made it all possible, to cut the ribbon, as breaking a bottle of champagne on it probably wouldn't be such a good idea."

To polite laughter, the Ambassador stepped forward to do the honors. It wasn't normal, of course, to have the UK's man in Washington open a cancer treatment center in an Oxford hospital, but the Ambassador's connections with the Trump administration had worked wonders. These new accelerators got the drugs to the tumors with pinpoint accuracy and were so much more effective than existing systems. And the best ones were being built in the States, where it was boom time for the medical technology industry after the repeal of Obamacare.

That was why Jonathan was struggling with the aftereffects of so many skilled staff disappearing over the Atlantic—or over the Channel to those Bond-villain clinics in Switzerland. The emerging global elite would pay any amount for the prospect of eternal life or as close thereto as was humanly possible—channeling their inner Gilgamesh—and the price and variety of new treatments on offer just kept going up.

Jonathan was political enough to hide the fact that he utterly loathed the man, but Farage had got them out of a hole. Negotiations had begun four years before when the price was already steep, but it kept going up as the pound spiraled gently downward. They'd had to settle in the end for a refurbished model from a Swiss clinic, but it was still a wonderful machine.

There were a couple of old Ukippers on the management team who knew him from the Referendum campaign, and the Ambassador was never one to shy away from a little good publicity. So, a few phone calls later, with a price and payment schedule crucially fixed in pounds, the machine was on its way. They were kind of renting it, but that didn't matter. Oxford was now the only publicly funded medical center in the UK offering state-of-the-art cancer treatment.

It was indeed a red-letter day, and the party was a good one. Decent canapés, good quality fizz for those who weren't looking at an afternoon shift, and, of course, some proper beer for the Ambassador.

▪ ▪ ▪ ▪

Strategic planning, later that afternoon, was a less cheerful occasion. A session made even grimmer given his text from Helen. The boys' school had been all over her. Andy had missed half of his morning classes. They may not teach so well, he thought, but they're good at keeping lists. (No surprise, the government paid for attendance, not performance.)

List-keeping was the most basic form of literacy there was. All the most ancient texts ever deciphered had turned out not to be more epics of Gilgamesh, but aids to managing resources. . . .

Lists—and the interaction between different lists—were really what they were dealing with at the meeting. Lists of funds coming in; lists of fixed annual costs; lists of necessary building repairs; lists of projected demand for different types of existing procedures; lists—with costings—of new treatments coming on stream; lists of desirable vacancies to be filled; lists of upcoming retirements and other staff losses.

Budgeting went on endlessly, but November and December were intense; it was when his team took time out of the daily grind to think systematically about the next financial year, beginning the following April. All based on figures given out in the Chancellor's Autumn Statement. This usually set strong guidelines, but this year there was more uncertainty. A White Paper on Health Care was due in early January, and much was left vague on health spending.

"OK, let's see what kind of overview we can get to at this point. Income . . . Dennis?"

"So far, the Chancellor's scraped together a 1.5 percent increase in cash terms, in line with his preferred measure of inflation, so the decline in real terms might be just over four percent."

Inflation in the health service, because of the cost for new treatments, had always run at 4 percent per annum. You needed a 4 percent increase to stand still (something governments didn't bother to tell the public too loudly; spending on the NHS should always be seen to rise). But since Brexit, it had increased to more like 6 percent.

"But," Dennis continued, "at least we're not looking at any major site repairs or construction work; there's nothing nasty in that woodshed."

"OK, so we've got maybe four percent less to work with. What are the projections on demand?" was Jonathan's routine question.

Maria, chief treatment analyst, took over.

"We've got a few major new treatments coming online, not least your new accelerator. The down payment came out of this year's acquisition budget, but there will be the scheduled repayments. We're hoping to recoup much of that from selling our services to neighboring trusts. The main mover we're expecting is a three percent increase in overall demand—due, as ever, to increasing longevity."

Longevity was now a pox on public health.

People really just need to be civic and die, was Jonathan's unspoken observation.

The Brexiteers had sold the public on the idea that immigrants and medical tourism were to blame for increasing financial pressures within the NHS. In reality, it was the fact that people were living longer.

"Staffing?"

"We're currently advertising for forty-seven consultant positions across all departments, and there is a shortage of medical staff down the line. Based on what's happened over the last three years, I would also expect us to lose at least another thirty doctors over the financial year."

As the value of NHS pay had declined in real terms since Brexit with the pound and inflation, and expected workloads increased, increasing numbers of—of course—the most highly trained staff had moved into less stressful, better-paid work with more luxurious public and private health care systems worldwide. Jonathan's Trust had a notional roster of about seven hundred consultants, but turnover was increasing, and, without good staff, all the equipment in the world was a waste of space.

Maria continued, "On the plus side—purely in budgeting terms of course—we also have to factor in staff shortages in all the diagnostic labs, which slow down the return of test results and hence of referrals, so that our front line staff shortages show up less clearly. . . ."

This was not a conversation Jonathan would like reported, but you can't begin to resolve a problem unless you're willing to state it clearly, and Maria was in her analyst mode.

His voice deliberately calm, Jonathan summed up. "So, the bottom line is a four percent cut in real terms and a three percent increase in demand. Ways forward?" This was the kind of summation, with slight variations, he'd been making in similar meetings for the last four years. . . .

Maria jumped in. "Recruitment of staff, particularly at the top level, is a high priority. But we can't pay more. If we give out any of the 1.5 cash increase in wages, the implicit cut to service provision will just be higher. There's not enough trained men and woman to be had within Britain; we're going to have to continue recruiting overseas, from southern Europe ideally (to whose financial position the departure of the then UK from the EU had brought no improvement) but also those parts of the developing world with reputable training regimes."

Yeah, good fucking luck hiring a German or Swede. . . . Now we go begging in Cuba. Jonathan's silent sarcasm mode was on full speed.

"Second," she continued, "we need to keep up the pressure to put more reality in governmental target-setting. Anything that doesn't come with a formal target and attached financial penalties, we're already rationing in practice. Free in vitro fertilization takes so long in referral and treatment that most women hit the age limit of forty before they get their three cycles. Hips get done in the end, but waiting times are longer, and it's the same with everything else too. The model's there. We gave them enough evidence on A&E waiting times, and they eventually cracked. Fining us money—so that we could do less—for not hitting an impossible target was so stupid that even politicians eventually had to acknowledge the point. And that's without thinking about how particular targets bend outcomes out of shape. Some non-emergency treatments generate very good quality-of-life outcomes, but we're having to ration them unduly because of the stress on particular targets, like cancer. There's no way with all the staff shortages in referral, testing and treatment stages that we can continue to pretend that we're going to be treating eighty-five percent of cancer patients within the sixty-two-day target time."

Long answer to a short question.

Jonathan valued the clarity of Maria's brain more than he could say. For the last five years, they'd been skimping and scraping. They'd effectively rationed non-essential services, and employed good, but not absolutely the best, staff. They'd also done everything they could to encourage those with money to take some of the pressure off by buying less expensive, non-essential treatments privately. He'd also accepted the fact that there was not that much his team could do about the diabetes and heart disease generated by sugar-powered ready-meals. As a result, they had just about managed to keep treatment times acceptable and had been able to incorporate many of the innovative procedures and medications opened up by new medical research worldwide.

Cancer and cardiovascular care seemed less negotiable than everything else. Those patients had an evil tendency to actually die—drawing unwanted oversight from system administrators. But, he knew Maria was right. The financial situation was forcing them to ration health care. It always had, of course, even if politicians would almost never admit it, but now the effects of the rationing were becoming more noticeable.

At least, he thought to himself, we're still ahead of America on all the key indicators like infant mortality. All he said, therefore, was, "Agreed. Every time we're asked, we tell it as it is and try to make the politicians see it. I'll also use all my joint meetings with other Trusts to push for a common line.

"Now, what about the White Paper?"

Bernard, the political liaison officer, took over.

"Whatever else they do, there's going to be *some* extra money. No politician goes anywhere near Health without announcing some kind of increase. But it won't be much; their room for maneuver is imperceptible."

The promise of an extra £350 million per week for the NHS had disappeared from the Leave Campaign website less than twenty-four hours after the Referendum. An old guard within the Parliament succeeded in maintaining increased spending commitments previously made by the Cameron government through 2020. This was, however, a mere bandage on a gushing wound.

Medical inflation expenses and continued increases in demand meant money never went as far as expected. And the overall financial context grew increasingly tough as GDP declined.

Not only had Hard Brexit proved politically unavoidable—this being the one thing that British Brexiteers and Brussels's Eurocrats had ever agreed upon—with damaging effects for the 80 percent of the British economy geared up to services—but no new trade agreements had yet been negotiated.

This was partly due to the protectionist climate ushered in by the Trump administration's trade war with Canada and Mexico, but also reflected the fact that Britain didn't offer that much to potential partners anyway, not once the big banks started to leave London.

And then, over the last three years, all that extra money had had to be found for flood defenses. Everyone had been worried about the Greenland ice sheet, but it was the west Antarctic that began to collapse. Sea levels had already risen a meter and a half, with more to come. Many thought the worldwide rush into cheaper fossil fuels stimulated by the Trump administration's backing for coal and fracking had been the trigger.

Perhaps, but Trump only facilitated a climate disaster begun with Great Britain's industrial revolution—some 150 years ago. A petty argument—cause and process no longer seemed to matter. Coastal eastern England and downtown London were already awash.

A problem made all too evident when the Parliament's foundation collapsed—causing Big Ben to crumble in a collection of dust and broken stone. England's most famous landmark destroyed; something even Hitler never accomplished.

"There's no way they will be able to find enough money to make a serious difference for us, so there's really only one issue. What are they going to do about social care?"

The NHS front line—hospitals—had been protected, but everything else cut. The short-lived May government had already set itself along the path of borrowing through the short-term political consequences of a Brexit-generated economic downturn. A policy that left England worse off than at the end of World War II. The UK's deficit wasn't quite up to Japanese levels yet, but it was fast approaching 185 percent of GDP and counting. . . .

The big problem for Jonathan's team, and every other Trust, was that the hospitals relied on other institutions so as to discharge patients who didn't need emergency beds but weren't fit enough to look after themselves. Subsidies for nursing homes and local social-care budgets were all politically easier targets in desperate times, and, over the past five years, it had become steadily harder to get people out of the hospital. Which is why 50 percent of the beds, rather than 40 percent, were now occupied by patients ready to be discharged.

"All the Trusts came into line on this one," Jonathan responded. "We submitted detailed evidence for the White Paper and spoke with complete unanimity. Everyone agrees that there needs to be an integrated system of hospitals for emergencies and intensive procedures, backed up by a mix of care homes, in-house assistance, and specialist treatment for the elderly. The present mess is fucking inefficient. All the Trusts agreed. Even if it means a bit less for the

NHS, this has to be the priority. That's the best way to allow us to use our specialist resources effectively. Otherwise, we're stuck using expensive staff and equipment to nurse convalescents and the elderly."

One answer had been proposed by the Cameron government in 2014. Offer free care (at home, in sheltered accommodation, or at specialist facilities as appropriate) to everyone with less than £118,000 in savings, and cap the amount any single person had to spend—however long they lived—at £72,000. But this had been swept under the rug immediately after Brexit.

The aged died in hospital beds that should have been available to cure productive members of society. Longevity would be the death knell for NHS.

▪ ▪ ▪ ▪

"Happy Christmas, Dad."

Jonathan undid the wrapping and laughed out loud. Jake had bought him a box set of *Father Ted*. He'd had one years ago, but it had disappeared somewhere. He couldn't wait to reacquaint himself with the Holy Stone of Clonrichert being upgraded to a class-two relic. . . .

They'd started with the silly presents under the tree, then worked their way round to the real ones. Jonathan had bought Helen a beautiful scarf, Hermès of all things. Had to be eBay rather than brand new, but no less beautiful. Helen bought him a top-end set of pruning shears—three sizes, so sharp it made you wince just to look at them. Whenever he could, Jonathan found solace in his yard—listening to soccer preferably, but music if not. Like Gladstone but unlike Bismarck, he spent more time cutting wood than planting trees.

"Croissants?"

"Yes, please, and bacon. . . ."

It was an annual ritual they all loved. After that, it was time to get the bird in the oven as Helen's parents would soon be there, notionally for lunch, but they never actually ate before dusk.

At that point, Jonathan's cell phone rang, as he knew it would. It was Maria. She'd drawn the short straw this year and had the helm for Christmas Day.

"How're things?"

"Very busy in A&E. Lots of action overnight from all the Christmas Eve revelry, and the flu outbreak is continuing to build. Waiting time is still only five hours, but only because we've got plenty of bed space for admissions—no patients on stretchers in the corridors yet."

Like other hospital trusts, Oxford cut scheduled procedures to an absolute minimum over the Christmas period, which meant that there was lots of room. Unlike America, Britain essentially shut down between Christmas and the New Year. It made Jonathan stir crazy, but he was used to it. He often wondered what the hell Christmas tourists found to do all day. . . .

"Thanks, Maria. I looked at the forecast, and it's suggesting this cold snap will break up around the twenty-eighth, so fingers crossed. With luck, we'll be able to clear enough people out the beds by January second, when we really need to get moving again."

▪ ▪ ▪ ▪

It had been a lovely day. The boys were in good form, playful and engaged. Quite a lot of gaming, of course, but, then again, they'd got some new ones that clearly needed employment. And, being seventeen, they could put the educational sword of Damocles hanging over their heads to one side with all the difficulty of swatting a fly. He really did love his in-laws too. His own parents had died young—both of cancer—a loss and a shame they had never known his sons.

Helen's parents fed and dispatched, she bid him to join her in the kitchen. He followed.

"I did talk to them about the boys. They'll help, of course, but it's not going to solve the problem. Dad's pension has gone down in value so much, and they have to keep plenty in reserve for potential care costs.

"They can't afford to remortgage. The best they can do would be something like ten grand a year. But if the boys restart A-Levels, and do two years at a private school, that's going to be one-hundred-forty thousand pounds. Where do we find the other one-hundred-twenty thousand?"

They'd had some money from Jonathan's father, but that had been sucked into the house, and there were no other savings worth talking about.

▪ ▪ ▪ ▪

"Good morning; it's 8:00 a.m. on Monday the twenty-eighth of December." Goddamn clock radio. He couldn't even sleep in on holidays.

As Christmas had fallen on a Friday, the following Monday was a public holiday, and Jonathan had it off.

"This is the *Today* program on Radio 4, and these are the headlines from the BBC. It's official. This is the whitest, coldest Christmas in a hundred years. . . ."

Jonathan groaned inwardly as the announcer cheerfully reported that an incoming Atlantic low had been forced further north than expected, so the continental high pressure—originating somewhere in fucking Siberia, Jonathan thought to himself—was still in place. Temperatures were not at record lows—it once hit fifteen on Christmas Day in southern Scotland—but it was well below freezing.

"God Almighty. Why are the British so obsessed with the weather? Bloody caricatures."

"And why are you so grumpy?" came a voice from the other side of the duvet. Helen also had the day off. "It's sunny and beautiful for once, and there are excellent leftovers in the fridge."

"Sorry, I'll cheer up. Didn't sleep very well for some reason." He felt both slightly fuzzy and simultaneously hyper-alert. "What shall we do with the day?"

"Let's have a long, slow breakfast and then dress for a real trek."

"Very good. How 'bout you do the coffee while I check in with Bernard?"

"Deal."

"Morning, boss. Enjoying your White Christmas?" Endlessly cheerful Bernard.

"Fuck off, Bernard," he responded with evident pleasant sarcasm. Helen had been so quick that there was already caffeine in his system. "Actually, I slept really badly, so cheer me up."

"Well, the flu cases are still dribbling in. Not a stream exactly, but more than a trickle. They've got a few beds on the third and fourth floors, but A&E waiting is five and a quarter, and most of the discharge team are on holiday, of course, so it's not so easy to get rid of anyone. . . ."

"But OK for today?"

"Yes, I think so, unless there's some kind of horrendous pileup on the motorway. . . ."

"Fingers crossed then. I'm here if you need me and will be back in the office tomorrow to help clear the hospital. Hopefully, we can get back to the day job after next weekend. . . ."

▪ ▪ ▪ ▪

Except that he hadn't actually made it in the next day. Somehow he always forgot, but not sleeping was a classic sign that he was either unusually stressed or was getting sick.

His turn for the seasonal flu and, like so many others, he'd had the bloody vaccination. Obviously some little mutation somewhere along the line, which, combined with the cold weather, had been enough to power a large outbreak that was keeping all the hospitals busy. So, generally healthy beast that he was, it had been Friday before he finally made it back to the office.

With both Christmas and New Year's Day falling on Friday, the British midwinter shutdown this year was about as long as it could be. "I wonder how many people have shot their in-laws so far?" he mused, opening the meeting. But, as lame a joke as it was, that was about as light as things got.

They weren't due to start normal activities until next Monday, but that meant admitting on Sunday, and there just wasn't any room. Flu cases were continuing to trickle in, A&E waiting was five and a half hours, and about 58 percent of bed space was clogged up with people who really didn't need specialist care. At this point, they were facing the prospect of having to cancel 20 percent of Monday's scheduled procedures, and there was little they could do about it. Bob's people were on overtime—another expense—trying to clear space, but New Year's Day was not a promising moment to be sourcing care options. . . .

▪ ▪ ▪ ▪

"Happy New Year, Helen," he said, kissing her when he got back home. He'd left before anyone else was up.

"How are you feeling?"

"Still pretty crap. My brain's clear again, thank goodness, but everything still aches. . . ."

"Pills and coffee?"

"Yes, please; it's been four hours, so I'm allowed more. The boys?"

"In their bedrooms—playing together." Helen still found it odd that they played together online and hence, physically separately, shouting and laughing back and forth across the landing. And even odder, when they were online with more of their friends in team games, as familiar voices would come echoing down the stairs from an entirely absent space.

"Sit down and let's talk."

He knew what about.

"Really, Jonathan. What are we going to do?"

"As I see it, there's only one option. Sell the house and move somewhere smaller. Prices have gone down a bit without all those oligarchs wanting to launder their money through the London property market, but not so much. We could find somewhere that's still pretty nice while freeing up maybe 100K. I can make the Trust improve my performance package just a bit too, and then, with a little help from your parents and some extra belt-tightening for a couple of years, we should be there."

"But we all—and you especially—love the house, the garden, the countryside, all of it. And once it's gone, it's gone. We'll never be able to afford to buy back anything like it again."

He'd been through all those arguments himself. Both in bed with his head spinning and afterward when it had cleared. And he was sure Helen had traveled down a similar path. Because, in reality, there wasn't anything else they could do. If the boys were going to have opportunities in life, they needed a better education, and there was no other way to pay for it.

"It's going to be shit. We both love this place. But watching a lifetime's worth of mediocrity and disappointment settle over the two people we love most on the planet, when there is something we can do about it, is not an option. And, let's face it, this is one of those first-world problems, which fades into nothing compared to drowned children on Greek and Italian beaches."

Helen's look of resignation, tinged with a little relief, said it all. She'd come to the same conclusion and had been gearing herself up to lead him in that direction.

"There's no great rush. They'll have to restart the school year next September anyway, so that gives us the spring and summer to get it all sorted."

"And to tell them," Helen added. "They won't be thrilled to leave their friends. . . ."

▪ ▪ ▪ ▪

"Happy New Year, Prime Minister."

"You too, Michael."

Like most politicians, the two men utterly loathed one another, but this was decision-time on the White Paper, a moment in which they were compelled to cast off personal animosities for a greater good. Before Christmas break, they'd managed to argue through two draft versions. What remained was a 95 percent compromise—lots of stuff about health education, and new preventative, cost-effective strategies for heading off obesity and Alzheimer's.

But the two politicians remained deeply divided on the integration of general social care with NHS core missions. They could not reach agreement before the break, except that Prime Minister Leadsom's inner cabinet would go away and think about it, and that a decision would be reached on January first—when the meeting could be disguised from watching journalists as a social event.

"Health Secretary, you should kick off I think. . . ."

Michael Gove opened the folder in front of him. After his self-destructive treachery during the post-Brexit leadership campaign, it was no surprise the May government found no place for him. He'd instead cast his lot in with the radical Brexiteers and managed to crawl back into influence.

"I've thought about it long and hard, about pretty much nothing else, in fact. I really do think it's time to be bold. We can't go on treating the NHS and social care provision as separate fields of action. We've protected NHS spending while cutting everything else, but that has meant paring down every other form of care, everything from full-on subsidies for care homes to home help via sheltered accommodation in between. With the result that we've effectively turned our specialist hospitals and their highly trained staff into general nurses. It's a staggering waste of resources. We'll actually get much more out of our hospitals in terms of medical care if we switch some of their overly protected resources into social care."

Deputy PM David Davis indicated that he wanted to come in at this point.

"That's clearly put, Michael, and, in an ideal world, you'd have my support. But where we are is far from ideal. We won the Referendum on the claim that Brexit would provide more money—a *lot* more money—for the NHS. Then we levered Theresa May out on the basis that she was failing to deliver real Brexit—hence the extra resources for the NHS and the new job opportunities for our people—which is what people really cared about. You yourself came up with the slogan, 'Defend real Brexit, before Theresa wrecks it.' For us to turn around now and cut the NHS, having found the funds already promised for it in the meantime only by the skin of teeth, will be politically disastrous."

"Chancellor?" Iain Duncan Smith looked up.

"I agree with David, Prime Minister. The money's just not there. You can't tackle social care without doing something about provision for the elderly; in practice, most of those we can't move from hospitals are elderly. So the amount of money we'd need to take from the NHS to do a comprehensive refit of social care would be huge. In 2014, the Cameron government costed it at about six billion pounds spread over six years, but it would be much more now. Given all the cutbacks that have been forced on us since, we'd be starting any care expansion from a much lower base, and the population has been aging steadily, one consequence of our successes in cutting back the flow of migration. There's nothing else left to cut, and we've pushed borrowing as far as we dare."

"It's so potentially toxic," interjected the PM herself. "The fairly wealthy elderly are one core of our support, as they were of Brexit, so we'll get lots of love from them if we bite this bullet, especially if we can still cap overall lifetime care costs in some way. But the have-nots, especially the JAMs,[1] who have nothing like a hundred grand in savings, are an even bigger source of support. They're not going to see why the inheritances of the better-off need protecting in financially straitened times at the cost of cutting the NHS, when protecting it was why they voted Brexit. The NHS—hospitals, not broader systems of care provision—is the great symbol of what remains of national consensus.

---

1 "Just about managing": a new acronym that entered British political commentary in the early days of the ill-fated May government.

The claim to be defending it is what won us the Referendum, and it's the one thing that everyone still agrees on. Look at all the surveys and polls. For us to cut NHS spending could easily bring down the government."

She looked long and hard at all the faces gathered around the table. "But Michael, you want to come back in?"

"Yes, Prime Minister. In my view, what we have to do for once is actually lead. Thanks to Blair and all his focus groups, politicians have been chasing after public opinion for the last twenty years, not explaining to it what needs to be done—however hard—and why. The public needs to redefine its understanding of the NHS to include social care as well. That's what we have to explain. Get them to see that we're putting it all under one umbrella, and all we're doing is shuffling money around to achieve a much more efficient outcome, not cutting anything at all. . . ."

▪ ▪ ▪ ▪

Monday morning's situation meeting started his week off in the toilet.

They had to cancel a dismal 25 percent of Tuesday's scheduled procedures for lack of bed space. There was literally nowhere they could safely send large numbers of the non-acute cases who were now clogging up the Trust's beds. This was not only leading to sudden cancelations but also pushing up A&E waiting times.

A particularly nasty motor vehicle accident had also hit the M40 during morning rush hour—the first after Christmas, so maybe everyone's out of practice? was Jonathan's only thought—so that non-urgent cases were currently taking an average of six and a half hours to be seen. And, even without any more pileups, this was going to be the pattern for the rest of the week. Despite warming weather and flu numbers in decline, they'd be canceling unacceptably high numbers of operations for at least a week.

And that would have a domino effect for the rest of the financial year. He didn't like to think about what the potential fine might be for all the targets that were about to be missed.

"It's going to be tough, ladies and gentlemen, but that's what we're here for," he concluded. "It's our job to make the very best of what we've got and what we're dealt."

Then the strategy team had met at 2:00 p.m. to watch the Health Secretary introduce his White Paper live. It began promisingly enough.

▪ ▪ ▪ ▪

"Order. Order," intoned the Speaker. "The Secretary of State for Health, the Right Honourable Michael Gove MP. . . ."

The Minister stood up to the usual mix of cheers and jeers.

"His Majesty's government believes the time has come to take a much more holistic and integrated approach to the health of the nation. . . ."

Gove's introductory vision turned out to be more enlightened than the rest of the speech. Aside from a host of small measures on health education—most of it already announced but repackaged into a supposedly new policy trajectory—there were two main measures.

To loud Tory cheers, Gove laid out the first.

"Even in these difficult times, the NHS is safe in our hands. His Majesty's government is proud to announce a further increase in spending on the NHS in the coming financial year of one percent above and beyond the additional 1.5 percent already announced in the Chancellor's Autumn Statement. This will ensure that the service can continue to maintain the highest possible standards of health care."

But on the crucial issue of social care, there was no joy at all. Gove turned to it right at the end of his speech.

"His Majesty's government has fully taken on board all the evidence submitted by our different stakeholders, not least the NHS trusts themselves, that the prevailing regime of social care provision requires an urgent and radical overhaul. This is such a complex, crucial, and, if I may also say, controversial area that it simply must be done correctly. I am pleased to be able to announce to the House, therefore, that, with immediate effect, a royal commission will be established to collect evidence from all the interested parties and advise government on the formation of its future plans."

■ ■ ■ ■

"A royal commission!" Bernard exploded, echoing all their thoughts. "They've bloody dodged it again. The last royal commission on the long-term care of the elderly took over two years to report in the 1990s, and then its main recommendations were basically ignored. Which is why we are where we are."

Bernard was better on the detail of Parliamentary history than the rest of them, but they all knew that royal commissions were the classic delaying tactic. Deal with the immediately unpalatable by starting a long-winded discussion, and then hope that something will happen in the meantime to make the problem go away, or that some financial fairy will wave her magic wand to make a tolerable solution affordable.

The rest of the meeting had turned into a dispiriting exercise in deciding how they could best manage the effective three-plus percent funding increase, in the face of a hospital that was going to be no less full of non-urgent care cases for the foreseeable future. As a consequence, A&E waiting times, non-emergency surgery waiting lists, and even referral and treatment times for more serious conditions were all bound to take a further hit.

The greatest good for the greatest number in the face of limited resources had always posed horrible dilemmas—never an easy job. But when the politicians ducked their responsibilities and made everything so much more difficult—well, that was just dispiriting.

■ ■ ■ ■

Jonathan threw himself into his chair. There was a sympathetic message from Helen who'd picked up the gist of Gove's speech at work. She'd also started calling real estate agents about selling the house. Which didn't make him feel any better at all.

"Bad news, then boss?" James brought some papers to sign.

Jonathan was really struggling here.

"You know, James, behind these bureaucratic targets are real human beings. Improvements we've fought so hard for in mortality rates from cancer and cardiovascular disease have been flattening out over the last few years, despite all the wonderful research going on elsewhere, because we can't afford all the latest treatments. And now that we're going to be able to do even less for at least the next three years, they might even start to rise again. And who the hell decides what an emergency is anyway? If you're a healthy older woman with a broken hip, then it's an emergency to you, and already too many die from complications while waiting their turn."

James knew better than to say anything.

"Even so, it would still be worthwhile if politicians would be honest. How could it not be? Using whatever you've got available in the best possible way, to improve the lives of the greatest number of people, is an utterly worthwhile way to spend your life, even if it's not possible to give everyone absolutely the best of everything. That's got to be better than America, where they seem to think it's perfectly OK for the poor just to die, while the rich can get everything they want. But when the politicians are too weak to have these difficult conversations with honesty, let alone make the difficult decisions, it rips the heart out of you."

James nodded sympathetically and beat a hasty retreat. There wasn't anything he could say.

Just then, the phone rang. It was Bernard.

"I really don't know how to tell you this, Jonathan, but, under cover of all the fuss about the Health White Paper this afternoon, the government made a second policy announcement."

"Go on. . . ."

"The Home Office has stated that all publicly funded bodies, explicitly including hospital trusts, will be required to reduce the non-British element of their workforce to a maximum of twenty-five percent of the total. There'll be a transition period of three years from next April, and I expect we'll be able to push them up a bit by negotiation when we point out the degree of chaos it's going to cause in their beloved NHS. But it's going to be hugely popular with the Brexit-supporting public, and we will certainly have to implement it to some degree. . . ."

After Bernard hung up, in black despair, Jonathan pulled out an opened envelope from under his blotter. The first of the regular stream that had been arriving since last summer, it had a Swiss stamp. He took out the letter, rereading what he knew was there.

> Dear Dr. Lawrence,
> We're writing to you, after conducting a worldwide search, because of your stellar record as both oncologist and medical administrator. The Paracelsus Klinik in Bern is planning to establish a brand-new, state-of-the-art cancer facility in the spring of 2022, and we would like to invite you to interview, potentially to head up the process as its new director. The overall budget for equipment and staff will be unlimited, and your own salary is entirely negotiable, but will be fully commensurate, of course, with those paid by our competitors worldwide. . . .

Jonathan pulled out his cell phone and called Helen.

"Forget the real estate agents; I've just had enough. I'm going to pursue the offer from Switzerland. . . ."

First Brexit, then the collapse of the financial sector, now an end to NHS. There was no reason to remain a citizen of Britain's tottering democracy.

## EDITOR'S AFTERWORD

BY ERIC C. ANDERSON

> *"Democracy suits Europeans today partly because it is associated with the triumph of capitalism and partly because it involves less commitment or intrusion into their lives than any of the alternatives. Europeans accept democracy because they no longer believe in politics."*
>
> —MARK MAZOWER,
> *Dark Continent: Europe's Twentieth Century*[1]

Before you cast Mazower aside as a gloomy historian reminiscing on the fate of Europe in a century that is now twenty years behind us, I would offer the following from Ian Bremmer. Bremmer, founder of the Eurasia Group—an international consultancy—put this on paper in February 2018: "Those of us who still believe citizens should only be governed with their consent are left to wonder what it would take to persuade a younger generation that we're right . . . The real crisis for democracy looks much more likely now to originate from within."[2]

Add to that the most recent work from a pair of Harvard professors, *How Democracies Die*. "Institutions alone are not enough to rein in elected autocrats. Constitutions must be defended—by political

1 Mark Mazower, *Dark Continent: Europe's Twentieth Century*, New York: Vintage Books, 1998, p. 397.

2 Ian Bremmer, "Is Democracy Essential? Millennials increasingly aren't sure—that should concern us all," NBC, 13 February 2018.

parties and organized citizens, but also by democratic norms."[3] What are those norms? Well, if the wise men from Harvard are right, they would be mutual toleration and institutional forbearance. In other words, accept your rivals and their right to compete for power—the latter norm boils down to "avoiding actions that, while respecting the letter of the law, obviously violate its spirit."[4]

All easily said, far more difficult to realize. Ideology, religion and time have no beginning or end. They are continuums that are temporarily intellectually transformed through the work of cogent philosophers who occupy a bit of academic and physical space as ideas and evolution continue to whirl by. Please note, that is *by* not *past*. There is no *before*, *during* or *after* in the realm of ideas and spinning clocks. . . . There is simply *now* and then another *now*.

That is what we seek to impart through the publication of *Fractus Europa*.

Who would be so bold as to argue Plato did not discuss his ideas on governance with other informed thinkers? Yet, modern American students contend he invented democracy. I suspect not. Plato likely debated a lively collection of thinkers who simply neglected to publish. And they did the same with forbearers who also remain nameless. The point here is that there is no "day one" or "zero hour" for democracy or any other form of governance. We just like to think Darwin's observations on evolutionary biology apply to political science.

Allow me to demonstrate. In 1989, Francis Fukuyama, a former RAND analyst and then–deputy director of the State Department's policy planning staff, published an essay titled "The End of History?" Written as the former Soviet Union visibly collapsed and China's dalliance with capitalism transitioned into a permanent state of affairs, Fukuyama's piece heralded "the total exhaustion of viable systemic

---

3 Steven Levitsky and Daniel Ziblatt, *How Democracies Die*, New York: Crown, 2018, p. 7.

4 Ibid., p. 106.

alternatives to Western liberalism."[5] More specifically, Fukuyama told his readership:

> What we may be witnessing is not just the end of the Cold War, or the passing of a particular period of postwar history, but the end of history as such: that is, the endpoint of mankind's ideological evolution and the universalization of Western liberal democracy as the final form of human governance.[6]

In this brave new world, national governments would be "liberal insofar as [they] recognize and protect through a system of laws man's universal right to freedom, and democratic insofar as [they] exist only with the consent of the governed."[7] A noble vision—and one that won much acclaim, even among American political scientists.

In September 1989, Lucian Pye, a renowned sinologist and then-president of the American Political Science Association, stood before his assembled colleagues and declared they were witness to the "crisis of authoritarianism." Pye insisted political science needed to get busy studying and explaining the imminent demise of what he argued were "all manner of authoritarian systems."[8] According to Pye, authoritarian regimes were fundamentally challenged by the rise of global communications systems, expanding educational opportunities, international trade, and the effects of contemporary science and technology. Furthermore, he was willing to argue that "the presumed advantages of totalitarian practices for economic development have

---

5 Francis Fukuyama, "The End of History?" *The National Interest*, No. 16 (Summer 1989), p. 3.

6 Ibid., p. 4.

7 Ibid., p. 5.

8 Lucian W. Pye, "Political Science and the Crisis of Authoritarianism," *American Political Science Review*, Vol. 84, No. 1 (March 1990), p. 5.

apparently evaporated."[9] All of which led him to conclude, "The long historical trend that favored the strengthening of centralized state power has seemingly come to an end, and the trend now favors the pluralism of decentralized authority."[10] For Pye, like Fukuyama, the future promised national governments who worshiped at the West's temple of free markets and liberal democracy.

As it turns out, everyone was not reading from the same script. The economic success realized by China and the so-called Asian tigers (Hong Kong, Indonesia, Japan, Malaysia, Singapore, South Korea, Thailand and Taiwan), coupled with their clear deviation from the principles espoused by Western liberal democracy, caused some academics to wonder if there wasn't another option.

The living embodiment of this so-called authoritarian capitalism was Lee Kuan Yew, Singapore's prime minister from 1959 to 1990. According to Lee, while there was much to respect in the West's concept of liberal democracy, there was also no end of shortcomings. In an interview published in *Foreign Affairs,* Lee declared:

> [There are] things that I have always admired about America . . . a certain openness in argument about what is good or bad for society; the accountability of public officials; none of the secrecy and terror that's part and parcel of communist government. But as a total system, I find parts of it . . . unacceptable: guns, drugs, violent crime, vagrancy, unbecoming behavior in public—in sum the breakdown of civil society. The expansion of the right of the individual to behave or misbehave as he pleases has come at the expense of orderly society. In the East the main object is to have a well-ordered society so that everybody can have maximum enjoyment of his

9 Ibid., p. 7.
10 Ibid., p. 8.

> freedoms. This freedom can only exist in an ordered state and not in a natural state of contention and anarchy.[11]

Needless to say, Lee's regime and his comments drew significant flak from the West—particularly from academics who took umbrage with his contention that individualism and materialism might undermine "Asian values" and thereby detract from the tigers' economic performance.[12]

The critics, however, faced a steep uphill battle. While they could criticize the authoritarian practices resident within many of the tiger governments, it was difficult to dispute their economic successes. This argument was rendered even more difficult by a 1993 World Bank report titled *The East Asian Miracle: Economic Growth and Public Policy*. According to the World Bank, "the East Asia miracle—achieving high growth with equity—is due to a combination of fundamentally sound development policies, tailored interventions, and an unusually rapid accumulation of physical and human capital." But, the authors continued, there was more to the story.

In most of these economies, the government intervened—systematically and through multiple channels—to foster development, and in some cases the development of specific industries. Policy interventions took many forms. Policies to bolster savings, build strong financial markets, and promote investment with equity included keeping deposit rates low and maintaining ceilings on borrowing rates to increase profits and retained earnings, establishing and financially supporting government banks, and sharing information widely between public and private sectors. Policies to bolster industry included targeting and subsidizing credit to selected industries, protecting domestic import substi-

11 Fareed Zakaria, "Culture Is Destiny: A Conversation with Lee Kuan Yew," *Foreign Affairs*, Vol. 73, No. 2 (March–April 1994), p. 111.

12 For instance, see: Christopher Lingle, *Singapore's Authoritarian Capitalism: Asian Values, Free Market Illusions, and Political Dependency*, Fairfax, Virginia: Locke Institute, 1996.

tutes, supporting declining industries, and establishing firm- and industry-specific export targets.[13]

Stated more succinctly, in addition to maintaining good social order—which frequently meant suppressing individual political activities—the Asian tiger leadership frequently, and in some cases successfully, intervened in Adam Smith's marketplace but chose to maintain the fundamentals of a capitalist system.

Academic and policymaker interest in this authoritarian capitalism might have continued to flourish had it not been for the 1997–98 Asian financial crisis. The International Monetary Fund's $40 billion bailout package—coupled with that organization's call for afflicted governments to implement strict monetary and contractionary fiscal policies—called into question the staying power of this emerging governance model. More than one academic claimed the entire fiasco could be attributed to "crony capitalism,"[14] and Paul Krugman, an economist who subsequently was awarded the Nobel Prize, declared the growth realized in Asia's tiger economies was probably caused by an "extraordinary mobilization of resources" rather than authoritarian policies.[15] In short, by the late 1990s, many Western policymakers were convinced authoritarian capitalism was a temporary phenomenon, a stage in the gradual evolution to liberal democracy. They were wrong.

Rather than fading away, the authoritarian capitalists appeared to develop a remarkable staying power. Vladimir Putin's perceived rescue of Moscow's moribund economy and China's continued high growth rates suggested that perhaps there was more to the story.

---

13 Nancy Birdsall, Ed Campos, W. Max Corden, Chang-Shik Kim, Howard Pack, Richard Sabot, Joseph E. Stiglitz, and Marilou Uy, *The East Asian Miracle: Economic Growth and Public Policy*, *World Bank Policy Research Reports*, Oxford: Oxford University Press, 1993.

14 Helen Hughes, "Crony Capitalism and the East Asian Currency Financial 'Crises'" *Policy*, Spring 1999, Wellington, New Zealand: Center for Independent Studies, pp. 3–9.

15 Paul Krugman, "The Myth of Asia's Miracle," *Foreign Affairs*, Vol. 73, No. 6 (November–December 1994), p. 62.

Instead of disappearing, the authoritarian capitalists actually seemed to be thriving. This disconcerting development was brought to the fore for Washington's policy elite in July 2007, when *Foreign Affairs* published Azar Gat's "The Return of Authoritarian Great Powers." Gat, the Ezer Weizman Professor of National Security at Tel Aviv University, used his essay to argue Russia and China's rise suggested "capitalism's ascendancy appears to be deeply entrenched, but the current predominance of democracy could be far less secure."[16] As Gat put it, "all that can be said at the moment is that there is nothing in the historical record to suggest a transition to democracy by today's authoritarian capitalist powers is inevitable."[17]

In George W. Bush's Washington, these were fighting words. The first shot across Gat's bow came from Michael Mandelbaum, the Christian A. Herter Professor and director of the American Foreign Policy program at the Johns Hopkins University School of Advanced International Studies. In an essay titled "Democracy without America," Mandelbaum hoisted the torch for those who believed authoritarian capitalist states were simply at a waypoint on the path to democracy. According to Mandelbaum, "the key to establishing a working democracy . . . has been the free-market economy. The institutions, skills, and values needed to operate a free-market economy are those that, in the political sphere, constitute democracy."[18]

For Mandelbaum, free-market capitalism did more than build institutional and social skills requisite for a democracy. The Johns Hopkins professor went on to argue that participating in a free-market economy cultivates two habits essential for democratic government: trust and compromise. His bottom line: "For a government to operate peacefully, citizens must trust it not to act against their most important

16 Azar Gat, "The Return of Authoritarian Great Powers," *Foreign Affairs*, Vol. 86, No. 4 (July–August 2007), p. 59.

17 Ibid., p. 66.

18 Michael Mandelbaum, "Democracy without America: The Spontaneous Spread of Freedom," *Foreign Affairs*, Vol. 86, No. 5 (September–October 2007), pp. 34.

interests and, above all, to respect their political and economic rights."[19] So, where is Europe in this process?

Mandelbaum dodges the question. While he focuses on Beijing, his observations certainly apply to Europe as it approaches the third decade of our twenty-first century. To paraphrase Mandelbaum, Europe has undergone a "dizzying change" that has installed "many of the building blocks of political democracy." And yet, there is an elite that is "determined to retain its monopoly on political power."[20]

Mandelbaum recognized that most members of our "civilized" society are loath to be plunged back into the chaos that characterized post–World War I Europe or Russia following the collapse of Mikhail Gorbachev's regime. This does not mean Mandelbaum thinks Moscow will be able to ward off democracy forever. Revealing his determinist tendencies, Mandelbaum ultimately concludes democracy may come because pressure for adopting this form of governance "grows wherever nondemocratic governments adopt the free-market system of economic organization."[21]

Unfortunately for Mandelbaum, this predilection for democracy in free-market economies does not appear permanent. As Larry Diamond—co-editor of the *Journal of Democracy*—noted in March 2008, "If democracies do not more effectively contain crime and corruption, generate economic growth, relieve economic inequality, and secure freedom and the rule of law, people will eventually lose faith and turn to authoritarian alternatives."[22]

I should be so lucky as to study at Larry Diamond's knee.

So how to avoid this predilection for authoritarian governance? Diamond contends democratic institutions "must listen to their citizens' voices, engage their participation, tolerate their protests,

19 Ibid., p. 35.
20 Ibid., p. 38.
21 Ibid., p. 39.
22 Larry Diamond, "The Democratic Rollback: The Resurgence of the Predatory State," *Foreign Affairs*, Vol. 87, No. 2 (March–April 2008), p. 40.

protect their freedoms, and respond to their needs."[23] The assertion here, of course, is that dictatorial regimes do none of these things—a premise known to be erroneous. In fact, Beijing appears headed down the very path Diamond would have us believe essential for any democracy—"rigorous rules and impartial institutions."[24] This would lead me to believe we are coming full circle, and Gat was right; we are preparing for a revival of authoritarian great powers.

But not before "The End of History" fans get in their two cents. In January 2009, Daniel Deudney—a professor of political science at Johns Hopkins—and G. John Ikenberry—the Albert G. Milbank Professor of Politics and International Affairs at Princeton—took their shot at rebutting Gat's hypothesis. In an essay bluntly titled "The Myth of Authoritarian Revival: Why Liberal Democracy Will Prevail," Deudney and Ikenberry contend "the proposition that autocracies have achieved a new lease on life and are emerging today as a viable alternative within the capitalist system is wrong."[25]

Phooey, but let's hear them out.

According to the two professors, today's authoritarian regimes may be more competent and capitalist-compatible, but they remain "fundamentally constrained by deep-seated incapacities that promise to limit their viability." What are these "incapacities"? Deudney and Ikenberry identify three: corruption; inequality; and limitations on governmental performance due to weak accountability and insufficient flows of information.[26]

Here's how this argument works. First, on the issue of corruption, Deudney and Ikenberry declare authoritarian regimes struggle with bribery and graft because officials are not restrained by institutional

23 Ibid., pp. 41-42.

24 Ibid., p. 45.

25 Daniel Deudney and G. John Ikenberry, "The Myth of Authoritarian Revival: Why Liberal Democracy Will Prevail," *Foreign Affairs*, Vol. 88, No. 1 (January–February 2009), p. 78.

26 Ibid., pp. 84–85.

checks on state power. Liberal democracies, they claim, solve this problem with constitutions and the rule of law.

I'm not buying that argument given recent developments in Hungary, Spain, South Korea or the United States. But let's continue.

Inequality, Deudney and Ikenberry continue, is resolved in a democracy through universal franchise and the rise of political parties that cater to various socioeconomic classes within a society. Authoritarian capitalists, for the two professors, have no such option and thus are at a stage "where the other shoe has not dropped in their political evolution." And the limits on performance? According to Deudney and Ikenberry, "closed political systems are prone to policy mistakes arising from bad information." Liberal democracies, on the other hand, are said to "flourish" as a result of a capacity to "mutate in the face of new problems."

At this point, the cynic is allowed a loud guffaw.

A review of the *Washington Post* or *New York Times* indicates the same three flaws abound within liberal democracies. Washington's continuing battles with campaign finance abuse, lobbying, and members of Congress under criminal investigation suggests there is no shortage of corruption in liberal democracies—even one as open and mature as the United States.

The debate over socioeconomic inequality has also not been successfully addressed—witness the labor unions' continuing battles with corporate America or the sad plight of many African Americans. And poor government performance? The ongoing international financial crisis—largely a result of lax government regulation—clearly indicates poor policy can be crafted even with full access to all the information. (We shall pass on a conversation concerning the limits and filters on information making its way to elected representatives on Capitol Hill—suffice it to say all voices are not granted an equal hearing; normally those with money get the final say.)

Back to Deudney and Ikenberry. Given these fundamental "incapacities," the representatives from Johns Hopkins and Princeton become advocates of a determinist philosophy. Like Mandelbaum, the two professors believe that authoritarian capitalist regimes are little more than an evolutionary stage en route to liberal democracy.

To wit, they argue, "autocratic capitalism is not an alternative model; it is only a waystation" on the path to liberal democracy.[27] As such, Deudney and Ikenberry recommend the policy community do little more than acknowledge authoritarian states' grievances and "inherited vulnerabilities" and then "mollify and ameliorate them." "A successful foreign policy," Deudney and Ikenberry continue, "should also seek to integrate, rather than exclude, autocratic . . . powers." Why? "The foreign policy of the liberal states should . . . be based on the broad assumption that there is ultimately one path to modernity—and that is essentially liberal in character."[28]

In short, we should not be surprised the European or US policy community does not know how to deal with a rise in nationalism and desire for authoritarian governance—they have been repeatedly told these social phenomena facilitate their own obsolescence. But what if this advice is wrong? What happens if the Chinese or Russian abandonment of Marx, Lenin and Mao has set the stage for establishment of a permanent fixture? That is to say, the authoritarian-capitalist model may not be an evolutionary waypoint but rather a viable means of governance.

What does this mean for Europe? How will we know it is coming? Answers to those questions were given in these pages. *Fractus Europa* takes us where academics and think tank philosophers typically dare not tread. Examined from the perspective of those who must live these conditions on a daily basis, *Fractus* leaves me sleepless—and worried about my children's future.

Eric C. Anderson
March 2018

---

27 Ibid., p. 93.
28 Ibid., p. 93.